D1020210

THE LIBRARY MACHINE

ALSO BY DAVE BUTLER

The Kidnap Plot

The Giant's Seat

THE EXTRAORDINARY JOURNEYS OF CLOCKWORK CHARLIE

THE LIBRARY MACHINE

DAVE BUTLER

ALFRED A. KNOPF
NEW YORK

THIS IS A BORZOI BOOK PUBLISHED BY ALFRED A. KNOPF

Visit us on the Web! rhcbooks.com

Educators and librarians, for a variety of teaching tools, visit us at RHTeachersLibrarians.com

Library of Congress Cataloging-in-Publication Data is available upon request.
ISBN 978-0-553-51303-5 (trade) — ISBN 978-0-553-51304-2 (lib. bdg.) —
ISBN 978-0-553-51305-9 (ebook)

Printed in the United States of America
September 2018
10 9 8 7 6 5 4 3 2 1

First Edition

FOR SUNITHA AND DAVID GILL

PART ONE

THE SPIRIT STONE

It was a hot day. So hot that if you dropped a lump of dough on the street, it would be bread before you could pick it up. God had made it that hot, as a sort of a test for Avrohom, you see? How would he react? And Avrohom sent Eliezer—he was a giant, you know, and he was also called Og—out to look for travelers. And when Eliezer couldn't find any, Avrohom went out to look himself, because that was Avrohom, always the hospitable one.

—from Isaac Ginzberg, *Tales My Uncle Told Me*, "The Angels' Visit"

"You knock, Ollie," Charlie said. "I need my hands to hold the divining rod."

The divining rod was a length of metal wire with his brother Thomas's scarf wrapped around it. It had been enchanted by the dwarf dowser Thassia, so it indicated the direction of Thomas. Charlie and his friends had used the rod to follow Thomas across the North Sea (stowed away in crates in the hold of a cargo ship) and western Germany (mostly on foot, but once in the back of a hay wagon) to a town called Marburg (according to a sign at the edge of town). All the people calling out across the boulevard on which they stood, or chatting to each other as they strolled beneath green trees, were speaking a language Charlie didn't understand.

German, probably.

Ollie raised an arm to rap on the door, but hesitated. "Only what if they don't speak English?"

Charlie and his friends stood beside a neat house, three stories tall. The house sheltered in a green garden, lovely with ordered shrubs and rows of vegetables. To one side rose a retaining wall of enormous stone slabs propping up the side of the mountain. Above the wall climbed tier upon tier of wood-and-plaster houses, and at the top Charlie saw the spires of a castle, built of orange stone. On a second side of the house and its garden loomed a squared-off, high-gabled stone building with tall, peaked windows and multiple rooftops. Its door was tiny and shut, but the building was sunk into the side of the mountain, so perhaps it had other doors, higher up. To the third side was the boulevard, paved with bitumen concrete and trafficked by steam-puffing carriages.

On the fourth side stood a building of astonishing beauty. A cupola rising above its center showed eight circular windows, each with the stained-glass image of a six-pointed star; another six-pointed star jutted from a metal rod above the cupola, like a weather vane. The main body of the building beneath the cupola bore further six-sided stars in stained-glass windows, and had a rooftop that rose and fell in a symmetrical pattern that created a shape like a star with eight sides. Broad steps climbed from the pavement in front of the building up to its main entrance, a grand set of recessed double doors.

"Someone better knock, boyo," Lloyd Shankin said. "I've

an uncomfortable feeling on me, and it's got something to do with that big machine."

The Welsh dewin—the word meant "wizard," and like other Welsh wizards, Lloyd Shankin sang all his spells—nodded down the street past the large building. Entering town along the same boulevard Charlie and his friends had traveled came something that looked like two gigantic gearwheels, rolling forward and holding suspended between them a metal carriage. The machine reminded Charlie uncomfortably of the London Eye, the gigantic leisure wheel where his bap had died.

And it had a skull and crossbones painted on the side.

"I'll do it." Heaven-Bound Bob's grin was as wide as her face. "I'm accoutered to people misunderstanding me."

"Accustomed, Bob," Ollie said.

Bob shrugged and knocked on the wood, worn smooth with age. Dark timbers framed the walls of the house, which were plastered white. A lamp hung on each side of the door, and the two stories above the ground floor each jutted slightly out, supported on more dark timbers, creating a sheltered porch on which Charlie and the two chimney sweeps stood.

Lloyd Shankin, who was taller, stood on the walk behind them. Natalie de Minimis, the fairy warrior and rightful heir to the throne of the pixie realm of Underthames, hovered beside him.

From inside the house came the steady *rum-pum-pum* of percussion instruments, and strings being played over them.

Charlie lowered the rod, tried to make it look inconspicuous. Too bad it was a wire; a length of wood might have looked like a walking stick. Instead Charlie appeared to be carrying a bent rapier, or a fire poker.

But the dowsing rod had definitely pointed at this house. He'd walked around it three times to be sure, and the rod continually tugged at the earth when pointed at the house. And, specifically, at one of the upper stories.

Thomas was inside; there could be no doubt.

The string instruments stopped, though the drums continued.

A man with trimmed facial hair and a small round cap answered the door holding a violin and its bow in one hand. He gave a similar impression to the house: his waistcoat was elegant, but worn like the dark timbers, and although his shirtsleeves were white, a couple of the buttons looked slightly mismatched. His beard was dark, but streaked with hints of gray. White tassels hung down beneath his waistcoat in a neat fringe.

"Guten Tag!" His eyes twinkled merrily, and his voice boomed. Charlie thought *Guten Tag* must mean "good day" or "hello" in German; he'd never heard anyone say good day and sound so much like they meant it.

"'Ere now." Bob stuck her hands in the pockets of her peacoat and smiled. "Any chance you speak English?"

"But of course!" the violinist cried.

"Ain't no *of course* about it." Ollie grimaced and dug at the wood of the porch with his boot.

"Are you not German?" Charlie asked.

The man laughed, then looked thoughtful. "That may turn

out to be a very good question." He brightened. "But England, I love England! I'm a Cambridge man myself."

"A toff." Ollie frowned.

"A toff can be an excellent chap, my china," Bob chided her friend.

Ollie snorted.

"Excuse me." Lloyd Shankin removed his broad-brimmed black hat from his head and pressed it to his chest; this made him look less like a scarecrow and more like an undertaker, dressed in black and pale from working indoors. "Are you a rabbi?"

"I am!" The violinist's answer burst from him with a joyous smile. "Levi Rosenbaum, at your service."

"Lloyd Shankin." One of the dewin's eyes swiveled around as if he were trying to look at his own ear.

"What's a rabbi, then?" Ollie asked.

"Like a preacher, or a priest. A Jewish one." Charlie's own knowledge of rabbis came strictly from books, but he wanted to show Rabbi Rosenbaum he wasn't totally ignorant. "Sort of like Lloyd."

"Like Lloyd." Ollie nodded. "That might be all right, then."

Rosenbaum and Lloyd Shankin both looked up the boulevard at the cog-wheeled machine grinding its way in their direction. The teeth of its wheels tore up stone as they dragged their way forward, and when a wheel drifted to one side or the other, it shattered trees and smaller carriages in its path.

"Please come inside." Rabbi Rosenbaum stepped back as an inviting smell of fish, furniture polish, and citrus drifted out the door.

The chimney sweeps Bob and Ollie scooted in first, followed by Charlie and Gnat, and Lloyd at the rear. Charlie limped, as he had ever since Bob had opened his chest under Waterloo Station and accidentally bent one of the pins in his mechanism. "Is that your synagogue?" the Welshman asked.

"It isn't *mine,*" Levi Rosenbaum protested. "But it's *ours,* yes. Gorgeous, isn't it?"

"I would love to see the inside," Lloyd said. "See the stained-glass windows with light shining through them."

"I'll give you a tour," the rabbi said. He stepped into a parlor to one side of the entry hall, moving around a cello propped on its stand and a gramophone that cranked out a steady waltz-time stream of drum and tuba. With the violin bow he eased aside white drapes to look out toward the boulevard. "Why don't we let these gentlemen pass by first? They don't seem like university types, do they?"

"University?" Lloyd asked.

"The tall building with all the roofs," the rabbi explained. "It's a very old university, with a very famous library. Which is not to say that a person driving a war machine might not be interested in reading books, but, well . . . those men seem intent on something else."

"Who were you playing with?" Lloyd pointed at the cello. "I thought I heard two players."

"My daughter, Rachel," Rosenbaum said. "She's somewhere about. Now *she's* one to have immediately gone and buried her nose in a book. She likes to know the details, that girl." He raised his voice to call her. "Rachel!"

A dark wood stairway led up within the entry hall. Charlie

had put his foot on the bottom step—it was sneaky of him, and rude, but Thomas had to be upstairs—when Ollie hissed to get Charlie's attention.

He turned to look. The sweeps stood in a library on the opposite side of the entry hall from the parlor. Shelves lined the walls from floor to ceiling and groaned with the weight of the books standing on them. Most of the titles were gibberish to Charlie, and many of the characters on the spines weren't even the letters Charlie knew.

But Ollie pointed insistently at a specific book, so Charlie stepped closer to look. When he read the spine, he stopped.

The gold letters stamped into the cover identified the book's title as *Almanack of the Elder Folk and Arcana of Britain and Northern Ireland* and its author as *St. John Smythson,* but there was something wrong with the volume. Despite the familiarity of the title, the book had a green cover, rather than the red Charlie knew. And it was too big.

Too big by half.

It must be the first edition. This was the book Grim Grumblesson and his fellow trolls had suppressed after publication, the book that had information so sensitive that the hulders hadn't wanted anyone to read it.

And here was a copy, sitting in a rabbi's library in Germany. Ollie dragged the big volume off its shelf.

Charlie looked back to the parlor. Lloyd and the rabbi were facing away from Charlie, toward the window, and their voices dropped as if they were discussing something that made them feel concerned.

"Those aren't the landgrave's men," the rabbi said.

"What's the landgrave?" the dewin asked.

"The local ruler. The human ruler, at least. The hulders meet at their Thing and of course the fairies have the Undergraviate. Every folk rules itself, you see? A landgrave is like an earl, or a baron. His men wear all black, as does he. His heraldry is a red-and-white-striped lion; you'll see that all over Marburg."

"Whose heraldry is a skull and crossbones?" Lloyd wondered. "They look like pirates."

The men were engrossed in their conversation.

Charlie crept up the stairs.

Gnat joined him, flitting ahead and then waiting on the landing. She still wore around her neck the tooth of the Hound of Cader Idris, a half-mechanical beast she'd defeated in single combat on the slopes of the Welsh mountain. "Have you tried the dowsing rod again?"

By way of answer, Charlie raised the rod and rotated slowly in place. When it pointed at a closed door, the rod dipped. He swung it back to check the result and it dipped again.

Thomas was on the other side of the door.

Gnat nodded, and Charlie tried the brass doorknob. The door opened, and they slipped inside.

Within, a simple wooden bed sat beside a small table with a crumpled black cloth lying on it. A few charcoal drawings hung on the walls, and the window to the outside looked up at the big building with peaked windows. The university, the rabbi had said. A shortish man with bright red hair that shot straight up rushed across the grass toward the university.

Fleeing the rabbi's house?

Charlie thought he heard the short man sobbing.

But there was no sign of Thomas.

Gnat flitted down to look beneath the bed and shrugged.

Charlie raised the rod and swept again—

It dipped, indicating the table.

"That can't be right." Charlie lifted the black cloth.

Underneath it lay a pale hand. It was attached to nothing, and its wrist was ragged, as if it had been torn off by violence. Metal wires showed around the steel wrist bone.

Charlie raised the dowsing rod over the severed member, and it dipped, touching the hand itself . . . and became abruptly inert.

A girl's voice spoke behind them, from the doorway. "What are you doing in here?"

Og had failed, but Avrohom found three men. Only what he didn't know was that they were really three angels, and they had come so he would have someone to show hospitality to.

—Ginzberg, *Tales*, "The Angels' Visit"

"What have you done with Thomas?"

Charlie grabbed Thomas's hand and whirled around. He raised the hand and pointed its finger at the newcomer like an accusation.

She looked the same age as Bob and Ollie and had long dark hair. Over a blue dress she wore a coarse brown apron that was spotted with dirt here and there and contained a garden trowel in its single large pocket. She held a musical bow, like the bow to a violin. Or a cello.

"You shouldn't have come up here uninvited." The girl spoke English with only a little more of a German accent than her father. "That's prying."

Charlie wanted to say something about how impressed and

surprised he was at her English, but he was flustered. She was right, he *was* snooping. But she also had Thomas's hand, and she didn't want to talk about it. She was hiding something from him, and that made Charlie angry. He set the dowsing rod down on the table—it was useless now—but he wrapped Thomas's scarf around his own neck. He waved Thomas's hand. "Did that man take Thomas somewhere?"

Rachel stepped to the window in time to see the red-haired person duck into a door in the university's wall. "That's just meneer doktor yon vie more. He didn't take anybody anywhere."

"Doctor what?" Charlie asked.

"Meneer Doktor is his title. That means 'mister doctor,' in English. The university people like to pile on lots of titles. Meneer Doktor is actually the short version. Yon, spelled J-A-N, that's his given name, and his family name is spelled W-I-J-M-O-O-R. Jan Wijmoor."

"Oh." Charlie felt slightly mollified. "Is he a professor at the university?"

Rachel shook her head. "He's an engineer. He maintains the Library Machine."

Charlie couldn't get distracted. "And where's my brother?"

"Brother?" The girl frowned.

"Our friend, he means." Gnat flew between the two of them. That only made Charlie angry again.

He brushed the pixie aside and waved the hand. "Stop hiding things from me. This is his hand, so we know he's here somewhere. Where is he?"

Rachel hesitated, but then looked at her feet. "He might be

up on the mountain. In the *Altstadt,* that means 'old town,' the original part on the hill. At the castle."

Charlie rushed down the stairs.

"I'm sorry," he heard Gnat saying behind him. "Charlie's under some strain."

Ollie slammed the *Almanack* shut with a guilty look as Charlie passed. Bob whistled innocently, standing in the library door to give Ollie cover, but Lloyd and the rabbi didn't even notice. Then Charlie was out the front door and heading up the mountain.

He found a staircase that climbed the retaining wall almost invisibly, hidden in a crease in the stone. At the top, he passed under an arch and emerged into an open plaza.

The square was cobbled and sloped up toward the castle, which was visible at the top of the hill, dissolving into several narrow streets before getting that far. Charlie's end of the plaza was lined with tall, square buildings, mostly plastered or of half-timbered construction; to his left, the largest seemed to be some sort of town hall, built out of stone, sporting an explosion of windows and bearing a single tower in its center, with a door on the ground floor and a blue-and-gold clock face at its summit. At the upper end of the square a large fountain hurled jets of water from several spouts in an erratic pattern. Beyond the pool rose a half-timbered tower with a roof so pointy, all Charlie could think of was a witch. Or maybe a sharpened pencil.

Some of the buildings were restaurants, and diners sat at tables in front wearing leather pants and suspenders while they drank large mugs of beer and ate sausage. Some were booksellers, and students in gowns and caps poked slowly through the shelves of books standing outside in the sunshine. Others sold clothing or shoes, and customers walked out their doors looking down at themselves with smiles of satisfaction. Men in short boxy hats and fur-lined capes stood in small clusters in front of the town hall and conferred in low tones.

BONG! BONG! BONG! A copper carriage rushed in front of Charlie, the bell on its nose clanging. Hoses clung coiled along its sides, and men in India rubber coats and steel helmets crouched on top of the vehicle or hung off the back. Charlie had seen a similar carriage in London, when a hat manufacturer had caught on fire. In London, people who put out fires were called fire bobbies. What did they call them here?

The fire bobbies and their carriage raced away to the left, where, beyond them, Charlie saw smoke rising from a burning building.

Marburg had a large number of hulders. The male trolls seemed to favor fur hats resembling black cotton balls, and the women wore similar headgear with the addition of a pair of long horns. The hats made the jotun women and men resemble each other a little more; Charlie smiled.

Charlie also saw kobolds, though not in huge numbers. A few pixies flew along Marburg's streets, which cheered his heart. Every pixie he saw wore a dress, even the men, which was the reverse of what he'd experienced in England. Gnat usually wore clothes Charlie thought of as old-fashioned men's clothing—a tricorn hat, shirt and trousers, and buckled shoes.

The shopping pixies flew up and down as much as they flew horizontally. Charlie followed the flight of one pixie to see where they went, and realized that the upper stories of many buildings had their windows open and goods laid out on their windowsills for sale to fairies.

Marburg was a vertical town, climbing up multiple levels. How many levels *down* did Marburg go?

And if the humans of Marburg could use their upper stories to accommodate their pixie neighbors, what might be happening underground? Might the fairies have a space in their realm that welcomed humans? That thought made Charlie feel warm inside.

Charlie was taking in all the sights when a hideous *hee-YONK!* blared behind him. He dived left, scattering a knot of the caped men, and then looked back to see three mechanical donkeys roll past. Their barrel-shaped bodies, pinched in the middle to accommodate saddles, were mounted on three axles with large India rubber tyres. The tyres rattled up and down on the cobblestones and even over potholes while the riders—three young men with green felt hats—stayed level.

And then, looking at the donkeys, Charlie's eye fell on something on the other side.

Thomas.

There he was, walking along by himself. He wore a long red cape Charlie had never seen before, but Charlie knew Thomas's appearance as well as he knew his own. Pale skin, dark hair, short and slight.

Could it really be him?

As the donkeys neared, Thomas turned to look, and Charlie got a direct view of his face—and the Iron Cog pin at his shoulder.

Charlie scooted to his feet and ducked behind several of the caped men. For his trouble he got cursed out in German and kicked away, but he managed to shuffle directly backward, keeping the men between himself and Thomas.

When he had regained his balance and was out of range of kicking boots, he looked across at Thomas again. His brother was walking away, his red cloak spreading behind him.

And for a moment, clearly visible, Charlie saw that Thomas had two hands.

Gnat flitted close to Charlie. Charlie turned to look and saw Bob, Ollie, and Lloyd. They had followed him up the mountain.

"Did you see?" Charlie asked them.

"Aye, I saw him." Gnat's stern expression reminded Charlie that she was Natalie de Minimis, and that her foremothers had been the baronesses of the pixie realm of Underthames since time immemorial. Since Boudicca, Gnat had said. "And I saw his hands. Both of them. That's not Thomas."

Ollie and Bob crept over to join Charlie. They crouched, probably intending to stay out of sight, but all that really did was make them look very conspicuous in a crowd of midday eaters and shoppers. Lloyd walked at a more leisurely pace, singing something under his breath.

"You've got that look in your eye, mate," Ollie said.

Charlie had a look? "What do you mean?"

"You're going to do something crazy." Bob tugged her bomber cap tighter by the straps. "We're in."

Charlie shook his head. "No, there are too many of us. Lloyd, can you . . . I don't know, sing me invisible?"

"I don't think so, boyo," Lloyd said. "But I'm doing my best to sing that person—whoever he is—into a calm stupor of trusting, sheeplike peace."

"I don't quite know what sheep have to do with it, but that'll do." Charlie looked uphill, at the orange castle. Was that where the real Thomas was? "I think I'd better do this alone. I'll be less conspicuous. Let's meet back at the rabbi's. His daughter knows something, and maybe he does too."

He jogged after the false Thomas.

Thomas took a right turn at the top of the square. At the corner Charlie shot a glance after his quarry; the red cape was still moving steadily away, so Charlie had time.

The shop at the corner was a hatter, and Charlie picked a green felt hat with a feather in it from the rack. He still had a roll of banknotes from his father's shop, one of the few things he'd salvaged from the wreckage. They'd survived in his coat pocket to Wales and now to Germany, never used. He slapped the hat and a one-pound note onto the wooden counter of the shop.

The shopkeeper, a square man with a square head and a square mustache, looked at the note, looked at Charlie, and said something in German, shaking his head.

Charlie sighed and added a five-pound note. He thought maybe he was supposed to sign the back of a note that large, but he didn't do it, and the square-faced man didn't ask him to. The shopkeeper took the bills and pushed the hat across to Charlie.

He'd paid too much. How useful would it be to speak German?

Charlie put on the hat and limped after Thomas again.

Here the houses got wider as they got taller, with each new story cantilevered up and out above the one below it. The houses resembled upside-down pyramids, and over his head as he raced down stone steps, Charlie saw short enclosed walkways connecting houses on opposite sides of the street.

Thomas stopped at the bottom of the steps, where the narrow street opened onto a wider road. Charlie turned right and grabbed the merchandise he happened to be standing in front of, pretending to inspect it.

Out of the corner of his eye, he watched Thomas. Across the intersecting street was a storefront with a sign that said KAFFEEHAUS LANDGRAF VON HESSEN. His fake brother sidestepped a rider on a zebra and went inside.

Charlie put the merchandise back. He had been handling a broad leather belt with an iron bell hanging from it. Not a belt: a collar, for a horse or a cow. A thin woman with a pockmarked face and a warm smile said something to Charlie in German. He smiled back and left.

The kaffeehaus had large windows on two sides; Charlie walked once around the building and spotted Thomas. He was sitting at a table in the back of the shop, talking with someone who wore a black cloak, with the hood up.

Pressing his back against the wall of the building, Charlie

considered. Thomas had lost a hand, and now someone who looked just like him was walking around in the same town where Thomas was.

Or was Thomas here at all? Had Charlie been following a severed hand all along?

But no, Rachel knew Thomas. She'd said he was here on the mountain.

Charlie looked up and saw another enclosed walkway, connecting the kaffeehaus with a building across the alley. That was perfect—he'd climb the stairs inside the other building, cross the walkway, and sneak down inside the kaffeehaus to get a good look at Black Cloak and the false Thomas.

But then he walked around the connected building and found its only door shut and locked.

Frustrated, Charlie looked up again.

The enclosed walkway had glass windows, and one of them was open.

Charlie looked around quickly to be sure no one was paying any attention to him, and then he started to climb.

An ordinary boy would have found the climb impossible, but Charlie was no ordinary boy. He gripped the corner timber of the kaffeehaus with both hands and leaned out, bracing his feet against the plaster and practically walking up the wall. Climbing this way meant his fingers had to be very strong. Insanely strong, even.

And it turned out that Charlie had very strong fingers.

Upon reaching the second story, Charlie grabbed the cantilever, the carved wooden support that branched out from the vertical timber to support the building's wider second story.

He easily pulled himself up and got his fingers around the timbers of the second story's face, and thereby climbed up to the bottom of the third story.

Here there was no visible cantilever. The third story simply jutted out horizontally, three feet beyond the second. Charlie looked for a way to climb safely and saw none. Bracing himself and counting down from three, he jumped up and out—

missed his catch—

started to fall—

and jammed the fingers of one hand into the plaster of the wall. White powder rained down, and Charlie coughed a cloud of white dust away from his face, but his fingers had found something more solid, and he held.

By one hand, feet dangling.

Thomas's scarf slipped from his neck and his hat fell from his head. Charlie grabbed for either, and missed both.

Someone below shouted in German. Charlie didn't want to look down, because it would only give people a better view of his face. Instead he looked up as he dragged himself hand over hand across the timbers of the kaffeehaus's third story until he could scramble into the walkway's open window.

Charlie crouched, hiding from the view of anyone trying to watch him from the street. There was no door stopping him, so he waddled forward until he was inside the kaffeehaus proper, and finally stood.

The top floor of the building was furnished as living quarters: the rooms Charlie peeked into held beds. He slipped down the stairs to the ground floor, estimating where he was in relation to where he had seen Thomas and his companion.

At the bottom of the stairs, he found himself in a perfect position, where he could see both faces—or he could have, if Thomas's face had been visible, but his hood was now up. He could see the other man's face, though, and he knew it.

Gaston St. Jacques. The Sinister Man. Agent of the Iron Cog, and the man who'd shot and killed Charlie's bap.

The false Thomas, who now just looked like a red cloak, leaned forward as the two talked and sipped coffee. The red hood hid his face completely.

Charlie waited; he didn't *like* holding still, but he was good at it.

He did wish he could hear what they were saying, though. With the hood down so far, he couldn't even try to read Red Cloak's lips, and St. Jacques's face was turned slightly too far away from him.

And then the Sinister Man left. Charlie heard the ringing of coins as he threw money on the table.

Still Charlie waited.

Red Cloak finished his coffee, set down the mug, and stood.

Charlie got a short, but clear, look inside Red Cloak's hood. Thomas's features were gone. Red Cloak's eyes were black on black and shiny. And Red Cloak had no nose, no visible mouth, no eyebrows . . . nothing but two pure-black eyes in a totally smooth face.

There once was a widow woman with a single child, a son named Mathias. The other children of the village mocked Mathias for having no father, and so he made no friends and was lonely.

One day the widow looked out her kitchen window and saw Mathias playing in the forest with a new child. The new child wore a bright blue bonnet that hid her face, and when the widow asked her son about his new friend he said nothing, other than that he was happy not to be alone anymore.

And indeed he was happier, and his teachers at school and the village priest both told his mother so. And so every morning the widow watched her son and this child playing out in the forest, and because her son was happy she said nothing more about it.

Until one day, when Mathias refused to get out of bed in the morning. The widow urged him to rise and reminded him that his friend would miss him, but the boy only said that he felt ill and needed to sleep. The widow prodded his belly and found it swollen tight, so she made Mathias some tea and let him sleep.

The boy slept three days. On the fourth day, the widow awoke to find her son sitting on a stool beside her bed, looking at her. "What's wrong?" she asked.

"Nothing," he answered. "I am only thinking how hard you work for your son, and what a burden life must be for you, and how good you look."

The widow went about her work, and though he seemed well, Mathias stayed indoors and followed her about, watching her. On the fifth day, she awoke to find Mathias watching her again. When asked what he was doing, he gave the same answer.

—Jacob and Wilhelm Grimm, *Children's and Household Tales*, "The Stranger"

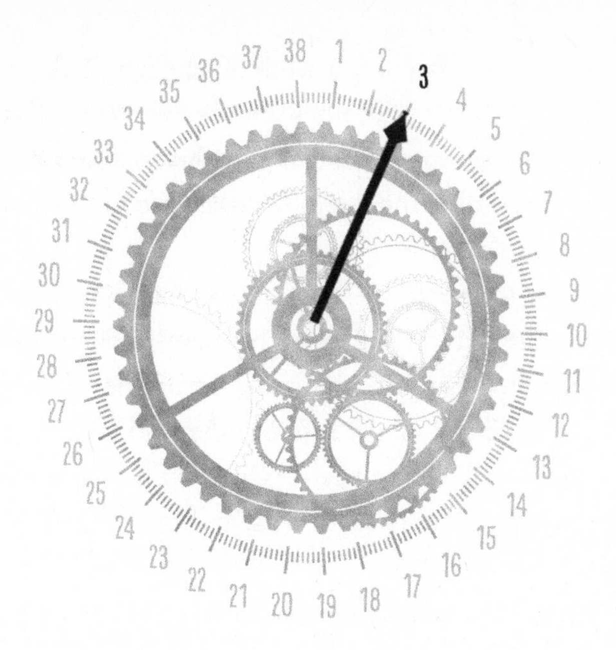

Charlie held very still.

The faceless person—or thing—turned immediately and went from the kaffeehaus with measured paces.

Charlie let his head drop back against the wall with a *plonk*. What kind of creature, person, thing, or devil was Gaston St. Jacques consorting with? It was possible, of course, that the meeting had nothing to do with Charlie, Thomas, or his friends.

No, that was ridiculous. The creature had looked like Thomas!

Charlie crept to the long windows and peered out. Seeing no sign of Red Cloak or the Sinister Man, he straightened up and walked out the door, trying to look calm.

Something had happened while he'd been in the kaffeehaus. Every corner of Marburg's upper town now had at least two, and in some cases four, men in black uniforms. They carried rifles on their shoulders. Charlie tried not to make eye contact.

The town square of the high city had the same shoppers and loiterers it had had earlier, with an eye-catching addition: twelve men stood at attention in front of one of the booksellers in the corner of the square. They wore black jackets above cream-colored trousers, with skull-and-crossbones patches on their cylindrical fur hats, and they leaned rifles on their right shoulders, too.

These were the same men who had been in the rolling war machine. Or men from the same group.

A man in a similar uniform, but with a slightly different combination of patches and medals on his jacket, stood among the shelves and dug through the books. Was he an officer? Other shoppers stayed several steps away, creating a void around the officer and making him impossible to miss.

When he had finished, the officer held three volumes tucked under his arm. Saying something crisp and loud, he paced along the length of the shelves and pulled another half dozen books off, dropping these on the ground and stomping on them with his boot heel. He looked coldly into the eyes of the bookseller—who looked away—and then turned and marched off.

Charlie kept walking. That the soldier was stealing and destroying books was not his business. Everyone seemed to see it, and no one was doing anything, including the men in the black uniforms. Were they the landgrave's own soldiers? He scrutinized the uniforms for any sign of an Iron Cog insignia. He saw none. Did that mean he could trust these men?

But of course not. They were at least strangers, and they could be enemies to Charlie even if they weren't agents of the Cog. For that matter, they could easily be the Iron Cog's men. There was no guarantee that every person in the Cog's service bore its insignia. In fact, the idea that they might was ludicrous now that he considered it. They were a secret society, not an army.

Charlie descended the hill quickly. Just in case, he hid himself in a recessed doorway at the intersection of two alleys to watch for signs that he'd been noticed or followed. After five minutes of ordinary foot traffic, he dropped down the stairs to the rabbi's house again.

He'd lost Thomas. He needed to regather his friends and find out what the girl Rachel knew about his brother.

The rabbi opened the door as Charlie's foot touched the step. "Charlie!" He sounded concerned, like Bap always had when he worried Charlie had been out of the house too long, but his voice lacked the note of scolding that Bap's voice had generally had.

Charlie stopped, and his shoulders slumped. He produced Thomas's hand from his pocket and showed it to the rabbi. "I should tell you that I took this from your house without permission."

Levi Rosenbaum laughed. "Well, that isn't exactly my

property, is it, Charlie? Come on in, before someone sees you."

Without waiting for agreement, the rabbi grabbed Charlie's shoulder and pulled him into the house, shutting the door behind him.

Charlie's friends sat in the study. Thomas sat with them, his face drawn into lines of worry and his single hand and both feet fidgeting. Charlie held himself back from running and giving Thomas a hug—Thomas was shy, and it might embarrass him—but he smiled at his brother. Rachel wasn't there.

"I guess my friends told you my name," Charlie said.

"Yes," the rabbi agreed. "But what no one told you, because you left before anyone could, is that Marburg isn't safe right now."

"It's filling up with soldiers." Charlie remembered what the rabbi had said to Lloyd Shankin. "The landgrave's men, who dress in black. And another group of soldiers, who wear a skull and crossbones."

"Those men are Prussian. From eastern Germany," the rabbi said. "They are here because Bismarck—he's not the kaiser, but he basically rules Prussia—wants the landgrave to join him in invading France."

"That doesn't sound like a good idea," Charlie said.

"Apparently, it seems like a good idea to Bismarck. Land is involved, and mines, and wealth. Also pride. But there's never been any shortage of people who want to rule and control other folk, even with good intentions. And I'm sure Bismarck would tell you how good it would be for Marburg to be part of the kaiser's state."

"I'm just here to get Thomas," Charlie said.

"I'm here to get . . . something else." Thomas looked down at his feet. "Something the landgrave has."

"You can stay as long as you like, Thomas," the rabbi said, "whatever it is you're looking for. You're a delightful houseguest—this week has fairly flown past."

The door opened abruptly, and Rachel came in. Behind her followed a short person with fine features—a kobold, though a tall one. Bob and Ollie leaped to their feet, and Charlie sprang back.

"You never said he was a broken!" Bob cried.

The kobold wore a long white coat, in the breast pocket of which was a series of metal prods. Other pockets clanked softly with other tools. Bright red hair shot straight up around the kobold's big ears. Craggy red eyebrows furrowed but then rose up in surprise, revealing icy gray eyes beneath. It was Jan Wijmoor, the library engineer Charlie had seen crossing the lawn earlier.

The kobold looked at Thomas, and then at Charlie. His lip trembled, and his eyes filled with water as if he were struggling with some powerful emotion. Finally, he sniffed and rubbed his nose on the back of his sleeve.

"Broken?" Wijmoor said. "I am certainly not broken."

"Broken home, gnome." Ollie was breathing hard. He looked like a bull about to charge. "On account of you're a gnome. It rhymes, see? Plus, it's kind of a joke about redcaps. You know, your wizards who break things."

The kobold tut-tutted, seeming to get his emotions under control. "Yes, I am a kobold. My name is Meneer Professor

Doktor Ingenieur Jan Wijmoor." That was even more titles than Rachel had given him. "And whatever you've heard about my people, we are not all redcaps. Very few of us specialize in breaking machinery; I think I can safely say that, Nondisclosure. *I* make and repair things, *exclusively.* I keep my duty of Compliance. Yes, that's one thing you can certainly say about me: I keep my duties. I'm very good at repairing machinery, in fact, and I've retrieved my tools and come back to repair the Thomas unit."

Nondisclosure? Duty of Compliance?

"Thomas ain't a unit," Ollie growled. "He's just *Thomas.*"

The kobold blinked. "Fine. Shall I reattach its hand?"

"His," Bob said. "*His* hand."

"*His* hand." Wijmoor shook his head. "Though I have not heard such dangerous talk as this for many years. This is Library Machine talk, and I don't like it. Not outside the library, Nondisclosure."

"No one thinks you're Zahnkrieger," the rabbi's daughter said gently. "Would you please repair Thomas's hand?"

"Zahnkrieger?" the rabbi murmured.

Charlie tensed up, fighting a sudden urge to knock the kobold down and run. Heinrich Zahnkrieger was the real name of Henry Clockswain, the kobold whom he had known as his father's business partner, but who had betrayed Bap to his death. "Zahnkrieger?" He tried not to shout. "Heinrich Zahnkrieger?"

The kobold took lunette-shaped spectacles from a coat pocket and perched them on his long nose, staring through the lenses at Charlie. "Are you also a Thomas unit?"

"I'm . . . My name is Charlie. Charlie Pondicherry. I once knew a kobold named Heinrich Zahnkrieger. Is that the same person you're talking about?"

"I taught Zahnkrieger," the kobold said slowly. Water returned to his eyes, and he blinked it away. "I was his advisor, his mentor. I urged him not to tamper with the Library Machine. And when I had to, I testified against him before the Internal Auditor at his terminal review. I think I can safely tell you this much, yes."

"You don't sound quite like old 'Einrich," Bob said grudgingly.

"I'm from the Dutch division of the Marburger Syndikat," Wijmoor said. "Formerly of the Eindhoven Conglomeraat, before the merger. Zahnkrieger is German, from the Marburger Kompanie."

"But—" Ollie started.

"And that is all I will say about Heinrich Zahnkrieger," the kobold said, his mouth snapping on the other kobold's name like a trap slamming shut. "Nondisclosure."

He sobbed once and looked away.

Charlie felt a hundred questions boiling up inside, but before he could ask any of them, Thomas pushed past Bob and Ollie and took his hand from Charlie's grasp. "Please, Doktor . . . Professor . . . Doktor Wijmoor."

"The short form of address is Meneer Doktor," Wijmoor said.

"Meneer Doktor." Thomas was trembling. His father, the inventor Isambard Kingdom Brunel, had designed Charlie to be shy and fearful on purpose. "I don't care whether you think of me as a unit or not. Will you please fix my hand?"

The kobold took a deep breath and sighed. "Of course I will . . . Thomas. And . . . the other thing?"

"Yes," Thomas said. "That too."

"What other thing?" Charlie asked.

The kobold jabbed an index finger at the ceiling, his fine-featured face breaking into a grin that, under his tall red hair and with his eyes puffy from crying, made his face look like a clown's. "I'm going to teach Thomas to speak German!"

◆ ◆ ◆

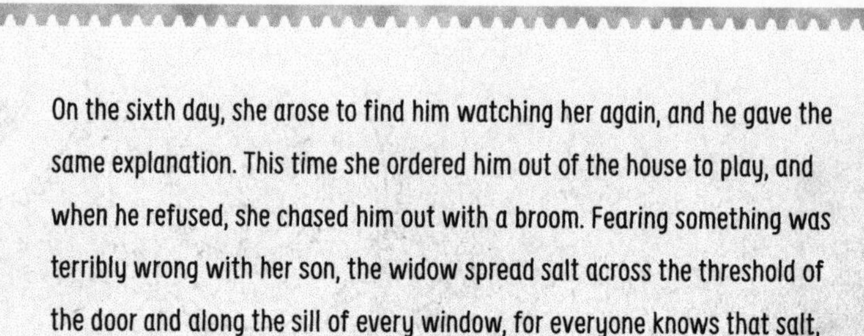

On the sixth day, she arose to find him watching her again, and he gave the same explanation. This time she ordered him out of the house to play, and when he refused, she chased him out with a broom. Fearing something was terribly wrong with her son, the widow spread salt across the threshold of the door and along the sill of every window, for everyone knows that salt, which is used to bless water, will repel evil spirits.

The widow searched her son's bedroom and found nothing, except that underneath Mathias's bed was his friend's blue bonnet.

When she returned downstairs, Mathias stood outside the door. "Why don't you come back in now and I will feed you some soup?" she asked him.

"The doorstep is so filthy, Mother," the boy said. "If you sweep it first, then I will come in."

"You are not Mathias," the widow said. "You are a stranger to me."

She threw a handful of salt at the boy, and when it struck him, he shrieked as if he had been burned. He bared long teeth, sharp as needles, and the widow threw salt at him again. This time some of the salt got into the boy's mouth, and he turned and ran away, screaming so loudly that the widow heard him for three hours.

The widow never saw Mathias again, and neither did anyone else.

—Grimm, *Tales*, "The Stranger"

"I'd like you to teach *me* German," Charlie said. That would let him understand what people were saying on the street around him. "If you can. I mean, if you can do it for me, too."

Could he trust the kobold? After all, Wijmoor knew Zahnkrieger. On the other hand, he wasn't making any secret of knowing the other kobold, and he seemed pretty tortured by that relationship. Also, the Rosenbaums trusted Jan Wijmoor, and they both seemed honest and friendly.

And Charlie really wanted to speak other languages.

Plus, his friends were here. If something went wrong, Lloyd and the chimney sweeps could intervene.

"Ha-ha!" Wijmoor snapped his fingers and pointed at the ceiling. "Mind you, I won't be *teaching* it to you, not exactly. And it won't be just German."

"I understand." That was a lie: Charlie didn't quite follow what the kobold was saying. "That is . . . what will you do, exactly?"

Jan Wijmoor chuckled. "I'll install a piece of technology in you, you see. It goes right back to Jacob Grimm, though it's not the Library Machine, per se, and it's called the Babel Card."

"Babel has something to do with lots of languages, right?" Charlie said.

"It's from the Bible, boyo," Lloyd Shankin answered. "The Tower of Babel is an old story about why there are so many languages in the world."

"Mmm," Levi Rosenbaum agreed. "This Babel Card sounds like a very nice thing to have. I might be able to use it myself, when I have my meeting with the landgrave and the Prussians tomorrow."

"That will be in German, surely?" Lloyd Shankin asked.

The rabbi spread his hands. "I've been told the undergravine and some of her fairy advisors will attend. Might there also be French people? Hulders? Diplomats from the Low Countries? The more people who are there to talk, the better, I say. The more people talking, the fewer shooting."

"Why is it a card?" Bob asked.

"Good question." Wijmoor snapped his fingers and pointed at the ceiling. "That has to do with how a unit like—with how Charlie processes data."

"You mean 'ow 'is brain works?"

"Right! Charlie's brain reads patterns punched into tiny cards made of finely hammered gold."

"You're going to stick a gold card into Charlie's brain, and that will let him . . . what?" Ollie asked. "Speak German?"

"And Thomas's, too. It will let them speak any language," Wijmoor answered. "Or almost any language. Even *read* the languages, I think."

"You'll insert the Babel Card in my head and then I'll understand and speak German," Charlie said. "And Dutch."

"And anything else the card's algorithms can unravel." Wijmoor nodded vigorously. "I expect any human language, and maybe the languages of some other folk to boot. I doubt you'll get a perfect mesh with Pixie, for instance, due to all the nonverbal elements. And Ghoul . . . well, is that even a language? The Babel Card still needs field testing."

Charlie wasn't quite sure what an *algorithm* was, but it sounded magical. He wanted what the kobold was describing. "And you'll do this . . . as a gift?"

Jan Wijmoor's lip trembled and he bit it. "Hmm, oh no, I'll have to charge you. Both of you, really. Best Efforts, you know. What do you have to offer?"

"I have money." Charlie showed the kobold the remainder of his bap's banknotes.

"Hmm, not worth so much around here, though."

"So I've learned."

"Tell you what." Jan Wijmoor snapped his fingers and pointed at the ceiling. "I'm helping you with the Babel Card, so how about you owe me an equal assistance? When I get in a pickle, will you and Thomas come help me out?"

"That seems fair," Levi Rosenbaum said. "They seem like boys who would honor that promise."

Charlie nodded.

"You drive a hard bargain, Charlie Pondicherry." The kobold grinned.

"What's an algorithm?" Thomas asked. Charlie was happy he wasn't the only one who didn't know the word.

"Algorithms are bits of complex math that the card will teach your brain to do. The algorithms aren't instantaneous; they take a little time to decipher, and they build on your existing vocabulary as well as contextual clues. The card lets you learn as any baby learns, only much faster. That's why the Babel Card will allow you to understand any language—or most languages—rather than just one. Would you like to see the card?"

Charlie nodded.

Wijmoor pulled a small wooden box and a pair of fine-nosed pincers from two separate pockets. With the pincers, he extracted something from the container. Moving slowly, he turned to show his prize to Charlie and Thomas.

Charlie saw a flake of gold, thin as the thinnest foil he could imagine, and no larger than one of his fingernails. Squinting closer, he saw that the foil was dimpled all across its surface in an elaborate pattern.

"What do we do now?" he asked.

Wijmoor made eye contact with the rabbi. "May we use your library? That seems like an auspicious room for it, all things considered."

"I would feel bad if you didn't."

"Come over here with me." Wijmoor led Charlie into the

library, in the center of which stood a broad coffee table. Ollie clutched the green *Almanack* under his arm as if it were a permanent part of him. The rabbi laid two sofa cushions on the table, and the kobold patted one with his free hand. "Lie down here. On your stomach."

"Like for a doctor, innit?" Bob asked.

"Yes," Wijmoor agreed. "Not strictly necessary, because I could insert the card with the—with Charlie and Thomas standing up. But this will be more comfortable."

Charlie stretched himself out on his belly on the upholstered table. He shoved a hand into his coat pocket and wrapped his fingers around the two broken halves of his bap's smoking pipe. "What now?"

Wijmoor tapped his foot on the carpet. "You too, Thomas. I'll work you in at the same time, here."

Charlie turned his head to watch Thomas climb up onto the table next to him. He smiled at his brother as he felt the kobold's long, slender fingers touch the back of his head, and then his vision went black.

*

Charlie stood in a deep pit. With a start, he realized that he'd been here before.

Ribs of stone arched upward gradually all around him. Overhead, Charlie saw a tiny spot of light, somewhere far away.

When had he been here before?

He heard soft weeping. Turning around, he saw a mound

of earth, as long as a person was tall and heaped up six inches high. At its head was a stone. There were characters on the stone and Charlie tried to read them, but somehow they were slippery. The characters shifted as he looked at them, flowing from one letter into another in a way that prevented Charlie from making any sense of what was written.

But the low mound had to be a grave.

A person knelt at the side of the mound, wearing a dark coat. The sobbing sounds came from this person, and each sob was louder than the one before, and made the mourning person's body shake.

"Don't be sad," Charlie said. "Your loved one will always be with you."

He touched the weeping person on the shoulder, and the person turned and looked up at Charlie.

The person weeping was Charlie himself.

Charlie stepped back, and as he did so, the face on the mourner shifted and flowed into another face, as the characters had flowed from one letter to another. By the time Charlie had regained his balance, the person kneeling had Thomas's pale face and dark hair.

"Papa?" Dream Thomas reached for Charlie.

"I'm your brother," Charlie said. "Not your father, do you understand?"

Dream Thomas stood. "Why?" he pleaded with Charlie. "Why would anyone do such a thing?"

"I don't know what thing you're talking about. Who did it? What did he do?"

Dream Thomas grabbed Charlie's wrists, but instead of the small hands he expected, Charlie found himself looking down at adult-sized hands, with skin that was pale almost to the point of being translucent but that felt like India rubber, and fingers with no nails.

Charlie tried to pull away but couldn't. He looked up—

and Thomas's face was gone.

In Thomas's place was Red Cloak. The featureless lower half of Red Cloak's face writhed as if the monster wanted to say something, and it stared furiously at Charlie with its all-black eyes.

Charlie jerked his hand away—

*

Charlie rolled over and fell off the coffee table—and slammed onto the floor.

"Ow." The carpet was beautiful, an interlocking pattern that was reminiscent of leaves, but it wasn't especially thick. He lay still, facedown.

"Charlie, *wie geht es dir? Wie fühlst du dich?* How do you feel, Charlie?"

Charlie hurt from the fall, but not too much.

And then he realized that Jan Wijmoor was speaking to him in German, and Charlie was understanding.

He tried speaking some back. "I good am. I am good. I'm well. I feel good." He pushed himself up and climbed to his feet.

"Well, my china," Bob said. "Either that worked, or you're doing a surprisingly good impression."

"Yeah, mate." Ollie rubbed his eyes. "I'd swear you was jabbering in German."

"It works!" Jan Wijmoor clapped Charlie on the back; Charlie was a little embarrassed at the dust cloud that came off his coat. "Charlie speaks German. And, in time, many other languages."

"But not Pixie, you say." Gnat folded her arms proudly across her chest, and she smiled.

"Well, Charlie, we may have to get a bit of Welsh into you. We Cymry call our tongue the language of heaven, you know." Lloyd smiled at Charlie.

"Steady on, mate." Ollie flared his nostrils and raised his eyebrows. "I've been to Wales. It was many things, but heaven wasn't one of them."

"Welsh in due time," Charlie said. "But for now, German is good." He looked at Thomas, who sat on the upholstered table and grinned.

Thomas smiled, opening and closing the fingers of both his hands, firmly attached to his wrists. "Now I'm ready."

"I'm coming with you," Charlie said. "Whatever it is you're planning."

"In the morning, gents," Bob said. "I for one need a bit of Bo."

The kobold stared at Bob.

"Bo Peep, sleep," Ollie explained to Wijmoor. "Bob's a Londoner, born and bred. Sometimes it takes a Londoner to understand him."

In London, Charlie had accidentally learned that Bob was a girl. She had sworn him to secrecy.

"Rhyming slang!" The rabbi clapped his hands. "Isn't it marvelous? You can get all the Bo you want right here, my friend! We have beds, don't we, Rachel?"

The rabbi's daughter nodded. "The girls can sleep in my room, and we can put the boys in the room where Thomas was."

"Girls!" Bob snorted. "What girls? If you mean Gnat, there's only one of 'er! Ollie an' Lloyd an' I can sleep on any old bit of floor you got!"

Rachel hesitated, but nodded.

"I must go!" Jan Wijmoor cried, snapping his fingers and pointing at the ceiling. "Compliance!"

Wheat, barley, ginger, and malt
The witch forgives and the priest finds fault
An iron nail and a pinch of salt
Never look in the mirror
Wheat, barley, ginger, and rye
A lonely child must never cry
So if you want to grow old and die
Never look in the mirror

—Francis James Child, *The English and Scottish Popular Ballads, Including Certain Lyrics of Britain's Ancient Folk*, No. 117

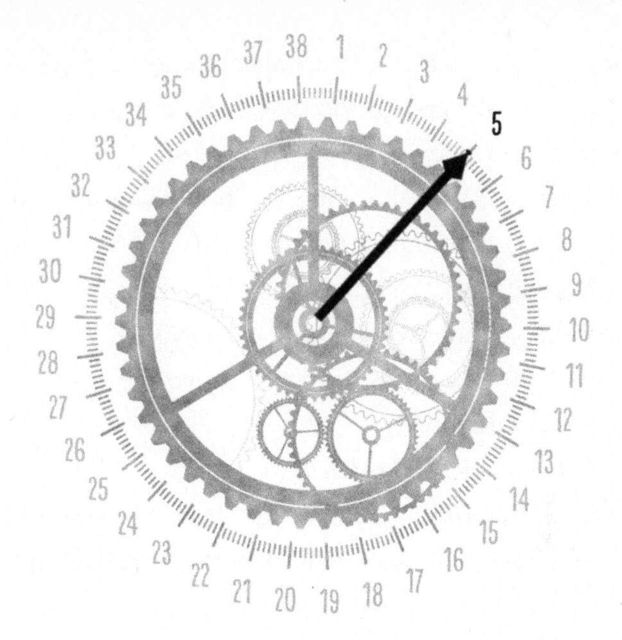

The kobold Wijmoor left, shuffling quickly across the rabbi's garden and disappearing into the door in the side of the tall square building. At least he wasn't crying anymore.

Charlie's friends settled in for the night, though for Ollie that meant huddling over the copy of the *Almanack* and poring over its pages by a little light that came from the hall. Charlie was surprised that Ollie, of all people, should be this attached to a book.

What was he so interested in?

Charlie and Thomas settled down to wait out the darkness. They sat in the shadows of the rabbi's porch with the lights off, to avoid attracting the attention of the armed men who rolled back and forth along the boulevard all night.

The landgrave's men? Prussians? Someone else? At one point, a fire broke out on the mountain, and they heard the clanging of the fire carriage.

And what was the rabbi supposed to do, with the clouds of war gathering over this small town?

But Charlie had other questions to ask Thomas.

"How did you lose your hand?" was his first.

"I was trying to sneak into the university library, and I caught it in a door."

"That tore your hand off?"

"*I* tore my hand off, trying to run away. But Rachel found me in the library and took me to Meneer Doktor Wijmoor. He cried a lot, but he promised to fix me."

"He seems anxious to help," Charlie said. "And weepy. What was Rachel doing in the university's library?"

"She's a reader, I guess," Thomas said. In the darkness, Charlie heard crickets chirping.

"You got here several days before us," Charlie said, trying to stimulate more conversation.

"I knew where I was going," Thomas explained.

"Thomas," Charlie said. "I want to help. If we're going to stop the Iron Cog, we'll need to work together. You need to explain more to me."

"I . . . I have a hard time trusting," Thomas said.

"I know." They sat silently for a while. "You're very clever, Brother," Charlie finally said. "You figured out something I haven't yet."

Thomas flinched. "What's that?"

"You got yourself all the way here, and your mainspring can't possibly have stayed wound the entire time. How did you do that?"

Thomas's faint grin was visible in a splash of light from a window across the boulevard. "It was easier when I had both hands."

Charlie tried to smile back. "Losing a hand must have hurt."

Thomas nodded. "I know you . . . tried to save me. I don't mean to run. I'm sorry. I'm just made that way."

Charlie squeezed his brother's arm. "I can't reach my mainspring with my hands, and yours is in the same place mine is." Charlie had seen his brother's mainspring when he and Bob had wound Thomas in an abandoned fairy barony underneath a Welsh mountain. "Are your arms more flexible than mine?"

Thomas shook his head. "I took two spanners from the wreckage of my father's home. With a mirror and a little bit of work, I could turn the spring myself."

That didn't sound comfortable. "Can I . . . see?"

Thomas hesitated, then nodded. He shrugged out of his coat, which dropped to the porch with a clank. Stooping, Thomas collected two heavy spanners from one coat pocket. "Lift my shirt."

Charlie raised his brother's shirt and saw his mainspring. Even in the darkness, he could see that the skin all around the circular grip was battered and torn.

"Like this, see?" Holding the spanners, Thomas stretched his arms over his head and reached back with the tools. It took him three tries, but he managed to get the heads of the spanners into the mainspring winder. “I can’t do it with one, but with two spanners I can slowly wind the spring.”

“Thanks, Thomas.” Charlie took the spanners and pulled his brother’s shirt back down. He put an arm around Thomas’s shoulders. “You don’t have to do that anymore, okay? We’re here for you.”

Thomas was quiet for a moment. “Okay.”

They waited in silence awhile longer, and then Thomas began talking. “I knew I could come here because the dwarfs who collected objects for my father talked about this place,” he said. “The landgrave has a famous collection. To do . . . the thing my father built me to do . . .”

“Cast your spell,” Charlie said, trying to be helpful. “That will bottle up the demon of technology again and stop the Iron Cog.”

“And us,” Thomas whispered.

“Probably,” Charlie agreed. “Yeah. Most likely it will stop us, too.” His heart hurt.

“I have to do it anyway. I was made to do it. I think about it all the time, going to Russia and helping my father cast this one spell I was made to cast. And then I remember that my father’s dead. And that his spell will shut me down forever.”

“Your father loved you.” Charlie said it because he wanted it to be true.

Thomas shrugged.

“What objects?” Charlie asked. “What did the dwarfs say was here?”

"There are three worlds," Thomas said. "Or, anyway, some old wizard said so. Like a three-layer cake. There's the intellectual world, the celestial world, and the elemental world."

"Those are weird names for worlds."

Thomas shrugged. "I guess we live in the elemental world. And the celestial world, that's the stars and the sun and the planets and such. And the intellectual world is above that, or inside it, or something."

"And what's in the intellectual world?" Charlie asked.

"God, I guess," Thomas said. "Or the gods. Demons, angels, that kind of thing. Ideas. And to cast the spell, I need to find the three nails, or the nails of the three worlds. There's a unicorn's horn here, and that's the nail of the elemental world. And then I need a piece of meteoric iron in the right shape; that's called the nail of the celestial world. And then . . . I'm not sure about the nail of the intellectual world."

"Your father had all those things." Thomas's father was Isambard Kingdom Brunel. Though he had collected the materials he and Thomas would need to cast the spell that would defeat the Iron Cog—sealing back into its Russian pit the demon whose release had loosed a flood of invention on the world—a traitor in the Cog's service had killed him and destroyed the airship carrying the precious items.

"Yes," Thomas said. "They're not unique, only really rare. I can get the horn here. And I think in the library I can figure out where to find the other two nails. I don't know quite what the Library Machine is, but maybe it can help me. I don't have all the pieces just yet."

Only later did the sliver of hallway light behind them disappear. Ollie had finally gone to sleep. Had he listened to Charlie and Thomas talking?

*

As the sun cracked over the forested eastern hills, Charlie and Thomas trudged up from Marburg's *Altstadt* and across the platform on which the castle stood.

At a stable near the edge of the platform, Charlie grabbed a barrow full of dung by its long handles and pushed. The barrow's two iron-rimmed wooden wheels ground a constant rattle on the gravel, punctuated by the steady crunching of the boys' shoes. Thomas picked up two long muck forks.

They'd agreed they'd sneak in, pretending to work at the castle. There must be lots of boys who worked there, too many for anyone to notice.

They'd also agreed they'd leave first thing in the morning and let their friends sleep. Ollie especially looked exhausted, mumbling in his sleep.

The castle proper was a single very large building, connected to a smaller one beside it by an elevated, enclosed walkway. The walkway was a larger version of the one Charlie had used the day before to sneak into the kaffeehaus, large enough to be a long room in its own right, built of the same orange stone as the rest of the castle, and resting on stone columns.

Charlie stopped at a flower bed in the shadow of the smaller part of the castle. "You think the horn is in there?"

Thomas handed one fork to Charlie and with the other

started slowly transferring dung to the flower bed and forking it into the earth. "In that walkway"—he pointed—"there's a guard. So I think the purpose of the annex is to house the landgrave's collection."

"Collection of what?"

Thomas shrugged. "Objects. Including one unicorn horn."

The annex had a door beneath the walkway, which was the only visible entrance other than the walkway itself. Charlie looked around to see whether he was being watched—he saw no one on this side of the castle, and no faces in the windows—and then tried the door. It was locked, and when he pulled hard it didn't even budge.

Stepping back and looking up at the windows of the walkway, Charlie saw the head and shoulders of a man in a crisp black uniform, marching back and forth. A rifle rested on his collarbone.

"I'd rather not fight the guard," he said. "It's dangerous, and it could get noisy. We don't want to be chased out of Marburg unless we're sure we can do it with the unicorn horn in our hands."

"The annex has windows." Thomas pointed. "But they're on the second and third floor."

"And the rainspouts angle directly off the roof, so there are no drainpipes to climb up." Charlie examined the main building of the castle. "But over there is an open window, surrounded by ivy. How do you feel about sneaking and climbing, Thomas?"

"I've lived most of my life hiding on a mountain." Thomas

shoved his fork down into the earth and left it there, quivering. "Sneaking and hiding are the two things I do best."

They brushed themselves off and straightened each other's coats. Beneath the walkway, opposite the barred door into the annex, was a wide gate that opened into a rectangular courtyard. From all four walls, tall, thin windows looked down on the courtyard and its cobblestones, and two wooden enclosed walkways clung cantilevered to the stone at the level of the third story. Several doors, all painted red, opened into the castle proper.

The center of the courtyard was a hive of activity. Pyramids of paint pails and soap buckets were assaulted by workers in rough brown smocks, who rushed their supplies into the building and raced out with empty pails afterward.

Charlie grabbed a bucket. He picked the smallest door into the castle and charged ahead.

"The important thing here," he whispered, "is to give the impression that you belong."

He found a narrow spiral staircase and climbed it. At the top, a man with short-cropped blond hair and a thick mustache, dressed entirely in plain black, examined a sheaf of papers. He looked up from his reading and stopped Charlie with a hand on his shoulder. "You have an errand?" The words were German.

Charlie showed his bucket and bowed.

The blond man frowned and stepped aside. "Ah, yes."

Charlie walked on.

They circulated around the third floor of the castle. The building had enormous rooms, swarming now with some teams scrubbing flagstones to a sparkling shine and others whitewashing walls.

Workers were laying a thick blue carpet over the stone floor of a long central hall. The carpet was so thick and heavy that the team managing it had to be comprised entirely of hulders, and their sweat made the hall smell like a cattle barn, even with a breeze blowing through.

Charlie looked for an open window. He found a dining hall first, with a high ceiling, a narrow table down the center of the room, and tapestries on the walls. The dining room's windows were wired shut, though, so Charlie moved on. Around the corner he found the open window he was looking for. Setting his bucket in the corner of the room, he climbed out onto the vines.

The ivy growing up the wall was as thick as Charlie's wrist, which was good, since Charlie and Thomas were both heavy. But they clambered up the ivy, the vines held, and in a few seconds both boys stood at the edge of the castle's rooftop.

The roof was steep and peaked and covered with black shingles. Crouching, Charlie and Thomas crept along the edge, turned the castle's corner, dropped onto the roof of the walkway, and crossed to the annex. From there it was a simple process to ease out along a narrow ledge of stone to the nearest window.

The window was latched shut. Charlie would have preferred to find it open. "Here goes." Gripping the lead edge of the frame with one hand and clutching the stone lip beneath with the other, Charlie pulled the window hard.

Sproing!

The window swung open and the latch fell. Charlie grabbed for it—

missed—

dropped—

and Thomas caught him by the back of his coat.

Charlie watched the tiny lead latch bounce on the gravel below. "Pull me up. Let's take a look at what's inside."

The landgraves of Hesse are known for their obsessive collecting. During the Thirty Years' War, Landgravine Amalie Elisabeth of Hanau-Münzenberg fielded an entire battalion equipped exclusively with medieval arms and armor.

—from Hermann Völpel, *Biographical Dictionary of Germany and the Low Countries*, "Landgraves of Hesse"

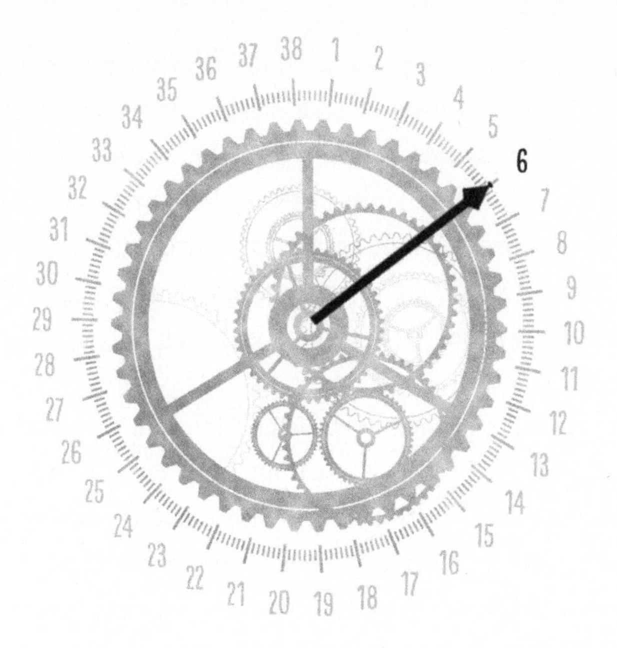

Thomas hoisted Charlie over the windowsill with a vigorous yank. Was Charlie that strong? He was heavy, being made of metal, and Thomas seemed completely indifferent to his weight.

Charlie grabbed the window frame as he passed through it, catching himself so he wouldn't tumble to the floor. After lowering himself quietly, he extended a hand and pulled Thomas in after him.

"We're quite a team," he told his brother.

"We're strong, fast, and clever. And we can wind each other's mainsprings."

"You forgot *handsome*."

Thomas grinned.

Charlie took a long look around. They were standing in a room filled with weapons. In a rack of blades, he could have pointed out the scimitar and the falchion, but he had no words for distinguishing the eight different lengths and thicknesses of fencing swords. A stand of ten polearms stymied him even more—one of them had to be a halberd and probably one was a pike, but he didn't know which was which. And what were the rest of the long, pointy weapons in the stand?

Two files of plate armor stood at attention. Rows of matchlock and flintlock guns leaned out from racks on the walls. Knives, long and short, straight and curved, one- and two-bladed, square and wavy, glittered under panes of glass.

Here and there, Charlie noticed empty slots. Were some of the weapons on loan to a museum, or on display elsewhere in the castle?

"Any of this look like a unicorn's horn?" Charlie asked.

Thomas shook his head, but they paced the entire room to be sure. The armory included axes, shields, mail, hammers, maces, spiked balls on the ends of chains, and stranger things Charlie couldn't identify. A second large room on the same floor was full of tapestries, hanging both on the walls and on the heavy wooden screens that subdivided the room into four.

A spiral staircase at one end led up and down. Beyond the staircase was a broad wooden door with a viewing hole protected by an iron grille. By gripping the grille, Charlie could pull himself up and look through: he saw the interior of the covered walkway.

The walkway was quiet, so he was about to drop down, when he realized something was missing.

"The guard," he whispered. "Where's the guard?"

Thomas took a turn at the window. "Maybe he's stepped away."

"Yeah, maybe. But let's keep our voices down, in case he's come in here." Charlie looked at the steps. "If you were the landgrave, where would you keep your unicorn's horn?"

"Up." Thomas mounted the steps.

Charlie followed. "Maybe the guard was needed to help paint one of the rooms."

"Maybe."

On the next floor, which Charlie guessed to be the fourth, the landgrave kept an impressive collection of musical instruments. Charlie saw curled horns he didn't recognize, water organs, harpsichords, a glass harp, and a piano whose strings ran up vertically behind a white linen curtain. There were cases of toys, including dolls, puppets, balls, penknives, oddities on string, sculpting wax, and building blocks whose paint had faded almost entirely to gray.

Charlie and Thomas got separated in the room full of clothing. Charlie heard high-pitched humming, a strange melody that must have been coming from Thomas. It was a lovely sound, and a lonely one.

Some of the clothing was pinned flat, either to the walls or to vertical boards, but most of it was worn by headless mannequins. To judge by what Charlie was seeing in this room, for the last two hundred years the landgraves and landgravines of Hesse had always dressed from head to toe in black. The sole exception was the white of their enormous ruff collars and the white lace poking out of the black sleeves of their jackets. Their children had dressed much the same, little stern copies of their parents who generated little stern headless mannequins.

Thomas emerged from a cluster of mannequins that seemed engaged in an extremely somber dance.

"Are these people as joyless as they seem?" Charlie asked.

Thomas shrugged. He stopped to examine the ruff collar of the nearest mannequin, tugging idly on the collar with one hand while he tugged at the end of his scarf with the other.

Charlie smiled at his brother.

Something was wrong, though. Something bothered Charlie.

Was it the missing guard?

Thomas smiled at Charlie again, a closed-mouth smile. He started walking toward Charlie, hands pulling on both ends of his scarf.

His scarf. Something about the scarf was wrong.

Thomas had left his scarf behind in Wales. The dwarf dowser Thassia had built it into a dowsing rod for Charlie to use to find his brother. And then Charlie had lost the scarf, trying to climb into the kaffeehaus.

"Thomas," Charlie asked. "Where did you find that?"

Thomas attacked.

Charlie knocked a mannequin into his attacker's path. Thomas bowled into the black doublet and outrageous white frill of some seventeenth-century landgrave and went down in a ball, rolling and hissing. Charlie stumbled back to gain some room to maneuver, nearly falling over when he knocked down a screen pinned full of little girls' black dresses.

"Thomas!" Charlie yelled.

Was this his brother, possessed or corrupted by some evil force? Or was it a shape-changer who had already killed his brother and had now come for Charlie?

Thomas came up in a crouch, ready to spring. Charlie immediately bolted sideways. He put mannequins and a screen between himself and his attacker, and it paid off when Thomas jumped at Charlie but fell to the floor, tangled up in black hoop skirts.

Charlie darted back into the previous room, looking for a weapon. He dug among the brass instruments and found a tuba. He heard racing footsteps behind him—

he spun and raised the tuba—

and *bong!* caught his attacker's head in the flaring bell.

Charlie charged toward the stairs, pushing his enemy by the tuba shoved around his head. With a final heave, he hurled his attacker down the spiral steps.

"Thomas!"

No answer.

Charlie bounded down the stairs after his opponent. If it was Thomas, he wanted to help his brother. And if it was some kind of impersonator, Charlie was afraid it would find the real Thomas and hurt him.

As his feet touched the stone of the third floor, a wrong shadow warned Charlie. He dropped to the floor and rolled, and his attacker crashed into the wall where Charlie had just stood.

Charlie scrambled toward the nearest wall-hung tapestry.

It was modern-looking, for a tapestry, and depicted two men in puffy hats (the kind Charlie had seen on pictures of Henry VIII and Thomas More) sitting at a table talking. One of the men pointed up and the other pointed down, and other men sat in a circle around the table, watching intently.

Only the faintest scratch on stone behind him warned that he was about to be attacked, but it was enough—Charlie balled both his fists into the thick tapestry and kicked off the wall with his feet, pulling the tapestry free and hurling it behind him.

The scratch was silenced as Charlie caught his attacker under the tapestry. Charlie didn't hesitate; he ran into the next room and grabbed a mace off its stand. The mace was a heavy spiked iron ball on the end of an iron handle, with a brittle leather strap wound around the bar to create a grip.

Charlie raced back into the tapestry room. The tapestry he'd pulled to the floor was rumpled to a large peak in the center, and Charlie rushed forward, swinging the mace down over his head—

BOOM!

The mace slammed to the floor, the violence of its sound echoing through the annex. Charlie's attacker wasn't under the tapestry, then. Where was he?

Charlie bolted up the stairs again. He heard a cracking sound and felt sick with worry. His mechanisms strained and heated as he pushed himself to throw one foot in front of the other as fast as he could.

Pounding back into the room full of mannequins, Charlie

saw a strange sight. Thomas lay on the floor. One arm was broken, snapped nearly off through the upper arm. Thomas crouched over him, or rather, Not-Thomas did, its hands around Thomas's neck.

Charlie threw the mace.

CRUNCH! He scored a direct hit, nailing the attacking creature right in its forehead. The monster rolled back with the force of Charlie's attack, crashing onto the keyboard of the vertically strung piano.

Charlie didn't let up. Snatching the mace off the floor, he hit Not-Thomas in the chest, knocking it up over the keyboard and through the piano's strings.

As the creature sprang to its feet on the other side of the piano, Charlie got a good look at its face. Most of the features were Thomas's, but where Charlie had hit the beast, its skin had turned translucent and rubbery-looking. And instead of Thomas's eyes, it now had eyes that were completely black.

Red Cloak. Charlie was fighting Red Cloak.

What kind of monster was it?

Charlie brought the mace down hard on top of the beast's head. It fell to the floor groaning, but it wasn't dead, or even unconscious. As it whimpered a complaint, Charlie grabbed his enemy by the ankle and dragged it to the nearest window. He saw forest outside, so he was facing away from the castle.

With a running start and the biggest heave he could muster, Charlie hurled the creature into the window. Glass shattered as Charlie's antagonist dropped to the castle grounds.

Charlie leaned on the windowsill to see the result. To his

disappointment, Red Cloak hit the ground, rolled, and then rose to its feet. With a hiss and a last flash of black eyes in Charlie's direction, it dropped over a wall into the forest below.

Charlie's legs trembled.

Not good. He rejoined his brother.

"Thomas."

"I'm sorry. I . . . had to hide."

"Don't worry about it. I understand."

"Thanks, Charlie."

Charlie nodded as his legs jerked twice, hard. "You'd better wind my mainspring, and then we need to get out of here."

The great questions of the day will not be settled by means of speeches and majority decisions but by iron and blood. Especially iron.

—Minister President of Prussia Otto von Bismarck, "Blood and Iron"

Thomas's upper arm turned inward where Red Cloak had broken it. This left the limb twisted across the front of his chest at an unnatural angle, so Charlie tucked the broken arm inside Thomas's coat and buttoned the coat with only the good arm in a sleeve. He thrust the end of the empty sleeve into one of the coat's pockets.

It didn't look quite as natural and inconspicuous as he would have liked, but it was better than having the arm visible.

"Charlie," Thomas said, "we can't leave without the horn."

Charlie nodded. He picked up the mace again, just in case, and they searched the rest of the annex. They found art and even chunks of masonry taken out of Marburg's oldest churches when they had been renovated. They found furniture.

They found maps of Marburg, and Hesse, and Germany. They found paintings and sculpture.

And finally, not on the highest floor of the annex, but on the lowest, they found the unicorn horn's display. The display included other natural wonders, including a mandrake root, a lamb born with two faces, a bottle full of human kidney stones, and a display comparing the skull shapes and sizes of various folk, including hulder, pixie, dwarf, alfar, kinnari, and djinn. The djinn skull was particularly fascinating, not for its stubby horns, but because it was only visible directly from the front—when Charlie stepped to the side and tried to look at it, the skull disappeared.

The landgrave's collection included a hand of glory (the pickled hand of a hanged man, converted into a candle), a stuffed mermaid (who looked a lot like a monkey with most of a fish stitched to its lower half), a pair of shoes once worn by Saint Elizabeth of Hungary (who had surprisingly big feet), and an orrery (a model of the sun and planets that moved when Charlie turned a crank in its base). And a pedestal marked HORN DES EINHORNS. As Charlie looked at the note, its letters rearranged themselves until they spelled UNICORN'S HORN. Thereafter, looking at the words, he seemed to see both German and English words simultaneously.

And there it was, the unicorn's horn. The nail of the elemental world.

"Shouldn't it look more . . . magical?" Charlie asked.

Thomas shrugged. "It looks like the one my father had."

The horn was as long as Charlie's arm, a straight spike the

color of old ivory, with a faint spiral twist running around the outside of it. Charlie took it and tucked it under his arm.

"Okay. Now let's get you looked at."

Charlie opened a third-story window and prepared to jump, but Thomas grabbed his elbow. "That's a long drop."

Charlie laughed. "Remember when you threw me off the mountain, Thomas? Trust me . . . this drop is nothing."

Thomas hugged his broken arm to himself and said nothing.

"Okay," Charlie said. He looked out the window and found a ledge running below it, around the building. "We'll go back through the castle."

He climbed out along the stone shelf and Thomas followed.

The ledge led them back along the elevated passage, and then the two boys were creeping along the outside of the castle's main building.

"Look," Thomas called from behind.

Charlie turned back to peer through the window. Within was the long, narrow dining table they'd seen earlier, from the other side.

Various parties filed into the room and began to sit.

Charlie pressed himself against the wall, and Thomas did the same. They stood on opposite sides of the window, both unseen by the people inside.

Charlie pointed at the ground. Should they jump down now?

Thomas shook his head.

Charlie sighed and peeked through the window.

Along the table to his right Charlie saw a row of people.

Nearest to him were the landgrave and two counselors, all dressed in severe black. The landgrave was the man Charlie had met earlier in the castle, the man who had waved Charlie along when Charlie carried a bucket of paint and pretended to have work to do in the castle. He seemed more tired now, and he sat between two men older than him, with less hair and long beards, who leaned in to make soft comments to their leader.

Beyond the landgrave were three kobolds in high-collared formal wear. They shuffled the papers in front of them, reading and rereading the same passages. None of them was Jan Wijmoor, but Charlie guessed they must be leaders of the goblin community . . . What had Wijmoor called it? The Marburger Syndikat?

On the far side of the kobolds sat a company of fairies. Their leader was a woman with an exploding mane of bright blue hair and wings that were streaked orange and yellow. She had to be the one Levi Rosenbaum had called the undergravine, and she also had two companions. All three of them wore plate armor that looked like blue tortoiseshells, and they perched on high, tiny-seated stools.

Beside the kobolds a single hulder hunched forward on a low bench, wearing one of the fur caps Charlie had seen in the *Altstadt* and an ornately stitched white shirt under a leather vest.

On the left side of the table sat fewer people, all men. Charlie saw the skull-and-crossbones commander he'd seen in the square, the thief and destroyer of books. He saw the Sinister Man, Gaston St. Jacques. And he saw himself.

He and Thomas locked eyes briefly; then Charlie stared again at himself. Or, rather, at the person who looked like him. He was even wearing a hat just like Charlie had recently worn.

Or was it the very *same* hat?

That had to be Red Cloak. The monster, the shape-changer. How had it joined this meeting in the castle so quickly? Was it the same Red Cloak—or were there two of them?

At the head of the table, facing Charlie, stood Rabbi Levi Rosenbaum. He wore a long white shawl over his shoulders, striped with black and fringed at the ends. The rabbi held his hands pressed together and kept turning to look at Not-Charlie, struggling to keep a baffled expression from his face.

"I should probably begin by thanking you all," Rabbi Rosenbaum said. "I was surprised at the invitation, but my community is honored. And personally, of course, I am flattered."

He spoke German, and Charlie understood perfectly.

"*We* didn't invite you," the Sinister Man said.

"Shh." The hulder glowered at him.

One of the landgrave's advisors, a man with a bulbous nose, spoke up, waving his index finger in a slow circle. "*We* invited the rabbi, Monsieur St. Jacques. This realm has a long history of including all its folk in its deliberations. Given the goodness of our purpose here, and how the rabbi's folk too shall gain from Hesse's neutrality in the upcoming conflict, his participation, and indeed a short invocation by him, seemed appropriate."

"Don't be so quick to commit yourself to neutrality," the

book thief snapped. "You'd be well advised to fully inform yourself of your options first."

"We are grateful to you, I am sure," St. Jacques said, "for including all your folk in these proceedings. We think *all* your people will be interested in what we have to say."

The pixie's advisors seemed to be urging her to patience, but she hissed at them and they bowed. "What's that, Frenchman?" the blue-haired pixie asked. "I'm ready to listen now."

St. Jacques smiled. "We should hear the rabbi out first."

"You know, I find myself in this interesting position," Rosenbaum continued. "I'm a guest here. I'm a stranger of sorts. My people have lived here a few generations, but we're recent arrivals. The landgrave's family has been here for centuries."

"I thought the rabbi was going to say a prayer and leave," the thief said. "That would have been tedious enough. This is worse."

"But then I think," Rosenbaum continued, "after all, what is a German? To the Romans, a German just meant 'one of those barbarians who live over across the river where there used to be Celts.' And that's me: I'm one of the barbarians over the river. I'm a German. Yes, I'm something else, I'm a Jew also, but I'm German. I speak German in my home; I love my German neighbors; I play German music.

"And I'm Hessian, too!" The rabbi bowed slightly in the landgrave's direction. "I live in Marburg, in Hesse. I pay my taxes to the Landgrave of Hesse."

One of the kobolds sputtered. "Yes, yes, this is elementary

taxonomy. You are also a rabbi, and a human. So what? I am a German, and a Hessian, and a kobold, and an engineer."

"Exactly!" Rosenbaum clapped his hands together. "So maybe, I think, it's perfect that I've been invited. Maybe the landgrave and his counselors have chosen me for a very specific, a very symbolic reason. Even if they didn't intend it, because of course some of the most powerful symbols come right out of that part of our souls that we don't see very well. My presence here—the presence of a stranger, an outsider, but someone who in other ways is very much at home—should maybe remind you that we're all strangers. And we're all family at the same time. And everybody can belong to many kinds of folk at the same time. That's fine, that's normal: nature makes overlapping circles and crisscrossing lines. The strange thing would be if there were no overlaps, if everybody were either a complete stranger, or family.

"Instead, everyone is a little bit a stranger, and a little bit family. And that's all good—that's a beautiful thing! Because if you and I are a little bit family, then we have things in common; we have shared ideas; we know how to talk to each other. Common ground, you see. But if we're also a little bit strangers, then you know things I don't. So I can learn from you. And maybe—I don't want to be presumptuous, so I'm saying maybe—there are things you could learn from me, too.

"I think this is what my presence here should remind us all. And so now we have visitors from the east, from Prussia and the kaiser. And you're a little bit strangers to us: you're driving big vehicles we've never seen before, and you speak our language with an accent. But you're also family. We're all Germans. And we're all people. So whatever you've come to discuss—"

"We have declared war on France," the book thief said.

"Nooooo!" the jotun lowed.

Rabbi Rosenbaum's hands fell to his side. "Yes . . . but . . ."

"Declarations are just paper." The landgrave leaned forward over the table to address the thief. "Words. Don't rush. We would be happy to smooth over trade issues, land, access to steel and coal. We know the French. As the rabbi says, we're family; we can work these things out. This very castle is famous for being a place to resolve difficult issues. When Martin Luther and Ulrich Zwingli disagreed—"

"You fail to understand," the book thief said. "We do not go to war over *economics.* We certainly do not go to war over silly issues of *superstition.* We go to war to *fix this broken world.* Today France, tomorrow the rest."

"And if I would not be fixed?" The pixie ruler shot off her stool into the air and raised her voice to a stern shout. "Would you go to war with me, human?"

"A new world is coming," the book thief said calmly. "The rabbi is wrong. It's not a strength that we're all strangers; it's a weakness. A new world is coming, and in it we will be one folk. One state. Everyone reading the same books, everyone believing the same truths. Everyone taken care of and served by machines."

"That has a kind of superficial beauty," the landgrave said. "But it's wicked nonsense."

"Is it nonsense?" the thief asked. "Do you know how pixies decide who will rule in their realms? Violent combat, like some medieval story. Do you know what displaced hulder youth do when machines and big businesses take over more and more of their farming work? They drift into the big cities, like garbage blowing on the wind, and drink themselves into a stupor with milk. Dwarfs won't live in houses and won't even say each other's names, because they're afraid of some ancient enemy that, as far as I can tell, doesn't even exist! Of all the elder folk, the alfar are the wisest—they just hide from the rest of us! And that's not even to mention human beings."

Charlie frowned. What the thief said had some truth in it.

"And what gives you the right to judge those folk?" the landgrave asked steadily. "What makes you so sure your ways are superior? If you wish to talk to dwarfs and invite them to live in houses, or try to explain to them that houses are superior, no one will stop you. Indeed, I would welcome such a conversation in the landgraviate, with open arms. But you didn't come here with bulletins and debaters. You brought soldiers and guns. If you are going to compel the world to live as you see fit, what will be the cost?"

"The time for talking is over," St. Jacques said. "Now it is time for deeds."

"We'll all have to become Prussian, you mean!" The bulbous-nosed man was nearly shouting.

St. Jacques shook his head. "What comes now didn't start in Prussia. It started everywhere. Prussia is merely the hammer, the tool in the hand that will move us forward to the next phase. In the future there will be no Prussia, no France, and no Hesse."

"There will be no *them,*" the thief added. "We will all be *us*. Doesn't *that* sound lovely, Rabbi? No overlapping, everyone just in a single circle? All of us acting together for the common good? All of us living wise and protected lives, making good choices because the bad choices—or at least the worst choices—are taken away from us? Every person living in leisure and served by machines?"

"You are offering to conquer us." The landgrave smiled gently. "This has been attempted before. If you read the history of the Thirty Years' War, you'll find that Hesse—"

"Hesse will come into the new order of things," Gaston St. Jacques said. "What you are offered is the chance to join peaceably, and spare your subjects the death and misery that must otherwise rain down upon them."

"I am prepared for you!" the fairy snapped. "Go back to your cold eastern hell, and take your clanking minions with you! My allies and I will not surrender!"

"Please," the Landgrave of Hesse said. His young face was deeply lined with care. "You are all my guests here, as you are all strangers. *We* are all strangers. Rabbi Rosenbaum has spoken words of real wisdom. We can learn from each other, and to do that we should begin by forgetting these hostile words. Let us allow the threats to fall to the ground and disappear, blow away in the breeze. Let us find our common ground and the place where we can share a peace that we can all honorably choose. You. Us. France. The Syndikat. The undergraviate."

"You are not with us." Gaston St. Jacques laughed. "War it is."

Thomas gasped.

Charlie looked to his brother just in time to see Thomas slip in astonishment and fall off the ledge.

Charlie jumped down after him.

I have been in a multitude of shapes,
Before I assumed a consistent form.
I have been a sword, narrow, variegated,
I will believe when it is apparent.
I have been a tear in the air,
I have been the dullest of stars.
I have been a word among letters,
I have been a book in the origin.

—from *The Book of Taliesin*, VIII, "The Battle of the Trees"

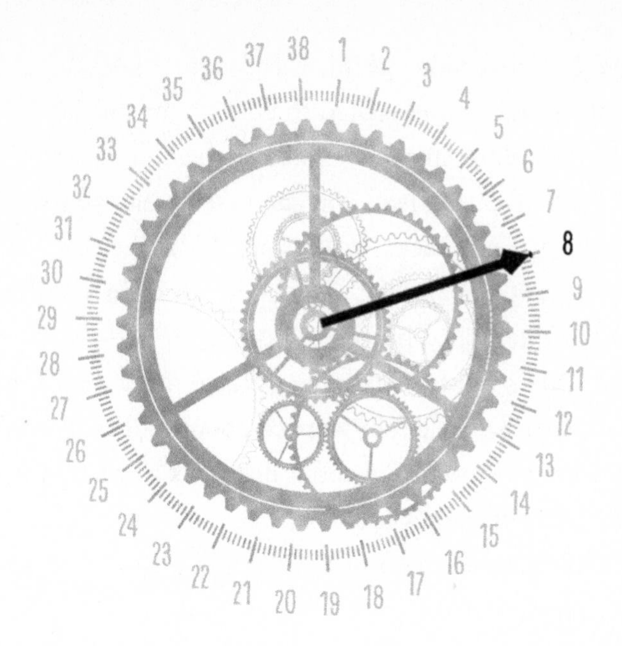

Charlie opened the door to the Rosenbaums' house and nearly bumped into Bob. Ollie stood at her shoulder, Lloyd behind them, and Gnat fluttered a few feet away to one side.

"Good," Charlie said. "I could use your help."

"Mate, you can always 'ave my 'elp."

"*Our* help," Ollie added.

"Only, Charlie, we'd be able to *'elp* you more if we knew where you *was.*"

Charlie was about to object, but he realized his friends were worried. It was a good thing he had friends who would worry about him, but that didn't mean it was a good idea to make them worry unnecessarily.

"Sorry, Bob. Sorry, Ollie . . . Gnat . . . Lloyd." Charlie

shrugged. "I just didn't think it through, I guess. *We* didn't think it through. I was excited to be with my brother."

"Also, you don't like feeling bossed around, do you?" Ollie grinned. "You're a big lad—you can take care of yourself."

Charlie grinned back. "Yeah, something like that."

"You're a hero, Charlie. We know you can take care of yourself." Ollie tipped his hat to his friend.

"Aye, Ollie's right." Gnat's wings fluttered faster. "Only remember, Charlie, we're not worried about bullies in a Whitechapel alley. We're worried about Bismarck's Prussian soldiers and their war machines."

"'E's the kaiser's monster," Bob said. "Runs the government, 'as started a few wars."

"Minister," Lloyd Shankin said. "Otto von Bismarck is the kaiser's chief *minister.*"

Bob crossed her arms over her chest. "When 'e came in, Prussia was a little place, didn't own other parts of Germany, an' now it does, lots of 'em, because it took 'em. 'E picked a fight with France, too. Plenty of people 'ave died so Bismarck could 'ave what 'e wants. Sounds like a monster to me, but if you want to use a different word, I ain't fussed."

Ollie grunted. "Those gents with the skulls and crossbones? They're his. And it turns out we're not so far from France or Switzerland or the Low Countries here. So Rabbi Rosenbaum is worried Bismarck's got another war in the offing, and maybe his boys are here to bully the landgrave into going along, or put the lads of Marburg into uniform and send them off to fight."

"Bismarck does have another war in the offing. I think he declared war on the landgrave just now." Charlie told his friends about hearing Levi Rosenbaum make a plea for peace, and his plea's failure. To explain what he and Thomas had been doing on the window ledge, he then had to go back and explain the landgrave's collection in the castle's annex, the unicorn's horn (which he produced from inside his coat) and the three nails, and the attack by the shape-changer Red Cloak. While he was narrating this last part, Ollie looked down at his feet. As Charlie finished, Thomas limped forward, clutching his injured arm. The chimney sweeps both gasped at the frightful wound.

Bob shook her head. "It's just too strange, mate."

"I want to go into the library," Charlie said. "Thomas has told me what we're looking for, and I want to try to find it. Also, I want to figure out more about this shape-changer. What is it? How do I stop it?"

"Could it be a shaitan?" Lloyd Shankin asked.

Charlie shook his head slowly. "Don't those take a person's shape after they've eaten him? And no one's eaten Thomas yet. Or me. Also, I don't think a shaitan would *want* to eat me or Thomas."

"We'll go with you, mate," Ollie volunteered. "I ain't never been in a library, but Bob here has. And I know a thing or two about shape-changers, so maybe I can help." Ollie moved his arms vaguely in circles, a gesture suggesting to Charlie that Ollie had no real idea how he could be of use in a library.

"Yeah," Bob said. "Ollie can tell us the names to look up.

Plus, I keep 'earing about a Library Machine. I've got to say, that 'as peached my curiosity."

"Piqued, Bob," Lloyd said.

"*Peach* means to rat someone out," Ollie added. "You know that, Bob."

Bob shrugged. "I admit it seemed a peculiar turn of phrase."

"Jan Wijmoor can get you into the library," Rachel said thoughtfully. "And he can fix Thomas's arm, too."

*

Their request prompted a shower of tears from the kobold, which started unexpectedly and ended just as abruptly. After he finished crying, the engineer was quiet for a minute and seemed to be thinking.

"You won't take anything?" he asked. "I have a duty of Loyalty."

"It's a library," Bob said. "It's for *borrowing* only, innit?"

Jan Wijmoor nodded slowly.

"Of course, I cannot condone your entry into the library. The library is the property of the landgrave and the university, and the Marburger Syndikat only maintains it. But fortunately, my forbidding you is totally pointless, since you will be utterly unable to get into the library without a card such as this one." The kobold waved a thin brass card with dozens of rectangular holes punched into it.

The little metal sheet reminded Charlie of the Babel Card, only larger and thicker. After Charlie got a good look, Wijmoor conspicuously dropped the card into the pocket of his white coat, then removed the coat.

Rachel, Thomas, Charlie, Lloyd, and the sweeps stood in the kobold's office. Gnat fluttered in the air. The office was a windowless room on a long hall in the university building. Rachel had brought the others there directly, knocking on the small door facing her garden to get admittance.

"I need a card to get in?" Charlie now asked the kobold.

"That don't seem right. 'Oo exactly are you trying to keep locked out an' ignorant?"

"The purpose of a library is to preserve and protect the knowledge stored within it in the form of books. Letting everyone in to do everything they wanted inside the library would be just as foolish as if you removed the roof of the building." Wijmoor hung his coat on a peg on the wall. "The card safeguards the library for all future users, and therefore I cannot give it to you."

"Nondisclosure and Compliance," Charlie said. "And I guess Loyalty."

"Yeah, yeah," Ollie grumbled. "There's always an explanation, ain't there? And still someone's always getting locked out."

Jan Wijmoor laughed as he snapped and pointed at the ceiling. Then he turned his back and busied himself with a row of metal valves on a shelf. "Lie down on the table, Thomas. We'll get right to work on your arm."

"I'll stay with Thomas," Lloyd Shankin offered, one eye diving left as he said it.

"Aye, and so will I. And we'll take care of that horn for you—you'll need a bigger pocket, to be carrying that thing around."

Thomas climbed onto the table. Rachel stood beside him and held his good hand.

Charlie put his hand in his pocket and gripped the broken halves of Bap's pipe.

Then he took the card from the kobold's coat. "It would be good to know which doors enter into the library. You know, so we don't accidentally open them."

*

Charlie, Ollie, and Bob followed Jan Wijmoor's directions, which were simple. In short order, they stood before a brass door, polished to a dull orange gleam, with no window and a slot in its exact center, a little below Charlie's eye level.

Charlie pulled on the brass handle of the door with no effect.

"Well, I guess it must work like the ticket-vendor automatons at the Sky Trestle." Charlie inserted Wijmoor's card into the slot.

"Welcome, Meneer Professor Doktor Ingenieur Wijmoor," said a soft female voice.

Chunk. The door popped open.

"I think I can just about handle a talking door," Ollie said. "But if the toilets around here use that same voice, I believe I'm going to feel uncomfortable."

The library was built around a single shaft. A colored glow filtered down from tall stained-glass windows several stories over Charlie's head. More light came from a column that hung down the center of the shaft, extending a third of the way down from the ceiling, glowing brightly. A single long ramp wound around the inside of that shaft, like the threads on a gigantic inverted screw. The inside of the ramp was bounded with a brass banister running along the top of a low, white-plastered wall.

The outer wall was lined with bookshelves from floor to ceiling, all along the ramp. The shelves were mostly full, and along the bottom of each shelf was printed a neat reference number. Jutting out from the wall were additional bookcases, each shelf labeled and filled with books. These additional shelves were built around long stone ribs that ran up the side of the chamber like supporting columns. The perpendicular shelves occupied six feet of the ten-foot-wide ramp, leaving a four-foot curving aisle between the ends of the shelves and the banister.

Here and there, the bookshelves were punctuated with doorways.

The floor was covered with a dark blue carpet, thin and tough, with gold numbers woven into it every few feet. To Charlie's left the number appeared to be 1, while to the right the number was 4. Spaced one quarter turn apart on each level were reading areas, created by replacing a pair of perpendicular shelves with two armchairs and a small sofa. The door by which they'd entered came into the library through just such a reading nook.

Charlie stood and stared.

"I ain't exactly disappointed it's just books," Bob said, "but where d'you reckon the machine is?"

Ollie held the banister and stretched his neck out for a

look. “What is this, twelve levels? How many books do you think it holds?”

Charlie joined Ollie at the rail and looked down. “Maybe the machine’s down there.” At the bottom of the shaft he saw a series of boxy shapes. They glowed brass under a ring of six gaslights on poles, so maybe they were machines.

Bob looked too. “We could just roll down, but maybe there’s a better way.”

They started down the ramp. After half a turn, they came to a reading nook behind which was a sliding glass door marked AUFZUG, which Charlie soon saw as LIFT. Bob eagerly pressed a button labeled BERUFEN even before Charlie could see the word meant SUMMON, and cables behind the door brought up a carriage. Inside, a row of buttons corresponded to floors, their current floor being 4 and the lowest being 12.

The pressing of another button brought them down to the bottom of the pit.

As Charlie had seen from above, six gaslights on poles illuminated the shaft’s floor. Three long brass boxes stood among the poles, and each box had a series of control panels, with each panel consisting of ten toothed brass wheels. Each control panel had a single word stamped in the brass above it: the words on one box all read SCHREIBER, and on the second THEMA, and on the third TITEL. Thanks to the Babel Card, Charlie’s eyes quickly resaw those words as AUTHOR, SUBJECT, and TITLE.

A bull-like male hulder, a female kobold, a long-bearded dwarf, and three women stood at control panels, all wearing student robes. A student would move the toothed wheels and pull a lever to the right, and then a slot beneath the wheels printed out a long strip of paper. Having collected enough such strips, the student would take them and depart by taking the lift or by trudging up the ramp.

"Reminds me of a thing I used in a library once," Bob said. "A card—"

The nearest library patron, a robed kobold, spun to shush her.

"Yes, Bob?" Ollie whispered.

Bob stroked her chin and lowered her voice. "I was going to say *caterpillar,* only I 'ave the distinct sensation that ain't right."

"Catalog," Charlie said. He'd read about card catalogs, though he'd never seen one. "It does look like a card catalog. Except there are no drawers to hold the little cards. Let's take a closer look."

"Shhhh!" hissed a glaring dwarf student.

"Library people are so sensitive," Bob mumbled. "Discourages the asking of 'elp, it does."

"What'll it be?" Ollie squinted at the machine. "A scriber? A tittle?"

"Subject." Charlie stepped up to a THEMA control panel.

Each tooth of each wheel had a character stamped in it. Spinning the first wheel experimentally, he saw that he had a complete alphabet and the numerals zero through nine. A little further investigation showed him that the other wheels were identical. A groove ran through the brass at the center position of all ten wheels, and again by trial and error he found that by putting the wheels into the position he wanted and reading along the groove, he could form a word.

"Shape-changers, that's what I'm looking for." Spinning the wheels, Charlie spelled out *SHAPECHANG*. He had to stop after the *G* because he had run out of wheels, but maybe the device would have enough information to know what he was seeking.

Should he try to research the three nails and their possible locations first? He didn't feel like he knew enough to ask the right questions about that subject yet. He'd learn how to use the library first, and then come back with Thomas later.

"Is this the Library Machine, then?" Bob asked.

Charlie pulled his control panel's lever.

The machine made a soft *whirrrr*.

A short strip of paper emerged from the slot. Charlie tore the strip free and looked: the paper was blank.

If it *was* the Library Machine, Charlie was failing to use it properly. He ground his teeth and considered the possibilities. His spelling looked right. Maybe the machine used a different word? He tried *SHAPESHIFT*.

Same result.

"Charlie." Ollie leaned gently against the brass box beside Charlie's control panel. "I know you well, don't I, mate?"

"I think so."

"So I know you don't take kindly to bossing. So this ain't bossing."

Charlie waited.

"And I know it's ironic that I should be the one to have this idea. But I'm the one who's had it, and I think I have a responsibility to share the idea with you."

"Ollie," Charlie said, "this is a lot of words. I promise I won't be angry with whatever it is you're going to say."

"Good." Ollie nodded. "In that case, how about you try entering the word in German?"

Charlie laughed out loud. With quick fingers he set the dials to spell *METAMORPHO,* the first ten letters of *Metamorphose,* which seemed to him to be a German word for shape-changing. Then he pulled the lever.

This time, following the whir, the machine spat out a strip of paper as long as Charlie was tall.

SHAPE-CHANGING

Generally	MTPH730000
In classical literature	MTPH730010
How-to manuals	MTPH730001
As illness or curse	MTPH730307
Shape-changing species	MTPH730030
—Loups-garou	MTPH730032
—Shaitans	MTPH730033
—Yokai	MTPH730031
In folklore, generally	MTPH730070
—in American folklore	MTPH730071
—in British folklore	MTPH730072
—in Chinese folklore	MTPH730073

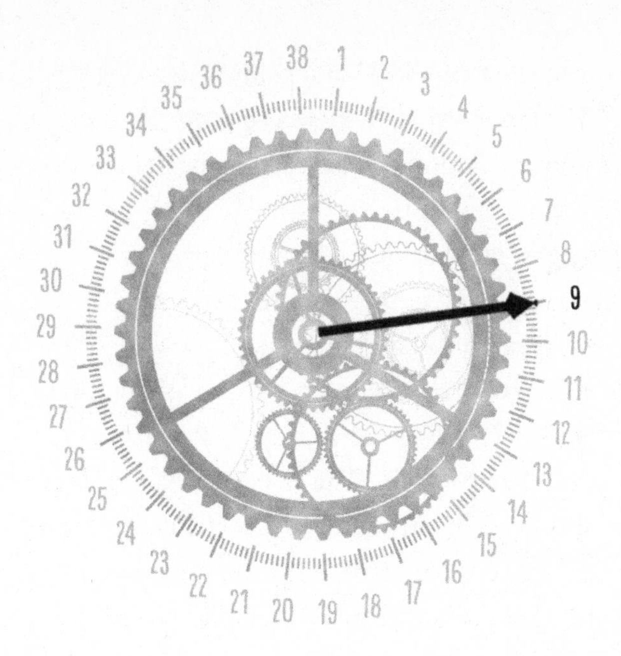

"I'm not going to say 'I told you so,'" Ollie said.

"Okay," Charlie said.

"Never mind, I lied. I told you so."

"Yeah, Ollie, you did indeed." Bob leaned in close to the machine, examining the alphanumeric wheels and the lever.

Charlie inspected the strip with a sinking heart and a growing sense of confusion. Even though the Babel Card had sorted it into neatly comprehensible English, he still had trouble following what he was reading. Two columns marched down the strip. The column on the left listed different kinds of shape-changing, or different aspects of shape-changing. The column on the right seemed to be in code.

It was too much.

No, it wasn't too much. Charlie forced himself to focus.

He scanned the entire left-hand column, looking for anything that said *shape-changers, dangerous* or *with black eyes and rubber skin* and saw nothing. To be certain, he did it a second time and got the same result.

"Here, give me that." Ollie took the paper and read it carefully, chewing his lower lip. "I think I've got it."

"I am prepared to be impressed," Bob said. "Indeed, I am prepared to bestow upon you a certificate of librariology if you 'ave got it right."

Charlie looked at Bob. "You've become quite eloquent."

Bob shrugged. "I am a chap as is prepared to admit 'is limitations an' strive to do better."

"Right, then." Charlie turned back to Ollie. "Tell us what you're thinking."

"Simple." Ollie pointed at the right-hand column. "There were numbers under every shelf, remember?"

"You think those are shelf numbers?"

"Bob's your uncle."

"Am not."

"How do we tell where the shelves are?" Charlie looked up, feeling the enormity of the library weighing on him.

"We'll just have to look, won't we?" Ollie cleared his throat. "I expect we'll find the *MTPH* section quickly enough, and then we can narrow down the search."

Charlie looked up again. "So I guess we just ride the lift up one level at a time and see what's shelved each time we get out?"

Bob slapped Charlie on the back. "No, mate, there's a much faster way than that. We ride the lift all the way to the top."

"Why is that faster?" Charlie asked.

Ollie laughed. "Because if I ain't mistaken, Charlie, my mate Bob intends us to *slide* down."

They rode the lift to the top of the library and slid down the banister. Charlie and the sweeps passed each other in leap-frog fashion, and Charlie stopped to look at the shelves when he was ahead and then slid when he was behind until he came out first again.

They never found an *MTPH* shelf. Every shelf's label was a string of numbers only, and the numbers repeated themselves.

The sliding was fun, though. Charlie felt giddy as the air rushed past his face and ruffled his hair. A quarter turn was just barely enough distance on the banister to really pick up speed, and then he dropped to his feet on the carpet to examine the shelves.

He didn't look down while sliding. Especially at the top, where a fall might have meant death even for Charlie. Ollie and Bob didn't seem to think twice about the heights. Was it their experience as chimney sweeps? Or with Bob's flyer, now destroyed and lying somewhere on the side of the Welsh mountain Cader Idris?

In addition to the shelf numbers, Charlie learned that each quarter turn had a number. Between the lift at each level and the next reading alcove downhill of it, the number 1 appeared woven into the carpet every few feet. From that alcove to the next was 2, and then 3, and then the section preceding the lift's return was 4.

Stopping and looking at shelves randomly, Charlie found only two books on shape-changing: Ovid's *Metamorphoses* and a thick dusty tome the Babel Card identified as *A Brief History of the Influence of Hussite Werewolves on the Reformation in Bohemia.* Charlie took one look inside that and sneezed from the dust. The books next to it on the shelf had no obvious connection with shape-changing either, being all about sixteenth-century eastern Continental history. It also had woodcut illustrations, most of which seemed to show people being impaled.

Halfway down the library shaft, when he was in the lead, Charlie waited. Rather than rushing to look at the shelves where he stood, he waved to Ollie and Bob to join him. Ollie grinned as he dropped to the carpet. Bob's bomber cap was in her hand and her long hair snapped out behind her as she rode the banister; stopping, she staggered a few steps as if tipsy and then pulled the cap onto her head without tucking her hair underneath.

She looked very much like a girl.

Ollie didn't seem to notice. He lay on his back on the carpet and took deep breaths.

"Bob," Charlie said, "I'm pretty sure you do not owe Ollie a certificate of librariology."

"That was obvious after the first floor, mate." Bob laughed. "But I might owe him a certificate of unspeakable fun instead."

"Hush!" A hulder in a student gown stalked by, holding a big finger to his bull-like lips and blowing spittle past it.

Bob giggled, and the hulder moved on.

Something about what Bob said stuck in Charlie's head. First floor, Bob had said. That was right. They had entered on the library's level 4, but its floors went from 1 to 12. Each floor had four sections, numbered 1 to 4. That meant that each quarter section could be identified with a unique number that combined the floor number with the quarter number.

So 1-1 would indicate the very highest quarter section of the library's ramp. And 12-4 would indicate the very lowest.

And within each section, shelves were numbered in order, from uphill to downhill, top to bottom. So that meant that every shelf would have a unique three-part number, 1-1-1 being the top shelf on the very first bookcase at the very top of the ramp.

He explained this to the chimney sweeps, who stopped giggling and listened. Bob tucked her hair into her cap as Charlie talked, and looked her usual boyish self by the time Charlie had finished.

"Okay. So we're on the sixth floor, and the carpet says we're in quarter section two." Ollie inspected the nearest bookcase. "And this shelf here is number two seventy-one. So what?"

Charlie stared at the shelf. It was three-quarters full and contained books on domestic economy, including at the far left a German translation of *Mrs. Beeton*. Something tickled at the back of Charlie's mind.

"You know," he eventually said. "It's possible these books have to be shelved not only on the right shelf, but in a consistent order."

"It's certainly possible," Ollie agreed.

"Let's assume that's true."

"Oh, good," Bob said. "An 'ypothesis."

Charlie and Ollie both stared at her.

Bob shrugged. "Can't a bloke try?"

Charlie returned to his thought. "If our hypothesis is true, then not only does every shelf have a unique number, but every book has a unique number."

Bob pointed at *Frau Beeton.* "So you're saying that book there would 'ave the number six . . . two . . . two seventy-one . . . one. Yeah?"

Charlie checked the floor, section, and shelf coordinates to be sure he and Bob had the same ones. "Yes."

"Fine," Ollie said. "So how do we find out if that's true?"

Charlie shrugged and took *Frau Beeton* off the shelf. He saw nothing on the book's cover to suggest his guesses were right, so he opened the book.

There, inside the front cover, neatly inked onto the flyleaf, were the numbers *6:2:271:1.*

"Charlie," Bob said, "I knew you were a man of action. Now I've got to start thinking of you as a man of science."

"Or a detective," Ollie added. "Blimey."

Charlie laid the strip of paper from the THEMA machine against the flyleaf. "Only now we just have more questions."

Ollie nodded. "Such as why the letters and numbers on this strip don't look anything like the number inked into this book."

Bob frowned and started counting off on her fingertips.

"The letters and numbers in the column must not identify books, right?" Charlie concluded. But then what did they identify?

"Ha!" Bob snapped her fingers. "Charlie, am I right to remember that when you entered the word into the machine, you 'ad ten wheels?"

Charlie thought carefully. "Yes. So I could only enter ten letters. That's why I wrote *Metamorpho* instead of *Metamorphose.*"

"Right." Bob plunked her finger down hard on the paper strip, nearly knocking *Frau Beeton* from Charlie's hand. "An' those wheels you turned to select letters would 'ave let you select numbers instead, am I right?"

"Yes. But what are you . . . ?" Charlie looked down at the paper strip.

"Ten!" Ollie gasped. "Ten letters and numbers, all of them."

"These numbers don't point to books or to shelves—they point to more specific searches!" Charlie almost smacked himself in the forehead, he felt so stupid.

"To the lift!" Ollie raced to press the button.

"Clock that!" Charlie shoved *Frau Beeton* back into her spot on the shelf and threw himself on the banister.

The chimney sweeps rushed after him. Ollie quickly disappeared, which probably meant he had transformed into a snake and curled up in one of Bob's pockets or around her head. Bob raced after Charlie with reckless abandon.

But Charlie was ahead, and he had weight and gravity on his side. He whipped around the remaining curves on the library's banister with insane abandon, and by the time he reached the bottom he had so much momentum he tumbled nearly all the way across the floor, among the Library Machine's control panels and the gaslights, and through the knot of student researchers, coming to a halt just before bumping into the wall on the far side.

Charlie lay on his back and stared at the ceiling, trying not to laugh.

"Shhh!" Every single student using the machine put a finger to his or her lips.

Bob landed off-balance but with more natural grace than Charlie. She stumbled, pirouetted, and eventually caught herself against the side of a SCHREIBER control panel.

They met back at THEMA.

"Okay," Charlie said. "Cross all your fingers and toes."

He dialed in *MTPH730031,* the number indicated by the slip for *yokai,* and pulled the lever.

Whirrrr.

Another slip of paper was ejected from the machine. Charlie tore the paper off and looked at the first entry at the top of the slip.

```
Shinto Legends of Japan
M. Musashi
7:2:103:14
```

Sir Walter Raleigh was fond of showing close friends and associates a small leather pouch containing what he called "corpse powder." Two days prior to his beheading, a manservant of Sir Walter's was apprehended attempting to smuggle this very pouch into Sir Walter's cell. Before the servant could be interrogated, he threw the dust inside the pouch into his own face, and promptly died of convulsions. And although there is no evidence beyond mere rumor that Sir Walter took the shape of animals, there are multiple witnesses on record confirming that at night his eyes glowed like a cat's.

Can any sincere investigator doubt that Sir Walter was at least in league with a yee naaldlooshii, or skinwalker, if indeed he was not one himself?

—from Sir Blaine Fothergill, LL.D., *Skinwalkers in the Old World: Myth or Fact?*

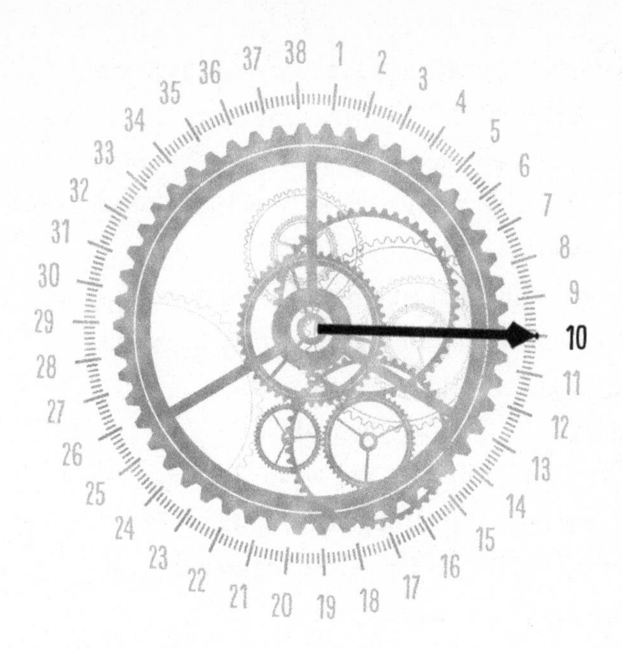

"That's a book, innit?" Bob asked.

"It looks like one," Charlie said.

"Only one way to find out." Ollie strolled cheerfully over to the glass doors against the wall and hit the button to summon the lift.

They found M. Musashi's book on the seventh floor, right where the slip indicated it should be. It was written in English. Standing huddled over the leather-bound volume, they leafed through its thick pages, taking in the full-color inked illustrations and reading the captions and sidebars.

"You figured out the library." Ollie doffed his hat to Charlie in a show of respect.

Charlie frowned. "Yeah, but all I've learned is that the thing that attacked us isn't a yokai. Or it's probably not a yokai, if this book is correct."

"That ain't a little thing, mate." Bob bounced with excitement. "That's 'ow science works, you know. You eliminate possible answers."

"Yeah," Ollie agreed. "So all we got to do is look at the books on every kind of shape-changer listed on that first list you've got, to try and eliminate each one."

"And if we eliminate them all?"

"Then what attacked you wasn't a shape-changer, was it? Could 'ave been something else, right?"

"An Italian illusionist," Ollie suggested.

"A demon," Bob added.

"I suppose another thing we could try is reading some of the books about shape-changers generally. Maybe they'll have indexes or chapter headings that will help. We can split up the list." Charlie gripped the slip to tear it into segments.

"Whoa, mate, you're forgetting something." Ollie grabbed Charlie's hand to stop him.

"It's getting late, isn't it? Do we need to get some food?"

Bob snorted. "You might not realize this about us, my china, but Ollie 'ere an' I 'ave skipped many a meal. There were times before you knew us, we might go three 'ole days without eating. We've got stamens, we 'ave."

"Stamina, Bob," Ollie said.

"Ah. An' there I was on a lucky streak."

"It's all right. I'm glad to have my mate Bob back."

"What am I forgetting?" Charlie asked.

"German, Charlie. That list's in German. We can't read it."

Charlie squinted down at the list. If he consciously thought about it, he could tell that most of the words in the first list he'd printed, the list of more narrow subjects, were German. The book titles, as he examined them, were in various languages.

"Okay," he said. "I will have to operate the Library Machine. I'll find specific books we want to look at and I'll give you those slips. You bring the books down, and if the book is in English, maybe you can do some of the reading too."

"Think of the possibilities," Bob mused. "The footnotes alone!"

"How do you mean?" Charlie asked.

"Well, if your writer was to say 'Loups-garou are notorious for their eating 'abits'—"

"Hey!" Ollie snapped.

"Ollie, you ain't a loup-garou. You're English, mate."

"Oh. Right."

"So if 'e says eating 'abits an' there's a footnote, you look at the footnote. An' the footnote might give you more detail, an' it might give you the name of another book."

"Bob, how do you know so much about libraries and research?" Charlie had never given footnotes any thought.

"'Ow d'you think I learned all my science?" Bob shot back. "I never went to school, but I snuck into a few libraries in my time. An' 'ere's another tip: if you find a good book on the subject you're investigating, take a look at what else is on the same shelf."

"This is quite a bit more exciting than I ever thought a library would be," Ollie admitted. "It's an adventure, ain't it?"

"Too right, Ollie. We get back to London, you an' I will go poke about in all the best libraries."

"All the best libraries might not let you and me in, Bob."

"Then we'll just let ourselves in, won't we?" Bob winked at Ollie. "Right, Charlie. What's the first book I should go get?"

Charlie quickly sent Bob for a book called *Hoyt on Spriggans,* and Ollie after the sensationally titled *Skinwalkers in the Old World: Myth or Fact?* Then he settled down to grind his way through more searches.

The Library Machine was clever, but it didn't seem all that mysterious. The way Rachel Rosenbaum had talked about it, Charlie had imagined something more exotic. Something that had to be protected from outsiders.

Didn't there just *have* to be something more?

Charlie quickly eliminated spriggans, whose only shape-changing ability seemed to be getting bigger and smaller. Skinwalkers remained a possibility, mostly because Charlie couldn't find a book that described their physical appearance, and also because the writers generally agreed skinwalkers were dangerous and probably evil. On the other hand, not only were they American, but they were associated with the Navajo, a folk who lived in the American West, in places with ludicrous names like *Utah.*

If a skinwalker had attacked Thomas and Charlie, it had come an awfully long way to do so.

Apparently, and to the surprise of all three of them, there

were many tales of Welsh dewins changing shape. But after Bob skimmed through a medieval collection of stories from Wales called *The Mabinogion,* they agreed to eliminate dewins from the list, since the dewins always took the forms of animals, and in fact animals found in Wales: salmon, deer, falcons, mice, and so on.

"Old Lloyd Shankin will be relieved we don't think it was 'im. Though now I fancy I'd like to see 'im turn 'imself into a salmon." Bob took her next scrap of paper, for a book called *Werewolf Brotherhoods Among the Wends and Old Saxons,* and headed back to the lift.

Charlie pulled the lever of the THEMA machine to get another strip of books. Tearing it off, he was struck by an idea.

Charlie reset the machine's dials to spell *Bibliothek,* which was "library" in German. The resulting strip had many subjects relating to libraries, but none of them said *Bibliothekmaschine,* as he'd hoped.

He almost picked up his strips again to get back to finding books, but a thought stopped him. He'd been right about the library so far; he should have confidence that he was right about this: that there was more to the library than he'd yet learned.

And he should be like Bob. Bob's approach to research didn't depend on finding obvious answers in the Library Machine. She dug through footnotes. She looked on shelves.

Where else might Charlie look for answers?

He reset the dials to spell *Grimm.* Hadn't Jan Wijmoor said something that connected Jacob Grimm with the Library Machine?

The resulting list of subjects included biographies, bibliographies of published works, books about the stories edited by the Grimms, and even collections of political speeches made by them. Nothing directly mentioned the Library Machine.

He switched to the author machine, SCHREIBER.

Why did he care about this? Was this really worth his time, in the same way it was worth his time to figure out who was trying to kill him and his brother Thomas?

But it was a puzzle, and Charlie couldn't walk away from a puzzle. Why would an engineer whose work was with the Library Machine also be willing to repair Thomas? Might the Library Machine have something to do with Thomas . . . and therefore with Charlie?

What *was* the Library Machine, if not this book-cataloging system?

Charlie set the dials on SCHREIBER to *Grimm*. The slip that emerged gave him separate ten-digit codes for each brother, Jacob and Wilhelm, and a third code for books written by the brothers together. When he ran those codes, the list of books he came up with was innocuous. Nothing that suggested the Library Machine.

There were fewer and fewer students in the library. Did the library have a closing time?

Charlie stepped to one of the TITEL panels and tried *Bibliothek*. This time, the machine spat out a long list of books with *Bibliothek* in their titles. For good luck, he ran the English words *library* and *machine,* too. Then he spent ten minutes reading the very long strip of paper he'd accumulated.

Nothing.

Charlie felt stumped.

He heard the hum of the lift as it rose to get Ollie, and he decided he'd try one last search.

He stepped back to the SCHREIBER machine and entered, as the author, the word *Bibliothek.* It was a nonsense search, but it was like looking on the shelf next to relevant books. Maybe he'd find a book that had been entered incorrectly in the catalog.

Charlie pulled the lever.

Whirrrr.

A short strip.

Frowning, Charlie took the strip and read it.

```
Wilhelm Grimm
Bibliothekmaschine
7:1:7:7
```

A book by Wilhelm Grimm about the Library Machine? But how had it not turned up in his earlier searches? Someone had made a mistake.

He heard a soft footstep behind him and turned, expecting to see Ollie or Bob.

Thomas swung a length of pipe at Charlie's head.

Beth yw dy waddol, fy morwen ffein i?
Cymaint ag a welwch, o syr, mynte hi
Dau rosyn coch, a dau lygad du
Yn a baw a'r llaca, o syr, gwelwch fi

(What is your dowry, my fine maid?
As much as you see, O sir, she said
Two red roses and two black eyes
In the mud and the mire, O sir, look at me)

—"Ble Rwyt Ti'n Mynd," traditional Welsh song

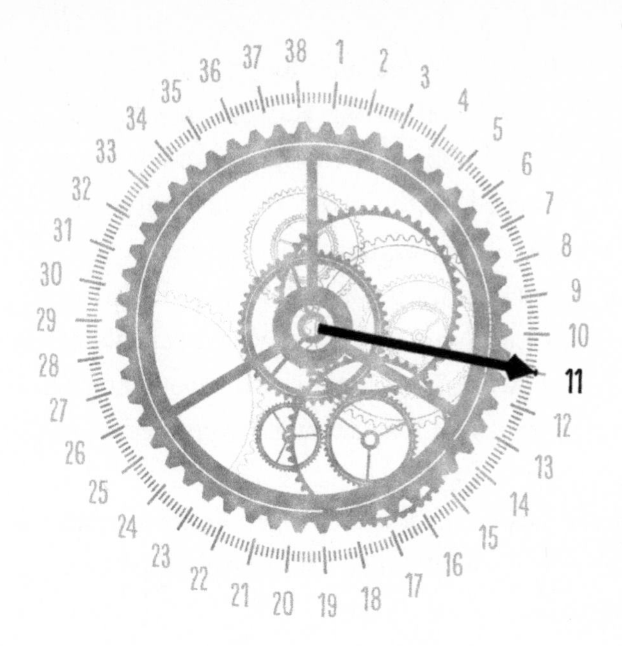

It wasn't Thomas, of course. It was Red Cloak.

Charlie punched.

Charlie was fast, but the shape-changer was already mid-swing, and the pipe hit Charlie right across the forehead.

Bong!

Charlie's blow missed. He staggered back on a floor that suddenly felt like the deck of a ship in a hurricane. He was off-balance, and Not-Thomas moved in for the kill, raising the pipe again—

"Shh!" A hulder in a student gown jumped between the shape-changer and Charlie. Charlie fell to the carpet and rolled. He bumped against one of the Library Machine cabinets and climbed to his feet.

Crack! Red Cloak smashed its pipe into the troll's knee. The hulder, every bit as big and bull-smelling as Charlie's friend Grim Grumblesson, whimpered and dropped.

Charlie shoved all the strips into his coat pocket and put his hands up in front of himself, expecting the shape-changer to charge him again. Instead the monster hurled itself on the fallen troll, mouth gaping and a row of needle-like teeth, like a shark's, all showing. The creature had a mouth, and it had teeth. Was its mouth just so lipless that it disappeared when closed?

The hulder screamed.

Charlie tackled the shape-changer. As his shoulder slammed into the monster's side, the creature reacted like a cat thrown into water. It hissed and raged, slashing at Charlie with fingernails like claws.

It bit Charlie's shoulder, and that hurt.

Charlie had been bitten before, but that had been by ghouls. It turned out that ghouls' teeth were much less sharp than this creature's fangs. Charlie felt his skin puncture and tear under pressure, and he smelled his attacker's breath. It reminded him of the tunnels beneath London, where Charlie had seen the rotting corpse of a horse lying in sewage.

Charlie arced forward, landed on his other shoulder, and rolled. He and Red Cloak tumbled together across the carpet, and Charlie heard the thudding feet of the remaining students running away. Maybe they'd call for help. But what help could possibly reach Charlie in time?

The shape-changer's skin looked like Thomas's, but it felt like rubber. Its bones were rubbery too, or at least, when Charlie smashed the creature to the carpet in his forward motion, it seemed to bounce and stretch beneath him. Where it banged on the floor, it stopped looking like Thomas and looked like the monster again.

As Charlie passed through the Charlie-on-the-bottom part of his roll and started to come up, he kicked his legs out flat to break his momentum. He also smashed his attacker in the face with his own forehead, right where its false, Thomas-like nose appeared to be.

The creature shrieked, tumbling across the carpet.

Charlie spotted the pipe and scrambled for it.

He'd never make it in time; it was too far away.

The shape-changer rose to its feet. It still looked like Thomas, but its legs were backward. The knees bent the wrong way and the creature hunched forward, claws extended.

Ding!

The lift doors opened. The shape-changer looked inside—the lift was empty.

Charlie grabbed the pipe.

The shape-changer turned back and crouched to leap forward—

Heaven-Bound Bob crashed on top of the creature. She came down boots-first and landed on its head, pounding it to the floor. She rolled off in one direction, and the monster rolled away in the other.

Charlie rushed forward, swinging the pipe. The shape-changer rose to its feet just in time to catch a blow from Charlie to its chest.

"Run!" Bob was already sprinting toward the lift as its door started to shut.

Charlie conked the shape-changer on top of its head and ran after his friend. He kept the pipe, just in case.

Bob thrust an arm between the glass doors of the lift and forced her way inside. The doors opened again, and Bob jammed her finger on one of the buttons repeatedly. "Run!"

Charlie threw himself through the doors just as they began to close again. He bounced off the wood paneling of the lift's back wall and spun to face the shape-changer, pipe in hand.

The monster was closer than Charlie had expected. It sprang as the doors closed, its face still mostly Thomas's but its eyes the glossy black of the monster's.

The door shut, the beast slammed into them, and the glass cracked—

but didn't break.

The lift began to rise. Charlie watched through the glass doors as the creature shook off the blow and ran for the ramp. It was astonishingly quick. The library's shaft was wide, but between the slow speed of the lift and the shape-changer's rocket-like velocity, Charlie realized that the monster was going to get to the next floor first.

There it would press the button and the lift would stop and open its doors.

Charlie hefted the pipe in his hand and prepared to do battle again.

He looked up, through the top of the glass doors, and just as they rose above the floor on the next level, the shape-changer skidded to a stop in front of the lift. It crouched to look down at Charlie and Bob through the glass, leering and licking its needlelike teeth with a long, bright red tongue.

"That is one 'ideous mess," Bob muttered. "Come on, Ollie."

"What does *mess* mean in rhyming slang?" Charlie asked.

"That wasn't slang, my china," Bob said. "It was a simple observation."

The shape-changer pressed its talons against the glass and sneered. The lift stopped.

"Come on, Ollie," Bob murmured again.

Charlie braced himself.

The doors started to slide apart, and the shape-changer shoved a long-nailed hand into the carriage.

Charlie struck the creature's forearm with his pipe, but that only knocked its groping talons against Bob. It grabbed Bob by her coat and dragged her into the opening.

She punched and kicked. "Let me go!"

Charlie wanted to swing the pipe, but he was afraid he might hit his friend.

The creature opened its mouth so wide it seemed impossible, too big for its head, and its teeth dripped glistening liquid as the beast leaned forward to bite Bob—

A chair shattered against the back of the creature's skull.

"Leave her alone!" Ollie yelled.

The beast went down. Ollie stepped out of hiding behind a bookcase and broke a second chair over its head.

For good measure, Charlie picked up the shape-changer by

its shoulders, took two steps to the banister, and threw it over the edge.

"'Urry up, Charlie!" Bob was jamming a button again: 5.

Charlie scampered between the glass doors as they slid shut.

Bob stood glaring into the corner of the lift. Ollie faced her back, his shoulders slumped.

Charlie grabbed them both and hugged them. "That was brave!"

Ollie shrugged. "Yeah."

Charlie peered through the glass but caught no glimpse of the beast. "That thing might still catch us."

"We 'ave an 'ead start now." Bob's face was red and her voice was quiet.

"What's on the fifth floor?" Charlie asked.

Bob snapped out of her sudden somber mood enough to grin a little. "You're going to like this, mate."

When Charlie stepped out onto the carpet of level five, he heard pounding feet.

Not far below. Probably one level. They had a few seconds, but no more.

"Psst!"

Charlie turned to the source of the hissing. A bookcase against the wall had swung out. The shelves were hinged as if they were a door, and standing in the open doorway was Rachel Rosenbaum.

"Secrets!" Charlie gasped.

Rachel blushed. "Yes. And I'm trusting you with this one. Because you and Thomas trust me with yours."

"I'll respect your secret."

Rachel beckoned Charlie to come toward her.

Bob and Ollie were already running toward the rabbi's daughter; Charlie followed.

Rachel pushed the door open a little farther to reveal the real Thomas and Lloyd Shankin, who hung on to a pair of ropes just within the passageway behind the door. The walls and ceilings of the passage were made of large stone blocks, dotted irregularly with glowing objects.

Charlie hurled himself into the passage. "How do I shut this door?"

"You don't, boyo." Lloyd and Thomas reached as high as they could, grabbed the same rope together, and sagged. The rope ran up and through a pulley a few feet over their heads, and as they fell, the bookcase door swung shut.

"Is there a lock?" Charlie whispered.

"Nay, this highway was built in trusting times, and to connect friends." Gnat appeared at Charlie's shoulder, a spear in her hands. She pressed her face to the closed door, and Charlie saw that there were a few eyeholes cut into it, to allow someone on this side to peer through the books.

He found another such peephole and looked.

Lloyd Shankin began to sing softly. *"Ble rwyt ti'n mynd,"* Charlie heard at first, but then the Babel Card turned the words from Welsh into English. Charlie didn't know the tune, but Lloyd's words were about a girl rejecting the attention of a man who only wanted her for money she didn't have.

The idea of avoiding unwanted attention was appropriate.

When the shape-changer ran by, it was so fast Charlie almost missed it.

"There it goes," Gnat whispered.

"Let's leave now before it realizes it's been tricked an' tries to find us." Bob was already tiptoeing down the passage. "I sent the lift on up to the top, but that will only give us a minute."

"Yeah, we don't know how good a sense of smell it has," Ollie added. "It might double back and decide it needs a closer look at this set of shelves."

Charlie watched through the peephole for a few more seconds and then followed his friends. He found himself bringing up the rear, with Lloyd Shankin. "I understood your words," he told the dewin.

"Oh, did you?" The dewin smiled, his eyes wandering in opposite directions. "Well, they seemed more or less right for the occasion. I just wanted to invite that thing not to notice us."

"Let's hope it keeps working now that you've stopped singing."

"I agree," Lloyd said. "Also, let's walk faster."

They stepped up their pace. As they went, Charlie saw that the light came from fruit. A dense growth of vines covered the ceilings of the passage and the highest few feet of the walls, and teardrop-shaped fruit dangled here and there from the vines, emitting soft light.

Beneath the vines on the walls he saw images from time to time. They were faded, and the light was poor, but he thought the pictures showed a joyous procession of pixies, kobolds, hulders, dwarfs, humans, and others, carrying armfuls of fruits and vegetables and various manufactured goods—shoes, harps, hammers, plowshares—and singing.

Was that the vision of the Iron Cog, everyone living in harmony? But at their meeting, they had talked about the life of ease everyone should enjoy, thanks to machinery, and the pictures didn't show a life of ease. They showed folk being different, working hard and working together, and getting along.

Carpet ran along the center of the hall; it had once been thick and luxurious, but it was now rotten. Charlie took careful steps, afraid that if he put too much trust on any one patch of the decaying carpet, it would give way and he'd fall.

A steep flight of steps led down to a landing from which three other staircases climbed up. Charlie stopped at his friends' heels, realizing that they had all come to a halt.

A squad of pixies held Charlie's friends at spearpoint.

Sources close to Parliament have today confirmed the appointment of a Committee for the Investigation of Anti-Human Crime. Prominent members of London's elder folk communities as well as humans have been identified as committee members, although the entire list of committee membership is uncertain.

"You have this all wrong," said Mr. Grim Grumblesson, a committee appointee. "One can investigate an alleged incident to prosecute a wrongdoer. One can also investigate an alleged incident to determine whether anything occurred in the first place, for the purpose of putting the public's mind at rest."

—*Daily Telegraph*, "Committee Empaneled," 14 July 1887

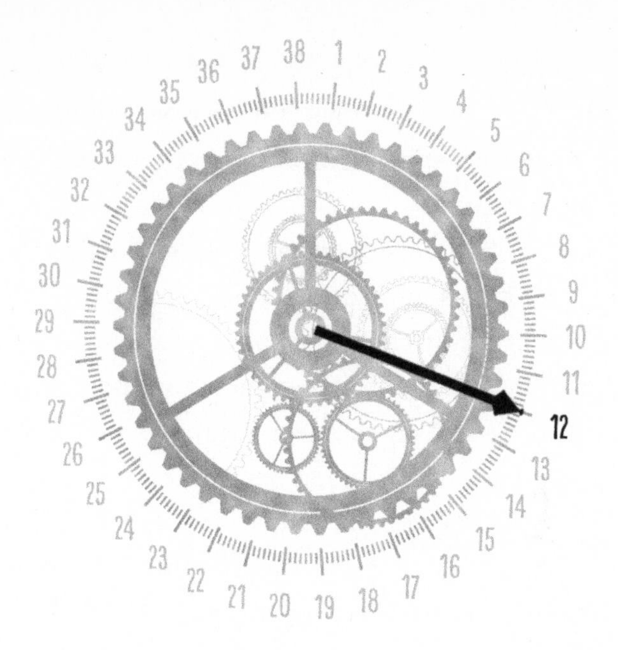

Like the fairies Charlie had seen in the castle, these pixies wore blue, and their armor resembled tortoiseshells. Their wings were mostly blue and purple as well, though Charlie spotted a dark green pair in the back of the group. He also saw the fairy with blue hair and orange- and yellow-streaked wings, the undergravine. Her hair was hidden beneath a helmet that made her look like a blue turtle. The pixies surrounded Charlie's friends in a U-shaped curve, spears pointed inward. Some of the pixies hovered over Charlie's head, so the U was really almost half a bristling sphere.

Like a hedgehog, only inside out.

Gnat shot forward, into the center of the bubble of doom. The spears shifted slightly, pointing at Charlie's friend. One wrong move, and she'd be skewered ten times.

Gnat began to speak. Her wings fluttered as she uttered unwieldy, harsh syllables that still rhymed and flowed like music. In Charlie's ears, the words didn't convert into sense, so his eyes wandered.

They stood at a crossroads, a meeting of four ways. Examining the four staircases, Charlie found that each arch of stones bore a different symbol. To Charlie's right, the stones had a carving of a lion standing on its hind legs; it was hard to be sure in the near darkness, but he thought the lions were painted with red and white stripes, now flaking off. To his left was the same six-pointed star he had seen on the outside of Rabbi Rosenbaum's synagogue. Behind Charlie was a stylized open book. And, behind the pixies, the stones were carved with a pair of crossed spears and butterfly wings. The same thick rotting carpet that lay under Charlie's feet covered the stairs ascending under each archway.

Gnat's words began to sound distorted, snagging as she spoke them. The pixie seemed increasingly agitated, the spears pointing at her trembled, and Charlie's other friends shrank back. Lloyd Shankin hummed something aimless under his breath; he was looking for a good englyn, a song-spell.

The tunnel marked by the sign of the book led to the library. The star-marked passage probably led to the synagogue, or maybe the rabbi's house. Surely the spear-and-wings sign marked the road to the fairy realm.

Underneath Marburg was a secret crossroads that connected some of its key folk. Charlie found that . . . hopeful.

It seemed to be a sort of explanation, or a reflection, of the rabbi's and the landgrave's inclusive, all-embracing desire not to fight, but instead to talk.

And Rachel Rosenbaum was a keeper of this secret tradition.

And then, suddenly, Charlie understood some of Gnat's words.

". . . my friend . . . machine . . . wicked . . ."

Charlie snapped his head around to pay closer attention. The fairy with the orange- and yellow-streaked wings was staring at him; the others focused on Gnat, and Gnat exchanged words and wing buzzes with a muscular pixie whose brilliant royal-blue wings matched his tortoiseshell breastplate. He was the sole fairy armed not with a spear, but instead with a saber.

". . . deny . . . secret purposes?" Royal Blue looked outraged and indignant.

Gnat snorted her irritation back. ". . . do you . . . lies? . . . London!"

Charlie met the undergravine's gaze. She arched her eyebrows at him. "The machine understands." She said it in German.

Gnat and Royal Blue shut up and spun around.

"I'm a boy." Charlie spoke German too. "I'm a machine, but I'm a boy."

"You're a weapon," the undergravine said. The other fairies had all fallen silent and moved to create a space around her. "Or a spy."

"You're the undergravine." Charlie nodded down the passageway behind the pixies. "Your realm must lie that way."

"The Undergraviate of Hesse." The pixie tilted her head to one side and frowned. "Juliet is my name." Her *J* sounded like a *Y*. "But since my disguise has fallen, you may address me as *Your Ladyship*."

"I'm not a spy, Your Ladyship." Of course, now he couldn't reveal where he'd seen the undergravine before, without looking *exactly* like a spy. "My name's Charlie. Charlie Pondicherry. I *am* a weapon, I think. It's complicated, but . . . the people who designed me to be a weapon are my enemies. They killed my father, and if I'm going to be a weapon, I'll be a weapon to defeat them."

"Charlie," Gnat whispered in English. "What's happening?"

"Oh, you're one to talk," Ollie grunted. "Everyone has been spouting gibberish for five minutes. I've been tempted to change shape just to get a little attention."

"This is . . . Her Ladyship." Charlie said to Gnat, pointing to the undergravine with a gesture he hoped didn't seem rude. "Juliet."

"Juliet Edelstein, Undergravine of Hesse." The undergravine fluttered up, rising above her soldiers as she switched to English. She handed her helmet to one of her warriors, unchaining the glittering blue hair that sprang from her head like a crown. Her chin rose, and the way she held her spear in front of her body made it resemble a scepter. She addressed Gnat. "And I have heard more than enough of my captain's semi-competent attempt to get information out of you. Tell me who you are and what this spying little device is, or we will destroy you both."

Royal Blue shrank at the criticism.

Gnat, though, rose higher in the air, to a level just inches below that of the undergravine. "Aye, my friend is a machine, but he's no spy, and he did not come here to threaten your realm. I am Natalie de Minimis." Her voice was surprisingly loud. "My mother and her mothers before her have been the baronesses of Underthames since the days of Rome, and I'll not suffer such threats from you."

The undergravine's eyes narrowed. "There is a de Minimis yet on the throne in Underthames."

"My cousin Elisabel." Gnat gritted her teeth, not mentioning that Elisabel had stolen Gnat's throne and murdered Gnat's mother. "How are you apprised of the affairs of Underthames?"

"Her emissary is here. She invites me to enter into the league with Underthames and its unexpected allies."

"Unexpected allies?" Gnat asked. "D'you mean rats?"

"Don't trust her!" Charlie blurted out.

Undergravine Juliet looked down at Charlie and frowned. "You have poor manners."

"Aye, Charlie sometimes has little sense of decorum." Gnat chuckled. "But he has a mighty heart."

"His mighty heart may get him skewered." The undergravine tossed her hair. From someone else the gesture might have seemed petulant; from her, it was terrifying.

Rachel Rosenbaum stepped forward, distancing herself slightly from Charlie's other friends. "My mother taught me that this road was a peaceful road. A road for friends and allies."

"The rabbi's daughter." Juliet flared her nostrils and gazed at the girl for a few moments, and then drifted downward toward the floor. "Your mother was right, of course."

"I didn't know I had come to Her Ladyship's attention." Rachel curtsied.

"Everything in Hesse comes to my attention." The undergravine turned her attention back to Gnat and Charlie. "You've not come here with the Prussian?"

"We're here on our own." Gnat drifted down, again assuming an elevation only slightly lower than the undergravine's.

Juliet pressed on. "And you're also not here with the Anti-Human League?"

"The Anti-Human League?" Charlie yelped.

Ollie laughed out loud. "No, you've got it all wrong. There's no such thing as the Anti-Human League . . . Your Ladyship."

"Right." Bob chuckled too. "That was just a pickled 'erring."

"Red herring, Bob." Ollie sounded hesitant.

"'Errings are always pickled." Bob's expression was grumpy. "Wouldn't want to eat an 'erring that wasn't, would you?"

The undergravine studied the faces of Charlie and his friends. "There is more here than you are telling me."

Ollie shook his head. "It's complicated."

Gnat threw back her shoulders and drifted slightly upward,

putting herself at the undergravine's level. "My cousin Elisabel de Minimis is a murderess."

"These are strong words." The undergravine arched an eyebrow at Gnat. "Can you stand the trial of words such as these?"

"Aye. In time, I aim to do precisely that."

Charlie couldn't help himself, and butted into the conversation again. "The Anti-Human League wasn't real. It was a red herring, as Bob says, to cover up the plots of the Iron Cog."

The undergravine narrowed her eyes. "I have heard this name, but not in recent years. The landgrave drove them from this city once. The present landgrave's father."

"They're scoundrels." Bob grimaced.

"The Iron Cog made me." Charlie shrugged. "Or they made some of me. But I think some part was made by my father. The Iron Cog wanted to use me, and other"—he hated to say the word—"*machines* like me to take over England."

"Only you refused." The undergravine drifted closer to Charlie.

Charlie nodded. "And they killed my father."

"So you're going to kill them."

Charlie took a step back. "No, I . . . I don't want to kill anybody." Was that true? Didn't he, in fact, want to kill Heinrich Zahnkrieger? Or the Frenchman, Gaston St. Jacques? They certainly were willing to kill Charlie and his friends. But no, he didn't want them to die. He just wanted them to go away. He wanted to stop them. Maybe he had been *built* to want to stop them, like Thomas had. "I don't want to kill anybody. But I want to defeat them."

The undergravine nodded. "The Prussian brought machine men. Soldiers made of metal."

"Not me," Charlie said quickly. "I'm no soldier."

"The pixie who told me these things was gravely injured by these same machine fighters. She lingers in her bed, and may yet die."

Charlie bowed his head. "I'm so sorry."

The undergravine took a deep breath. As she exhaled, she shuddered. "The Anti-Human League has offered me an alliance against the machine soldiers. I am inclined to take any ally I can find in such a conflict."

"Wait, no!" Charlie cried. "It's a trick!"

"What sort of trick, Charlie Pondicherry? My daughter was gravely wounded by a metal man. Now you, also a metal man . . . what trick would you warn me of?"

Daughter? The pixie who might die was the undergravine's daughter.

"The Anti-Human League was invented by the Iron Cog!" There were too many dots for Charlie to connect them all in a coherent picture on such short notice. "I know that if your daughter is injured, you must have very strong feelings right now. . . . I'm not sure how or why, but I think you're being misled."

"There is no trick." The green-winged fairy fluttered forward from the ranks, and suddenly Charlie recognized him. He wore a garment Charlie had never seen on a pixie: a long green tabard like knights in storybooks might wear, marked on the chest with a seal that showed two pixies holding between them a white shield quartered by a red cross. Beneath the shield was a scroll bearing the Latin words SICUT NOSTRAE MATRES ANTE, which the Babel Card rearranged for Charlie as LIKE OUR MOTHERS BEFORE. Charlie had met this fairy on entering Underthames, the fairy realm beneath Whitechapel. Then, the pixie had been a guard at the gate with a spear in his hands, but now he held a plain white staff.

"Cousin Hezekiah!" Gnat cried in surprise.

"There *is* an Anti-Human League," Hezekiah said. "We elder folk are banding together to defend ourselves against human aggressors. The Prussians are attacking here, and the Crown is oppressing us in Britain, others elsewhere."

"Wait," Charlie said. "What's happening in Britain?"

"Parliament is persecuting our kind," Hezekiah said. "New laws, trials, and secret committees."

"That ain't right," Ollie grunted.

"'Tisn't," Juliet agreed. "That is why we elder folk are resisting . . . together with other allies."

Ollie spat on the tunnel floor. "Rats."

"An' I reckon that makes old 'Ezekiah 'ere the pied piper," Bob added. "'E ain't come to save your children, Your Ladyship; 'e's come to lead 'em away."

Charlie recognized Bob's reference to one of the stories by the Grimm brothers, and something about it bothered him. No, something about the brothers themselves. Or, more properly, something about Wilhelm.

He dug into his pocket and found two strips of paper spat out by the mechanical catalog. One said:

```
Wilhelm Grimm
Bibliothekmaschine
7:1:7:7
```

And the other read:

```
Shinto Legends of Japan
M. Musashi
7:2:103:14
```

And suddenly, Charlie knew.

◆ ◆ ◆

There is little record of the brothers' last years. They ended their days at the University of Marburg as procurators of the university's library. Jacob Grimm invented the library's elaborate mechanical card catalog; his brother Wilhelm increasingly spent time in mystical studies and meditation. The only indication we have of the content of these reflections is in his extensive rewriting of earlier tales as well as annotations in the mythological and theological books in his personal library. Like many thinkers of spiritual bent, he seems to have spent much time pondering the nature of eternal life. We can only regret that we have no indication of the final thought of either brother.

—Völpel, *Biographical Dictionary*, "Jacob and Wilhelm Grimm"

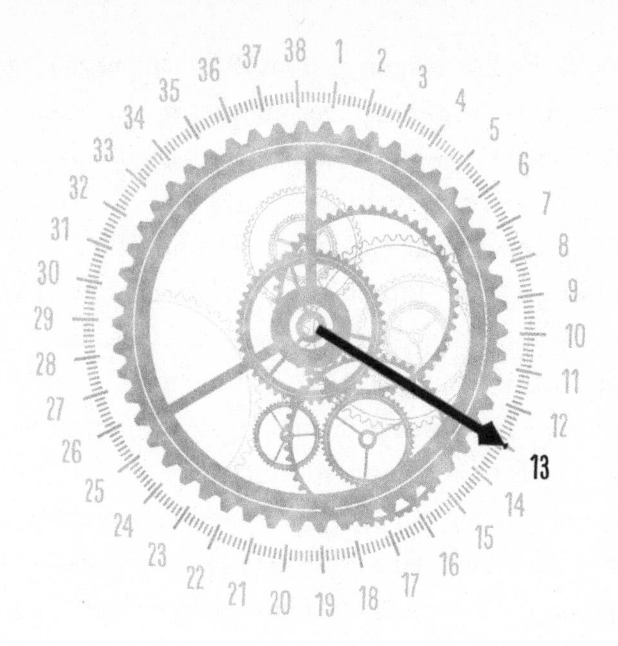

"I have to go," Charlie said. Then he turned and ran back the way he'd come, toward the library. The pixie warriors seemed surprised, but they looked to the undergravine and then let him pass.

Charlie was so preoccupied with his sudden insight that he didn't notice who had followed until he got to the secret door. Thomas was behind him, with Ollie wrapped around his neck like a scarf.

"The others?" Charlie asked.

Bamf! Ollie dropped to the ground in his boy form. He stared at the floor. "They stayed to talk to the pixies."

"You look sad." Charlie hesitated. "Did you want to stay to talk with the pixies too?"

Ollie shook his head. "Bob's mad at me."

Charlie tried to imagine reasons Bob could be mad at Ollie and couldn't think of one. "Do you want to talk about it?"

Ollie shook his head. "Nothing to talk about, mate. I made a . . . serious mistake, is all."

"What are we doing back here?" Thomas asked.

Charlie grinned. "I think I've found the Library Machine."

"Ain't you worried about the monster?" Ollie asked.

"I don't think it would have stuck around," Charlie said. "It's probably gone back to its masters, to St. Jacques. But just in case . . . the three of us need to stay together."

They peered through every peephole they could find into the library and listened for the sound of any creature or researcher on the other side before dragging down the pulley to open the secret door.

Charlie crept to the banister to survey the interior of the library. Eyes sweeping in a spiral about the empty central space, he looked for any sign of the monster. He also looked for signs of the machine men the undergravine had talked about. Nothing. Just students, going about library-type business, though some looked about nervously, as if they'd heard there had been a disturbance and worried it might be repeated.

"So what's your idea?" Thomas asked, crouching beside Charlie.

"We need to get to level seven," Charlie said. "Seven-one-seven-seven."

From their secret entrance it was a short stroll.

"Here it is." Charlie counted. They stood in a shadowed recess, shielded from the view of most of the library, although a person passing by on the ramp would have seen them.

"Seventh floor, first section—it has to be first and not seventh because there are only four sections per floor—seventh shelf, seventh book. And, because there are twelve floors, the line between the sixth and seventh floors is the exact middle spot of the library."

The three boys stopped and stared.

"There's no book there," Thomas said.

"There must be some mistake." Charlie consulted his slip of paper, 7:1:7:7. No mistake. Could someone have gotten here ahead of him and taken the book he wanted?

Could it have been the shape-changer? But what would the monster want with the book?

"What are the other books on the shelf?" The shelf was a little over the boys' heads, so Thomas stood on tiptoe to look.

Charlie imitated his brother. *"The Mahabharata. The Ramayana. The Cloud of Unknowing. The Gospel of John. The Walam Olum. The Voluspa. The I Ching."*

"What kind of library shelf is this?" Ollie asked. "These books seem random."

Charlie took one of the books off the shelf and looked at it more closely. *"The Meditations of Marcus Aurelius."* He opened the front cover and looked at the flyleaf, hoping a tiny hope that maybe the books had been shelved out of order and he could find the book he was looking for, in another book's assigned position. "Oh."

Written inside the book was its proper shelf position, 7:1:7:2. Also inside the front cover was pasted a bookplate. It read EX LIBRIS in large capital letters, which the Babel Card quickly rearranged into FROM THE BOOKS OF.

And in the center of the bookplate, in a neat Continental hand, was written the name Wilhelm Grimm.

Thomas looked over Charlie's shoulder. "That's strange."

"Maybe it's sort of a clue." Charlie put the *Meditations* back. "Let's check the other books."

They looked, and found a bookplate with the name Wilhelm Grimm inside every book on the shelf.

"These are Wilhelm Grimm's personal books," Charlie said. "His library. People give their collections to libraries sometimes when they die; he must have done that."

"But the book you want is missing," Thomas said. "What book is it, anyway? A manual on how the Library Machine works? A history of it?"

Charlie didn't know. "Maybe it got pushed back. Give me a hand?"

Thomas made stirrups with his hands and Charlie stepped into them. Thomas hoisted Charlie without effort. Charlie peered into the gap between the books, hoping to see the spine of the missing book, inadvertently shoved into the darkness by some overzealous librarian.

Instead, flat on the shelf, he saw a button.

It was hard to spot, because it was flat, but the shelves were dark-grained wood and the button was unmistakably a copper metallic color. Charlie pressed the button.

"What's going on?" Ollie asked.

Charlie listened for the sound of machinery and heard none. "I guess nothing is happening. Go ahead and let me down."

Thomas relaxed and Charlie stepped to the floor. Turning

to face the other boys, he was astonished to find that they were not alone.

Standing behind Thomas and Ollie was a man. Or, rather, there stood the image of a man, but the image was composed of something that was neither light nor smoke but was instead both. He was a thin man, elderly, and bald. He smiled in a kindly way and stooped forward with a slouch that suggested he was really just a big boy who looked like an old man, and he was about to share a secret.

Removing a long-stemmed smoking pipe from his mouth, the apparition smiled. "Hello." The voice sounded as if it were far away, or as if a wind were whipping at the words and making them hard to hear. "My name is Wilhelm Grimm."

"You can't be!" Charlie blurted out.

"I can't?" The apparition sucked at his pipe and held the smoke in his mouth, seeming to taste it. When he exhaled, the smoke left his mouth in a perfect, tiny ring. Rising, the ring expanded, and through it Charlie saw not the apparition claiming to be Wilhelm Grimm, nor the library in which they both stood, but countryside. Strangely, the countryside seemed to be constantly changing: one minute it was forest, and the next it was ocean, and then again it was a volcano. "Why can't I?"

"You're dead," Charlie pointed out. The apparition and Charlie both spoke English. The ghost's English had a pleasant accent with mild and educated tones.

The apparition looked down at the elbows of his tweed jacket, patched with dark fabric. "I don't *feel* dead. Do I *seem* dead?"

"Sort of." Charlie looked to Thomas for help, but Thomas was crouched beside him, his eyes darting in all directions. It made him look like a smaller version of Lloyd, and Charlie tried not to laugh.

The apparition harrumphed.

Charlie tried a different approach. "Just because you look alive doesn't mean you really are. That could be art, an illusion."

"Really?" The apparition blew another smoke ring. Charlie would have sworn he saw green grass and blue sky through the ring's center. "Couldn't I say the same about you?"

Charlie hesitated. What did the apparition know? Of course, to phrase the question that way conceded the argument to the apparition that it was alive. But someone knew something. He chose his words carefully. "I suppose you could say the same about any person."

"You could indeed, Charlie." The phantom's smile only made Charlie feel uneasy. "But I didn't say I was *alive,* did I? I said I didn't think I was *dead.*"

"How do you know my name?" Charlie's voice sounded tiny in his own ears.

"Of course, in the way we think of these things, it's hard to imagine what it could possibly mean to be neither alive nor dead. What are the alternatives, eh, my boy?"

Charlie felt distinctly uncomfortable.

"I was once alive. And you . . . well, I suppose this is what you've come here to find out."

"Are you the Library Machine?" Charlie asked.

"I don't know, Charlie," the phantom said. "Are *you*?"

The question made Charlie acutely uncomfortable. "You didn't tell me how you know my name. That's impolite."

The apparition that looked like Wilhelm Grimm shrugged. "Well, you didn't introduce yourself, even after I did. Isn't *that* rude?"

"I'm Charlie Pondicherry, Mr. Grimm," Charlie said. "This is my brother Thomas, and my friend Ollie."

"Hmm." A smoke ring. "Please, call me Wilhelm. I am far too old to be *Mister.* Or call me Papa Wilhelm, if you feel you must give me a title. And you two, Charlie and Thomas, are different from the other boys, aren't you?"

Charlie nodded reluctantly. "How do you know that?"

"You've been here before, Charlie. With your friends. I watched you." Charlie must have made a disconcerted face, because Wilhelm Grimm laughed. "Oh, nothing sinister, I promise you." He waved his pipe in a circular motion. "This particular spot is where I appear, when I am invited and I choose to come, but the library—all the library—is my home. I'm rooted here. Physically connected, don't you know, so I see what happens here."

"And what makes you say I'm different?"

Wilhelm Grimm blew a smoke ring so big, Charlie could see an entire village through it, and a flock of ducks swimming on a river. Was Wilhelm Grimm not an apparition after all? Was he alive somewhere and communicating remotely? But Charlie was sure the real Wilhelm Grimm and his brother Jacob had died twenty or thirty years earlier.

Although he'd thought Isambard Kingdom Brunel was long dead too.

"I can just see it in you," Grimm finally said.

"See what?" Charlie involuntarily clutched at the hole in his side. Maybe he should find another cream like his bap had once made him wear on his face.

"Myself," Papa Wilhelm explained. "I can see myself in you."

Thomas stood up straight.

Charlie was puzzled. "What do you mean? Is this some long way of saying you can tell I like reading books, because you saw me in the library before? What do you mean? What *is* the Library Machine?"

"Know this, Charlie Pondicherry." Wilhelm Grimm chuckled. "You and I are kin. Ah!" He raised a finger, heading off Charlie's objections. "It is true. We are kin because I live in this machine, this library. And we are kin because a part of me was stolen once. It was stolen by a person motivated by greed and ambition, but perhaps still something good has come of his act. That bit of me that was stolen passed through strange and dark hands, but it came to rest in you."

"Me and my brother?" Charlie asked.

Thomas stood still as a stone, staring with wide eyes.

Wilhelm smiled. "Yes. You and your brother. In a not entirely usual sort of way, one might say that you two are my children."

"By 'dark hands,' you mean the kobold Zahnkrieger, don't you? He stole something. He stole a . . . bit of you, whatever that means. Your technology, maybe. And he gave it to the

Iron Cog, and that ended up inside me. That bit, Papa Wilhelm. Whatever you're talking about."

Wilhelm smiled. "Yes. And there was a third, a rabbit. Or, rather, she was the first."

"Aunt Big Money."

"My hour is short, but I will tell you now that the thing that roots me is in grave danger."

Charlie thought Wilhelm Grimm's eyes flickered into the central shaft of the library. Was the apparition looking at the hanging light? Something on the other side of the library, perhaps?

"Can I save you?" Charlie asked.

Papa Wilhelm shook his head. "You don't have time, Charlie. You have to save something much larger than me."

"What's that?" Charlie asked. He had found, for the second time since his bap's death, someone who seemed to be a new father for him . . . even if, in this case, that someone was already dead. And just as he had lost Isambard Kingdom Brunel almost immediately, Wilhelm Grimm was already talking about his own imminent destruction!

"The world, Charlie. The ability of people everywhere to be free and happy."

"Are you talking about the Iron Cog, sir?" Ollie asked.

The sweep's question surprised Charlie, and especially the fact that Ollie had called Wilhelm Grimm *sir.* Ollie was never that polite to *anyone.*

Wilhelm brushed aside his question. "You have the unicorn's horn."

Charlie hesitated. He didn't have the horn; he'd given it to

Lloyd and Gnat, when they'd stayed behind with Thomas in Jan Wijmoor's office.

"I'm holding it," Thomas said.

"That is your nail of the elemental world," the apparition said. "Now do you want to go to get your nails of the celestial and intellectual worlds?"

"I'm not quite sure what you're asking," Charlie said.

"I am the Library Machine," Papa Wilhelm said. "I can take you anywhere, provided you have the right book."

"The . . . stars?" Charlie guessed hesitantly. He had no idea where to go to get the nail of the celestial world, but Thomas had said that that was the world of the stars. "Another planet?"

"Cairo," Ollie said suddenly. "We'll go to the Souk of Wonders."

"What book will take you there?" the phantasm asked gravely.

Bamf! Ollie turned himself into a yellow-green snake, but he lay coiled on the carpet only momentarily, and then he returned to his boy form in a second cloud of sulfurous smoke.

But when he reappeared, he was holding a book. And not just any book—the green copy of Smythson's *Almanack* from the rabbi's library.

"How did you do that?" Thomas asked. It was what Charlie had been thinking too. He'd never seen Ollie produce an object from thin air.

Ollie shrugged. "You know how when I'm a snake, I don't have clothes?"

The other boys nodded.

"Yeah, well, the clothes kind of go into a pocket."

"Snakes don't have pockets," Thomas said.

"Not a real pocket." Ollie grimaced. "But it's *like* a pocket. And when I'm a boy, I leave the snake in that pocket. And I can leave other things in that pocket too."

"What sorts of things?" Charlie asked.

Ollie shrugged. "I dunno. This is the first time I ever tried putting anything there other than my clothes, and it's also the first time I ever left anything in there while I wasn't a snake."

Charlie wanted to offer Ollie a compliment, but all he could do was stare.

"What?" Ollie shrugged. "If Bob can have hypotheses, I can experiment."

Wilhelm Grimm nodded. "The Souk of Wonders it is!" The scene behind him, which had been a hillside patchworked with plowed fields and low stone walls, disappeared, and was replaced by a haze of thick smoke.

The floor beneath Charlie shook suddenly. He caught himself on the nearest bookshelf and looked at his friends in alarm—Thomas had fallen flat to the carpet, and Ollie had taken the shape of a yellow garter snake and landed on top of Charlie's brother.

"What was that?" Charlie heard his own voice as a terrified squeak. "Earthquake?"

Papa Wilhelm shook his head sadly. "It's my end, coming for me. There's no time to waste now—come on through."

Charlie stepped forward into the light and smoke, and the library disappeared.

PART TWO

THE SOUK OF WONDERS

Jacob's first work as a mechanick seems to have been when he was a simple carter in Napoleon's Grande Armée. In the wake of the disastrous siege of Moscow, Jacob Grimm became one of the engineers who devised steam-trucks to carry the retreating French troops to safety.

—Völpel, *Biographical Dictionary*, "Jacob and Wilhelm Grimm"

Charlie coughed and waved a thick cloud of smoke away from his nose. "What is this place?"

Papa Wilhelm spoke in low tones. "It is a shisha lounge. The souk is outside."

Charlie, Ollie, and Thomas all sat on leather benches surrounding a low wooden table. The air was dense with smoke that reminded Charlie a bit of Bap's pipe, but had a sweet fruity tang to it as well. A curtain of beads separated the alcove from the rest of the lounge.

Papa Wilhelm stood on the table in a column of white light. "When you have the nail, come back here." He smiled a kind smile, and then he was gone.

"What if we don't get the nail," Ollie muttered, "and have to run away?"

They left the alcove and picked their way across a long, narrow room cluttered with small tables and people smoking water pipes. The air was close, and felt like the inside of an oven. Charlie turned back as they reached the front of the lounge, to be sure he knew exactly which alcove he had to return to, to find Papa Wilhelm again.

Then they stepped out of the doorway—there was no door, just an open space—and into blazing heat and light.

"Baksheesh, baksheesh!" three voices shrieked. Hands tugged at Charlie's coat from all directions. "Alms! Alms!"

"Get out of here, you!" Ollie exploded into a storm of kicks and swung fists, and the three beggars scattered. Charlie caught a glimpse before they disappeared around a corner—they weren't human, and they weren't any other kind of folk Charlie recognized. One had a bird's head and feet, the second was covered with scales, and the third was blue.

The three boys stood on a street of sand, surrounded by clay walls. A sun that seemed three times larger than it should have been hammered down from directly overhead, and the sand and clay seemed to bounce the heat right back toward Charlie.

The shisha lounge had been cool by comparison.

Carpets hung out of second-story windows in the clay walls. Goods for sale hung from long strings against those carpets: Charlie saw the dried bodies of small animals he couldn't identify, and glittering stones, and jewelry. Stacked against the walls on the sand were booths under awnings propped up on tent poles to ward off the wicked sun. The array of strange objects on the booths' tables was too much for Charlie to really take in, but he saw three-eyed and horned skulls, live two-headed fish blowing bubbles in a bowl of water, amulets carved with characters the Babel Card couldn't reorganize, vials of dark liquid, packets of dried herbs, curved swords engraved with magical symbols, stacks of books and scrolls, and more.

Beyond the clay walls, to all sides, rose enormous pyramids. At the nearest street corner, where five alleys seemed to meet in a jumble of irregular walls, Charlie saw a stone statue of the Egyptian dog-god Wepwawet, Opener of the Ways, and beside him the ibis-headed Thoth, writing on a sheet of papyrus.

Shoppers thronged the alleys, packed tighter than herring in a tin. Many wore long white robes that seemed to fit the setting, but Charlie also saw hulders in furs and wool coats, and kobolds in bright silks, and he thought maybe even an alfar in the distance. Sellers and customers alike yelled in a boiling soup of tongues. The Babel Card didn't tell Charlie what languages he was hearing, but it sorted the words out into sense over time.

"Potions! Love potions, half off, today only!"

"Free amulet for warding off the evil eye with the purchase of any two items!"

"Have you seen the new models of flying carpet, sir? They are now capable of flying forward *and* backward!"

It was like the landgrave's museum, only it stretched as far as he could see in all directions.

"The Souk of Wonders," Charlie said. "Where are we?"

"Cairo," Ollie said. "Sort of. If I understand correctly, it's a bit of Cairo sort of . . . stuck out of the ordinary flow of time. It's like a permanent, magical part of Cairo, if that makes any sense."

"It doesn't," Thomas told him.

Ollie shrugged.

"When did you become such a font of information?" Charlie asked. "Is this from the reading you've been doing?"

Ollie blushed.

"You need a guide, gentlemen!" A dwarf swept into view. He was dressed in a pale blue caftan. His beard was oiled to a point, and his hair was bound in a dark green turban. He spoke English.

"No baksheesh here, mate," Ollie growled.

The dwarf turned the backs of both hands to Ollie, showing that he wore gold rings on all his fingers. "Do I appear to you to be a beggar?"

Ollie harrumphed.

"Earth and sky, no!" the dwarf continued. "I am a guide. And I am not paid by you, but by the merchants with whom I will connect you. Only tell me what you seek, and I will help you find it."

"You're a dowser," Charlie said.

The dwarf tipped his head in acknowledgment.

"What shall we call you?" Thomas asked. Thomas had even more experience with dwarfs than Charlie did, since his father had employed several families of that folk to collect items for him.

Locating them in places such as the landgrave's collection and, perhaps, Charlie realized, this market.

"You may call me Sayyid," the dwarf said. The Babel Card told Charlie that *sayyid* meant "sir" or "mister."

"And if we must refer to you, we'll say 'the dwarf who brought us here,'" Thomas said.

The dwarf bowed. "Tell me your pleasure, my friends."

"Heavenly iron," Thomas said. "Meteoric iron, what they call cold iron. The oldest metal, the iron that falls out of heaven. And we need it in the shape of a spike."

The dwarf frowned and clicked his tongue.

"Is it not to be found here?" Charlie asked.

"I will take you to a man who has such a piece," the dwarf said. "But I warn you, he will ask a very, very high price. What you seek is rare, and costly."

"Everything here is rare and costly," Ollie said. "It's the Souk of Wonders, ain't it?"

"Yes," the dwarf agreed. "And that means you will find cold iron here. It does *not* mean that the cold iron will be cheap."

"I have money." Charlie straightened his back and raised his chin. "Take us to this man."

The dwarf's face brightened and he bowed. "Perhaps I can help you negotiate. I am but a humble child of the souk, a person of no worth or importance, but I have been known to strike a deal or two in my time."

"Maybe," Charlie said. "Take us to the shop, please."

"Follow me!" The dwarf waved his ringed fingers and plunged into the crowd.

The dwarf was short and so were all the boys, and that made staying together difficult in the crowd. Charlie kept his eyes fixed firmly on the flashes of blue from their guide's caftan and of green from his turban, and dragged Thomas and Ollie along in his wake.

Thomas shuddered and cringed at each contact with another person. Ollie still looked morose.

"What's wrong?" Charlie asked his shape-changing friend. "You said Bob was mad at you. That doesn't seem right; Bob's never angry."

"Yeah," Ollie agreed glumly. "Only I stuck my foot in my mouth today."

The dwarf led them around the corner, past Thoth and Wepwawet, into a broader avenue. Here tents stood in a row down the center of the street, splitting it into two. Charlie ducked to avoid the bite of an irritated camel. "What are you talking about?"

Ollie sighed. "I knew something about my mate Bob, you see. Something I wasn't supposed to know. And today I accidentally let on that I knew."

And Charlie remembered. When Ollie had smashed a chair over the back of the monster's head in the library, he had shouted, "Leave her alone!"

Her.

Ollie knew Bob was a girl.

Thomas didn't know, though. Charlie had to be careful.

"I know the secret you're talking about, Ollie." Charlie kept following the dwarf as he turned down an alley with no shops in it, so narrow Charlie could touch the opposite walls at the same time. "You're thinking Bob's angry because you accidentally told me."

Ollie's eyes narrowed. "Yeah . . . ?"

"But that can't be it," Charlie said. "Because I already knew. And Bob knew I knew."

"Then I don't understand!" Ollie almost shouted. "How can Bob be mad at me? I kept the secret! I played along with Bob's game, as long as we've been mates! What else was I supposed to do?"

"How did you find out?" Charlie asked.

Ollie laughed. "Mate, it was obvious from the start. No offense, but you've got to be half-blind not to see it. Or, in your case, a boy who's never been around . . . you know. Who never left the house."

Thomas jumped out of the way of the backward kick of a mule and knocked Charlie down. As they disentangled themselves and stood, Thomas frowned. "What are you talking about?"

"Nope," Ollie said. "I ain't making that mistake again."

"It's complicated," Charlie said slowly. "But I think you'll find out before too long."

Thomas looked hurt. What could Charlie say to him that wouldn't break his promise to Bob?

"This is it," the guide said.

The alleys had given way to a small plaza. The sand had been swept away or possibly covered over, leaving tight round cobblestones paving the square. The walls to all four sides towered over Charlie and his friends, four stories tall or more. In this suddenly open space, Charlie would have expected to see more shops against the walls, but there were none.

There was a single stone porch with a row of painted pillars and behind them two doors, lacquered red, which arced up to a single point. Standing on the porch with their arms crossed were two enormous men with bright red skin and stubby horns. Their chests were bare, they wore silk pantaloons, and at their broad leather belts hung wide, curved swords.

"Djinns?" Ollie asked.

Charlie thought of the skull in the landgrave's collection. "One way to find out," he said.

Charlie smiled to communicate that his intentions were good, and he walked to his left. Within two steps—as soon as he was no longer facing the djinns head-on—the two men abruptly disappeared. "Yeah," he said. "Djinns."

"What is this place, Sayyid?" Thomas asked. "Are we still in the souk?"

"We're at the souk's edge." The dwarf pointed farther down the alley along which they'd come. "A few steps that way, and space and time both begin to curve back, to return you to the souk."

Ollie frowned. "That makes the souk sound like a trap."

The dwarf smiled. "If you were able to find a way here, surely you can find a way out. Shall we speak to the collector?"

"Collector?" Charlie asked. "I thought you'd take us to a merchant."

"The collector is named Suleiman Abd al-Rahim," the dwarf said. "He is a mighty magician, and he is known to sell items from his collection . . . when he is offered a high enough price in return."

Charlie stepped closer. "Okay, Sayyid. Take us in."

Real artificial magic produces real effects, as when Architas made a flying dove of wood, and recently at Nüremberg, according to Boterus, an eagle and a fly have been made in the same way. Daedalus made statues which moved through the action of weights or of mercury. However, I do not hold that to be true which William of Paris writes, namely that it is possible to make a head which speaks with a human voice, as Albertus Magnus is said to have done. . . . Such forces and materials can never be such as to capture a human soul.

—Tommaso Campanella, *Magia e Grazia*

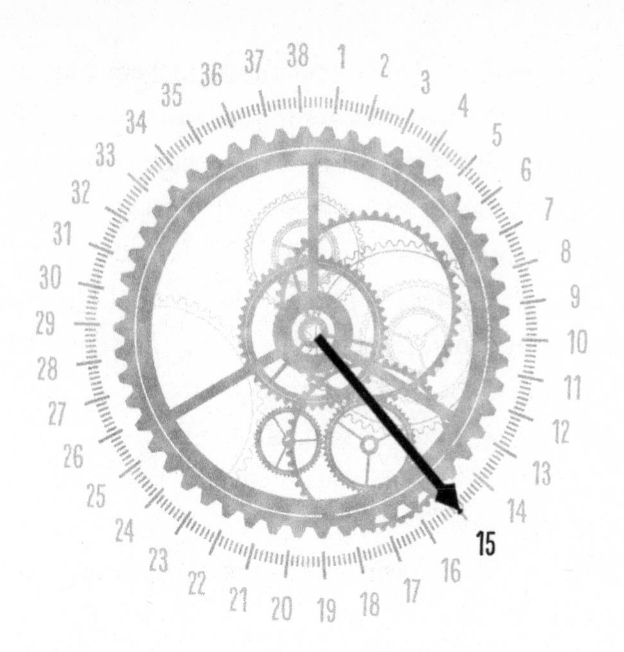

"Iftah, ya baabaain!" the dwarf shouted. *Open, doors!* Charlie understood.

With no apparent help, the doors opened, and their guide trotted up the steps to the porch. The two djinns bowed, and turned in to face the dwarf as he passed between them—which made them disappear to Charlie.

"Come along!" the dwarf called.

Ollie followed first, and Charlie and Thomas came after him. Charlie held Thomas's hand, but nevertheless his brother jumped as they passed between the two djinns, and the huge warriors appeared briefly, still bowing low.

Once past the doors, Charlie stopped. Around him, rows of arched columns ran in all directions. Walls to his left and right were wooden lattices, and through them came a cool, moist breeze—through the gaps in the lattice, Charlie saw not the sand and white-baked clay he expected, but blue water, and tall green reeds, and white lotus flowers.

"This Suleiman is a real magician." Ollie was staring.

"Upstairs!" The dwarf urged them forward. "The magician prefers to meet people in his throne room." The guide climbed a set of marble steps that went straight up.

"I don't know," Thomas said, pulling back.

"People make you nervous," Charlie said. "Your father made you that way."

Thomas nodded slowly. "Knowing that doesn't make me less nervous."

"Just keep hold of my hand," Charlie told him. "You'll be all right."

The brothers followed Ollie up the stairs.

"What's he collect, anyway?" Ollie yelled at the dwarf's back. "So far, I'm seeing quite a nice palace, but that ain't a collection, is it?"

"Magical things, mostly!" The dwarf stopped and waited at the top of the stairs. "Cold iron is the oldest magic. It fell from the sky, connecting the world of the stars with the world in which we stand, back when humans were scratching on cave walls and hulders were butting each other in the head to decide who was stronger."

"They still do that," Ollie muttered.

"Newer magic is different. Magic is changing in your century, and the collector Suleiman Abd al-Rahim is fascinated by it. He is studying the new magic to master it, as he mastered the old."

"See?" Ollie said to no one in particular. "You *can* master magic."

The dwarf chuckled.

Charlie and Thomas reached the top of the steps. Here too wooden lattices surrounded them, and here too cool breezes brought in the smell of the rushes and lotus flowers that Charlie could see growing just beyond the lattice.

Then Charlie stopped and scratched his head. "Ollie," he said softly. "Down below, did we seem to be on the ground floor? Level with the water and the plants outside, I mean?"

"Yeah, mate." Then Ollie whistled. "And we've come up the stairs and we're still level with the water."

"And as you go up again," the dwarf said, "you'll be level with the water still. Only it's different water each time."

Ollie sucked air through his teeth and said nothing.

"One more floor!" The dwarf turned and climbed another staircase.

"I ain't seeing much in the way of people," Ollie said.

"The magician is mostly served by his creations," the dwarf said.

At the top of the stairs were more columns and lattice walls, but also a clear avenue with a throne at the end, standing on a round dais. The throne glowed like brass in a soft light that bathed it from above.

The dwarf trudged to the seat, the three boys following. When he arrived, he climbed into it, turned, and sat.

"That seems rather cheeky." Ollie frowned.

"Suleiman!" Charlie gasped.

"That's not my name either," the dwarf said. "Obviously."

"But you *are* the magician," Thomas said.

"The more important a job is, the less you can trust it to a servant." The dwarf grinned. "And collecting is the most important job of all."

"The dwarf," Ollie muttered. "The dwarf is the magician."

"Are you a dowser, Sayyid?" Charlie asked. "That made sense to me when I thought you were someone who just found buyers for the merchants, but it makes sense for a collector, too."

"I began life as a mere dowser." The magician leaned forward, resting his elbows on his knees, and smiled. "Every magician starts somewhere. But I outgrew that at an early age."

"Too right," Ollie murmured.

"Why are you willing to sell us the iron we want?" Charlie had a sinking feeling in his stomach.

"Ah, yes, let me show it to you." The dwarf leaned back in his seat and pulled at some sort of control set into one armrest, out of Charlie's sight. Out of the other armrest rose a long triangular dagger, with copper wire pounded in a crosshatched pattern into the iron handle.

"Looks like a knife," Ollie said.

"May I see it?" Thomas asked.

The dwarf nodded, and Thomas came forward to examine the object. After a few seconds' inspection, he turned back to Charlie and Ollie. "This is it," he said. "This is what we need."

"Are you sure?" Charlie asked.

"I was made for this," Thomas said. Was his voice sad? "I'm certain."

Charlie pulled his bap's money from his pocket. "I don't know how much is here," he said, "but you can have all of it."

"Really?" The magician smiled and stroked his oiled beard. "This is what you offer, paper money from a country far away in space and time?"

"It's what I have," Charlie said.

"What use have I for that? Tell me." The dwarf's eyes glittered.

Charlie's sinking feeling got worse. "I won't give you the unicorn horn," he said. "We need that, too."

The magician guffawed, a laugh that shook his whole body. "What a delightful work you are! So innocent, so hilarious!"

Something about the way the dwarf said the word *work* bothered Charlie. "Thomas," he said softly. "Come back here, please."

Thomas didn't need extra encouragement. He retreated to Charlie's side, leaving the knife. The dwarf let him go, grinning broadly.

"So," the magician purred. "You understand what I want."

"Me," Charlie said, and he could see no other way. "You can have me for your collection."

"No!" Ollie and Thomas yelled together.

"Trade me instead!" Thomas suggested.

Charlie drew his friends in close to discuss. "It has to be me. Thomas is the one who knows the spell."

"Maybe you do too, mate," Ollie said. "Remember how you said you thought you might be the redundancy? The backup?"

Charlie frowned. "Are you suggesting I should give Thomas to this dwarf?"

Ollie blushed. "No, I don't . . . No! I don't want to give either one of you to him!" His shoulders slumped, and he stamped one booted foot on the floor. "Only, Charlie, it really hurts to think of losing you."

"I know," Charlie said. "But if I'm the redundancy, the backup plan, I don't know how to do . . . whatever it is I'm supposed to do, anyway."

Ollie turned abruptly to face the dwarf. "I have a counter-offer, Sayyid! Or Suleiman, or whatever you want me to call you."

The dwarf arched his eyebrows. "Speak."

"I'll be your apprentice. Give these lads the knife, and I'll be your servant. I'll help you add stuff to your collection, and I'll do whatever work you want, and you can teach me more magic, so I can serve you better."

"*More* magic?"

"Yeah." Ollie squirmed and then changed shape. *Bamf!* He was a long yellow cobra for a few seconds. *Bamf!* He took his own shape again.

The dwarf laughed. "You're a bold one, child. But I won't give you what you want in exchange for what you also want. That would make me a fool, wouldn't it?"

Ollie looked down at his feet.

"Besides," the dwarf continued, "I already have enough

shape-changers in my collection to fill a zoo. The largest shaitan community in captivity is right over your head, boy."

"I ain't a shaitan," Ollie grunted.

The dwarf turned back to Charlie. "Yes. The dagger for one of you. I don't care which."

"Me," Thomas blurted out.

"No," Charlie said. "Me." He looked at his brother. "It has to be me, and you know it."

Thomas's lip trembled. "But how can I possibly be brave enough to do what needs to be done without you? You're the brave one, Charlie."

"Ollie will help you," Charlie said. "And Bob and the others."

"Bob will help." Ollie grimaced. "Bob might not talk to me ever again, but Bob will help."

Thomas looked down at his feet. "Okay."

Charlie hugged his brother.

He didn't know what exactly his bap had built him for, but if Thomas succeeded and undid the very magic that had created Thomas and Charlie, Charlie would die anyway.

Why, Bap?

Charlie hugged his brother tighter.

"One more thing!" Ollie cried.

"Oh?" the dwarf asked.

"We give you Charlie, and you do two things. You give us the knife, and you show us your collection."

The dwarf's eyes narrowed. "Why?"

"I'm the same as you," Ollie said. "You started as a dowser

and you wanted more. So you kept your eyes open and you learned, and now you're a big wizard. I started as a shape-changer but I always wanted more. Show me. Let me see the magic."

"Hmmm." The dwarf chewed his lip.

Ollie laughed. "Oh, knock it off. You know you *want* us to see it."

"Ha!" The dwarf leaped to his feet. "You're right, of course. Come upstairs with me, all three of you, and I will show you marvels."

Shaitans are solitary predators by nature. They eat other folk, after stalking their prey for weeks and sometimes years. No reliable witness exists for the natural physical appearance of a shaitan, and it is unclear why. The folkloric sources vary widely.

—from Reginald St. John Smythson, *Almanack of the Elder Folk and Arcana of Britain and Northern Ireland*, 2nd ed., "Shaitan"

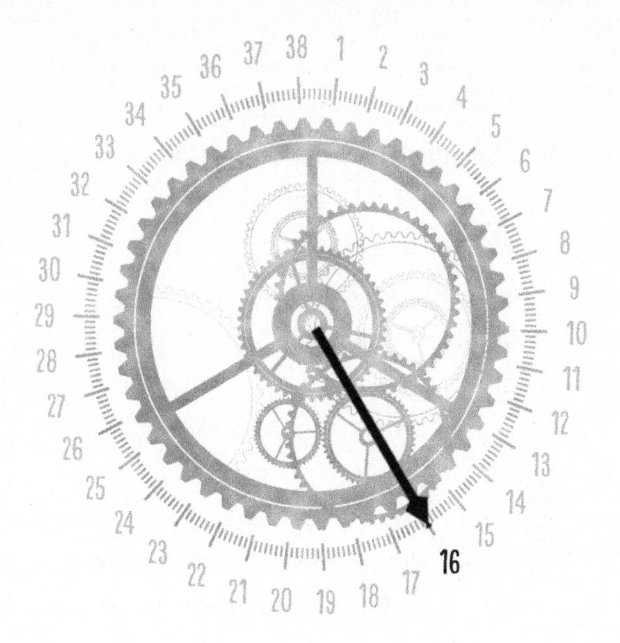

“Watch your feet,” the dwarf warned them as they reached the top of the next flight of steps. “Don’t cross any lines in the floor. The creatures within are trapped and cannot come out, and if you enter their cages . . . I won’t rescue you.”

Charlie held Thomas’s hand tighter.

As the magician had promised, this floor too seemed to be on the ground level, and through wooden lattices and deeply shaded balconies Charlie saw long bodies of blue water fringed with green and white, and, beyond, brilliant red sand.

With one small difference—*these* waters churned. Charlie squinted to get a closer look, and he thought he saw crocodiles and very large snakes.

“Blimey,” Ollie said.

After the landgrave’s collection and the souk, Charlie imagined he’d be dulled to wonder. He was wrong.

He saw a column of salt that sang—once the Babel Card sorted out its words—of a city burned by the vengeful fires of heaven. He saw a suit of lacquered blue armor that marched itself through military drills though no one was wearing it. He saw a bow that burned in seven colors and emitted a noise that made Charlie want to sing for joy. He saw a pair of polished ivory dice that rolled themselves over and over on a golden platter; at each roll, a shower of small objects burst from the dice and fell through slots in the floor surrounding the platter. Some dice results rained gold, pearls, silver, or gems; others threw out frogs, scorpions, snakes, or mice.

He saw a large plain boulder, and he pointed at it. “What’s that?” It seemed so out of place.

The dwarf chuckled. “That, my boy, is the Foundation Stone. It holds down all the waters of creation, and if it were to be lifted up, the flood that would burst forth would destroy the Souk of Wonders in moments, and the world with it by sunset.”

“Seems dangerous to keep around, don’t it?”

“Herakles and Samson together could not budge it an inch,” the magician snarled. “The only thing that can move that stone is the dancing of the king.”

“Which king?” Charlie asked.

“The true one, of course,” the dwarf answered.

“Good thing I don’t dance,” Ollie said.

And there were creatures. Charlie was very careful to follow the magician's instruction: each creature or group of creatures was in a space marked off by a thin black line on the floor, and the creatures, however much they might hiss and howl, never crossed the line. Charlie saw a seven-headed snake, a lion with fire for its mane, and a troop of little men with only one leg each, who hopped about or knit their shoulders together to stand in pairs. He saw owls with human faces, perched high in an oak tree that sprouted from the floor. He saw werewolves, which snarled and threw themselves at the line, only to be hurled back by an invisible force, yelping in pain. He saw a man with a scorpion's tail and sad eyes, who tried to sting himself but couldn't because his tail was weighted down with iron.

And then he saw four shape-changers.

"Red Cloak," he whispered.

The magician chortled. "I don't know that name," he said, "which probably means it's wrong. They're generally called shaitans, and sometimes rakshasas."

The four shaitans, squatting in a mound of filthy straw, stared at Charlie with their black eyes. As one person they opened their lipless mouths to show needlelike teeth and hiss.

Then they sang. It was a wordless song, like an open-mouthed hum. It was the same melody he'd heard from the shape-changer in the landgrave's museum, only now it had layers of harmony woven in above and below.

The song made Charlie want to sleep, and the thought of sleeping in the presence of such monsters made him shudder.

"But I thought a shaitan only took someone's shape after it ate him," he said.

The magician snorted dismissively. "No, that's nonsense. You've been reading all the wrong stories. A shaitan takes someone's shape *in order* to eat him, and then keeps it for a time afterward. Watch this."

The magician unwound his turban. The black hair underneath sprang outward in a tightly curled mane. After balling up the length of cotton, the dwarf threw it into the shaitan cage.

The shaitans leaped on it. All four seized the turban and tore away pieces. Hissing and snarling at each other, they retreated to the four corners of the cage, where each clutched a fragment of cloth to its chest and stroked it obsessively.

"Impressive," Ollie said. "They must have the strength of, what, a ten-year-old?"

"Wait."

Within the space of a single blink, all four shaitans changed. They all resembled the dwarf magician, and as one they smiled at him.

Charlie had been wrong. The creature in Marburg, working with the Prussians and the Iron Cog, had been a shaitan after all.

"Amusing, no?" The dwarf snapped his fingers; the scraps of cotton disappeared, and the shaitans returned to their rubbery, noseless look.

"Yeah," Ollie said. "I'm laughing hard."

Thomas squeezed Charlie's hand tighter.

“This will be where you sleep, Charlie.” The magician crossed a row of columns to where there was a small bed and nothing else. The bed was surrounded by a black line in the floor, creating a space ten paces long by ten paces wide.

Charlie was careful not to step over the line.

Around his cage, on this side of the columns, were machines. Charlie saw a pump, drawing up a continual stream of water that fell back through a grate in the floor. There was a pair of mechanical wings—very similar to the ones invented and built by Heaven-Bound Bob—attached to a silver ball, flapping up and down of their own accord. Mechanical legs ran on a band of India rubber that moved without stopping, creating a belt so the legs could run and yet remain stationary.

“The new magic of your time,” the wizard said. “I am learning it too, the art of ball bearing and crankshaft, the fine nuances of aerial geometry, the secret explosion of the combustion engine, the transformation of the four elements together—earthy coal, celestial fire, mundane water, and fine air—into motive power.” He looked at Charlie. “And you.”

Charlie released Thomas’s hand and stepped to one side. “When you deliver the dagger, I’m ready.”

But the wizard seemed to be in no mood to rush anything. “And who would have thought this would prove the strongest magic? By it the earth is tilled and food is grown in great abundance! By it man moves as fast as ever he did on any elf road, and as high as he could on any ifrit’s carpet! This flowering of invention will feed the masses and bring wealth to all—mark my words, in a century the poorest person in your England will enjoy luxuries never imagined by Henry the Eighth!"

The wizard's words caught Charlie up short. This magic-hoarding sorcerer who was about to imprison Charlie forever as part of his collection saw Charlie and the wave of invention of which he was a part as a *good* thing. Charlie stretched his mind back a few weeks to recall what Isambard Kingdom Brunel had said. "But what about . . . the bad side?"

The dwarf shook his head impatiently. "Technology has no good and bad side; it is just a tool. Does a shovel have a bad side?"

"If I bopped you on the head with a shovel, you might think it did," Ollie said.

The dwarf laughed. "The ill will, the evil, the harm, are all in you. In us. They're not in the tool. The tools give us power to do great things, according to what is in our hearts."

What the dwarf said made a great deal of sense, but Charlie struggled. If the worst weapons were taken away, people could harm each other less. "But . . ."

"Look at *you*!" the magician cried. "You're so charming-looking; no doubt your maker meant you as a companion, or a toy. But you don't breathe, do you?"

Charlie shook his head.

"And I'll wager you resist heat, too!"

"No need to experiment," Ollie muttered.

"What a worker you would make!" The magician clapped his hands against Charlie's shoulders with excitement. "You could mine veins of ore in places no human could ever go.

You could farm the bottom of the ocean. You could rescue stranded climbers in the Himalayas, in snow that would kill an ordinary man. You could perform delicate medical operations for hours on end, and your arms would never grow weary!"

"And you're going to take all that away from the world," Thomas said, "by locking him in here."

The dwarf hesitated, then sniffed. "It's a museum, a record. If the world outside loses this precious knowledge, it can come here and I will restore it."

"For a price," Ollie said.

"That's only fair!" the dwarf cried. "And besides, I'm only keeping one of you; I'm setting the other one free! That's generous!"

"You might be a bit confused about that word," Ollie suggested.

"Hand over the knife." Picking a fight with this magician didn't seem like a winning proposition. Charlie had made his deal and he'd keep it, but he had no intention of lying here awake for all eternity, watching the dwarf play games with the shaitans. He'd let his mainspring wind down, and hopefully the magician wouldn't know how to wind it up again, and Charlie could just sleep in blissful ignorance while his brother and friends stopped the Iron Cog.

Or maybe he'd dream again. That had been all right, dreaming.

"Get in your room first," the magician answered.

Charlie stepped over the line. The magician chanted several quick words, too quick for the Babel Card to catch, and snapped the fingers of both hands at the same time. Nothing obvious happened.

"Observe." The dwarf grinned, and then crossed the line, standing next to Charlie; then he exited again, and nothing happened. "Now, Charlie . . . your turn."

Charlie reached a tentative finger toward the space over the black line—

A force that felt like a steam train moving at speed knocked him to the floor and hurled him across the room. He landed in the bed, aching all over.

The dwarf handed the iron dagger to Thomas, who now held two of the three nails.

Thomas looked stricken.

"Trust Ollie," Charlie groaned. "Ollie and Bob and the others. They're your friends."

"I'm sorry we can't help you, mate." Ollie's voice trembled, but there was something flickering in his eyes, and it didn't look like sorrow. "We'll get the job done."

"I . . . I'll miss you," Thomas said.

"Don't worry." Charlie smiled. "I'll be fine."

"Yes, yes." The dwarf waved one hand, and Charlie's friends vanished.

Charlie struggled to sit up. "Did you—where are they?"

"They are unharmed! They are in the Souk of Wonders, and will no doubt shortly find their way back to wherever you came from." The dwarf walked a slow circle around Charlie's cage, smiling and nodding. "Tell me, Charlie; do you play chess?"

Charlie shook his head.

"I shall teach you," the dwarf said. "You and I are going to be in here together a very long time."

Waving a hand again, the dwarf himself disappeared.

Charlie lay down and stared at the stone ceiling, waiting for darkness to come.

After twenty long years working down in the mine
I've got shovels for fingers and a scythe for a spine
If I'd kept my mouth shut I'd be doing just fine
For twenty more years working down in the mine

—Child, *Popular Ballads,* No. 2

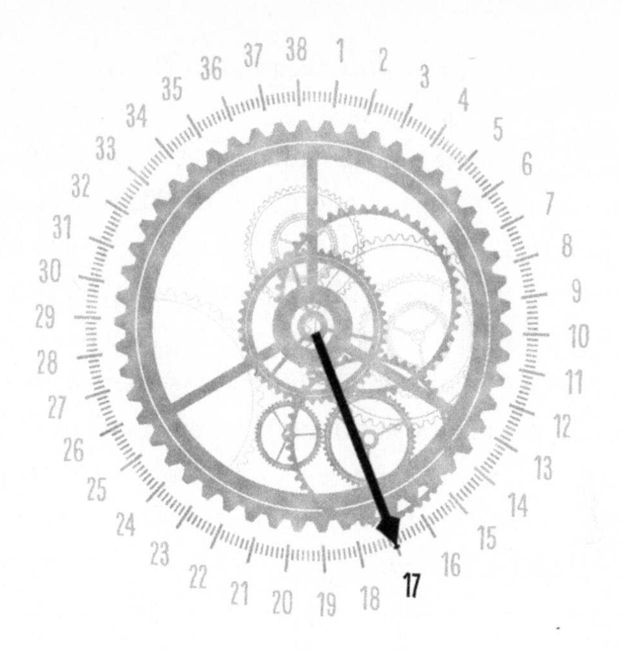

The sun set outside the wooden screens, and then the thrashing monsters in the water settled down. Not that that gave Charlie any opportunity to escape—he wasn't about to test the invisible walls of his cage again.

He watched the streaks of gold and crimson and then the deep indigo of the night sky with sorrow. This would be his last sunset. He had thought for some time—since learning on Cader Idris that Isambard Kingdom Brunel's plan involved the death of his son, Thomas—that he and Thomas had been designed to die. That doing what they'd been made for would result in their own death.

Or maybe *death* was the wrong word, but . . . Charlie would stop working.

Could he ever know what his own bap had thought? What Bap had planned for Charlie?

And not knowing his bap's mind, what should Charlie do?

Now he was facing not only death, but likely failure. He'd left his friends alone, and however much he encouraged Thomas, he didn't think his brother was as brave or persistent as Charlie himself.

He thought about Rabbi Rosenbaum's speech: the rabbi had said that all folk had things in common and differences, and that that meant people could learn from each other. The Prussians, on the other hand, and the Iron Cog, wanted to tell everyone what to do—and they said it was for everyone's good. And since people wouldn't willingly join them, the Cog was going to war. Then there was Brunel's view that the demon unleashed by the Romanovs empowered evil people, and his plan to stop the Iron Cog by traveling to Russia to end the very technology of which he was master and inventor. And now Charlie had the dwarf wizard's rant in his head too—Suleiman loved technology, but only because he wanted to keep it all, like he wanted to keep everything else. Charlie was a museum exhibit to the dwarf, or maybe a toy.

What was the truth? Whom should Charlie follow? He found himself in a world of visions that overlapped and competed and sometimes even fought to the death.

Charlie loved adventure, but it was beginning to seem that adventure was just another word for people getting hurt. Bap had been killed, and Brunel. Now Charlie was going to die. Had his father made him to love adventure? Did that mean his father had done a bad thing?

Charlie wished he had been made instead to love peace and quiet.

But some part inside him protested. He wasn't being entirely fair. Charlie liked having friends. He liked motion, and danger, but he didn't want to hurt people.

And the world the rabbi had talked about—the world in which people could be different and still be friends—didn't that world require defending sometimes?

It did. And Charlie had tried to be that defender.

Not that it mattered now. He was stuck in here, and would soon lose consciousness.

"Good luck, Thomas," he whispered to the ceiling. "Good luck, Bob. Good luck, Ollie."

Bamf! Charlie smelled the stink of rotten eggs.

"Thanks, mate. I reckon we'll all need it, and you and me sooner than the others."

Charlie rolled to sit, but a hand shot up from the floor and grabbed him, urging him to hold still.

"What is it?" Charlie asked.

"I don't know who's watching," Ollie whispered. "I reckon it must be someone."

"How did you get back here?" Charlie wanted to know.

"Mate, it was amazing." Ollie's whisper picked up speed. "Old Papa Wilhelm was waiting for us after all. We got back through his gate, and you'll never guess how much time had passed."

Charlie's heart sank. "Years?"

"Not even seconds," Ollie hissed. "Nothing, no time at all. I'd swear I saw my own boot heel disappearing *into* the Library Machine just as I was stepping out of it."

"Is that because the Souk of Wonders is . . . What did you say? Outside time?"

"Or is it instead because—now bear with me here, mate—we ain't in a real place at all?"

"That doesn't make any sense, Ollie."

"Doesn't it? Papa Wilhelm said we could go anywhere that was in a story, right?"

"He said in a *book*. That's different."

"Okay, but what if the place you had in the book wasn't a place in the real world? What if it was someplace made up, like the Isles of the Blessed, or Chichester?"

"Chichester isn't made up, Ollie."

"You ever been there, mate? No? Me neither. Anyway, what if it was a made-up place entirely? Would Papa Wilhelm say, 'Oh no, you can't go there; it ain't real,' or would he just sweep you on through?"

"I don't know."

"So I'm thinking maybe this ain't real either. I mean, how many pyramids did you see when we were walking around the souk?"

Charlie thought back. He had seen pyramids in all directions, he thought. "A dozen?"

"Right. So I ain't an expert, Charlie, but I'm pretty sure there ain't a dozen pyramids standing all together like that anywhere in Egypt."

"You did say we were out of space and time. And I thought the dwarf seemed to agree."

"Yeah. But now I'm starting to think we ain't in a real place, Charlie. Notwithstanding old Smythson put it in his *Almanack*."

"Then what is it? It certainly *feels* real."

"I think it's a story. I think the Library Machine is a door that moves you into stories."

Charlie lay still and tried to absorb that. "I don't know. That's . . . strange."

"Right? But it gets stranger, mate. Consider this: If you can move into a story land . . . how do you know you weren't in a story land to begin with?"

"That's easy," Charlie said. "I think. I feel. I get hurt."

"How do you know characters in stories don't do those things?"

Charlie shook his head. "That's crazy, Ollie."

"Maybe," Ollie agreed, "but it got me thinking. Hey, how's your mainspring?"

"I have no real way to tell," Charlie said. "But a lot of time has passed."

"Shall I wind you, mate?"

Ollie's bizarre line of reasoning had him curious. And maybe, just maybe, Ollie could get him out. "Okay."

Charlie rolled over onto his side, and Ollie climbed to his knees to wind Charlie's spring.

"So it got me thinking," Ollie continued, "about magic."

"I know you want to be a magician," Charlie said, "like Aunt Big Money, and like . . . Sayyid. But being a shape-changer is a great thing."

"Sure it is," Ollie said. "It's a good start. But what exactly is holding me back from doing more?"

The winding was done, and Ollie sat back on the floor in the darkness. Charlie cautiously sat up. He half expected lights to come on and the dwarf wizard to leap out of hiding, but nothing happened. "I don't know, Ollie," he said.

"Just the story." Ollie's voice sounded as if he might be crying, a little. "I think just the story is holding me back."

"Do you mean that you're held back by the limitations inside your own head?" Charlie asked. "Or do you mean you really think you're a character in a story?"

"Is there a difference?" Ollie replied.

"I don't think I'm smart enough to follow you," Charlie said. "But I'm very glad you came to visit me. It's very dangerous, though, and you probably shouldn't do it again. You should probably just leave me here to . . . just leave me here."

"I didn't come to *visit* you, mate," Ollie said.

"No?"

"I came to get you *out*."

Had Ollie become a full-fledged magician—was that what all his strange talk about stories and limitations meant? "How will you do that, then?"

Ollie sniffed. "Easy-peasy. I'll carry you."

"I don't think you're strong enough, Ollie. Remember how heavy I am? And even if you could lift me, what good would it do? Remember what happened when I touched the line myself?"

"Yeah." Ollie chuckled. "But Bob and I have a theory."

"Bob's speaking to you?"

"Yeah." The humor fell out of Ollie's voice. "She's still angry, scowls a lot. But she's talking to me." Ollie laughed suddenly. "And at least I can call her *she* now. Thomas was quite surprised, but I think he's adjusting to the idea."

"You have a theory." Hope was unreasonable, Charlie told himself. Whatever insane idea Bob and Ollie had come up with, there was no way it would work.

But he had nothing to lose by trying.

"Remember how I carried the book?"

Charlie thought back. "What did you say . . . that you left it with the snake? In the snake's pocket?"

"Yeah. So I'm going to try that with you. I'm going to try to leave you with the boy, like I do with my clothes, and slip on out of here. What's the worst that could happen?"

Charlie tried to imagine. "Sayyid's spell might tear you to bits, trying to push me back into the cage."

"Yeah, Bob said the same thing. But I reckon, what have I got to lose?"

"Your life, Ollie."

"I was afraid you might see it that way." In the darkness, Ollie grabbed Charlie's wrist.

Bamf! Ollie the boy was suddenly gone, replaced by Ollie the snake.

Only this time Charlie went with him.

Charlie had never experienced anything like it. He didn't *become* the snake, but he was *inside* the snake. Ollie's snake head was definitely out in front, so if Charlie had to assign himself to a part of the snake's actual anatomy, he'd say he was in its belly. He couldn't find his own body, but he was conscious that there were other things inside the snake with him: a bowler hat, a peacoat, rough-shod boots, and a book.

Charlie tried to will himself to be able to see the book and touch its pages, but he failed.

Was he just constrained by his own story?

But if he was in a story, then he had an author. And an author who would kill Charlie's bap, and give him the Iron Cog for an enemy, and finally stick Charlie in a museum to rot forever . . . *that* author deserved a punch in the nose, and maybe worse.

Ollie slithered toward the edge of Charlie's cage. Charlie felt the stone floor beneath him humming slightly, like the hum of tools operating in Bap's shop, or the vibration of the washers and presses in Lucky Wu's Earth Dragon Laundry, Whitechapel.

Then Ollie crossed the black line in the floor.

An invisible force suddenly pounded Charlie, as if a hammer had slammed him to the marble. He rolled, finding himself suddenly in his physical body and tumbling alongside Ollie, in boy form again.

They were both screaming in pain.

But they were outside the line.

They rolled to a stop, Charlie crouching and Ollie lying flat on his belly. The sweep groaned and whimpered.

"It worked, Ollie," Charlie whispered. "Where's the Library Machine? Where did you come through?"

"The dwarf's throne," Ollie moaned. "I found a reference to it in the *Almanack*."

"Can you be a snake?"

"Probably. Only I'm tired, Charlie. Magic takes a toll. The bigger the magic, the more tired it makes you."

"It's my turn to carry you. You can stay a snake for a while, and rest."

Ollie stopped arguing. *Bamf!* Charlie picked up the yellow-green garden snake and tucked it into his pocket, where it curled up and trembled.

Charlie tiptoed carefully across the floor. He left the machines behind and tried as best he could to stay away from the beasts, but he had to cut through the corner of their space to reach the stairs down. As he moved past the shaitans' cage, all four of them raised their featureless faces and sang.

In the darkness, they were, if anything, more frightening.

A faint light came up from below. Charlie crept down the stairs and saw the throne. In the glow that still bathed it from above he now saw wisps of smoke, and as he moved closer, Papa Wilhelm stepped forward from the smoke and reached out a hand.

Then, to each side of the throne, a djinn rotated into view. From facing each other they turned to face Charlie, and they held their long, curved swords in their hands.

For only Og king of Bashan remained of the remnant of giants; behold, his bedstead was a bedstead of iron; is it not in Rabbath of the children of Ammon? nine cubits was the length thereof, and four cubits the breadth of it, after the cubit of a man.

—Deuteronomy 3:11, Authorized King James Version

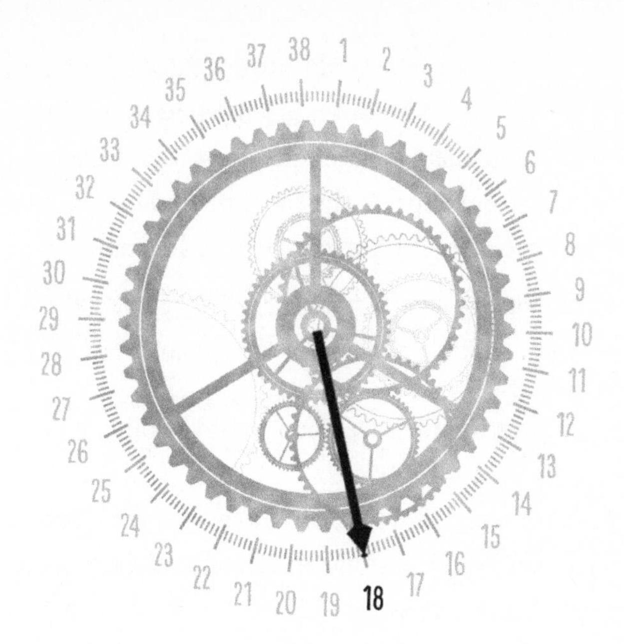

The djinns immediately rotated out of view again.

Were they advancing sideways toward Charlie? Were they watching him out of their peripheral vision, waiting for him to move forward?

He considered throwing Ollie into the Library Machine's glow, so at least his friend could escape. But he didn't know how good the djinns really were with their swords, and the mental image of one of them slicing Ollie the snake in half with his blade . . .

No.

He needed a way to know where the djinns were.

Charlie turned and ran back up the stairs to the collection. What would allow him to see djinns? What if he covered them in chalk dust—would that make them visible?

Or a mirror. If Charlie could surround the room with mirrors, he thought he'd be able to tell where the djinns were, by the reflection their faces made where they faced forward. Hearing heavy footsteps on the stairs behind him, Charlie ran faster. He was grateful Ollie had wound his mainspring, and he sprinted among the items of the collection in the shadows, looking for . . . what? A moving mirror? A wall of mirrors? A bag of chalk?

He found nothing that seemed to fit the bill.

Footsteps. Heavy footsteps.

Something wiggled in his consciousness as he ran past an enormous iron bed. It had no mattress, and each spring was as long as Charlie's forearm. The bed was thirteen feet long and six feet wide—what enormous person had slept in that? What *giant*?

He heard a footfall again, at the top of the stairs.

Their feet. If the djinns moved by walking, mustn't they disturb the ground?

Throwing chalk dust on the djinns might not reveal them, but if Charlie could cover the floor in chalk dust, that should reveal where the djinns were as they walked.

Charlie ran, looking for anything that would work. A mill that ground out salt? He had read an old story about such a mill, and that would have been perfect, but he couldn't find one here. A bottomless jar of jam?

What about the Foundation Stone? Charlie was quite strong. Was he stronger than Herakles and Samson put together? If he could flood the floor with water, that would show him where the djinns moved.

He turned in the dim light—

and a heavy sword slashed into his side.

A boy made of flesh and blood would not have survived. Charlie was knocked down and thrown across the floor to the Foundation Stone. "Clock me!" he cried.

Charlie squatted and reached to put his hands under the edge of the rock. It was a great flat boulder, dusty, and now that he saw it up close, he noticed grooves cut into its surface. He straightened his back, heaving with all his might—

he felt his springs wind down at an alarming rate—

and the rock didn't move.

Charlie released the boulder, staggering away from it. How far from him were the djinns? And in which direction? He feared every shadow.

He heard a loud hissing, and then the strange wordless song of the shape-changers. The shaitans were awake. That in itself wasn't so bad—he could probably avoid their cage—but their noise meant it was even harder to hear the djinns' footsteps.

Then Charlie remembered the pair of dice. They rolled themselves, and at each bounce they scattered a shower of small objects. Where had they been?

Charlie raced around the exhibits, seeing the singing pillar, a sword with two hands of its own, the giant's bed, a pair of boots with a snarling mouth in each toe, the boulder again, a glass bowl that contained a snowstorm inside, the animated armor—

The dice.

He grabbed them. They were larger in his hand than he'd

expected, and pearls burst from them and rained down around Charlie's feet.

It was getting lighter. The sun was coming up. That might mean the magician would wake soon.

Charlie needed to get out, and he needed to get out now.

A hand grabbed him, and suddenly Charlie saw one of the djinns, towering above him. The brute had a wide, toothy grin on his face, and raised his curved sword over his head—

The djinn screamed in pain and looked down.

Charlie looked too. A yellow-green cobra pulled back from the djinn's thigh, weaving as if exhausted. Blood from two fang marks ran down the djinn's leg, and the djinn released Charlie to clap its hand over the wound.

Charlie grabbed the cobra and ran, stuffing the snake into his pocket as he went.

He threw the dice at the floor, bouncing them just once and catching them again in his hand. Spiders scattered from the point of impact. He did it again and again, leaving a trail of fruit peels, rubies, worms, gold coins, thorns, pomegranate seeds, ashes—

Perfect—Charlie conceived a plan.

He swerved, narrowly avoiding the shaitans. He ran his trail another hundred feet and then ducked behind a pedestal on which a hen slept, brooding over a clutch of dully gleaming metal eggs.

He had maneuvered himself so that the giant's iron bed lay between him and the trail of riches and curses. On the far side of the trail hissed the shaitans.

He waited, listening. The hissing was too loud; he'd never hear the djinn's footsteps. He was entirely relying on the hope that the djinn would follow him more or less directly.

There it was. Charlie didn't see the djinn himself, but saw a small pile of silver coins scatter, as if of their own accord.

Charlie hurled himself forward, his legs trembling from the unwinding of his springs—

and slammed into the iron bed frame, sending it flying.

He saw a flash of the djinn's face and chest as the bed knocked his legs out from under him, swept him away, and carried him into the shaitans' cage.

The shaitans shrieked with joy and leaped onto the bed. Like monkeys they bounced up and down, and as they sank their teeth into the invader, they one by one took on the appearance of a djinn.

Charlie fell to his hands and knees, shaking.

"Ollie," he mumbled. "I'm sorry, but I need your help."

Bamf! Ollie was beside Charlie, also shaking. As Charlie fell forward onto his belly on the cold stone, he felt Ollie's hand grab the mainspring in Charlie's back and give it a single, uncertain twist.

And Charlie felt fine.

"Hold on, mate." Ollie's voice was ragged. "Let me give it a few more turns."

"Not too many," Charlie said. "There's another djinn."

Ollie turned the spring several times, and then they both climbed to their feet.

Then Ollie fainted.

Charlie grabbed the other boy before he fell.

"Ollie," he said.

Ollie was pale, and didn't answer. His breathing was shallow.

He needed help.

If only he had fainted in snake form, Charlie thought. At least then he'd have been more manageable.

But Ollie had come back for Charlie, and risked his life to do it. Charlie couldn't leave his friend now. He hoisted Ollie over his shoulder, turned, and ran away from the hissing of the shaitans and the screaming of the djinn, toward the stairs.

He threw the dice ahead of him, making a trail of djinn-locating small objects. Stooping at the top of the stairs without slowing down, he snatched the dice from the floor and threw them ahead of him again, down the steps, watching the small objects carefully as the sun came up on both floors, flooding the halls with sudden light.

A spray of rotten eggs bounced unnaturally. To one side of the dice's trail, eggs hit something unseen and either shattered in midair or fell straight down, cracking on the stone.

The djinn.

Charlie jumped over the banister on the opposite side of the stairs, feeling a sword swish through the air behind him as he fell.

Was that all he needed to do? Had he evaded two djinns, and there were no further obstacles?

The cloudy white light on the dwarf magician's throne

beckoned, and Charlie could see within it hints of the form of Papa Wilhelm, coalescing and reaching out to him again.

But what if there were more djinns, hiding in wait around the throne?

And worse, what if now those djinns had seen Charlie's trick with the dice?

Charlie raced to the foot of the stairs and scooped up the dice. Appropriate, since he was about to gamble. But really, all adventure was gambling, and all life was adventure. He just had to place his bet and try his hardest.

Charlie sprinted toward the space to the throne's left, as if the throne were at twelve o'clock on a clock face and he was charging toward ten. He desperately hoped that no djinn was lurking this far from the throne.

Thirty feet, he thought the distance was.

Reaching back with his arm, he threw the dice ahead of him, toward ten o' clock. He hoped that would give any waiting djinns the idea that he intended to run in that direction. He also hoped their eyes would follow the dice, which would distract them, even if only for a second.

At the same moment he threw the dice, Charlie turned right and accelerated.

He took three very fast steps, to close the gap a little more.

Then he jumped.

Horrible visions of himself and Ollie both being sliced right down the middle filled his mind.

He heard the *swoosh!* sounds of not one but two swords

whistling through the air. The first missed—his feint and his distraction had worked!

The second blow struck Charlie's leg and knocked him out of the air.

Charlie rolled, trying to shield Ollie's head with his body and mostly succeeding. When he stumbled to his feet at the foot of the throne, two djinns charged directly at him, swords high—

Charlie turned and jumped into the Library Machine.

The government's secretive Committee for the Investigation of Anti-Human Crime, which is being referred to by some as the Human League, has today named ten deputies. These ten, whom the committee has confirmed could be supplemented by further deputies as necessary, will be led by newly appointed Sergeant Egil Olafsson of the city's hulder community.

"The committee simply needs a fact-finding team," said Mr. Grim Grumblesson, the committee's deputy chairman. "This is not a law-enforcement body, and there is no intention that it should become one."

—*Daily Telegraph*, "Deputies Appointed," 16 July 1887

Charlie thought he felt Papa Wilhelm's hands carrying him through the cloud of white light, and then he and Ollie tumbled onto the carpet.

BOOM!

The floor beneath him shook, and Ollie stirred in his arms.

"What 'appened to Ollie?" Bob stood over the two boys, looking down. "'E don't look good."

"It's a long story," Charlie said, laying Ollie on the carpet and climbing to his feet. "But the point of it would be that Ollie saved me, twice, and was pretty badly hurt doing it."

Ollie cracked one eye slightly and raised his head. "That ain't the only point, mate. The much more interesting point is that I carried you inside me. That ain't shape-changing,

Charlie, that's wizardry, and I used it to beat old Suleiman at his own game. I won a wizards' duel, mate. I'm a magician."

Ollie's eye shut and his head fell again.

Bob bit her lip, sniffed hard, and stepped back.

Lloyd Shankin swooped down on Ollie like a crow and touched his head, singing an englyn under his breath with eyes fixed tightly on the chimney sweep. Something was odd about Lloyd, and it took Charlie a moment to realize what.

The dewin wore a long blue tabard, and he held in one hand a short white staff.

He couldn't worry about Lloyd's clothing now. Charlie tottered away. Was his limp more pronounced? Had he been damaged?

Thomas came from nowhere and hugged him. "Did you know Bob's a girl?"

Charlie nodded.

"Charlie, you've been damaged." Jan Wijmoor stooped to look at the cuts in Charlie's leg and side. "And there's an old wound here too." The kobold was shaking, and his face had turned nearly as red as his hair.

Charlie was a little surprised to see the engineer, but more surprised at the kobold's emotion. "What's wrong?" Charlie whispered.

"It's all my fault, Charlie," the kobold whispered. "All of this. It felt as if maybe helping you and Thomas would make up for my mistakes, but . . ."

Wijmoor took a deep breath and stood back.

The library balcony was crowded. In addition to Charlie, Thomas, the sweeps, and Lloyd, Rabbi Rosenbaum and his daughter stood nearby. The rabbi looked grief-stricken—he still wore the long white scarf over his shoulders, but it was scorched now, as if he'd run through fire, and his face was streaked with soot. Gnat hovered in the air beside her cousin Hezekiah and Undergravine Juliet, and behind them was a corps of pixie warriors.

Papa Wilhelm stood in the center of them all, ghostly and smiling.

"What's going on?" Charlie asked no one in particular.

"Humans," the undergravine said. "Humans couldn't leave well enough alone. Hesse was a land where all folk lived in peace, and that offended them."

Her words stung him.

"Not all humans." The rabbi's voice was heavy with sorrow. "Far more than I would have liked to believe, but not all of us. I will never believe that."

"Not all," the undergravine admitted. "Do you too wish to join my service?"

"Wait," Charlie said. "What do you mean, 'you too'? Gnat, did you—"

Gnat shook her head. "Not I, Charlie. My path lies with you still." She pointed at Lloyd.

Lloyd stood up. Ollie's natural color was returning and his eyelids fluttered, and Charlie got a better look at the Welshman's new clothes. He was dressed like a bigger, bluer version of Hezekiah, only his tabard bore a different coat of arms: crossed spears and a butterfly's wings, to match the emblem Charlie had seen at the underground crossroads.

"Aye," Juliet said. "I've taken the dewin as my herald. It

seemed it might be useful to have a human in my service at this time."

"I had to, Charlie," the Welshman said. "I had to help, because . . . well, because that's my journey. And I knew a song that I thought would heal the undergravine's daughter, but Undergravine Juliet wouldn't let me sing my englyn over her child until I agreed to enter her service with an oath. I think she worried I might do something harmful."

"You want to do good." Charlie nodded. "I understand."

Lloyd grinned, eyes wobbling. "And it worked."

"We fly!" The undergravine raised her spear, pointing at the tall stained-glass windows overhead.

"I don't believe I have the talent for that, Your Ladyship, either in wings or in magical strength." Lloyd bowed his head respectfully. "But if you tell me where to meet you, I can walk very fast."

The undergravine changed the angle of her spear, pointed toward the horizon. "We fly . . . low."

"Where?" Charlie asked. "What's that way? If your realm is being attacked, don't you want to defend it?"

"Iron men are already in the undergraviate," Juliet said, grinding her teeth. "We carry our eggs with us, but we are forced to march to war."

"The Anti-Human League assembles in London," Hezekiah said. "War is coming to Britain, as it has already come here. We will strike mankind from a unified position of strength."

"Don't do this, Cousin," Gnat pleaded.

Hezekiah's face was solemn. He reached forward to touch

the tooth of the giant Hound that hung as a trophy around Gnat's neck. "You can stop me. Three mighty deeds, and then challenge Elisabel. That'd make you baroness."

"Aye," Gnat agreed. Gnat had been exiled from her mother's barony, Underthames. To retake the throne, she needed to complete three mighty deeds and then challenge her cousin Elisabel to a duel.

"I do not ask you to do that," Hezekiah said. "That would be disloyal to Elisabel. And Seamus would never ask it either."

"I understand." Gnat's tears were so large they filled her eyes entirely.

The undergravine flew down the ramp and out a door Charlie couldn't see. With a last nod, Lloyd Shankin ran after them, blue tabard flapping behind him.

Following them with his eye, Charlie saw a mob lower down in the library, knocking over shelves and tearing books from the shelves. Were they students? "What's happening?"

"Marburg has fallen into chaos," the rabbi murmured.

"My end is here," the phantasm of Papa Wilhelm said behind Charlie.

Charlie looked up. From higher in the library, and descending toward him, he saw men in Prussian black and cream, with skulls and crossbones on their uniforms. They carried rifles with bayonets fixed to their ends, and Charlie saw with a start that they had mechanical limbs. Their arms and legs shone like brass—

and they ran fast.

"'Ey!" Bob pointed at the well of the library.

Charlie rushed to the banister to look down. The boxy brass machines of the card catalog had been unbolted and dragged from their places in the center of the floor, and a pit had been dug. Around the pit a crew of dwarfs in white-and-purple-striped trousers worked a pulley that hung by a tripod platform erected over the hole. The dwarfs had two donkeys tied to a rope that ran through the pulley, and they dragged the animals forward, pulling a large white stone out of the pit. Other dwarfs stood watching, with lit torches and metal cans in their hands.

The dwarfs all wore conical masks, which made them look a little birdlike.

"Don't breathe in the dust!" a dwarf cried. His voice sounded metallic through his mask.

Dust? Did the dwarf mean smoke from the torches?

A pair of dwarfs pushed a sledge under the tripod and above the hole. Without any further talk, the dwarfs holding the donkeys' halters backed the animals up, lowering the boulder onto the sledge. Charlie squinted at the rock—from this distance, it looked to be the size of a person. "What's that white stone?"

"That is the spirit stone." Papa Wilhelm smiled sadly. "That's my soul . . . on this earth."

"Why are they taking it?" Charlie asked.

"I'm afraid they can only have evil purposes, Charlie. The stone is the closest thing to spirit this mortal earth can hold."

"We've got to go." Ollie stood, taking a deep breath. "And much as I'd like to go back to the Souk of Wonders and do a bit of shopping, I don't want to run across Suleiman again."

"Last time, *he* was the one who found *us*," Thomas said, trembling.

Charlie snapped out of his thought. "Then where to?"

He was asking Papa Wilhelm, but Ollie answered. "Best guess, mate? Believe it or not, the Punjab. The *Almanack*'s got an old story about a demon lord named Ravana, and it mentions his nail. Demons come from your intellectual world, don't they? We want to go to Mayapore. Palace of the Rajah Amir Singh."

"Singh?" Charlie's father's real name—the name he'd never told Charlie—had been Singh. "You've been doing some studying."

Ollie shrugged. "I heard you and Thomas talking about the three nails, and I've been reading like a madman every spare moment since."

"What are they doing?" Rosenbaum pointed down into the well.

Charlie took a last look into the hole. The donkeys, reattached now to the sledge, were pulling the stone away. The dwarfs with cans sloshed liquid in a circle around the floor of the library. Charlie could smell the chemical stink of oil. "Fire. They're going to burn down the library."

He had no time to wait to see it.

"Papa Wilhelm," he said. "Can you take us to the palace of Rajah Amir Singh?"

Papa Wilhelm smiled. "I can." Behind the phantasm, the

white cloud of light swirled and coalesced into a lush garden. Its ferns and drooping trees were bathed in pale luminescence, and Charlie half imagined he could smell sweet tropical plants. "Goodbye, Charlie."

"I'll come back," Charlie said.

"You won't." Papa Wilhelm's face was sad. "I am in the spirit stone, Charlie, as the stone is in you. This is my final act, and you and I will not meet again."

As the stone is in you? What on earth could that mean? And why wouldn't Charlie come back—did Papa Wilhelm think Charlie was going to die?

Bang! Bang! Bullets whizzed past Charlie, disappearing into the white light. Were the bullets striking trees in a garden in the Punjab?

Charlie looked back toward the library and saw that the half-machine soldiers were coming around the bend. The foremost were charging, bayonets leveled to stab at Charlie and his friends. The ones in the rear crouched and shot with their rifles.

Bang! Bang!

"Get down!" Charlie shouted to his friends. "And get through the gate!"

"Charlie . . . ," Thomas pleaded.

Charlie pushed his brother into the Library Machine.

Papa Wilhelm flickered, was dark for a moment, and then reappeared.

"Go!" Charlie shouted.

"I must stay here, Charlie," the rabbi said. He spoke with

surprising deliberation, given that half-machine soldiers were charging him. "I can't leave my people now. I'm disappointed and I'm afraid, but I'll stay. My daughter could go with you."

"If I'm going to be in danger, Father, let me at least do it with you. Now go!" Rachel pushed her father down the ramp and toward the secret door.

Jan Wijmoor stared at Papa Wilhelm with tears running down his cheeks. "I am sorry," he said to the phantasm. "This is my fault. I took Zahnkrieger on as my apprentice, and I indulged him."

Papa Wilhelm flickered again but then smiled. "Sometimes our children do not love us as they should."

"Charlie," Wijmoor said. "I am in a pickle and I need to call on your assistance. My library is being destroyed. Will you help me?"

Charlie pushed the kobold through the gate.

"This would be a mighty deed," Gnat murmured, eyeing the charging machine soldiers.

"It would mean your death," Charlie told her. "What would be the point?"

Gnat nodded, and flitted into the white cloud.

The soldiers farther away continued to fire.

Charlie grabbed the nearest bookcase. It was heavy, but he found he could tear it out of the floor and wall, and he pushed it over in the direction of the attacking soldiers. That would slow them down.

A bullet struck Charlie, knocking him to the floor.

"You okay, mate?" Bob asked him.

"Just dented, I think." Charlie stood. "We need to go now!"

Papa Wilhelm flickered, disappeared. He reappeared again, but his light was much dimmer, a cloud of gray fog rather than bright white light. "Now!" the phantasm shouted.

Ollie looked at Bob and shook his head. "Bob, mate, I'm so sorry."

"This is not the time, Ollie!" Bob grabbed Ollie's hand and dragged him into the Library Machine.

Charlie jumped through last of all.

Except that as he came through the gate and landed in a heap on paving stones in a tropical garden, he felt that one more person had come through with them.

Papa Wilhelm, gray and blurring, looked down at him with smiling eyes. "Goodbye, Charlie."

Then Papa Wilhelm was gone.

Thunder crashed. A hot, wet wind shook the garden, and a ring of long, curving swords sprang up around Charlie and his friends.

PART THREE

THE INFIDEL PRINCE

There once was a carter who had a rare gift for his trade. He could pack a cart tighter than any other man, and the villagers said that when he whistled, his mules would hear and come to him, even if they were twenty miles away.

One day, the carter's prince demanded his service, and the carter went to war. The prince promised the carter that he only wanted to use the carter's gifts in packing and leading animals, and that the carter would never have to fight. The prince kept his word, but the war lasted many years, and although he never had to fight, the poor carter still wandered far from his home.

When he returned, the villagers were happy because there was much work for the carter to do. To their surprise, though, he did not once again hang out his signboard and take up carting. Instead, he hid himself away and made toys, which he never sold or gave to children, but placed on the shelves of his house.

When asked about his behavior or about the war, all the carter would ever say was "I have lost my gift for making carts. All I can do now is break them."

—Grimm, *Tales,* "The Carter"

A thick wash of rain hit Charlie in the face.

He raised his hands over his head in surrender, and the others followed suit.

Gnat threw herself underneath a broad green leaf, dodging the rain. Before Charlie could say anything about the men with swords helping her get inside, the rain striking him stopped and was replaced by a heavy drumming sound.

He looked up and saw a glass ceiling in the form of overlapping blades. They all sprouted out of the top of a large pole in the center of the garden, and as the rain fell, they unfolded downward, creating a shelter from the storm.

The men with swords wore their hair wrapped in navy-blue scarves, and on their feet they had long black shoes, decorated with gold stitching. A thin man with large hands and a thick mustache was speaking. After a few initial words, the Babel Card sorted out his speech for Charlie. "The rajah wishes to see you."

"I understand," Charlie and Thomas said at the same time.

"The rajah wants to see us," Charlie added as an aside to his friends.

"What's a rajah?" Bob asked. She stood at the far side of the group from Ollie, and her arms were crossed over her chest. She didn't look angry, Charlie thought, but confused and . . . sad.

"A king or a prince," Charlie said.

"Right." Ollie straightened his peacoat and brushed raindrops off his hat. "That's just who we want to see."

"You are English," the man with big hands said, switching to English himself. "Are you company men?"

Charlie remembered the stories his bap had told him, about the traders and soldiers of the East India Company. Sometimes it seemed as if those men were allies, friends, and trading partners with the princes of India, but sometimes it seemed—though Bap had never been one to dwell on unpleasant details—as if the relationship were darker than that.

Charlie had always identified with the company men. Suddenly, he wasn't so sure.

More to the point, he wasn't sure it was safe to be English here.

"We're from all over," he said. "Gnat's a fairy. Thomas is Welsh. Meneer Doktor Professor Ingenieur Jan Wijmoor . . . I think he's Dutch, but he lives in Germany."

"I am a kobold," Wijmoor added. He seemed to have regained his composure a little. "Of the Marburger Syndikat, of course in Germany."

"I'm English!" Ollie jerked a thumb at his own chest.

"Might as well own it," Bob added slowly. "So am I."

"I am the captain of the rajah's bodyguard," the big-handed man said. "Follow me now, please."

The captain went first, followed by Charlie and his friends, and then finally by the rest of the bodyguards, who never put their swords away. As they left the garden, Charlie heard a sudden rustling sound in the thick fronds to his right.

He thought of the presence he had felt, as if one more person than planned had come through the Library Machine with them. But he looked, and saw nothing.

"The garden is lovely," he said to the captain.

"It is called the Bibighar Garden," the captain said. "The rajah's father built it, and when it rained, he liked to stand out in the weather and get soaked. The rajah wished to protect the plants from the worst of the storms, so he built the pavilion." The captain pointed up at the glass covering, which was fully extended now and shielded all the garden from the tempest.

"Where I come from, it rains most of the time," Thomas said. "But if you protect the plants from the rain, won't they dry up and die? Don't they need the water?"

The captain turned to look at Thomas. His eyes glittered, and Thomas staggered sideways two steps, but when the man spoke, his voice was gentle. "In mild rains, the shield is not opened. And rain is always collected in cisterns and fed to the plants as they need it. As a result, the plants prosper.

They grow and produce all year round, rather than for a short season."

There was machinery and invention, benefiting people. Or at least benefiting gardens.

"So it must not always rain so much," Charlie ventured.

"It does not," the captain agreed. "But it is the beginning of the rainy season now, and we have weeks of storms ahead of us. You English have borrowed the word *monsoon* from Arabic to describe this weather."

"My father was from the Punjab," Charlie said.

"Ah." The captain nodded. "You didn't tell me that."

From the garden and its pavilion they passed into a long walkway. A roof upheld by two rows of columns kept the direct rain from soaking them, but the wind blew water sideways. Gnat flew high over Charlie's head, close to the walkway's ceiling, to stay dry and protect her wings.

The walkway led them into a palace. As they approached, Charlie looked through the arches enclosing him to note the white-plastered walls, the onion-shaped domes atop the towers, and the crenellations on top of the highest walls. The palace had no windows for its lower two or three stories, which suggested it was a fortress, and when Charlie and his friends passed from the walkway into the palace, they did so through a pair of double doors whose wood was thicker than Charlie's chest and banded with iron.

Two flights of steps and a final broad hallway led them into a reception room. Here a man wearing a long yellow coat stood with his hands clasped behind his back, looking out at the storm through open doors and a balcony. The yellow coat had elaborate red stitching about the waist and shoulders, and that embroidery was the man's only decoration. He wore red slippers whose toes curled up so much they pointed back at him, and his thick black hair was cut short; his head was bare; he smelled of flowers and cinnamon.

"Thank you, Captain," the man in yellow said in English. "You may send the others to their usual posts. Please remain here."

"Yes, Your Majesty." The captain saluted and waved to his men, who left.

The room was large but simple, and it was dominated by a library. Shelves ran up walls that must have been fifteen feet high and groaned from the weight of all the books that sat on them. A table near the center of the room held a short stack of red-bound volumes, and several additional books lay open, with inkpots, knives, compasses, and other small objects weighing down their pages.

The man in yellow—the Rajah Amir Singh, presumably—turned to face Charlie. He was fairer and taller than Charlie's father, but Charlie couldn't resist making his connection with the prince. "My name's Charlie," he said. "My father is from the Punjab. His name was Joban Singh."

He hadn't expected the rajah to light up and announce their near relation, but he was nevertheless disappointed by the prince's understated response. "Singh is a common name here. It means 'lion.' All Sikh men share that same last name."

"*All* Sikh men?" Charlie was only dimly aware of what a Sikh was. "Are your men Sikh too?" he asked.

"They are also all named Singh." The rajah nodded. "Carrying their famous swords and wearing their *dastars*—their turbans, you would say."

"Shouldn't you also have a dastar, then?" Charlie asked. "And a sword?"

Jan Wijmoor cleared his throat at length, and the captain stepped forward as if to seize Charlie, but the rajah raised a hand to restrain him.

And then the rajah smiled. "How direct."

"Sorry." Charlie shrank a little. "I sometimes don't know when I'm being rude."

The rajah paced, but he kept his eyes fixed on Charlie. "It is true, many people would find such questions rude. I do not. I was born a Sikh—Sikhism is a religion, and also a culture, a people—and so I am named Singh."

"So my father must have been a Sikh."

The rajah shook his head. "Not necessarily. People who are not Sikh may be named Singh. But if your father came from this land, then perhaps."

Charlie sighed. "But even if that's true, the name Singh won't help me find anything about him at all. All men are named Singh, so I can't know who my family are."

The rajah cocked his head to one side and frowned. "Or . . . all men are your family."

The prince's words struck Charlie so hard, he had nothing to say.

“I am Sikh, but here in the land of five rivers, in Mayapore, in my country, many people are Hindu, and many more are Muslim,” the rajah continued. “Do you know these religions?”

Charlie shook his head, still mute. His father had said very little to Charlie about religion.

“It doesn’t matter. Suffice it to say, each has its attractive face. Each has distinctive practices and teaches a unique path to walk in this life, and maybe in the next. Each teaches important truths and principles.”

“That sounds good,” Charlie said. “Truths and principles.”

“Does it? I don’t like principles much,” the rajah continued. “Principles cause people to sacrifice. They may sacrifice themselves, which can be very noble, but can also be tragic. Worse, principles may lead one to sacrifice others, which can be quite monstrous. Principles may lead a person to refuse to eat dinner with his neighbor, or refuse to trade with him, or become angry if his daughter wishes to marry his neighbor’s son.”

“Oh,” Charlie said. Could principles also lead someone to join the Iron Cog? If you believed strongly enough in principles, maybe you would think it was acceptable to force other people to follow them.

Might you be willing to kill other people, to force them to follow?

“All in all,” the rajah continued, “I would like fewer principles and more love. Any principles or practices that tell a person to choose God above his neighbor, I find unacceptable. And do you know what, Charlie?”

Charlie shook his head. He felt frozen in place.

"I think God finds it unacceptable too. And I will not wear a dastar or carry a sword, because although those things would tell my Sikh subjects that I am one of *them*—and this is true—it would tell my Muslim and Hindu subjects that I am *not* one of *them* . . . which is false. For this I am called heretic, unbeliever, sinner, infidel, and worse." The rajah shrugged. "So be it."

Charlie was silent. Rajah Singh and Rabbi Rosenbaum hadn't said exactly the same thing, but they had said similar things. He thought the two of them would get along well.

"You're a brave person," Thomas said.

"It's easy to be brave when I am surrounded by men with guns and swords who defend me." The rajah addressed Charlie again. "A light was spotted in my garden, a flickering light, full of smoke, and then people came through it. You people, in fact. To ask me such questions, you must be a stranger to my lands—why, then, are you here?"

"We came looking for the nail of the intellectual world," Ollie announced proudly.

The rajah shook his head. "What is that?"

Charlie's shoulders slumped.

"You may not know the nail, but you know the vessel it was built into," Bob said. "The Pushpaka chariot, the great pride of Viswakarman, archaeologist of heaven."

"Architect, Bob." Ollie grinned. "I looked that one up in the *Almanack* for my mate."

Bob looked uncomfortable and stepped slightly away from Ollie.

"Of course," the rajah said, "but I don't see how you can possibly reach the Pushpaka chariot now."

"Why not?" Charlie asked.

"It's underwater." The rajah pointed out the window as lightning flashed and the rain came down even harder. "And getting deeper underwater by the minute."

Seeing there is a Three-fold World—Elementary, Celestial, and Intellectual—and every inferior is governed by its superior, and receiveth the influence of the virtues thereof . . . wise men conceive it no way irrational that it should be possible for us to ascend by the same degrees through each World, to the same very original World itself, the Maker of all things and First Cause.

—Henry Cornelius Agrippa, *Three Books of Occult Philosophy*

They rode forth from the palace on elephants.

Each beast was guided by a mahout, a rider sitting behind its head. Each beast also had a canopy on its back, in which the rajah and Charlie's party sheltered, four people to each elephant. The canopies stopped the rain that fell down on them from the sky above, but did nothing to stop the rain that blew sideways onto them in hot sheets.

The rajah, Charlie, Gnat, and Bob rode on the first beast. Gnat was sheltering inside a large wicker basket to get protection from the water on all sides. As soon as she had seen that there was one space left on the first elephant, Bob had leaped up the stepladder beside the creature's belly without a word.

Avoiding Ollie.

Nine elephants carried the riders. Four additional elephants in the rear were burdened with large unmarked crates.

"Does this Pushpaka chariot belong to you, then?" Bob asked.

The rajah laughed. "No, it belongs to no one now. Once, it belonged to the demon lord Ravana. When he was shot down in battle, the chariot smashed a very deep hole in the earth."

"I don't really think of flying things when I hear the word *chariot*," Charlie said.

"No?" Rajah Amir Singh smiled. "And yet the sun was said by the Greeks to ride a chariot. Have you not read the story of Phaethon?"

Charlie shrugged.

"That's where you're taking us, then?" Bob asked. "An 'ole?"

"No, no." The rajah pointed along the side of the stone road over which his elephants tramped. "Tell me what you see there, young lady."

No one corrected him. Bob had simply, with minimal fuss, become a girl.

Bob leaned over the edge of the canopy and squinted. "Water. In a long stream, flooding over its banks."

"And does the stream look natural?" the rajah pressed.

"No," Bob admitted, "it's much too straight for that. You're talking about irritation, then?"

"I beg your pardon?"

"You mean irrigation, Bob," Charlie said.

"Course I do. This is rainy season now, so it's cats and dogs everywhere you look, an' it feels like the water will never end.

But when dry season comes, this place'll parch like a desert. So you get water around by irritation ditches. Which are right now overflowing, on account of the rain."

"Correct. In the dry season, we bring water down from the mountains. And in the rainy season, we try to capture all the water we can in deep wells."

"'Oles in the ground," Bob said.

"Yes. Perhaps not such as you imagine, but yes. And now we use pumps to bring water out of those wells and supplement the flow of water in the irrigation ditches with it. In the old days, in the dry season, you went to the well for water."

"And let down a bucket?" Bob asked.

"No." The rajah smiled.

"This was before pumps, though." Bob looked puzzled. "What, then? The screw of Archimedes?"

Charlie wasn't entirely sure *Archimedes* was the right word, but he didn't know what Bob meant, so he didn't correct her. He looked back for his friends and saw Ollie, struggling to keep Jan Wijmoor from falling off the back of their elephant. The kobold was fascinated by the canopy and was examining it, but his investigations kept carrying him too close to the edge.

"You will understand shortly." Rajah Singh nodded at the road ahead and a low, wide brick building, with brick towers at its corners. "We are arriving. But the point is that the well you are about to see was originally formed by the crashing of the demon lord Ravana's chariot into the ground. This chariot, or *vimāna,* was known as Pushpaka. The annals of my kingdom Mayapore tell us all this."

Bob nodded. "Yeah, I reckon that's what Ollie read me out of the *Almanack*. Back when you were up at the castle, Charlie."

They reached the building. The rajah whistled and the elephants came to a halt. The rajah himself climbed down first, taking along an umbrella from the elephant's palanquin and popping it open to keep the worst of the rain off himself.

Charlie did the same. The umbrellas were red and yellow and made of silk, so they didn't have the same mineral smell as the oiled-paper umbrellas Grim Grumblesson had had them use in London. Counting his friends to be sure they were all there, Charlie saw Gnat huddled under Ollie's umbrella, clinging to the sweep's shoulder to stay out of the rain.

Bob ignored Ollie.

The captain of the rajah's bodyguard seemed to have a brother in the regiment, another man with the same face and mustache, who climbed down off the back of one of the last elephants.

"This way." The rajah strolled through an open gate in the large brick building, and Charlie followed.

He found himself in a brick courtyard. The rain falling on the brick sounded like a cannonade. In the center of the courtyard was a pavilion, also of brick, and under the pavilion a crowd of people gathered around a cluster of pipes. The pipes sprouted from the ground, curved earthward, and emitted a steady stream of water. As they drew closer, Charlie saw that the water fell through metal grates in the brick and disappeared.

The people held large skins and clay pots, and they were collecting water. They weren't gathered in one crowd, Charlie now saw, but in three, with a clear aisle of empty space between the groups.

"One day we will run water from here directly into all my people's homes," the rajah said. "I have mixed feelings about that—coming to the well forces people to meet each other. But think of the time it will save. And any time a woman or a man doesn't have to spend coming here to collect water can be spent on running a business, or playing with a child, or writing a poem. Imagine the lives of my people then! It will be nearly as magnificent as the tractors!"

"'Old on," Bob said. "I believe I just 'eard you say 'as magnificent as the tractors.' What, are these tractors an 'undred feet tall?"

"No!" the rajah said. "They're very small, so all my people may have one, if they wish. And with this very small tractor, a farmer can plow and plant her field in a fraction of the time. And with the rest of her day, she can teach her children to read, or go dancing, or admire the stars. Do you not find that magnificent?"

Bob scratched her head.

Charlie looked at the pipes. "These draw water out of the well?"

The rajah nodded. "And the aquifer beneath, the water underground that is connected to the well. Marvelous invention, though, is it not? Even this pump saves my people the trouble and danger of going down into the well."

Charlie was confused. "But there's so much rain! Surely now is the time when your people *don't* need to come here for water!"

"You might think so," the rajah said. "But the rain is so violent and lasts so long that it washes mud into wells and cisterns, and where there are pipes it shatters them. So some of my people can gather water on their own rooftops or in barrels, but many of them still come here."

"This is just the pump, right?" Charlie asked.

"Yes," the rajah agreed, "and you're here to see the well. Come with me."

The rajah led Charlie past the pavilion, both of them raising their umbrellas against the rain. Charlie looked over his shoulder to see his friends following. The bodyguards brought up the rear, with the captain's brother lagging behind, last of all.

On the far side of the courtyard they passed through another brick arch, and then Charlie stopped in amazement.

What he was looking at seemed to be half pit and half palace. Like an inverted pyramid, the pit descended seven stories until it reached the level of the water. At each story, a square walkway circled the entire pit, and from each walkway down to the one beneath it descended multiple staircases.

Passages were bored horizontally into the earth at every level, and through their openings Charlie saw arches, pools, and verandas, as well as shallow canals leading the water from the main well along into the passages and their chambers. At whatever level the water lay, it would be surrounded by a shaded palace for lounging, bathing, and collecting rainfall.

"You could fit the entire library in that well!" Jan Wijmoor gasped.

The whole thing was built of brick and stone, and Charlie saw elegant statues everywhere of gods and goddesses he didn't know: dancing men with elephants' heads, four-armed men, women with skulls for heads, princesses seated on opening lotus flowers, muscular men with flaming spikes of hair and long, drawn-out tongues, snakes with human faces, and more. Water flowed down over the steps, and also out along stone rainspouts that turned into elephants' trunks or snakes or other features, channeling the rainfall down into the bottom of the pit, where brown water churned. The most prominent of these gargoyles were four enormous stone swans, sculpted into the uppermost tier, which leaped out from the center of each of the four walls, spreading their wings as if trying to meet in the center.

"This is called a stepwell," the rajah said. "So you see, it's a little more than a hole in the ground."

"The 'eck," Bob said.

"How far down does it go?" Ollie asked.

"It is hard to say for certain." The rajah shrugged. "I've never seen the well when there wasn't water in it. To my knowledge, no one alive today has ever seen the well when it was completely empty of water. Thirteen is a fortunate number for Sikhs, so if my Sikh forefathers dug this well, I would guess it to be thirteen levels deep."

"But?" Charlie asked.

"But this well is older than Sikhism, which after all was born only a few centuries ago. And besides, I've seen it with fifteen levels exposed to dry air, and a large pool of water yet in the center. One hundred eight, on the other hand, is an important number to my Hindu subjects. It stands for all the great teachers and teachings of their faith together. So if their forefathers dug this well, I might guess it to be one hundred eight levels deep."

"But?" Charlie asked again.

"But unless the walkways become ridiculously narrow, I don't think the stepwell is large enough to have one hundred eight levels."

"'Ow many levels do you reckon it 'as, then?" Bob asked.

"Some number," the rajah said, smiling, "between fifteen and one hundred eight."

"And the Pushpaka chariot is down there at the bottom?" Charlie stared at the water. It was brown and turbulent, thrashed by the rain, but also by water streaming down the steps into the well. "The Pushpaka vimāna?"

"I've been told this all my life," the rajah said. "I've heard old women and men swear that in dry seasons, when the waters are at their lowest, they turn golden. I tend to believe it's true."

Charlie stepped to the edge and looked down. "Bob, can you wind my spring?"

He felt a little self-conscious that the rajah and his men were watching, but Charlie steeled himself. If Bob could openly be a girl now, Charlie could openly be a . . . mechanical person.

"Amazing" was all the rajah said. "You are even more magnificent than a tractor, Charlie."

"There you are, mate," Bob said.

"I guess the good thing is that I won't have to swim back up," Charlie said. "Even underwater, I can just walk up the stairs."

And before anyone could say anything else, he took a running start along a stone elephant's trunk and threw himself like a cannonball into the water.

Equus unicornus (common name: unicorn)—The last credible written record of a unicorn sighting in Great Britain took place in the reign of Henry IV. Whether due to climatic changes, overhunting, or the obscure details of unicorn nutrition, the unicorn has ceased to be a British species and has become instead a British symbol. To us today a unicorn means fragility, beauty, otherworldliness, and elusiveness, whereas to our forebears it meant a head over the mantel and a delicate meat for Sunday roast.

As a side note, it is worth observing that a unicorn's horn is the repository of its magic, and not a weapon for fighting. Writers who maintain otherwise are knaves.

—Smythson, *Almanack*, "Unicorn"

Splash!

Charlie sank.

As the water closed over his head, he had the last-minute thought that the well could be bottomless, and he might now sink forever and never be found. Bottomless wells didn't exist in the real world, of course, but what if Ollie was right? What if passage through the gate of the Library Machine had brought Charlie into a land that only existed in a story?

In stories, there could be bottomless wells.

And how were Charlie and Thomas going to get to Russia? Without the Library Machine's ability to transport him instantly, he was back to riding in steam-trucks and stowing away on cargo ships.

He kept his eyes open.

At first he saw nothing but brown murk, and his eyes stung from the grit.

But then he sank enough to get past the cloud of sediment. Looking around, he saw a dark cloud of mud above him, like a roiling storm. To all sides of him, walkways and stairwells slid past. He wished he knew how many had gone by, but he must be fifteen or twenty levels down already, and sinking steadily.

And then the last stair and the final walkway passed, and the walls disappeared. Charlie still fell, and there was light coming from below.

He looked down, and was astonished at what he saw. This had to be the vimāna, but it looked *nothing* like a chariot. It looked like a palace, like a pyramid, only the vimāna's basic shape was circular rather than square.

And it glowed.

Charlie found that by waving his arms against the water and pointing his toes, he could direct his descent. He wiggled and squirmed, steering for the top of the pyramid. As he got closer, he saw that the peak seemed to consist of a small open platform surrounded by four enormous swans. The birds were sculpted of metal and leaped out from the apex of the vimāna in four directions, quartering the flying palace.

Did the stepwell's similar swans announce the presence of the vimāna below?

Bong! Charlie struck the metal floor in the center of the four swans, bounced once, and came to rest lying on his back.

From that position, he looked up—no light. No sign of the entrance by which he'd come to this watery underworld. No cloud of murk, no stepwell. Just darkness.

And then something moved in the gloom.

Charlie stood, wishing he had some better weapon than the broken fragments of his bap's pipe in his pocket. If he'd carried the unicorn horn or the cold-iron knife, he'd at least have something to stab with.

But then if he died down here, those would be lost with him. It was better that Thomas had them.

He saw the movement again, a flash of tail like that of a long fish or a sea serpent. And then another, and then more.

Was he surrounded by a school of fish, circling the vimāna?

The creatures came closer, and Charlie staggered backward a step.

They had the long tails of serpents, but from the waist up they looked human. They wore coats that might once have been a dark blue uniform of some sort, but most of the fabric had rotted away, leaving them all shrouded in blue strands like shirts made of spider's web. Their eyebrows were raised with excitement; the whites of their eyes showed. Their mouths were open, their teeth long, yellow, and sharp.

They circled Charlie, too many to count.

One of them broke from the school and moved toward Charlie. It was a woman, and as she came closer, Charlie saw that her skin was a dark emerald green, and it glowed. She opened her mouth, and to Charlie's surprise, he understood the words almost immediately.

"Are you the promised helmsman?" The language she spoke was close to whatever the rajah and his bodyguards used.

"What are you?" Charlie ignored her question. His own voice sounded far away, muffled by the water.

"We are nāgas." The first *a* in the word *nāga* was longer than the second. The tip of a forked tongue flickered out from between dark green lips to lick the nāga's teeth. Oddly, her voice was completely unimpeded by the water, as if she were speaking in ordinary air.

"Are you a folk?" Charlie asked, trying to delay answering her question. He was afraid she wouldn't like his answer. "Do you live down here?"

"We do not *live* at all." The nāga smiled, and through the green skin of her face, Charlie suddenly saw a skull. "When we lived, we were humans like you."

"Not like me." Charlie tried hard not to step backward, knowing it would only bring him closer to the nāgas circling at his rear. "I'm not a man."

"A boy." The nāga smirked.

"Yes. And no." Charlie enjoyed the confusion on the nāga's face, but he forced himself to focus. He needed a way back to the surface, preferably with the vimāna, before his mainspring unwound. He didn't want to get trapped in some riddle game. "What brought you here?"

The nāga gestured at the gleaming pyramid on which Charlie stood. "We sailed the Pushpaka vimāna for Lord Ravana. But when the helmsman was slain and the chariot sank, we died."

"And you're waiting for another helmsman? Someone to fly the vimāna?"

"We're trapped, dead inside the vimāna and beneath it. What you see isn't our flesh, but our spirits."

Charlie refrained from commenting on just how horrible and ugly those spirits *were.*

"Yes?" he prompted the nāga instead.

"Before leaving us, Lord Ravana promised he would send us another helmsman. A helmsman, Lord Ravana said, a flyer who could raise the vimāna from the deep, freeing us." The nāga lowered her chin and smiled, which only made her teeth look longer. "Are you the helmsman?"

Charlie had no idea how to fly anything, other than the flyer Heaven-Bound Bob had built, which had been destroyed on the slopes of the Welsh mountain Cader Idris. "I have flown," he said cautiously.

The circle of swimming nāgas came to an abrupt halt, so instead of a ring of wiggling tails, Charlie saw a circle of green snake-people, all baring their teeth at him. And extending long, razor-like claws in his direction.

Charlie nodded.

He examined the top of the chariot. Two rods rose from the floor to his shoulder height, each ending in a golden, glowing ball. They reminded Charlie of the control rods he'd seen on steam-carriages, including the steam-carriage that had carried Queen Victoria over Waterloo Bridge during her Jubilee celebration.

Only these rods didn't seem near a steering wheel.

Also, they seemed fixed in one position, riding perpendicular to the floor. He didn't think the rod would move if he touched it.

He was also afraid to touch it, because doing so might make his ignorance obvious.

"The steering mechanism," he said to the nāga. It wasn't a question, it was a statement designed to lure her into saying more.

"The steering mechanism," she said back.

"Steeeeeeering," all the nāgas wailed together. It was an eerie sound, with a strange interval between two long notes.

In the echo of the nāgas' word, Charlie thought he heard his name.

He cocked his head to one side and frowned at the nāga. "Did you hear that?"

"Are you the helmsman or not?" the nāga asked. She licked her lips. "Because if not . . . we are *hungry.*"

"Chaaaaaaarlieeeeeee!"

"No, I definitely heard something." Charlie looked up and saw an object that looked like a dark disk, falling slowly toward him.

A dark disk and, in the center of it . . . boots?

"Wait one moment," he said to the nāga, and he jumped.

Charlie didn't have to breathe, but he was too heavy to be much of a swimmer. Still, exerting his legs, he managed to leap far enough to reach the object—

which turned out to be a large brass bell, dropping through the water.

Clinging to the side of the bell, Charlie examined it. The bell was the size of a large closet or a small room. It sank slowly into the water because it was being lowered on an iron chain of enormous links. Two tubes, each as big around as Charlie's arm, attached to the upper surface of the bell and climbed, winding around the iron links.

Booted feet protruded from the underside of the bell, and Charlie knew the boots.

They belonged to either Ollie or Bob.

"Charlie!" He heard his name, muffled by the water. The voice was definitely Bob's.

Charlie rapped on the outside of the bell three times, and then pressed his hands and mouth to it to call to Bob. "I'm here. I'm going to guide you down. Hold on!"

The nāgas stared, but Charlie ignored them. By pushing off the bell, he got down to the vimāna's platform before it did, and then he grabbed the bell's lip. As it fell, he tugged hard and dragged it to the center of the vimāna's platform, so that Bob's feet came down right beside the golden rods and the bell settled on the backs of the swans, enveloping both Bob and the steering mechanism. That left a space about three feet tall between the top of the vimāna and the lip of the bell.

"What is this?" the nāga speaker hissed, and crept forward.

"The helmsman," Charlie told her. "Hold on."

He dropped to all fours and crawled under the bell. When he stood, he found that the inside of the bell was full of air, and Bob was sitting on a cushioned seat. She reached up to pull down a speaking tube from the wall of the bell and said into it, "I've reached the bottom, and Charlie's here."

Then she held it away from her mouth and Charlie heard the answer, in the rajah's voice. "Wonderful! Tell us when to pull you up!"

"What is this thing?" Charlie asked.

"A diving bell," Bob said. "Apparently, it's what the rajah 'ad stowed on those other elephants. 'E expected we'd be using this all along, an' was a bit surprised when you just up an' jumped in."

Charlie examined the inside of the bell. "One tube for speech. Another for breathing. Seats for two divers."

"Do you know you're leaking, Charlie?"

Charlie looked down at himself. Where his body had been pierced in various fights, he now leaked water. He grimaced, but there was nothing he could do about it. "Did Ollie not want to come with you?"

Bob's face was flat. "'E did, as a matter of fact. I told 'im not to bother. I told 'im I'd need the second seat for my mate Charlie when we came back up."

"You know Ollie's your friend, right?" Charlie felt ridiculous even saying the words.

Bob growled. "Yeah? So my friend knew my biggest secret, an' let me go on pretending, an' making a fool out of myself? Is that what friends do, Charlie? They yumiliate each other like that?"

Charlie looked at his feet, dark outlines on the glowing metal platform of the vimāna.

"What's all this, then?" Bob changed the subject. "Two poles 'ere, an' I'm standing on something shining."

"I think this is it," Charlie said. "The Pushpaka vimāna. And outside there are . . . well, ghosts, sort of."

"What do you mean, *sort of*?"

"Well, they're ghost . . . snake-people. With big teeth. I think they used to be the crew of this vessel, only they're dead and cursed, or something. And if we don't fly the Pushpaka vimāna, they're going to eat us."

Pushpaka flies like a bird, it holds souls like a city, and it commands the lightning. Pushpaka cannot be restrained and it cannot be measured. Of all Lord Ravana's marvels, the vimāna was the most astonishing. For these reasons, Lord Ravana himself greatly favored the vimāna, and traveled in it everywhere.

—Prashastapada, *Ninety-Nine Questions for Yudhishthira*

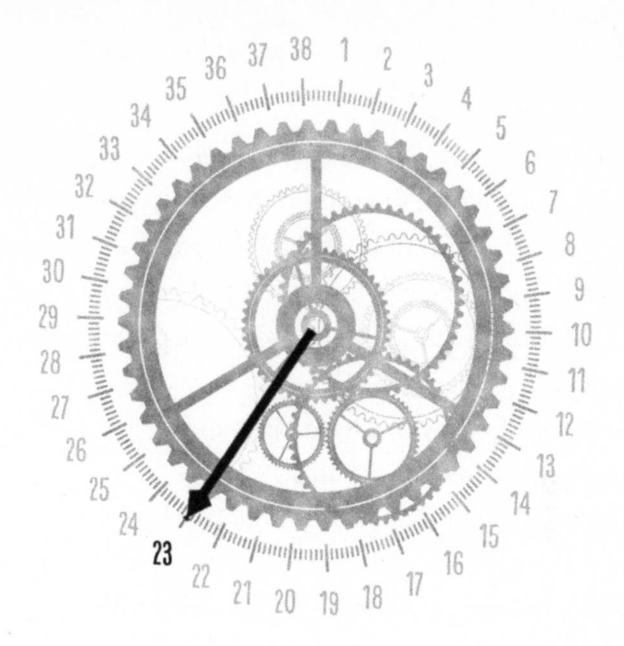

"Well," Bob said. "That ain't friendly, but it's much of a piece with the ghouls, innit? An' then there was that dog on Cader Idris, too. A monster wants to eat me? Bring it on, my china."

She stepped forward to the two rods and took them in her hands, gripping the poles. She pushed, and the rods didn't move.

Charlie waited.

She pulled on the rods, and still nothing.

Charlie whistled a few notes.

She pushed one rod and pulled the other.

Charlie smiled.

"Charlie, mate," Bob said to him. "You can't stand 'ere while I do this. You're distraining me."

"Distracting."

"What's *distraining,* then?"

Charlie shook his head. "I don't know."

"Right." Bob jerked her thumb toward the wall of the bell. "Get out of 'ere. Go find something else to do, an' if nothing else, go talk to the snake-ghosts. Tell 'em I'm working on it."

Charlie dropped to all fours and crawled back outside the diving bell.

The circle of nāgas had tightened, and they looked at him with wide eyes and open mouths.

Charlie locked his hands behind his back; it made him feel official. "The helms . . . helmsman is at work raising the ship."

"Heeeeeelmsmaaaaan," the nāgas keened together.

"What is the bell?" the spokesnāga asked.

"It is the helmsman's." Charlie straightened his back to maximize his authority. "He is at work inside. If you touch the bell, or if you enter, or if you disturb the bell in any way—"

"Lord Ravana will destroy us!" the lead nāga shrieked.

"Destroooooooy uuuuuuuuus!" the others wailed.

"Yes," Charlie said. "Destroy you. So move back, leave the helmsman to do her—that is, to do his work."

To his surprise, the nāgas retreated. To his sorrow, they didn't disappear entirely. How long would they wait before they attacked?

Not long enough, he feared.

And that thought gave him an idea. "How well do you know the workings of the Pushpaka vimāna?" he asked the head nāga.

"Workings?"

"I mean the machinery."

The nāga stared.

"How it functions. The inside."

"We know the inside," the nāga said. "We sailed this vimāna on all twelve winds; we know it as a vessel."

"Good. Tell me, then . . ." Charlie thought, and wished he had a better way to ask this question, but he didn't. "Where is the nail of the intellectual world?"

The nāga stared.

Charlie had no idea what the nail looked like, but he'd seen the other two. "It's as long as my arm," he said. "And it belongs to the gods. The world of the gods, and the demons." To protect himself, he added, "Probably. Did Lord Ravana leave a big nail behind somewhere?" He wished he'd asked Ollie for more of a hint before jumping into the stepwell.

The nāga blew bubbles of green vapor from its lips, a gesture that was picked up by the entire circle of nāgas. They drifted slowly inward, looks of suspicion on their faces.

"Back!" Charlie shouted, leaping forward.

The nāgas scattered, regrouping at the edge of the light, barely visible.

"I will consult the helmsman!" he announced.

Then he ducked into the water again and entered the diving bell.

Bob crouched in the water, working with her fingers at the bases of the long rods.

"How's it going?" he asked.

"Testing 'ypotheses. It'd be easier if I could see the 'ole machine." Bob shrugged. "'Ow's it going with you?"

"The crew hasn't eaten me yet," Charlie said, "but that's not for lacking of wanting to." Then he heard his own words and had an idea. "Keep it up."

He splashed back under the lip of the bell.

The nāgas had returned and were slowly circling the vimāna. The lead nāga drifted close to the pilot's platform, if that was indeed what the space between the swans was, and stared at Charlie through slitted eyes.

"You were the crew!" Charlie called to her, enjoying the sound of his underwater voice. "What part of the vimāna were you *not* allowed in?"

The nāga blew green bubbles. "Lord Ravana's chambers."

"Very good," Charlie said. Would the nāgas see his ignorance, and would that make them attack him? "Lord Ravana is pleased. Now lead me to those chambers."

The nāga speaker bowed, and then swam down the outside of the vimāna.

Charlie followed, walking along one of the swan's necks to its beak and then stepping off. He dropped, slower than the nāga swam, but fast enough to keep her in view.

They descended two levels, and then the nāga waited for him.

The walkway encircling the vimāna here bristled with metal poles pointing outward. They looked a bit like spears, only they weren't sharp at the tip. Coiled gold wire connected them all. From here Charlie could see the white sand at the watery bottom, on which the vimāna rested.

Long, eyeless fish moved back and forth just above the

sand. White crustaceans with multiple legs and eyes on long stalks scuttled beneath the bellies of the fish. Far enough away to be nearly invisible, something with tentacles retreated into darkness.

"This way," the nāga hissed. Then she swam through an open window.

Charlie clambered in after.

To his surprise, much of the interior of the vimāna still held air. Or at least it wasn't full of water—whether the air was breathable or not was a different question, and one Charlie had no ability to judge. When she led him through passages filled with water, the nāga swam; with equal facility, she slithered up onto dry floors to lead him across halls that were not submerged, dragging her human forepart forward by leaning on the palms of her hands.

Charlie also learned that the nāga smelled bad. Because of Ollie, he associated snakes with the smell of rotten eggs, even though he knew from his reading that snakes were very clean and didn't really smell like much at all, to an ordinary person.

The nāga smelled like decayed flesh.

At one point, Charlie stopped. "I think you're leading me in a very roundabout fashion," he said to the nāga. He pointed to a submerged passage to his right. "We could have come directly here by cutting through that passage; I'm sure of it."

"Yes," the nāga hissed. "But I can't go in that passage."

"Because it belongs to Lord Ravana?" Charlie asked.

The nāga hung her head. "Because our bodies lie there,

rotting." Again her skull shone through her emerald-green flesh, and when Charlie looked again at the submerged hallway, he thought he now saw it full of rib cages and skeletal hands.

A dull thud resounded from the vimāna itself; something had struck the vessel.

"Is someone interrupting the helmsman?" Charlie asked.

The nāga shook her head.

"Lead on," he told her.

"This door," she told him. "Behind here are Lord Ravana's chambers, and I may not go."

The door was enormous, easily five times Charlie's height. It was made of a dark, heavy wood that had been painted red. The antechamber in which Charlie and the nāga stood was not submerged, but sheer age had made all the paint on the door curl up into flakes that barely clung to the surface they had once covered entirely.

There was no apparent knob or knocker. A single hinge near the center of the door's height, the length of Charlie's arm, suggested that the door swung outward, but Charlie saw no way to grip the door.

A second thud, even louder. But the sounds seemed to come from the side of the vimāna, not its top. Probably Bob was still safe, and working.

Charlie was conscious of the nāga watching him. "Iftah, ya baabaain!" he shouted, imitating the dwarf magician Suleiman.

Nothing happened.

"Open sesame!" he tried next, partly as a joke for his own benefit, but partly because it worked in stories, so it might work in real life. Or, Charlie thought, he might *be* in a story, if Ollie was right.

The door stayed shut.

Charlie considered, and saw only one option. He examined the single hinge—fortunately, it was simple, a long white spike, made of something that looked like chalk, connecting interlacing gold loops, which were affixed in alternation to the door and the wall. Remove the spike, and the door should simply fall forward. Hopefully.

"What are you doing?" the nāga asked him.

"Can I stand on you?" Charlie asked. "I mean, will I fall through?"

The nāga bared all her teeth, which turned out to be a lot. "You may not stand on me. Are you Lord Ravana's servant at all?"

"You may stand on *me*," said a voice. Thomas's voice.

Thomas climbed out of the water, shedding streams of it from his black coat. His hands were in his pockets, which bulged—maybe from the unicorn horn and the cold-iron knife, Charlie thought, though those were long enough that they were probably hidden up his sleeves instead.

"You may climb on me, Charlie," Thomas said again.

"What sort of name is Charlie?" the nāga asked.

"Come stand by this hinge," Charlie said to Thomas. He shook a finger at the nāga. "As for you . . . do you wish to be freed, or don't you?"

The nāga backed down, cowed.

Thomas waited beside the hinge and Charlie clambered up his brother like a ladder, stepping first on his knees and then dragging himself up onto his shoulders. "Hold on while I push." Gripping the pointed tip of the spike holding the hinge together, Charlie groaned as he tugged it upward—

it resisted, and Thomas shuddered with the effort—

Charlie yanked, and the spike came free into his hands. It was pointed, as long as his arm and of a metal of strange color.

It looked just like a nail.

"Hey, Thomas," Charlie began, and looked down at his brother.

Thomas wobbled, trying to catch his balance, and Charlie saw into the stuffed pocket of his brother's coat. In the pocket, balled up, was Thomas's scarf.

His scarf.

"You're not Thomas!" Charlie shouted.

The shaitan shifted into its natural, black-eyed face, baring needlelike teeth and hissing. Adjusting its grip quickly, it dragged Charlie down and hurled him to the floor.

"Liar!" the nāga yowled, and pounced on Charlie also.

◆ ◆ ◆

The famous Seven Duties of the kobolds have been ordered in an overlooked passage of an obscure penny dreadful, *Napoleon's Tallest Teamster* (Joseph Monson, 1832). Despite his purple prose, narcissism, and fascination with melodramatic love triangles, there is reason to think the author was in fact present during the 1812 campaign and was party to the kobolds' so-called Prime Secret. We should therefore take seriously his suggestion that the key kobold duty is Compliance, which has three positive sub-duties (Best Efforts, Good Faith, Assignment) and three negative sub-duties (Loyalty, Noncompetition, Nondisclosure). Monson everywhere implies but nowhere explains the connection between the duties and the Prime Secret, so as to this point, we can make no comment.

—from Reginald St. John Smythson, *Almanack of the Elder Folk and Arcana of Britain and Northern Ireland,* 1st ed., "Kobold"

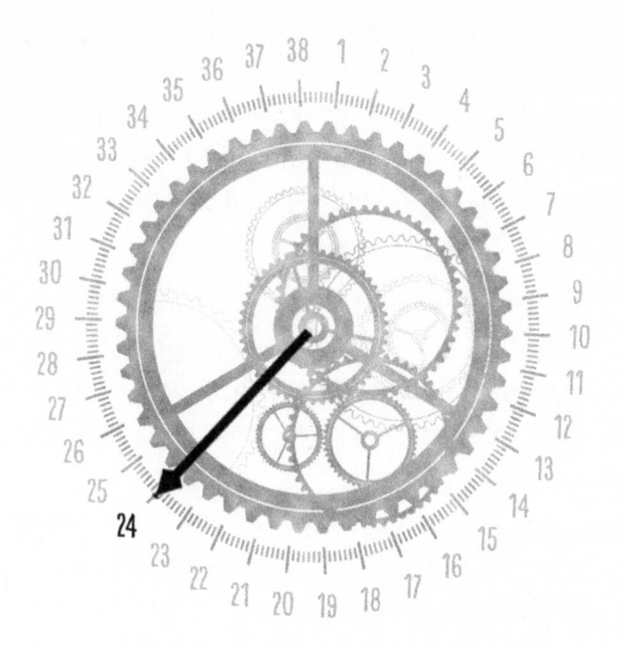

Charlie kicked, and his attack knocked the shaitan away. At the same moment, though, the nāga coiled her tail around Charlie's waist and sank her teeth into his neck. Charlie flailed and pounded her with his arms—for a ghost, she turned out to be very solid—but all he got for his efforts was hurt hands.

Hissing like a wet fire, the shaitan kicked Charlie in the side of the head. When Charlie raised his arm to block a second kick, the shaitan grabbed his wrist and began to pull.

The nāga stuck two fingers into one of the holes in Charlie's side and gripped his body. She, too, began to pull.

Charlie heard the groan of metal, and he felt himself beginning to be literally torn apart.

"De Minimis and Underthames!"

Gnat?

The pixie leaped past Charlie, holding a dagger high over her head. It wasn't the cold-iron knife, but something the color of ivory—the tooth of the Hound that Gnat had killed in Wales, now wielded as a weapon.

The shaitan turned too late, and Gnat stabbed it in the chest. Bright green blood sprayed out, and the shaitan punched the fairy. Gnat flew in one direction, trailing drops of water, and the shaitan sprang back the other way, clutching at its wound.

Charlie felt his chest bend out of shape. He slammed his forehead into the nāga's nose, but she didn't flinch.

Then, suddenly, her smile fell flat.

"Leave my brother alone!"

The nāga's tail was ripped from Charlie's body. The action tossed Charlie himself aside, and he banged into the metal wall of the vimāna and lay in a crumpled heap.

Thomas had come to Charlie's rescue with Gnat. His face looked as afraid as it was angry, but he had the nāga firmly by the tail and was swinging her in a circle over his head. The nāga gibbered and shrieked, and it swung its clawlike hands at Thomas, but it couldn't reach him.

Thomas threw the nāga against the door of Lord Ravana's chambers.

Bong!

The door shook on the impact. The nāga fell to the floor and lay stunned, shaking its head slowly. The door trembled, toppled slowly forward—*BONG!*—and landed on the nāga.

The door was so heavy it didn't bounce, and when it hit

the floor, whatever was left of the nāga was so thin, Charlie couldn't see it—the door seemed to be lying perfectly flat.

The shaitan hissed and jumped at Charlie.

Charlie hurt, and his chest and arms felt weak, but his legs were strong. He kicked them against the wall and hurled himself out of the shaitan's path.

Thomas's face still looked terrified, but that didn't stop him from leaping forward to butt the shaitan with his head and shoulders. Like an acrobat, the shaitan tumbled into the large, totally dark room behind the door.

Gnat leaped after him. She leaped, and didn't fly, because her wings were soggy with water. As she jumped, one of them fell off. She had no weapons in her hand, but her face shone with concentrated fury.

"Shut the door!" she yelled to Thomas and Charlie.

Charlie stood. "But that will leave you alone with the shaitan!"

The room behind the door had no furniture. The shaitan pounced toward the pixie warrior and seized her by her remaining wing. When she squirmed out of its grip, the wing came off in its hand.

"Do it!" Thomas squealed.

The door was enormous, but the brothers were strong. Gripping the door by its two corners, they heaved it back up and into place. Charlie felt his mechanisms whine in protest, but he and Thomas got the job done.

Stuck to the underside of the door, like a single sock, was the only sign of the nāga: the squished body of a sea snake.

The door fell into its frame with a soft *boom*.

"I could stand to have my spring wound," Thomas said.

"So could I," Charlie agreed. "And maybe some repairs."

Behind the closed door, they heard an ear-shattering howl, and then silence.

"Gnat?" Charlie called tentatively.

He heard a soft tapping on the door. "Aye, lads, 'tis I. You can open the door now."

Charlie remembered that the shaitan had appeared to be Thomas, and had even spoken with Thomas's voice. "How do we know you're our friend Natalie and not the monster?"

"You'll have forgotten this, but like all my kind, I see in complete darkness as well as I do in broad daylight. Blind, the shaitan was no match."

Maybe . . . but Charlie wanted more confirmation, just in case. "Tell me something only Natalie would know," he said.

"The day I met you, Charlie Pondicherry, Grim Grumblesson smashed his horns through your father's ceiling."

Charlie was convinced. He and Thomas wedged two of the nails between the door and its frame, one on each side, and they pulled the door forward again.

Gnat stood behind the door, on top of the shaitan's body. She was wingless and no bigger than a doll, but Charlie thought she'd never seemed taller. In her right hand, she held the Hound's tooth, green with the shaitan's blood, and in her left she raised the scarf that had once been Thomas's.

"I'll be taking this as my token, Thomas," the fairy warrior said. "If you don't mind."

"I'm proud that you'd take it," Thomas said shyly. "Also, that will keep it out of the hands of any more shaitans."

The mechanical boys wound each other's springs, and Charlie looked inside Lord Ravana's chambers while Thomas brought him up to full power. The ceiling was high and vaulted, and the hall was gigantic, but there was no art, and no furniture, and the walls were plain as could be.

"How did you get down here?" he asked Gnat.

She smiled. "When I saw that fellow grab a rock and jump in, I knew he must be the shaitan. So I picked up another stone and jumped in after him."

"I didn't need a weight," Thomas said. "I just jumped in like you did, Charlie."

"That was brave," Charlie told his brother.

Thomas grinned.

"And you knew you'd lose your wings," Charlie said to the pixie.

"Better than losing my friends."

"That was a mighty deed," Charlie said.

"Aye." Gnat laughed. "That's what I plan to tell the folk of Underthames."

As Thomas finished giving Charlie's mainspring the final crank, the entire vimāna shuddered.

"Bob!" Charlie shouted.

They rushed out. On foot, the boys were faster than Gnat, so the pixie rode on Charlie's shoulders, both in the passages and chambers where there was air, and in the submerged sections. She took an extra-large breath before they exited the vessel.

A flurry of activity crowned the vimāna. The nāgas lunged, time and again, at a figure who stood in the center, defending the diving bell. The outnumbered warrior had a curved saber in each hand, and he dodged the nāgas' attacks by disappearing repeatedly and then reappearing to slash at the snake-ghosts. He was nimble and quick, but his attacks were just awkward swings.

It was Ollie.

He wasn't disappearing; he was dodging by turning himself into a snake and back into a human, over and over again.

That had to be exhausting.

"Ollie!" Thomas barreled into the fight, kicking one nāga like a ball and knocking it entirely off the top of the vimāna.

Charlie almost joined the attack, but he knew Gnat would need air.

Why didn't Ollie need air?

Also, he wanted to see Bob.

The vimāna shook again as Charlie climbed under the lip of the diving bell. Gnat gasped and leaped into one of the bell's seats, the wet scarf dripping like a rain-soaked cloak about her, the Hound's tooth clutched in her hand, ready to strike.

Bob stood, holding the knobs atop the two rods and beaming. "I've almost got it, Charlie!" she cried.

"But the rods aren't moving," Charlie said.

She shook her head. "They *don't* move. It ain't that kind of machine, a vimāna. In fact, I ain't sure she's quite a machine at all."

"What does that mean?"

A nāga that had slipped past Ollie sprang up out of the water, leaping toward Bob—

Gnat sprang into the air to intercept it, stabbing the creature with her ivory weapon and falling with it into the water.

"She's got a mind, Charlie. I don't think the vimāna is a machine; I think she's a creature. Pushpaka is a spirit, or a demon, or a god, an' when I 'old these rods, I can talk to 'er. She doesn't want to fly—says she's too old, it's been too long—but I reckon she's about to come around. It ain't that easy, though; there's still the facts of aeronautics, wind an' gravity an' so on, an' she needs guiding."

"You're talking to her?" Charlie asked.

"Mostly I'm listening." Bob grinned. "Pushpaka is lonely. Also, she's pretty angry with the blighters 'oo crashed 'er 'ere in the first place. Some chap called Ravana, an' 'is pilot."

Charlie was so astonished, he found he had nothing to say.

Bob leaned forward, without releasing the knobs. "Just between you an' me, Charlie, I think she likes the fact that I'm a girl."

"So do I," Charlie said. "And you know who else does?"

A dead sea snake floated to the surface of the water, and then Gnat climbed out.

"'Oo?"

"Ollie," Charlie said. "I'm pretty sure Ollie kept your secret, just like you kept his. Only he kept it so well, he didn't even tell *you* that he knew. And I think he did that because he knew you wanted to keep your secret from him."

"Yeah." Bob sniffed, but she nodded, and a hint of pride crept into her face. "Yeah, I reckon you're right."

"We'll go help Ollie," Gnat said. "You fly this demon."

Gnat gulped air again, and she and Charlie both exited the bell.

Ollie continued to fight, but the nāgas closed in—until, with a sudden lurch, the vimāna rose.

The nāgas froze and were almost instantly left behind. The last Charlie saw of them, their faces bore expressions of gratitude, and then heads and upper bodies disappeared, and sea snakes scooted away.

"Hold on!" he shouted to his friends, voice muffled by the water, as he grabbed Gnat and clung to one of the swan's tails. Thomas anchored himself to another swan, and Ollie slipped into snake form and wrapped himself around Thomas's neck.

The vimāna shot straight up.

CRASH!

Bricks smashed into Charlie as the Pushpaka vimāna battered its way through the lowest, tightest levels of the stepwell. He hunched over Gnat, shielding her with his body, and grunted in pain as the masonry struck him in the head and chest.

The diving bell protected Bob.

Then the bricks were gone, and the water was a muddy fog.

Then the water was gone, and Charlie was shooting straight up into the monsoon on top of Pushpaka.

Over the pouring rain, he heard a mass shout of astonishment.

Then a loud groan of iron, and the diving bell was suddenly ripped away. Bob crouched with a mad gleam in her eyes, clinging to the two control spheres.

"Charlie!" she shouted. "Get off! Pushpaka ain't used to flying, an' this wind is too strong for 'er!"

Charlie and Thomas both obeyed. They ran down the levels of the vimāna, leaping from walkway to walkway until they reached the bottom. As the vessel shook and swayed back and forth, they hurled Gnat and Ollie (still in snake form) into the water of the stepwell.

Then they dropped.

Charlie hit the gravel around the stepwell hard, and bounced. After landing facedown in a puddle, he immediately flipped himself over to look for signs of Bob.

He raised his face just in time to see the Pushpaka vimāna framed against the dark monsoon clouds and glowing with a golden light. And then the storm snatched it away, and Bob and Lord Ravana's demon chariot both disappeared.

PART FOUR

THE DEMON PIT

No gift like a pixie's gift. No vengeance like a pixie's revenge.

—Eirig Johansson, *Proverbs of Field and Furrow*

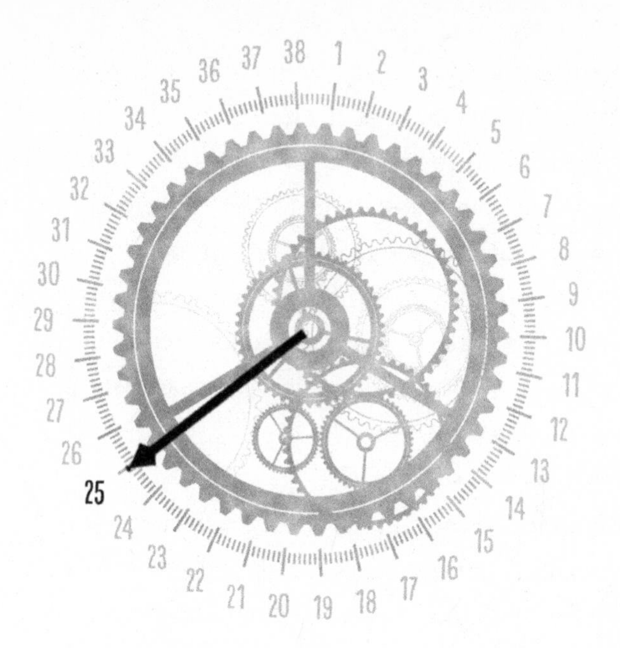

"The rajah! Rajah Singh!" Charlie heard.

He staggered to his feet. Whatever the nāga had done to his chest, it had aggravated Charlie's limp. He followed the crowd to the stepwell and stopped at the edge.

The lower parts of the well were completely destroyed. The stairs and porticoes and walkways of the upper part were cluttered with the rubble the vimāna had generated as it smashed its way out.

Jan Wijmoor stood at the edge of the destruction and stared at the rubble, a look of dismay on his face.

The crowd of people—no, the three separate crowds of people—who had been standing around the stepwell's pumps to collect water now streamed down into the stepwell. Whatever the divisions had been among them, they were now forgotten as the rajah's subjects linked arms to create a long human chain that anchored itself to one of the top-level swans and descended all the way to the water, down the last shaky, disintegrating steps, to extend to the rajah, who, still in his long yellow coat, thrashed in the brown mud.

Not far from him, Charlie saw the diving bell. It lay on its side atop a pile of the chain that had lowered it into the water, and the giant spool around which the chain wound, and the crank that moved the spool.

Bamf!

Ollie stood beside Charlie at the lip of the stepwell, staring at the sky. Gnat trudged up the steps behind him.

"Bob?" Ollie's face was twisted, and he shook.

"She . . . she'll be back," Charlie said.

Ollie stared at him. "Will she? How do you know?"

"Because she's Heaven-Bound Bob." Charlie wished he felt as certain as he sounded. "And, Ollie . . . she wasn't taken by some monster; she was flying an airship."

"Biggest bloody airship I ever saw." Ollie still trembled, but he nodded and grinned. "Big as a museum. Big as a village. I only wish those royal aeronaut toffs she always wanted to impress had seen her."

Down in the stepwell, the rajah's people had managed to grab his coat and were pulling him to safety.

"She'll be back," Charlie repeated. "How did you get down into the well, by the way? And how did you stay down there so long without air?"

Ollie shrugged, and something like a smile crept into the corner of his mouth. "I'm a wizard, ain't I?"

Charlie stared.

"All right, then, mate. I borrowed—that is to say, I *stole*—swords from two of the rajah's men. Then I turned into a snake and slithered down the air tube into the diving bell. Got there just in time, because some of those beasties were about to jump Bob. I reckoned my only chance was to keep them off guard by changing into and out of snake form. I discovered that when I did that, I kept finding air."

"In the same pocket where you kept the *Almanack,*" Charlie said. "And me."

"Same place," Ollie agreed. "Also, the fact that I was a snake, of all things, seemed to impress the monsters."

Charlie whistled to show that he was impressed.

"Too right," Ollie said. "Show me the loup-garou who can do half of that, mate. I ain't French."

Once he was certain that the rajah's people had extracted their prince from the well, Charlie gathered his friends around the pump. The bodyguard captain joined them and provided white cotton towels.

As wet as they were, Charlie expected to see everyone shivering. But it was a hot rain, and a warm wind that blew it sideways under the pavilion, so instead of huddling against the cold, his friends wiped off rain and sweat as they talked.

"You've all come with us on a long road," Charlie said. "And I think this is where it ends for the rest of you."

"No way, mate," Ollie said. "To borrow a phrase from my friend Bob: the 'eck. I ain't stopping here."

"Nobody is," Gnat agreed. "Besides, what do you imagine I'll do here, wingless and alone? And I've a third mighty deed to perform." She grinned recklessly. "I expect my best chance of meeting fearsome monsters is to stick with you lads."

"We have to go to Russia now," Charlie said. "That's where Brunel said he and Thomas were going. I don't even know how we're going to get there, unless Bob shows up again with the Pushpaka chariot. I guess we'll walk." As he spoke, though, another possibility occurred to him.

"Where in Russia?" Gnat asked.

"Thomas knows." Charlie turned to his brother.

"No, I don't." Thomas looked at his feet.

Charlie was stunned. "What? But . . ."

Thomas shrugged. "I don't know. I tried to tell you: I know the magic, but I don't have all the pieces."

"I thought you meant you didn't have the nails," Charlie said. "But we have the nails now."

"I don't know where the pit is." Thomas shrugged again, and he looked tiny.

Charlie turned to Ollie. "What about the *Almanack*?" he suggested.

"I haven't seen it, mate, and I read the article on Napoleon and the Romanovs. I can look more, but . . ." Ollie raised his hands to show he was helpless. "It might not be in there."

Charlie shook his head slowly. "Russia's a long way away. I guess we can just go in that direction, and try to find someone who knows where it is when we get there."

"Russia's also very big," Ollie pointed out.

Jan Wijmoor made the noisiest sigh Charlie had ever heard, an exhalation so large it nearly knocked the kobold over. "I know where the pit is."

"You?" Charlie and Thomas spoke together; Charlie *felt* as surprised as Thomas *sounded.*

"But this is not an easy thing for me to tell," the kobold said. He pointed a finger at the pavilion overhead. "Non-disclosure, you know!"

"I *don't* know," Charlie said, "but I've heard that from you before."

The corners of Wijmoor's mouth tugged down. "I am not permitted to share the secrets of the Syndikat. But even more than that, I am not permitted to share the secrets of my folk."

"You're short, and you break stuff," Ollie muttered. "What's to share?"

"Shh," Charlie hushed his friend. "Go on," he said to the kobold.

"Some of us have a great gift for stopping and wrecking machines," Wijmoor said. "Many more of us have a gift for making them."

"Or for both," Charlie said. "Like Heinrich Zahnkrieger. He worked with my father to make things in the shop, and he did it very well. But it turned out he was also a redcap, a wizard with the special gift of making machines malfunction."

Wijmoor nodded. "And to be a redcap is seen among my folk as an illness, or a curse. A redcap is exiled by any right-thinking cooperative, and not spoken of afterward. But my folk's gift was not always with machines at all. Once, we had a great gift for working with animals."

Ollie wrinkled his nose in surprise.

"You understand, I am violating my duty of Nondisclosure in telling you this."

"You keep talking, mate, or I might have to violate my duty of not punching you in the face." Ollie shook a clenched fist.

"Relax, Ollie." Charlie put an arm around his friend's shoulder, which was hard, because Ollie was taller than him, but he could stand on tiptoes and just make it. "I miss Bob too. She'll be fine."

Ollie sobbed once and stepped away from the circle.

Wijmoor nodded heavily. "We were the world's greatest muleteers, and equerries, and mahouts. We handled beasts."

"It is true." The captain nodded. "The old stories tell that it was the little people of the woods and rivers who guided all our elephants. But it has not been so since my grandfather's time."

"Since 1812, to be precise," Wijmoor said. "When my people managed the carts and wagons for the greatest invading army the world has ever known, the Grande Armée of Napoleon, and helped him attack Russia."

"This is starting to make sense," Charlie said. "I remember reading in the *Almanack* that the last tsars summoned a demon from some pit when Napoleon attacked Moscow. So some of your folk were present when the Romanovs' demonologists freed the demon, or the spirit or whatever, that lived in the pit."

"We were there," Wijmoor said. "And in its emergence, the demon changed us. We lost our gift with animals, and so Napoleon's retreat was a rout. The mules wouldn't cooperate; what horses were left pulled up their pickets and bolted; the goats would no longer give milk. We thought our gift had been stripped from us as punishment."

"Was that not it?" Charlie asked.

"Who can say?" Wijmoor rubbed his hands together. "But as steam trains, and telegraphs, and airships have exploded into use over the last century . . . we have learned that we have a *new* gift. We are gifted with the things of the new world, their use and also their obstruction. Did a demon force a bargain on us? Did the demon's emergence simply overwhelm our talent and impress us with a new power?"

"Or did you make a willing bargain with the demon?" Ollie suggested.

Wijmoor shrugged. "Who can say?"

"Were you all standing in the pit when the demon was summoned, then?" Gnat asked.

Wijmoor shook his head. "Only a few of us. But the underlying rule of magic, its single most basic principle, is that all things are connected. What affected those few gnomes in witness affected us all."

And if Charlie and Thomas rebottled the demon, what would happen? Charlie looked at his brother, and the look of worry on the other boy's face told him that Thomas was having the same thought. Charlie and Thomas themselves might cease to function. And would all kobolds lose their gift, and become nothing more than short humans?

And what about the pumps that brought water to the rajah's people, and his plans for pipes to bring the water directly to their homes? How much of that would go away?

And the tractors he liked so much?

And the library in Marburg, and all the marvelous knowledge it contained? It had been burned, but if the technology was possible, couldn't it be rebuilt?

"I know this is all very sensitive," he said to the kobold. "Thank you for telling us."

"And I know where the pit is," Wijmoor said. "We all do."

"What, like an inborn memory?" Ollie returned to the group, sniffing slightly and red around the eyes.

Wijmoor shook his head. "No. It's an important part of our story, and our managers tell it to us over and over, from a very early age. It's in Moscow. The pit is in one of the longest-occupied places in Moscow, one of the city's oldest buildings. It's in the deepest cellar beneath the palace called the Kremlin."

Thomas's face brightened, but then fell again. "Well, that tells us where to go, to put an end to this. But it's still a long way away."

"I have an idea," Charlie said. "The Path of Root and Twig."

"The what?" Ollie asked. "Do you mean that elf road you took in Wales? I don't see how that can help you here."

"Charlie's right," Gnat said. "If he can find alfar, they can put him on the Path. The Path is everywhere, at the same time that it's nowhere. At least, it's everywhere where there are trees."

"The Kremlin's a palace," Ollie said. "It's got to have trees. Every palace I ever saw had a garden."

"How do we travel on the Path, though?" Charlie thought

out loud, looking at the elephants huddling under the pavilion to shelter from the rain. "I was thinking we could ride elephants, but Moscow's cold, isn't it? It seems like it would be cruel to take an elephant there and possibly have to leave it."

"We can't just walk?" Jan Wijmoor asked.

"I don't think so," Charlie said. "Plants on the Path sort of . . . tear at you. The donkeys didn't like it very much, and I think it might hurt. I think we need something like a cart."

"I'll get you a cart," the captain said, stroking his mustache.

Thomas clapped Charlie on the back. "And you and I can be the donkeys!"

Charlie laughed, thinking of his friend Syzigon, and how the dwarf had called Charlie Donkey when they'd first met. "Perfect!" He turned to the captain. "And one more thing. Can you tell me where to find standing stones? You know, like menhirs, or some other kind of megalith? Preferably surrounded by trees . . ."

Miss Ingrid Björnsdottir and Mr. Grim Grumblesson

∞ regret to announce ∞

∞ the postponement of their nuptials ∞

∞ previously announced in these pages ∞

∞ two weeks ago today ∞

∞ there will be NO party ∞

—*Daily Telegraph*, "Announcements," 16 July 1887

The standing stones were different from the ones Charlie had seen in England. Each was only about his height, a solitary column of black slate. He counted forty-one of them, in a circle large enough to accommodate all thirteen of the rajah's elephants, had he wanted.

Instead the rajah's elephants had stayed away, out of sight on the other side of a low rise. Charlie wasn't sure, but his sense was that the alfar, who lived in forests and seemed almost like trees themselves, valued their privacy and would prefer that the smallest number of people possible see them. Only the rajah and his captain—at the rajah's request—had followed Charlie to the edge of the circle. They each held an umbrella, though the rajah was so wet from having fallen into the stepwell that his scarcely mattered.

At the last minute, Charlie hesitated. "Does anyone else want to do this? Does anyone have experience with the alfar, or knowledge of them?"

"Mate, are you joking?" Ollie asked. "I'm from London."

"Aye, my folk are also urban," Gnat said.

The kobold only shrugged.

Rajah Singh shook his head. "My people know them as yakshas, but we have no ordinary commerce with them. When we see them, as we occasionally do, we regard it as a good omen for the next growing season."

It was up to Charlie, then. "Does anyone have a good gift?" he asked. "Something that a tree might like?"

They all shook their heads, other than the rajah.

"Yes," he said. "I might."

"Will you . . . give it to me?" Charlie asked.

"No." Rajah Amir Singh laughed. "But I will come with you to meet the yakshas, and I will offer it to *them*."

The rajah whispered something to his captain, who smiled broadly and left. Then Charlie and the rajah crossed to the other side of the stone circle, where an arm of lush green forest enveloped three of the stones.

Charlie rapped his knuckles on a stone, and thought back to when he'd seen Syzigon the dwarf do this same thing. "I wish to speak with the people of the woods!" he cried in English. For good measure, he called the same thing a second time, in the rajah's tongue.

As he finished his final word, two alfar strode from the woods and approached.

The rajah stared, eyes wide.

Like Pithsong and Tenderroot, the alfar Charlie had seen in England, these creatures were clearly trees, while at the same time they were obviously people. The first had dark, mahogany-colored skin and a riot of green hair like tiny leaves paired on long stems, falling down about a slyly grinning face. The second exploded in elongated red flowers, resembling bright bottle-cleaning brushes.

"Yakshas," the rajah murmured.

The tree people smiled. "Greetings, Prince. How prospers the plowed land?" asked the bottle-brush tree-person.

The rajah shook his head slowly. "Not as well as I would like, O yaksha. But every year a little better."

"And you," the mahogany tree-person said to Charlie. "You are an unusual person, and we do not know what words to say to you."

"I'm Charlie."

"I am Broadshade," said the dark tree.

"Blossomjoy," said the one with red flowers.

"And I am Amir," the rajah said.

"We have heard only once of a person such as you," Blossomjoy said to Charlie. "And that was far from here."

"I have met the people of the woods once," Charlie said. "Two of them. Their names were Pithsong and Tenderroot."

The two alfar made a creaking sound that resembled laughter, and leaned sideways, though into wind rather than away from it. "Then we have heard of you."

"We have . . . that is to say, Amir has . . . brought you a

gift." Charlie shot the rajah a sidelong glance, and the prince nodded his affirmation.

The rajah straightened his back and bowed his head, which had the strange effect of making him look both majestic and humble at the same time. "I have brought a gift, O yakshas, that is as low and simple as you can imagine. And yet it is a gift such as only a prince can give."

"Is your gift a riddle, then?" Broadshade asked.

"No. Behold!" The rajah flung his arm to one side, pointing at the far end of the stone circle. The captain of his bodyguard approached, at the head of a line of thirteen elephants.

Elephants? Charlie had a sudden vision of two offended alfar tearing him limb from limb. What would they possibly want with elephants?

But the alfar leaned and laughed again, and their sound was joyous. "This is a princely gift indeed, O Rajah Amir!" Blossomjoy bellowed.

Charlie felt a little silly, so he said nothing and just listened.

"For how long may we keep them?" Broadshade asked.

"They and their children are yours forever," the rajah said. "I believe they will live happily among you."

More alfar laughter. Charlie scratched his head.

"Their dung will warm our knees!" Broadshade cried.

"We will plant our saplings in it, and they will grow to be mighty trees, even as the trees of old that once covered all the lands!" Blossomjoy added.

Dung. Elephant dung.

Charlie found he had to shut his mouth to avoid looking as silly as he felt.

The alfar shivered with delight, and then Blossomjoy leaned in close to Charlie and the rajah. "And what gift may we give you, friend Amir and friend Charlie?"

"We would travel the Path of Root and Twig," Charlie said. "To a city far from here, called Moscow, and to a palace in the city called the Kremlin."

"We do not know this place," Broadshade said.

"We shall inquire," the two alfar said together.

Then they fell silent. Charlie looked to the rajah, but the rajah bowed his head and folded his hands together. It made him look like a supplicant, and that struck Charlie as a good posture. He bowed his own head and folded his hands.

The rain crashed hard upon them, and the warm wind blew so fiercely, Charlie was afraid it might knock over the stones themselves.

"The gift you ask is great," Blossomjoy said, "and we grant it with all our hearts. We do not fully understand your quest, Charlie, but some of the farthest-seeing members of the great world-forest, the redwoods and the baobabs and the oaks, speak up on your behalf."

"Thank you," Charlie and the rajah said together.

"The Path begins there." Broadshade pointed at the thickest tangle of dark green leaves at the edge of the circle, and then the alfar both stepped back and fell still. If he hadn't seen them moving and talking only moments earlier, Charlie might have taken them both for trees.

"Safe journey, Charlie." The rajah extended his hand in farewell. "May the winds always blow softly upon you."

"Thank you, Your Majesty." Charlie shook the offered

hand. "May the waters of your kingdom always be drinkable and gentle."

The bodyguard captain brought Charlie the cart, bowed, and then led the thirteen elephants into the forest. Charlie thought he saw the trees parting to let the herd enter.

The long pole extending in front of the cart had a crossbar at its end for yoking two draft animals. Charlie picked up one side of the crossbar, and Thomas picked up the other. Thomas looked nervous.

"You're going to love this," Charlie assured his brother. "When the forest catches you . . . just let it."

Thomas smiled weakly and nodded.

Gnat, Ollie, and Jan Wijmoor climbed aboard and hunkered down, getting as low as they could within the rickety wooden sides of the cart. "Wave goodbye, everyone!" Charlie shouted. "Here we go!"

He and Thomas ran onto the Path of Root and Twig, dragging the cart behind them.

Broad, dark leaves parted to make a way for them. Charlie was only a dozen steps into the forest when tendrils rose from the ground and from the undergrowth at either side to wrap themselves around his feet, ankles, and calves. They did the same to Thomas, and, looking back, Charlie saw that tendrils had also gripped the cart.

"By the Wheel!" Jan Wijmoor gasped, and then he collapsed below the edge of the cart and disappeared.

Ollie and Gnat remained looking at the path, faces peeping over the wood.

A final blast of hot, wet monsoon air slammed Charlie and his friends, and then a green curtain fell shut behind them and the wind was blocked, as if by a door. The temperature dropped noticeably, to a comfortable coolness. A green glow from no discernible source bathed the cart and its occupants.

The tendrils passed Charlie and Thomas forward. The wagon followed, also borne on the plants. Its wheels no longer rolled, because it wasn't touching the ground. In fact, looking down, Charlie wasn't certain there *was* ground beneath him.

"I don't know about this, Charlie." Thomas's eyes were shut, and he was frozen as if in fear.

"Just keep your eyes closed until you're ready," Charlie said. "Imagine that you're on a merry-go-round, or taking a ride in a steam-carriage."

Thomas said nothing.

Charlie leaned forward. His chimney-sweep friends had once joked about Charlie being the figurehead, the image carved into the front of a sailing ship. Now he imagined he *was* one, and that as he stretched outward, he could feel not only the cool ocean air but also the stinging salt slap of waves on his face.

He almost *smelled* the ocean.

And he almost forgot that he was racing to get to a pit underneath a palace in Moscow to cast a spell that would end his own life, as well as the life of his brother. That the spell would take away the kobolds' gift, and would also destroy the machines Rajah Singh used to improve the lives of his people.

Was this really a good plan?

But was there any alternative?

"Charlie, you're right!" Thomas cried.

Charlie opened his eyes and looked. Thomas lay forward almost horizontally. Tendrils wrapped around his belly and even his arms pushed him along, and he grinned at the Path ahead.

"That looks painful," Ollie grumbled.

It would have been, for a flesh-and-blood boy. Anything more tender than one of Syzigon's donkeys would arrive at the end of the Path of Root and Twig scratched, bruised, and maybe worse.

But Thomas was laughing merrily, and for a moment, that took all Charlie's cares away.

And then suddenly he found earth beneath his feet, and so did Thomas. They leaned forward into the crossbar, and the cart rolled easily behind them. A thick wall of branches parted before them, and the two boys pulled their friends out into a thickly forested park, beside a red brick wall. On the other side of the wall rose several towers topped with onion-shaped bulbs.

"That's it!" Jan Wijmoor pointed at the towers, his finger and his voice both shaking. "We've arrived."

◆ ◆ ◆

The palace and Her Majesty's government have both denied that rats have been admitted as emissaries to the Court of St. James.

—*Daily Telegraph*, "Rats in Carriages?" 19 July 1887

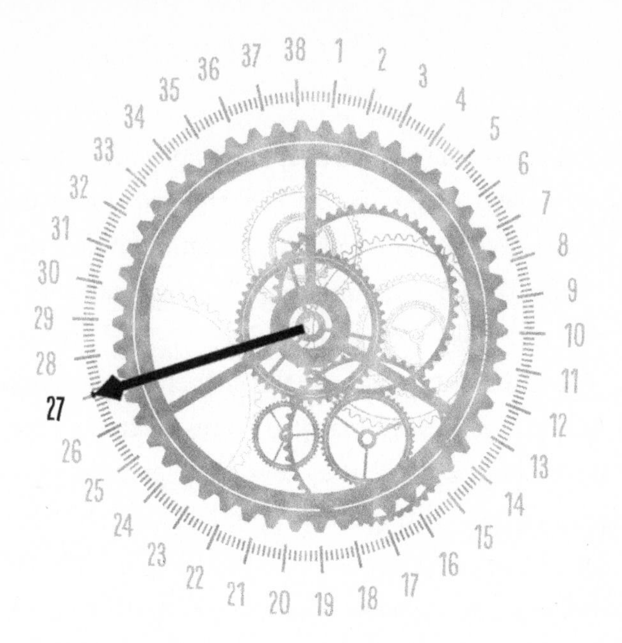

"Just tell me what I'm looking for, mate." Ollie pulled his bowler tight over his head.

"Are you sure about this?" Jan Wijmoor asked. "We could all go together."

Night had fallen. Ollie had volunteered to scout out the demon's pit and was now preparing to leave.

"All of us wandering around together like a circus looking for a tent is just asking to get caught," Ollie said. "I'm a professional; leave it to me. I only wish my mate Bob were here. He—I mean, *she*—was . . . I mean, *is* a dab hand with a lock."

"You're looking for the chapel," Jan Wijmoor said.

"Yeah, of course the demon pit is under the chapel," Ollie agreed. "I always figured every vicar I ever knew was up to no good; just goes to show you."

"The Romanovs built the chapel over the pit on purpose," Jan Wijmoor said. "A long time ago, they used to offer human sacrifices to the demon. The chapel was put there as a sort of a plug, or maybe a bandage. To heal the bad things that had once happened there, and to keep the demon in."

"A bit like the Foundation Stone," Charlie murmured.

The kobold looked at him blankly.

"How will I know I've found the chapel?" Ollie asked.

"Many, but very, very many, pictures of saints. The Russians are famous for this: they love their pictures of saints." Wijmoor snapped his finger and pointed at the sky. "An altar. Lots of gold paint everywhere. A little thing like a tower with a handrail looking down over it all, or a stage that will only fit one person."

"What's that for, then?" Thomas asked.

They all looked at each other and shrugged.

"Right," Ollie said. "Stay hidden; I'll be straight back."

With a puff of sulfurous smoke, Ollie was gone.

"What do you think your dad's plan was, once he got here?" Charlie asked Thomas.

Thomas shook his head. "He never told me, but just to guess by all the rockets and guns he had built into the mountain and into his airships . . . I expect he planned to shoot his way in. Or maybe only threaten to shoot, to get access. Or maybe he had a device that would dig a burrow? He had a lot of machines."

Charlie looked at the towers. "Maybe we could just knock, and ask whoever lives here."

"That would be the tsar," Jan Wijmoor said. "Alexander the Third. He's a very big man, and not very nice. They say he walks through doors without bothering to open them."

"I'm not sure about nice," Thomas said, "but that doesn't sound very *smart.*"

"Maybe," the kobold agreed. "But imagine someone who *can* walk through a shut door."

"Grim Grumblesson," Charlie said.

"Aye," Gnat agreed. "I was thinking the same, and wondering how the old bull was doing."

"That's right," the kobold said. "Think of a hulder without horns. And because his father was assassinated, Alexander believes his people have had too much freedom, and has spent his time on the throne taking that freedom back."

"He doesn't sound like a person who would welcome us," Charlie agreed.

They fell silent and listened to the whistling of night birds and the droning of insects.

Ollie returned without warning, standing up in a cloud of smoke. "I've found it. All we need's a bit of rope, easy-peasy."

"Aye, and if I know *you,*" Gnat said, "you've already got a rope."

Ollie chuckled. *Bamf!* In quick succession he was a snake and then a boy again, only this time he had a length of rope coiled over his shoulder.

They climbed the wall and dropped into a courtyard. Ollie pointed out the pacing guards, and then led them across cobblestones under a nearly full moon, hiding them in the dark shadow at the base of one of the towers. "That old moon'll help us," he assured the others. "It'll make the darkness darker, if you know what I mean. Now stay here just three minutes."

In snake form, Ollie slithered off.

Charlie and the others kept their silence, and then suddenly the end of Ollie's rope fell among them. The top of it disappeared into a tall, narrow window, several stories over their heads.

Ollie slid down the rope in snake form. "Now I'll go distract those guards. You all get up the rope quick as you can."

Gnat went up first, and then Jan Wijmoor, practically pushed by Thomas coming after him.

Ollie used the moonlight. He hid behind a steam-carriage out of sight of the nearest guard, but slowly danced, casting a long and moving shadow. When the guard approached—back turned to Charlie and his friends—Ollie changed into snake form and slithered away under the carriage.

He did a similar thing beside a lamppost, and then again atop the brick wall, and then it was Charlie's turn. He climbed the rope, and when he looked back, two guards in tall bearskin hats stood in the corner of the courtyard talking to each other and shrugging.

Ollie's shadow antics kept the guards looking the wrong way.

Then he came up the rope quickest of all and pulled it after him.

They descended the tower and walked through a couple of large rooms and a hall. Charlie immediately lost track of what turns he was taking, because the palace, even with its gaslights turned down low in their sconces, was an eye-dazzling assault of opulence. White columns, gold window frames, shining tiles that looked like the ocean itself, paintings and sculpture everywhere—this was what *real* wealth looked like, colossal wealth, and not the wealth accumulated by a merchant like the Iron Cog speculator William Bowen. This was the wealth of *kings.*

Charlie was impressed, but he also asked himself what these kings, these tsars, had done for their people.

Had they done as much as the Rajah Amir Singh wanted to do?

And if Charlie and Thomas bottled up the demon, would the rajah become just another king who lived in wealth on the backs of his people?

The chapel was as Jan Wijmoor had described it. The walls were absolutely covered with pictures of saints. Charlie knew they were supposed to be more than human because they all had golden halos painted around their heads. The paintings were sunk into recesses and separated by gold frames cast in the shapes of leaf-bearing vines.

And there was the strange little platform, but what interested Wijmoor was the altar. "Can you push this aside?" he asked Thomas and Charlie.

It was a heavy piece of stone, but together they could move it.

Under the altar, steps led down into darkness.

"Gnat will be able to see," Charlie said. "But what about the rest of us?"

"Don't you worry, mate," Ollie said. "I've got you covered. You ever heard of a snake called the moonbeam snake?"

"No," Charlie admitted.

"This is what we wizards do in our spare time." Ollie tapped one finger to his temple. "Reading. Only we call it *research*."

Bamf! Ollie transformed into a snake, paler than his usual coloring, a whitish green. Other than the distinctive shade, Charlie saw nothing out of the ordinary, until Ollie the snake slithered down the steps into the darkness—

and began to glow.

The snake hissed and descended. Charlie and his friends followed.

The demon's pit was shaped like the inside of a jug: the steps spiraled down a narrow well, uneven and rough, and then the well opened up into a larger cavern, and the steps tumbled eventually to a flat stone floor.

Ollie slithered out into the center and coiled up, acting like a light.

Grooves crossed the floor in a pattern Charlie couldn't decipher, but all of them ended in a deeper pit, a ragged hole in the center of the floor. Charlie looked into the grooves and saw thick brown grime, something now coagulated that had once flowed across the stone to fall into the chasm.

Three dimples in the stone surrounded the pit at equal angles, like the points of an equilateral triangle. Thomas walked promptly to the one farthest from him, pulled the unicorn horn from his coat, and knelt to push it into the hole.

"Is that all there is to this? To the spell?" Charlie wanted to resist. Or at least to wait, to think about it a little longer.

The world had turned out to be so much more confusing than Charlie had ever expected when he'd passed his nights reading books in the attic above Pondicherry's Clockwork Invention & Repair. Many of the books he'd trusted to teach him about the world had turned out to be wrong, or partly right, or accurate but so offensive that well-meaning people destroyed them. And people he admired and respected had terrible ideas, while other people who seemed like villains to him claimed to be acting from benevolent motives, or said things that seemed to be true.

His head was spinning, and if he took a wrong step now, the magic that fueled him might stop working. Of course, if he made a different wrong step, the Iron Cog might destroy London.

He wanted to slow down and think it through.

"No," Thomas said, "there's more. We pound in two of the nails. I know some words, and a sort of . . . dance. Those will summon the demon back into this hole, and then we pound in the third nail. And then it's done."

"It don't sound safe, being down here with a demon," Ollie grumbled.

"It won't be safe." Thomas looked at Charlie. "I think my father planned to do the magic himself, and I was only a backup. And I don't think he planned to survive."

Charlie nodded. "And once you've done it, you and I . . ."

"We'll have done what we were made for. What our fathers created us to do. We'll be successful, Charlie; we'll be heroes. We'll have stopped the Iron Cog."

"*We* won't survive."

And Charlie wasn't certain that was why his father had made him anyway.

Jan Wijmoor wept softly.

Why had he wanted to come along with them, really? Why not stay in Marburg, like the Rosenbaums?

Thomas walked to a second hole in the floor—

"Thomas!" Charlie cried.

Thomas ignored him. He knelt and pushed in the cold-iron knife.

"You're very brave, Thomas," Charlie said. "You're braver than I am."

"Maybe we'll stop." Thomas's face looked stricken as he spoke. "Probably. But this is the thing I was made to do. It's the thing I *have* to do."

Thomas was willing to die.

And Charlie realized that *he* was willing too. But he also realized that his own death wasn't really what was bothering him.

"Forget about *us,*" Charlie said. "What about the rajah and his people? Won't their pumps stop? And their tractors?"

Thomas nodded.

"And the mechanical libraries. And the airships. And the Sky Trestle in London, and Big Ben. All of it will stop. And all the inventions that *could* happen, in the future. Who knows what those could be? Travel to the moon . . . cures for terrible diseases . . . tractors that make food cheap and plentiful." He thought of the rajah and smiled. "The dwarf wizard was right, at least in this one thing he said. Magic isn't good or evil;

inventions aren't good or evil. Those things are just tools. Taking the tools away from the world may take away someone's power to do evil, but it also takes away someone else's power to do good. Of course, Suleiman wanted to lock up all the technology for himself, and that isn't the right answer either. If we really trap this demon, all those good inventions will stop."

"And so will the Cog," Thomas said. "With their part-machine soldiers and their part-machine beasts."

"Will they *stop*?" Charlie asked. "I know that was your father's idea, but what if he was wrong? Will the Cog give up, or will they just find a different way to accomplish what they want? Their goals sound lovely—peace and plenty—but to get there they want to control everybody. They're trying to do it using machines, and I don't really entirely understand how, but if they lose the machines, won't they just try the same thing another way?"

"What other way?" Thomas took two steps toward the third hole in the floor. If he began to chant or dance, what would Charlie do? Would he tackle his brother and try to stop the magic?

"War," Charlie said. "They've already shown they're willing to go to war, and they don't need fancy machines to do that. Guns, knives, poison, clubs, fists. There are lots of ways to hurt and bully people, Thomas. Whatever we do today won't put an end to people being cruel. But we can make it harder for the rajah's people to get water, and for the students in Marburg to learn. We can take Thomas out of the world, and that would be a loss."

"Yes, there's war," Thomas said. "There's war coming to *London,* the pixies said! We can do something about it. Are you saying we should do nothing instead? That doesn't really seem like my brother Charlie. Or is this just your nature? My father made me shy to keep me out of the hands of his enemies. You told me once that your father made you disobedient for the same reason. Are you sure you aren't just resisting because your bap designed you to resist?"

Charlie laughed. "No, I'm not sure. And are you sure you aren't just following your father's plan, because that's what *he* made *you* to do?"

Thomas shook his head slowly. "I'm not sure of anything."

"I'm sure of one thing," Charlie said. "My brother Thomas is as magnificent as a tractor, and the world is better off because he is in it."

Thomas smiled. "What do we do, Charlie?"

Charlie thought for a moment. "We try to do what Papa Wilhelm said. We try to make a world where people can be happy, and where they can also be free."

Thomas nodded.

Charlie gently took the third nail, the nail of the intellectual world, from his brother's hands. "I'll hold this, in case we need it. But I think if we go back to London, we can find another way."

"What's in London?" Thomas asked. "Besides the danger?"

"My friends Ingrid and Grim. Lloyd, I think. The queen—she doesn't know me, but she's seen me."

"And is that enough?" Thomas asked. "Is that enough friends and allies to stop the Iron Cog?"

"Maybe not," Charlie said. "But I think we have to try."

"Okay, Charlie. I'm willing to try." Thomas looked briefly at his feet, but then he looked up again, smiling. "I've never been to London."

Charlie grinned. "We're world travelers, you and I."

"And so am I!" cried a new voice.

It belonged to Heinrich Zahnkrieger, the kobold Charlie had once known as his father's partner, Henry Clockswain, but who had spied on Charlie's father and betrayed him. Zahnkrieger wore a bulky airman's suit and goggles, as if he'd just stepped off an airship, and a large rucksack strapped to his back. He climbed slowly down the stairs into the chamber, pointing a brass wand at Charlie.

"I'm glad to see you, my friends," Zahnkrieger said.

He muttered quick words—Charlie didn't hear them clearly, and the Babel Card didn't help—and Charlie felt his body freeze.

Gnat leaped forward to attack, and an arc of blue light leaped from the tip of Zahnkrieger's wand. It struck the pixie in mid-leap and knocked her to the cavern floor.

She groaned.

"I came directly here from Cader Idris." Zahnkrieger smiled. "It's about time you caught up."

Having voted in full session, and noting expressed dissent, the Committee hereby orders as follows:

1. That no nonhuman may travel the highways and byways of London between sunset and sunrise.
2. That individual creatures of the following species shall require a license, which may be issued by a borough council upon a showing of non-hostility: krakens, dragons, giants, mastodons, and any insect greater than six feet in length.

The foregoing measure is adopted for the safety of our law-abiding elder folk, and shall remain in effect until withdrawn by this Committee.

—Committee for the Investigation of Anti-Human Crime, Order No. 1

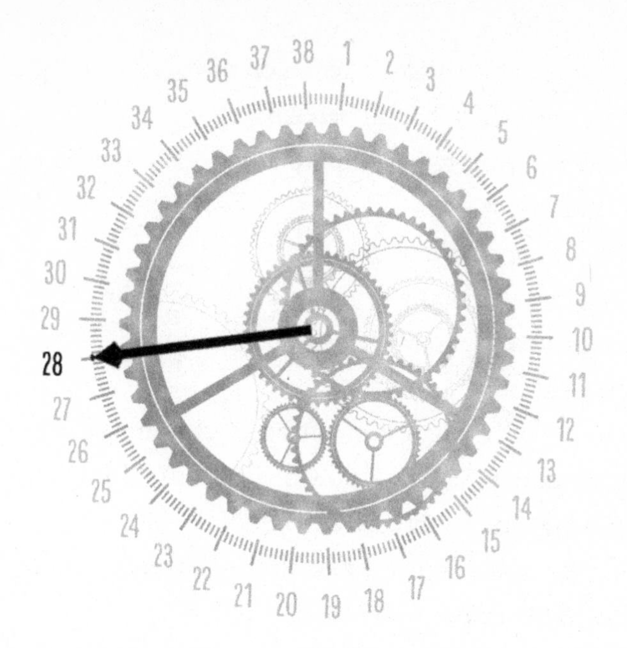

"Heinrich," Jan Wijmoor said. "Please don't do this."

"Do what, *Meneer Doktor*?" Zahnkrieger asked. His sneer twisted the other kobold's titles into an insult.

"You can make the world a better place in many ways," Wijmoor said. "But not this way. Not forcing people."

"How odd." Zahnkrieger reached the bottom of the stairs and stopped. He smiled at Wijmoor, stroking the straps of his rucksack. "That's not what you said when they were stripping me of my degrees and titles, and beating me with carter's whips, and throwing me out of the Syndikat."

"I was wrong." Wijmoor gulped. "As you are wrong now. I've regretted it since, and not only because it drove you into the arms of those people. But at the time, I did what I thought I *had* to do. For the Syndikat."

"As I do what I think I have to do now." Zahnkrieger nodded. "For the world. For all peoples."

The redcap muttered obscure words that the Babel Card didn't translate.

"Hey!" Thomas shouted.

"What are you doing to my brother?" Charlie yelled.

Zahnkrieger tightened one shoulder strap. "If he resists, he'll only get hurt."

Thomas's head wiggled in outrage, but from the neck down he was absolutely still as Zahnkrieger plucked the nail of the intellectual world from Charlie's hand.

Then the kobold turned and threw the chalky spike down the hole in the center of the floor.

"There," he said. "Fixed."

"You can't take away everyone's right to disagree," Wijmoor said.

"Psh, *right.*" Zahnkrieger laughed. "You have gotten so metaphysical, Meneer Doktor. When did my old thesis advisor cease being an engineer and become a professor of philosophy?"

"I'm still just a grinder of gearwheels and polisher of ball bearings," Wijmoor said. "I've made plenty of mistakes. But I know what's wrong. And I recognize madness when I see it."

"We're not going to take away from anyone any *right.*" Zahnkrieger continued as if Wijmoor hadn't spoken. "We're going to take away the *ability* to disagree. From everyone. For their own sakes."

"What makes you think you'll get out of this pit alive?"

Gnat looked up from the floor, gripping the Hound's tooth hanging from her neck.

Zahnkrieger patted the strap to his rucksack. "I have a device," he said. "But if I die here, the Cog carries out the plan without me. I am completely redundant at this point."

"But if *I* die here, my folk will never stand for it," Gnat snarled.

"Ah, yes, Underthames."

"You *are* mad," Charlie said. "What you're talking about is impossible."

"You of all people—or should I say, of all *things*?—ought to know better, Charlie." Zahnkrieger rubbed his hands together. "You were built to *disobey,* but that was a perversion of the technology Joban Singh was working on."

Charlie felt cold all over. "You're lying."

Zahnkrieger shook his head. "The first generation of experimentation was Wilhelm Grimm, who trapped his own soul in a device with the help of his brother. The second was you two, Charlie and Thomas, the creation of a new soul in a device. And of course the rabbit, which was how Brunel tested the broadcasting technology."

Broadcasting? Charlie thought of the visions Aunt Big Money had given him, and the dreams. "What do you mean?"

But Zahnkrieger pulled at a thread on his airman's suit and continued, ignoring him. "The third generation was the Hound, and now the machine soldiers. The use of the spirit stone to connect a living soul to a part-flesh and part-mechanical body. The fourth generation, and where we have been going all along, is the use of a machine to control living souls, through the medium of the powdered spirit stone."

Charlie stared.

Zahnkrieger smiled. "A little bit inhaled, Charlie, just a little of the same substance that makes you so marvelous. Breathed in or swallowed, in a glass of water. Don't you want everyone else to be as wonderful as you are? But the little bit we'll put into them will take away their power to disobey. We will broadcast, and everyone who has taken in the spirit stone will do as they are told. For their own good, of course. You know what I'm talking about, Charlie. The constant war between rats and pixies will end when the rats and pixies are all under our control. Everyone benefits; everyone prospers. That oaf Grim Grumblesson will stop fretting about who marries whom once he's no longer making the decisions."

"You would enslave my people!" Gnat stood.

"We'll try. Anyone too stubborn to surrender to the powder will have to be controlled . . . or put out of the way . . . by other means."

Gnat hissed.

"Heinrich here was my student, Charlie." Jan Wijmoor's voice creaked with pain. "Many years ago. And his thesis—the research he wanted to do—was on the Library Machine."

"You don't mean the card catalog," Charlie said. "You mean Papa Wilhelm."

"That's exactly right. Wilhelm Grimm managed to connect his spirit to a white stone, which let him live beyond his natural death."

"He called it the spirit stone," Charlie said. And then Charlie realized what Papa Wilhelm had been trying to tell him, that part of the magic that made Charlie work must be that a bit of the spirit stone was inside Charlie himself. And another bit was inside Thomas—that was what really made them brothers, and Papa Wilhelm and Aunt Big Money their family.

"His brother Jacob found it. The stone also connected Wilhelm to mechanical devices," Jan Wijmoor continued. "Such as the projector and the gate that you know. Such as the card catalog, which Wilhelm powered. You saw the spirit stone—it was buried beneath the library. And Heinrich believed that the same connection could be used to control people."

"I did not *believe*." Heinrich straightened the front of his suit. "I inferred from the data. And Singh and Brunel proved me right!"

"He stole pieces of the stone." Wijmoor's shoulders slumped. "We never found it—the evidence wasn't conclusive, as I testified on his behalf—but at his review, the Internal Auditor determined that he should be terminated."

"Killed?" Thomas asked.

"Exiled," Zahnkrieger snarled. "But then the pebbles for which I had risked my life and my career were stolen from me, by those ingrates Joban Singh and Isambard Kingdom Brunel."

Gnat took a step forward.

"Stop!" Zahnkrieger barked. "Or I leave, and seal you in."

"That's the stone inside me," Charlie said. "And Thomas. And Aunt Big Money."

Jan Wijmoor looked at Charlie and smiled sadly. "You boys have souls, I believe. Or maybe you have a portion of Wilhelm Grimm's soul, but who's to say that isn't the same thing?"

"And then, after testifying on my behalf," Zahnkrieger growled, "which is to say, telling the board of directors that they were probably right that I was a thief, but that without definitive proof they should *merely* demote me and put me on probation—"

"You *were* a thief!" Wijmoor shouted.

Zahnkrieger smiled slowly. "Very well. You were then content to *control* me, to take away *my* freedom, to meddle in *my* destiny. You were perfectly happy to side with the Internal Auditor and the board and see me thrown to the wolves."

"The wolves didn't eat you," Wijmoor observed, pointing a slow and weary finger at the ceiling. "You joined their pack."

Heinrich Zahnkrieger threw back his head and laughed. "So true. But don't worry, soon enough there will only be sheep, one happy bleating flock to be regularly sheared and occasionally, happily, eaten."

"Did my father know you were in the Iron Cog?" Charlie was afraid of how the rest of Zahnkrieger's story would go.

Zahnkrieger shook his head. "I'll give you this gift, Charlie, to prove my good intentions. Your father and Brunel were innocent men. They knew the Cog as an honorable association of thinkers and noblemen, with the aim of benefiting all people—which is true, of course. We brought them to the work and kept its full nature hidden from them, believing that they would scruple at some of the plan's details. So your father believed he was creating artificial life, for purely disinterested and benevolent purposes. And when he found schematics that revealed to him what we were truly attempting, he and Brunel both fled."

"But *you,*" Charlie said. "He must not have known *you*. Or he never would have taken you as his business partner in the shop."

"I supervised him in secret," the kobold agreed.

"And the fake Queen Victoria?" Charlie asked. "You needed my father to activate her. It."

"That's true." Zahnkrieger nodded. "We chose Singh and Brunel because they were the best engineers we could find working on simulated persons. But since the events of the Jubilee, we've been able to recover the false Victoria and reverse engineer the work your father did. We've deployed it in Prussia, for instance."

"Bismarck," Jan Wijmoor said. "You've replaced him with an automaton, and the automaton has declared the war you wanted."

"Which very conveniently let us take Hesse and Marburg. We have the stone now," Zahnkrieger continued, still talking to Charlie. "And we've mastered the technology. So we don't need your father or Brunel. And we don't need you."

"You just came to stop us from stoppering up the demon." Charlie's heart sank.

"I've been waiting here for weeks. Since I last saw you." Zahnkrieger raised his hands. "My fingers still hurt from you stomping on them, as does the back of my head from that bottle." He glared at the pixie.

"Aye, I'll be sure to use something sharper this time," Gnat growled.

"There will be no 'this time.'" Zahnkrieger twisted one of his suit's buttons. "Your journey ends here."

"And how will you escape," Gnat asked in a suddenly sweet, calm voice, "if you cannot see?"

It was a signal to Ollie.

Bamf! Charlie smelled rotten eggs, and with the disappearance of the moonbeam snake, the cave was plunged into near-complete darkness. A faint glimmer of yellow light filtered down from the gaslights in the chapel above.

Thud! Pffffffffffffft!

A hissing sound filled the room, and then Charlie heard Gnat cursing. Something spherical blocked off the light, and then came the patter of Gnat's feet.

"Light, Ollie!" Gnat cried.

Bamf! Ollie dropped back into his moonbeam snake shape, and Charlie could see again.

Gnat sprinted up the circular stairs as fast as her tiny legs could take her, but it wasn't going to be fast enough. Jan Wijmoor now rushed after her, but he was even slower.

Ollie hissed in frustration.

Where Heinrich Zahnkrieger had stood, a steel canister lay on the floor. A balloon had sprouted out of the kobold's rucksack, and it now carried him quickly up to the top of the chamber. The kobold had to duck and bring in his arms and legs to be small enough for the bottleneck, but he grinned as he did so.

"Goodbye, my friends!" he cried.

Then, as the kobold neared the ceiling, he unclipped an object resembling a pocket watch from his belt and touched it with his other hand.

Ka-boom!

Starting ten feet in front of Gnat and running all the way to the top of the cave, the stairs erupted into billows of powdered rock. Charlie turned his face away, still unable to move his body, as rock chips struck his skin and stung him.

Gnat stopped at the edge of the cloud. Wijmoor caught up to her and stood at her shoulder; they both looked anxiously into the dust.

Heinrich Zahnkrieger escaped up the hole in the ceiling.

With a heavy scraping sound and a bang, the glimmer of light from above disappeared.

The dust settled, and the stairs were gone.

Whitehall has confirmed today what the *Telegraph* has heard from its foreign correspondents: the kaiser and his power-mad minister president, Otto von Bismarck, have declared war on France.

—*Daily Telegraph*, "Prussia Declares War on France," 18 July 1887

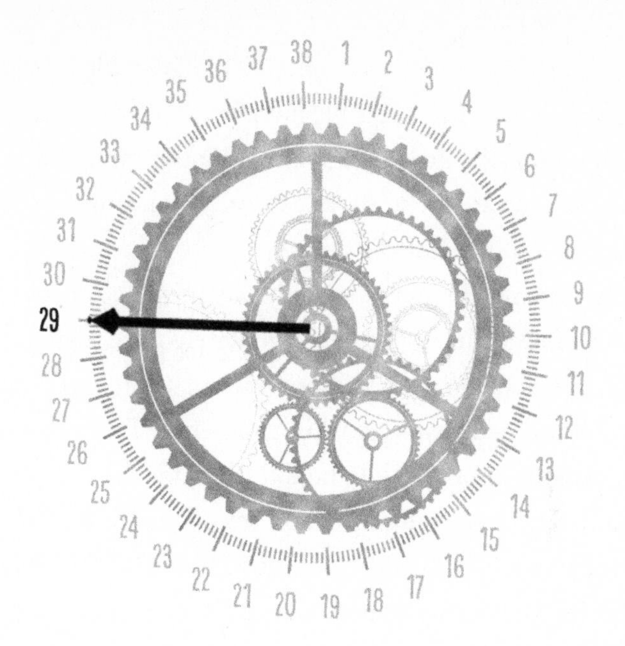

Bamf!

The cave went completely dark.

"You rotten little kobold!" Ollie shouted. "Liar! Thief! Weasel! Traitor! I knew when I first met you that you deserved to have your nose punched, and when I get out of here, that's the first thing I'm going to do!"

When he fell silent, his words echoed a few seconds longer.

"Aye," Gnat agreed. "Well said."

"I had to get that off my chest," Ollie said. "Shall I turn back into the snake, so you can have some light?"

"I don't need it," Gnat said.

"I can't move anyway," Thomas added.

"I can't either," Charlie said.

"He must have had a machine," Ollie grumbled. "No way he could move that altar on his own."

"If you give us a little light," Jan Wijmoor said, "I'll restore the lads. I'd do it in the darkness, only I'm afraid of falling into the hole in the floor."

Ollie became the glowing snake again. Gnat checked the stairs and found the upper half completely gone, which made the exit unreachable. Jan Wijmoor opened a hatch in Thomas's back and reached inside; within moments, Thomas had regained full movement. Then he did the same for Charlie.

The friends gathered at the bottom of the stairs, and Ollie returned to boy form. In the darkness, they sat and thought.

Back on the mountain of Cader Idris, Aunt Big Money had told Charlie that he had heaven and hell both within him. At the time, he'd thought those were poetic words, but now he understood they meant something rather specific, and strangely contradictory. His machinery was demonic—though from a demon whose works benefited people in amazing ways. And his spirit was from a magical stone—though one whose power could apparently be used to deprive large masses of people of their free will.

"You know, Meneer Doktor," he said. "I thought of you as a person who had come into my story, but more and more it seems like *I'm* a person who has come into *your* story."

"Yes?" The kobold's face was glum.

"My story is about a boy who couldn't save his father, and is trying to save the world instead," Charlie said.

Jan Wijmoor sniffed and trembled.

"Nay, lad." Gnat's voice was gentle. "You're far too hard on yourself."

Charlie continued. "But your story started first. Your story is about how you tried to stop your student from breaking the Syndikat's rules."

"I should have lied," Jan Wijmoor said. "If I'd lied to cover for him, he wouldn't have been punished, and I could have won him back from the Iron Cog."

"Maybe," Charlie said. "But maybe not. Instead you told the truth and asked the Internal Auditor to show him mercy. But the punishment he got was too much for him, and you've been sad ever since."

"I feel responsible." Wijmoor sighed.

"That's why you've been so willing to help me and Charlie," Thomas said. "Helping us is a bit like helping your old student."

"My story is about a teacher who didn't protect his student when he should have," Wijmoor said. "So when the teacher got a second chance, he jumped at it."

"How is it, Thomas," Gnat asked, "that you led us straight to Marburg, and the place where Heinrich Zahnkrieger was a young engineer?"

Thomas shrugged. "The dwarfs who brought my father his things told me about Marburg and the landgrave's museum, so I knew there was a unicorn horn there."

"Those dwarfs—they wear purple-and-white trousers—work for the Cog," Charlie said. "So they may have heard about Marburg from Heinrich himself."

"All true stories go in circles," Ollie said. "A good story ends where it started, don't it?"

"And there's a part of the story in the middle," Wijmoor added, "a part I don't know. About how Heinrich advanced his research by manipulating your fathers, boys."

"Aye. Until they discovered the true nature of the conspiracy and fled."

They were silent awhile. "Speaking of stories," Ollie said, "I don't reckon your kobold stories know about a way out of the pit? I mean, other than the one in the ceiling."

"No," Wijmoor said glumly.

"Give me a couple of days, and I'll regrow my wings," Gnat said. "Then I can go look down in the hole."

Nobody said anything to that, but they all must have been thinking what Charlie was thinking—there could be no exit down in the hole, and if there was, it surely went to someplace even worse than this. A demon world of some kind.

"I think I'm strong enough to push that altar aside, even from below," Charlie said.

"Yeah," Ollie agreed, "I reckon you are. Which is why Zahnkrieger took care to get rid of the stairs, so you couldn't even reach the altar."

"Could we jump?" Thomas suggested.

So Ollie became the moonbeam snake, and slithered about the chamber while Charlie and Thomas tried jumping. With a running start, Charlie found he could leap high enough to bump against the underside of the altar, but not with enough impetus to move it aside. Thomas couldn't quite reach the altar. They took turns winding each other's mainspring to refresh themselves after their efforts, and then they resumed their conversation in the dark.

"Could we dig out?" Jan Wijmoor asked.

"The walls are all rock," Gnat said. "And we have no tools. I think not."

"Maybe there's a way for something smaller to get out," Charlie suggested. "Such as a snake. And if Ollie could get out, he could bring help."

"Already looked, mate." Ollie's voice sounded distracted in the darkness. "There's no snake holes or rat holes or anything I can get out through, unless they're down that pit in the floor."

"Perhaps I could make a machine that would help us," Wijmoor said. "Something like a mechanical lever. And if I could build it, then in two days, when Gnat has regrown her wings, she could fly the lever up to the top of the cave and use it to remove the altar."

There was a moment's silence.

"Build a machine out of what, exactly?" Thomas asked.

There was a longer silence.

"Well," Wijmoor said, "I'd have to use parts from you and Charlie. I'm not sure how many. Maybe I could take both your legs, and use them to build a lever. Or at most, I think, I could disassemble just one of you; that would be enough."

"Disassemble . . ." Charlie grabbed his bap's broken pipe in his pocket and squeezed it. "And could you then reassemble me?" He said *me* deliberately. If one of the mechanical brothers was going to sacrifice himself, it would be Charlie. It was

Charlie's fault they were in this mess, since it was Charlie who had talked Thomas into hesitating, and not casting the spell he'd been designed to cast.

"Physically, yes." The kobold hesitated. "I don't really know how the white stone works. I've seen it inside you, and I see the connections it makes, but . . . once I've pulled it out, I'm not sure I could make it work again."

"I'm willing to take the risk," Charlie said quickly, to forestall Thomas from volunteering. "Unless . . . there's anything else we could try."

"Yeah," Ollie said. Suddenly his voice sounded very weary. "It was a wizard who brought you down here, and I reckon I know how a wizard can bring you out."

Charlie imagined some trick with the metaphysical space that surrounded Ollie. "Maybe you could put us all where you keep the snake," he said, enthusiastic with the hope that he wouldn't have to die so his friends could escape, "and then push us out somewhere else."

"I dunno about that, mate. I have a different plan. Here, I'll give you a bit of light, and I suggest you all crouch down in the corner of the room and keep your heads low."

"What are you going to do?" the kobold asked, but Ollie had already become the moonbeam snake.

Charlie, Thomas, Gnat, and Jan Wijmoor huddled at the base of the stairs, and then the room returned to darkness again.

"Right," Ollie said in the darkness. "Here goes nothing."

Bamf! The sulfur stink was stronger than Charlie had smelled before, and Jan Wijmoor coughed.

“I don’t know what good that will do us, Ollie,” Gnat said. “Though you’re impressive, to be sure.”

Bamf! “Give a fellow a chance, Baroness.”

What was Ollie doing?

“Nay, I’m not the baroness, and I may never become it.”

“I reckon you’ll have to,” Ollie said, “if you want to save your people.”

Bamf!

“Aye, that’s a good trick!” Gnat said. “But I still don’t see . . . Oh, lad, do you really think you can do it?”

Bamf! The rotting-egg smell was so thick that Jan Wijmoor gagged, retching into the corner of the room.

Ollie groaned. “This ain’t as easy as it looks.”

“It doesn’t look easy,” Charlie said. “I can’t see *anything.*”

“I’m changing shape,” Ollie told him. His voice was slow and heavy.

“Yeah, I can smell *that*!” Charlie snapped. “What are you doing?”

There was a long pause. “One more try,” Ollie said.

“Will you survive it, lad?” Gnat asked.

“Dunno. Too big a spell can kill a magician; there’s lots of stories about that. But since *none* of us will survive me *not* doing it . . . I reckon I’ll try. And I’ve done the research. I’m a wizard, Gnat. I’m a wizard or I’m nothing. I’ll give it a try.”

Gnat was slow to answer. “Aye, lad,” she finally said. “Do it.”

“Do what?” Charlie nearly yelled.

BAMF!

Jan Wijmoor vomited from the stench.

"By all my mothers before me!" Gnat murmured. "Ollie?"

A jet of orange flame appeared near the ceiling. It began small, but even at its smallest, it cast enough light to illuminate a vast scaly bulk, with four legs, gigantic claws, and a long, sinewy tail.

Then the jet grew longer, in a whoosh of hot air like an exhalation. Charlie saw the long neck, the thick tufts of hair on the shoulders, the batlike wings that, even folded, were vast, the head that was half horse and half iguana . . .

And, improbably, the tiny bowler hat perched on top.

Ollie had transformed into a dragon.

"There." Ollie's voice was much deeper and rumbled around the cavern, but it was unmistakably Ollie. "That feels . . . much better."

"Ollie!" Charlie leaped to his feet. "You did it!"

"I'm a wizard," Ollie roared. "And I ain't French."

"Be careful, lad," Gnat urged Ollie the dragon. "If you knock down chunks of stone, it may crush us."

"Also," Thomas added, "you don't want to lose your hat."

"Yes." When Ollie opened his mouth to speak, he revealed a ball of fire that burned steadily at the back of his throat. As Ollie spoke, that light flickered on and off in the cavern. Cautiously, Ollie raised his torso off the floor, creating a hollow under his gigantic scaly armpit that was shielded by his dragon body. His voice still sounded tired, but it also sounded enormous. It sounded elemental, as if Ollie were closer at this moment to being a mountain or a storm than he was to being a boy. "Come take shelter under me."

They all scrambled to hide beneath Ollie's body, but Charlie couldn't resist crouching at the edge, most of himself protected behind the vast wall of scaly muscle Ollie had become, but his face out. So he could watch.

Ollie the dragon rammed his head up the bottleneck. In a single thrust, he knocked aside the altar and shattered the cavern's ceiling. Chunks of stone and gold-covered furniture began to fall into the pit, and Charlie jumped back under Ollie for safety.

CRA-A-ASH!

Rubble blocked their view. Then they heard more and louder crashing sounds, then silence.

"This dragon smells a little sweaty," Thomas said. "I'm not complaining; I'm just noticing."

With a single sweep, the dragon's tail wrapped itself around the rubble and thrust it aside, freeing Charlie and the others.

"Climb onto my shoulders," Ollie told them.

They did. He was as big as two omnibuses and his scales were mostly very smooth, but Ollie lay on his side to make it easier for them. Their going got easier once they reached his spine, where there were spikes to grip, and they settled themselves in his tufts of black shoulder hair, as large as bushes.

Ollie's hat was battered and dusty now, but it was still on his head. "Where shall we go?"

"To London!" Charlie called.

Ollie craned his long neck around to look at his friends and nodded. "Hold on."

Then Ollie the dragon straightened out his neck and body. The hole above them had become large, and Ollie had apparently smashed part of the palace, too, because Charlie looked up along the dragon's neck at the full moon.

He heard shouting, which the Babel Card quickly organized into "Foreigners! Subversives! Criminals! Kill the beast!"

Ollie leaped into the air. He might have been as big as two omnibuses and tired to boot, but he was fast and strong, and in a single bound he was out of the pit and two stories above the earth. Guards in bearskin hats raised rifles and pointed them at Ollie.

He flapped his wings, and the rush of wind knocked the guards flat—

and launched Ollie high into the air.

In the moonlight, Ollie glowed bright yellow.

"Ollie!" Charlie cried, yelling over the wind in his face as the lights of Moscow grew tiny below him. "You're made of gold!"

Ollie roared wordlessly, breathing a column of fire into the cool night air.

Soon the lights below them disappeared entirely, leaving only the moon and the stars.

When the sun rose, it was at their backs, and before them lay the mouth of the Thames and London.

PART FIVE

THE COG CITY

The Ministry of Defense has announced today the deployment of a new type of soldier. Called Mechanically Augmented Fighting Units, these soldiers will be instantly recognizable due to their possessing one or more mechanical limbs, permanently integrated into their flesh. In an initial testing phase whose duration has not yet been determined, the MAFUs have been deployed in the capital as policemen and fire bobbies.

—*Daily Telegraph*, "New Troops Deployed," 20 July 1887

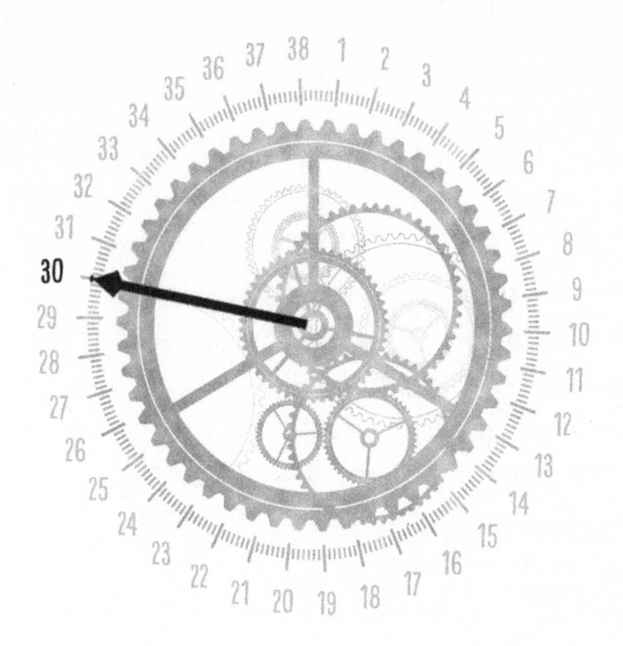

"Maybe we should land somewhere out of the way," Charlie suggested as Ollie began to descend. "Somewhere outside the city, for instance, and ride in on a train. So as not to attract attention, you know."

Ollie laughed, a boom so loud it shook Charlie's body. "Oh, we're going to attract some attention. I'm going to Westminster, mate. Straight to Parliament, and we're going to set everything right."

Charlie gripped Ollie's shoulder fur tight and leaned out to look at the city below. He thought he recognized Whitechapel, including Irongrate Lane and maybe even the Gullet. Then he saw the dome of St. Paul's Cathedral.

"Stop!" Charlie cried.

Ollie flapped his wings once to brake and rise, circling slowly back. "What for?"

"I saw Grim," Charlie said. "On Ludgate Hill. By the cathedral. He was with . . . I don't know, he looked very official."

"Grim?" Gnat laughed. "Nay, that doesn't sound right."

"Who is Grim?" Jan Wijmoor asked.

"He was Charlie's lawyer." Ollie laughed, a sound like rolling thunder.

Ollie settled on the stone wall over Ludgate. As the crowd babbled and stared, he lowered his long neck so that Charlie and the others could climb down it and onto the ground, onto the steps of the cathedral.

Down the street and on the other side of it, smoke belched from the broken front window of a shop. A band of fire bobbies in their helmets and long coats pumped water through the front window.

Some of the fire bobbies wore conical masks, like the beaks of birds. Something about that seemed familiar to Charlie, and troubling, but he couldn't immediately figure out what.

Two police carriages, a dozen policemen, and a somber group of people who looked like lawyers stood interviewing a shopkeeper in the shop next door to where the fire burned. Holding back the crowd of spectators was a handful of rough-looking trolls in long brown coats.

Two of the serious people were hulders, and one of them was Charlie's friend.

"Grim!" Charlie cried.

But something about the scene made him hang back. Grim

looked haggard, and reluctant, and even from behind, Charlie thought he knew the other hulder too.

Grim turned. "Charlie." Grim's face looked tired, his eyes red. He crossed the street to Charlie. "When did you get back to London? Where are Bob and Ollie?"

"We just landed." Charlie pointed at Ollie the dragon.

Grim frowned. "Gnat, what happened to your wings?"

"What are you talking about, Grumblesson?" Gnat crossed her arms over her chest and glared.

The other hulder strolled in their direction, steam puffing from his shoulder. It was Egil One-Arm! Charlie stared, and Grim sighed.

"Yes," he said. "Many things have happened in a short time. Maybe you shouldn't have come back. Egil and I work with a committee to—"

"Grim!" Charlie whispered. "The Iron Cog have a plan to take over the city!"

Grim furrowed his brow. "We caught the Frenchman St. Jacques sneaking into England in an unregistered montgolfier. I had him in a cell, but he escaped. Not sure the committee would have let me hold him, anyway."

Committee? Egil hadn't quite yet reached them, so Charlie continued softly. "There's this powder. And if they can make people breathe it . . . or maybe drink it, or both, then—"

Ollie launched abruptly into the air, shrieking.

Egil arrived. "Is that dragon licensed?" he asked.

Grim looked at Ollie. "Haven't had a chance to ask. It has no military insignia. Is it wild?"

Egil pointed. "Don't worry, they've got it."

Two other dragons, each as large as Ollie, but one black and one green, sped from west London. They wore regimental colors, and each had a rider seated on its back like an elephant's mahout, behind a rotating turret with a gun mounted on it. The green and black dragons chased after Ollie, who flew straight up.

"Grim," Charlie said, "that yellow dragon is *Ollie.*"

"Ollie?" Grim frowned. "Ollie!"

"Look, you're under arrest," Egil said. "The pixie and the kobold and, for good measure, the metal boy." He waved at Thomas. "You too, while I'm at it. Conspiracy and abetting to violate licensing provisions, if nothing else. If the committee decides it wants to, it can release you later."

"What?" Wijmoor trembled.

"Yes," Grim agreed. "I'm sorry, but you'd best come along." He sighed. "It's for your safety. We can sort this out away from the public view."

Egil grabbed Thomas with his mechanical arm, and Grim put a hand on Wijmoor's shoulder. The kobold stared at Charlie, eyes big with fear.

"No, Grim," Gnat said. "This is wrong."

"Shut up, you wingless twit!" Egil One-Arm reached for Gnat—

and, quick as a wink, she ran.

Charlie turned and ran with her. "What are you doing?" he called to Grim over his shoulder.

"Restrain these two," Grim ordered the swarm of bobbies

with him, handing Wijmoor and Thomas into their keeping. Then he lumbered after Egil, who was already chasing Charlie, who followed Gnat—into the cathedral.

Charlie rushed past pews and large columns, hearing the stomping of the two trolls behind him.

"Wait!" Grim roared.

The dawn's light shone in through tall stained-glass windows. Suddenly Gnat turned right into a side room and began sprinting up spiral stone steps. The trolls were getting closer, so Charlie ran a little faster and scooped Gnat up. "Where are we going?" he whispered to her as she ran.

She looked over his shoulder. "Up."

At the top of the stairs, they were on a sort of balcony that traced all around the inside of the cathedral and, following its rough cross shape, looked down on the inside of the church. Bobbies swarmed in. "Why?" Charlie asked.

"Because it will even the odds, lad."

"Grim's afraid of heights," Charlie said.

"Aye, as you and I have learned."

The next set of steps was of iron, and Charlie charged up it. As he raced ahead, he shot a look backward.

To his credit, Grim ground doggedly up the steps, not looking down. "Charlie!" the troll bawled. "Stop! We need to talk!"

Behind Grim, Egil hollered too. "You're all under arrest!"

The next level was an iron-railed ledge around the base of the cathedral's dome.

"Here?"

"Higher." Gnat's voice was determined.

"I don't want to hurt him!" Charlie blurted out.

"Aye, I don't either," Gnat said. "I want him to stop in fear."

Charlie raced up a further spiraling staircase, the two trolls puffing behind. "I'll need my mainspring wound," he said.

"I can do that," Gnat agreed.

Charlie looked back at Grim. The troll gripped the hand railing of the stairs and climbed with his eyes squeezed shut.

Charlie and Gnat reached the next level. It wasn't the highest—the stairs climbed a little farther, into a tiny belfry—but at this level Charlie and Gnat passed through a doorless opening onto a circular walkway outside the church, and at the top of the dome.

Higher than he'd been on the Sky Trestle, almost as high as he'd been in Bob's flyer or on Ollie's back, Charlie gazed down on London. From here, and in this neighborhood, it looked like an elegant maze of white stone palaces. Sky Trestle tracks swerved close to the cathedral, never quite reaching it, but adding energy and movement to London's rooftops.

"Gnat, look!"

Gnat spun on Charlie's shoulder just in time to see what appeared to be the final strokes in a duel between the green and black dragons on the one hand and Ollie the yellow dragon on the other. They rolled over the Thames, and Ollie and the black dragon clutched each other with their claws as if wrestling, and spun around and around in midair.

The green dragon's gunner-mahout took careful aim. *Bang!* and *bang!* and *bang!* again he fired his big gun.

Ollie *ROARED!*—

threw himself away from the black dragon—

and disappeared.

"Ollie!" Charlie screamed.

"You're under arrest!" Egil One-Arm bellowed again.

"Charlie," Gnat whispered into his ear. "Throw me up there!"

Charlie did as he was told, tossing Gnat to the belfry. She alighted easily and perched, looking down.

Egil charged, panting, through the door and stooped to grab for Charlie.

Charlie shrank—

Gnat jumped—

grabbed Egil by one big cowlike ear—

and dragged his face into the iron railing.

Bong!

Egil sank to the stone walkway, dazed. His mechanical arm swung in a slow circle, like a boat that had lost its pilot.

"That leaves one, Charlie!" Gnat cried. "Follow me!"

They left Egil muttering to himself in a choked voice and raced back down the stairs. Grim, dragging himself upward one step at a time, heard them coming and cocked a single eye.

"Egil? Eh, Gnat, Charlie! Stop!"

"Arrest *me*, will you?" Gnat cried. She leaped from the steps to the handrail, protected from falling to her death by nothing but her own agility, and then she leaped toward Grim's face.

Grim tried to grab her but missed, which was no surprise,

given that his eyes were closed. Gnat landed with her feet on Grim's forehead and gripped his two long horns, vaulting herself over his top hat.

Grim leaned back, swatting at the pixie who had once been his clerk.

Charlie slid, feetfirst, beneath Grim, and grabbed Grim's ankle as he passed.

Grim was off-balance already, and Charlie was heavy and moving fast. With a roar that passed through a choking sound and became a high-pitched yelp, Grim fell forward onto his face on the steps.

Crunch.

The steps bowed beneath the weight.

Charlie hesitated and looked back.

"We've got to run!" Gnat called.

Grim lay facedown on the iron steps, groaning. The iron groaned now too, and Charlie saw several of the bars in the framework beneath Grim begin to bend.

Charlie leaped forward, grabbing Grim's belt with one hand and the undamaged portion of the staircase with the other.

Crack!

The stairs gave way beneath Grim, and he and Charlie fell. Charlie's grip on both the troll and the stairs held, though it felt as if his arms might come out of their sockets.

Grim yelped and squirmed, hands over his eyes.

"I've got you, Grim!" Charlie grunted.

Another length of the staircase bent, and they fell twelve feet. In descending, though, they came closer to the walkway at the base of the great dome. Bobbies in blue uniforms waited there, shouting directions to Charlie.

Other bobbies, he saw, were shoving Gnat into a device that looked like a birdcage.

"Can you catch him?" Charlie called to the bobbies.

They looked at him as if he were mad, but he felt the next level of the stairs straining and about to go. His arms, too, felt overextended. Grunting with the strain, Charlie rocked his friend Grim out away from the policemen and then began swinging him back in the other direction—

the stairs gave out again, and they dropped—

and Charlie released Grim, hurling him into the crowd of bobbies.

At that moment, Charlie's own arms and legs jerked violently, and he lost his grip. He fell, policemen and others scattering out of his way, and bounced on the stone floor. Standing, he managed to totter, limping and shaking, half-way to the front doors of St. Paul's before he pitched over, unconscious.

Throughout this text, I shall scatter warnings to the beginner, and even to the more adept practitioner. Magic is fraught with danger, because it is freighted with power. Here is the first, and most basic warning: magic will always cost you something. If you create a little effect, it may cost you only a small amount, but heroic efforts will demand heroic sacrifices.

—from Adelbert Philotheles, *First Principles of Wizardry,* "Introduction"

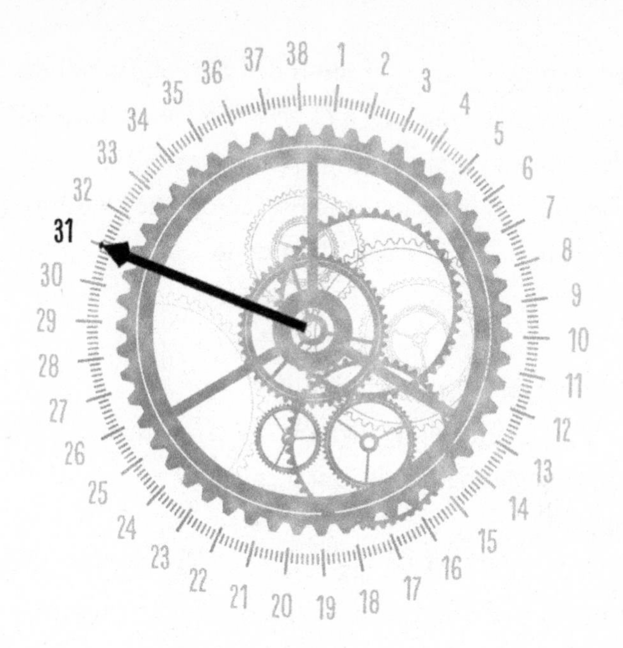

Charlie sat on a stool, facing his bap.

Bap sat on another stool, facing Charlie. They were in the reception room of Pondicherry's Clockwork Invention & Repair, and Charlie dimly thought there was something wrong with that.

He couldn't quite put his finger on the problem.

Between them, hanging on the wall, was Bap's portrait of Queen Victoria. The queen looked back and forth at Charlie and his father and frowned. It wasn't a frown of disapproval, but more of fear.

Charlie went to stand up, but stopped. There was no floor between him and Bap, but only a yawning chasm, dark and spitting out a boiling mist. Down deep in the abyss, Charlie heard a wailing sound that reminded him of the sounds made by the nāgas, but somehow he knew that this call was made by an older beast, and one that was more terrifying.

"Charlie," his bap said, reaching across the chasm to pinch Charlie's thigh. "Your work is not done."

*

Charlie opened his eyes to dim light.

Not the organic glow of gloom-moss, with its tiny humanoid figures wiggling inside, but a pale white illumination cast by a bulb.

"Hello, Charlie," Thomas said.

Charlie sat up and found he was on moldy straw, in a niche set into a stone wall. Thomas had just finished winding Charlie's mainspring and stepped back, smiling ruefully. Overhead, a single long tube emitted a weak gray light and a faint audible buzz.

Jan Wijmoor sat on another bed niche. Like Charlie, he leaned forward to avoid banging his head on the wall. In a third niche, Charlie saw Natalie de Minimis. She was small enough to fit inside entirely, with her knees up and her arms crossed over the top of them.

"Hello, Charlie," Wijmoor and Gnat said together.

The room with the sleeping niches held the four of them prisoner. Beside an iron door, a rusty pail and a wooden pitcher rested on the floor.

"We're in gaol," Charlie said. "Did Grim . . . ?"

"Aye," Gnat said. "Grim is with the police now, Charlie. He

had us arrested, and here we are. We're to be tried for something called Violation of Committee Order Number One, if you can believe it. Subsection two."

"I never heard of that," Charlie said.

"Nay, nor have I. It sounds like nonsense." Gnat sighed. "And yet here we are."

"I wish we had the sweeps," Charlie said. "Bob could pick that lock."

"And Ollie could turn into a dragon and knock down the entire prison," Thomas added.

"He's not the same Ollie I first met," Charlie said thoughtfully.

"No?" Gnat asked.

"In good ways, I mean," Charlie said. "He's learned things. Although it turns out that, in a sense, he was never the Ollie I thought he was. He knew Bob's secret for . . . I'm not sure, donkey's years, I think, as he would say . . . and kept it. He even kept Bob's secret from *her.* What kind of person would do that?"

"A devoted person." Gnat looked at the ceiling of her sleeping niche and sighed again. "A person who would risk himself for the one he loves."

"But just because Ollie and Bob aren't here doesn't make us helpless." Charlie stood and walked to the door. It was a steel rectangle, with rivets around its outside edge every three inches, and a barred viewing window just barely low enough for Charlie to look through. "Come on, Thomas, let's give this a try."

Thomas looked down at his feet.

"What is it?" Charlie asked.

"I didn't do what my father wanted," Thomas said. "We collected the three nails, but then we didn't seal up the demon."

"Because we had a better idea," Charlie said.

Thomas shook his head. "*You* had a better idea. *I* was *afraid*."

Charlie nudged his brother. "It's not over yet, Thomas."

Charlie and Thomas both wrapped their fingers around the little window in the door, and each braced himself with a foot against the wall.

"On three," Charlie said. "One, two, three."

They pulled.

Nothing happened.

"Harder," Thomas grunted.

They strained, and Charlie felt his mechanisms spinning within him, and the door didn't budge.

"Nay, 'tis too strong a door."

Charlie sighed. "You're right."

The boys rewound each other's springs.

Charlie was just finishing winding Thomas when he heard voices in the corridor.

"Will you all be at the grand opening of the pumping station, then?" This voice was a troll's, but Charlie didn't recognize it. "Hampstead Heath is a bit posh for a water tower. Not quite sure what they'll do there—might break a bottle on the side of it, like they do with a ship. Cut a ribbon, maybe. Mmm, taken a wrong turn. Not sure, but I think it must be one of these doors. Ah yes, here it is."

"Well, if you've an innocent pixie in your gaols, she needs to be freed immediately." This sounded like Heinrich Zahnkrieger. Charlie wanted to say something about finding the kobold here, but all he could do was stare at Thomas, open-mouthed.

Thomas stared back with the same stunned expression.

"Immediately!" This was a fairy, and Charlie recognized the voice but couldn't quite place it.

"Couldn't agree more," the hulder rumbled. "We're supposed to be arresting people who commit anti-human crimes, and not elder folk in general. Obviously, I mean—look at me. A mistake, I'm sure."

When the door opened, a troll stepped theatrically aside and waved at the cell. The troll wore a long brown coat and held a club in his hand. He was one of the trolls who had been holding the crowd back from the burning building at St. Paul's, or he looked like one of them.

"Here's the pixie," he said. "One of yours, no?"

Three small people entered the cell, two of them flying. Gnat turned to face them.

Heinrich Zahnkrieger, now dressed in a navy suit with pinstripes and a red cravat, wheeled and looked at the troll with suspicion on his face.

Juliet Edelstein, the Undergravine of Hesse, flitted back in surprise.

Elisabel de Minimis, Gnat's cousin, hovered beside her. The Baroness of Underthames wore a tricorn hat and breeches, and her face was twisted into a mask of anger.

"What is this, you idiot?" Zahnkrieger snapped at the troll.

"Said he was from Underthames, that's what I was told." The troll cleared his throat. "This fairy is a troublemaker and it was quite hard to arrest him. Her, rather. Isn't she one of yours, Baroness? Underthames, no?"

"I should have known better than to trust a jotun," Elisabel de Minimis growled.

"This fairy must stay locked up." Heinrich sniffed, tugged at his jacket sleeves, and turned.

"Herr Doktor," Jan Wijmoor said.

Heinrich stopped and fussed with his high starched collar, but he didn't leave.

"I did you wrong," Wijmoor said. "I should have guided you, and I should have taken more involvement in your work. I should have spoken up more vocally on your behalf, Herr Doktor Ingenieur Zahnkrieger, and if you had to fall by the Internal Auditor's memorandum, then I should have fallen with you."

"Yes," Zahnkrieger said slowly, and he pivoted on one heel. "You should have. But you didn't. Did you?"

Wijmoor looked down. "I am sorry."

"Your regret is not enough." Zahnkrieger's eyes smoldered.

"We chose not to take away your gift," Charlie said. "Remember that. We could have summoned that demon and bottled it up, and you would have lost your magic. But we didn't."

"Was that your consideration?" Zahnkrieger wheeled on Charlie. "Generosity toward *me*? Or was it rather pity for *yourselves*?"

"We chose compassion toward everyone." Charlie tried to

stay calm, and was becoming aware that Elisabel and Natalie de Minimis were engaged in a staring match, eyes locked and jaws furiously clenched. "For you and for ourselves and also for all the people in the world who today benefit from hospitals, and airships, and factories, and water pumps, and tractors."

Zahnkrieger played with the knot of his cravat. "Good. So you're coming around."

"I challenge you!" Gnat howled. She stood on the edge of her sleeping niche, head and shoulders rising out of the alcove, making her about the height of her cousin, though Elisabel flew and Gnat was still wingless. "I call all here to witness, Elisabel, that I challenge you!"

The ferocity of Gnat's demand sent both kobolds and Charlie stumbling back. Charlie thought he even saw the troll's hair blown sideways by the force of the pixie's anger. Gnat herself trembled; how did she not fall?

"By what right?" Elisabel's voice was an equally ringing shriek, and her wings hummed a low bass note below her response.

"By the right of my mother's rule!" Gnat cried. "And by my own three mighty deeds!"

What deeds? Charlie wondered.

"Have you witnesses?" Elisabel demanded.

"I slew the Hound of Annwn," Gnat said, "a fell beast, part machine, that stalked the slopes of Cader Idris. I slew that beast with my spear, in single combat."

"I saw it," Charlie said. His words felt a little plain, after Gnat's.

Elisabel snorted.

"I dove, alone, into the waters of creation in a monsoon," Gnat continued, "to board the Pushpaka vimāna, flying city-ship of the demon lord Ravana. There I slew a shaitan murderer alone in a closed room."

Charlie tried to be more eloquent this time. "I was witness."

"So was I," Thomas said.

Elisabel scoffed, but she seemed less certain of herself.

"And I defeated not one, but two hulders, atop St. Paul's Cathedral this very day," Gnat cried. "Armed only with my bare hands and my mother's cunning, I rendered one unconscious and the other helpless."

"I was witness," Charlie repeated. Technically, he'd been there to help, but he wasn't going to undercut Natalie now.

"Sneak! Fraud!" Elisabel yelled at the hapless troll. "You tricked me here!"

The hulder shrugged, a bewildered expression on his face.

"I will not permit you to address the warrior throng," Elisabel said to Gnat through gritted teeth.

"You must," said Juliet, the Undergravine of Hesse, and there was iron in her voice.

Elisabel only stared, her mouth falling slightly open.

Had someone sent this troll to bring the two pixie noblewomen here to give Gnat a chance to issue her challenge?

"Now really," Heinrich Zahnkrieger spluttered, fidgeting with the buttons of his jacket. For a moment, caught off guard, he looked like the old Henry Clockswain whom Charlie had known in his father's shop, a fussy, obsessive kobold who was rude to Charlie but friends with his bap. "We have no time for this pixie nonsense!"

"We *always* have time for honor!" Juliet snapped. She fixed her eyes on Elisabel, but her words seemed to be addressed to Zahnkrieger. "If you wish us to be part of your league, you must respect our customs."

"I think this can be settled quickly," Charlie said. "Speeches to the warriors and then single combat. Am I right?"

Elisabel's glare was icy. "Follow me," she said. "We're not far from Underthames."

She turned and led the way, Juliet at her side. Everyone else followed. The hulder gaoler looked confused and dismayed. Heinrich Zahnkrieger looked thoughtful.

Much has been made of the kobolds' so-called Prime Secret. Nothing could be less sensitive. The Prime Secret is simply *lorem ipsum dolor sit amet, consectetur adipiscing elit, sed do eiusmod tempor incididunt ut labore et dolore magna aliqua.*

—Smythson, *Almanack*, 1st ed., "Kobold"

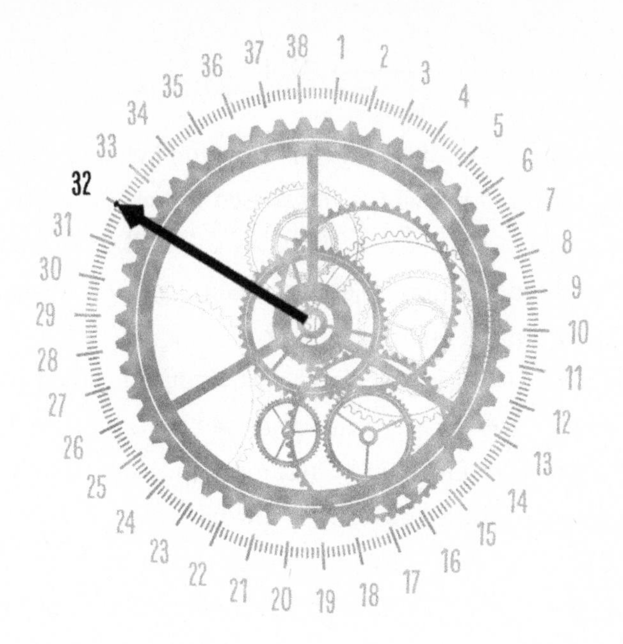

Charlie pressed himself to Gnat's side.

"Will your deeds count?" Charlie whispered. "I mean, defeating Grim and Egil—is that a mighty enough feat?"

"Only the warrior throng can decide." Gnat held her head high. "I hope they're impressed by the trophies."

They followed Elisabel into Underthames. They left the sewers after several minutes of fast walking, moved along a natural passageway a short, gloom-moss-lit distance, and came to a gate.

The four pixies at the gate shocked Charlie: they wore padded vests and brass helmets with smoked-glass visors covering their faces, and they carried short rifles. Stranger still, the gate was also guarded by four rats. The rats were armored and armed too, with leather flaps hanging from their bodies and sharpened sticks in their paws.

At the first sight of them, Charlie stumbled and nearly fell. Elisabel fluttered her wings and passed unbothered, but eight sets of guards' eyes fixed on Gnat as she walked through on foot. Natalie de Minimis held her head high and looked forward, ignoring the guards.

The pixie realm looked mostly as Charlie recalled it from his first visit, the very day his father had been kidnapped and he had turned to Grim and Gnat for help. Underthames was still a series of linked caverns with high ceilings. It was still lit by glittering gems, full of birdlike nests and streams of flowing water. But rats now slouched where the fairies scampered and flew, some of the streams looked gray and fouled, and the corners of some caverns were heaped high with refuse. The stench of rotting meat washed over Charlie in a wave.

Elisabel de Minimis brought Charlie and the others to a place Charlie remembered, a low mound with a circle of broken-topped white pillars around it. At one end sat a stone chair, pixie-sized, and all the paths of Underthames flowed together and converged on this plaza and its throne.

The two kobolds stood together, apart from the others. Jan Wijmoor watched his old student with sad eyes, and Heinrich Zahnkrieger stared resolutely away.

The hulder gaoler stood at the far edge of the crowd, shifting from foot to foot and snorting.

As Elisabel approached, pixies who had been lounging

suddenly stood. Those included Hezekiah and Seamus, Natalie's love, and several warriors in blue tortoiseshells—the only pixies who seemed to retain their traditional spears, rather than use the new rifles. Lloyd Shankin stood up with them, still dressed in blue and carrying a white rod; his eyes were fixed on Gnat.

Lloyd began to sing, and Charlie understood the words through the Babel Card. "O cuckoo, O cuckoo, where have you been?" the dewin sang. He smiled at Charlie, though only faintly.

Elisabel flew to the height of the cavern and then alighted atop one of the pillars, spinning down gently like a pirouetting dancer. When she came to a stop, she sneered at Gnat. It was an insult, Charlie realized—he remembered how embarrassed Gnat had been at the loss of her wings.

But Gnat showed no shame or hesitation now. She sprang to the lowest of the broken columns, and then up to a second, and with a third leap she came to perch at the height of one of the tallest pillars.

"Dear little Natalie," Elisabel clucked. "My poor cousin, come home with her uplander friends. Will you tell us your cause yourself, or have you a herald?"

Gnat stood, straight-backed, to face the crowd—

"She has a herald!" Lloyd Shankin cried. "A herald and a bard and a dewin!"

Juliet Edelstein raised a single eyebrow but showed no other sign of surprise.

Elisabel frowned.

"Hear the three songs of Natalie de Minimis!" Lloyd called. Then he raised his hands over his head and began to sing:

I sing you a warrior princess, brave as has ever been found
On the slopes of the giant's mountain, she slew death's only hound

Charlie found his own mouth forced open, but what came out were not words. A melody rushed from his lips, and borne on the melody like autumn leaves upon a stream came images. Above Lloyd's head, the green and gray slopes of Cader Idris arose, and out of Charlie's soul somehow came the image of the Hound chasing him and his friends down the slope. The pixies saw and emitted a collective shudder. Then the image showed them a shattered Aunt Big Money, and they wept, and finally as Gnat single-handedly—and without wings—killed the Hound, the pixies of Underthames sent up a cheer.

The blue-clad fairies looked to their undergravine, whose eyes narrowed.

Gnat raised the Hound's tooth over her head. "My first token!" she cried.

Elisabel stared fury at her cousin, but the other fairies of Underthames cheered louder.

Lloyd continued:

I sing you the baroness's daughter, in the palace of the demon lord
She slew the fiercest hunter, and now claims her reward

More melody and further images flowed out of Charlie. Startled, he realized that Lloyd's magic had picked him up off the ground and was holding him in midair as it pulled this story out of him. It raised Thomas, too, and from the two of them together came the second story of Gnat's heroism.

This time, Charlie saw above Lloyd's head the image of the Pushpaka vimāna, a glowing circular pyramid lying at the bottom of a dark sea. The hideous nāgas circled it, and suddenly the shaitan plunged past them, holding a boulder to ensure its swift descent. Gnat followed, unnoticed, until she assaulted the nāga and the shaitan, and then ordered the mechanical boys to shut her in. The vision showed the pixie and the shaitan as white outlines only against featureless black, and when the shaitan pounced for the fairy, she deftly stepped and stabbed it with the Hound's tooth. Then she took the scarf from its neck and wrapped herself in it.

Gnat raised the scarf above her head. "My second!"

This time the undergravine smiled, and the pixies of Hesse joined the English pixies in roaring their applause.

Lloyd sang a third couplet:

I sing you a lethal dancer, fearless, in control
I sing you a pint-sized warrior who can dominate a troll

Charlie continued to hang in the air, but Thomas fell to earth, looking shaken but delighted.

From Charlie burst the images of himself and Natalie de Minimis running through St. Paul's Cathedral, followed by

Egil and Grim. The pixies stared, and Charlie watched them closely. Would it be enough for them? The church grew and shrank as the running figures raced up within it. As they watched Gnat single-handedly stun Egil One-Arm, the gathered pixies sucked in a collective breath—and as she leaped over Grim, yanking him off-balance so Charlie could drop him to the stairs, they cheered.

The rats, Charlie noticed for the first time, hissed among themselves and slunk to the edges of the crowd.

Before it could show the staircase breaking under Grim's weight, the vision faded into white light. "And have you a token, Natalie?" Elisabel asked. Her tone was sarcastic, but Charlie thought the sarcasm hid fear.

"I am Natalie de Minimis's third token!"

"Grim!" Charlie nearly fell over in surprise.

The voice was his troll friend's, and the hulder lawspeaker barged into the circle of pixies. When he reached the broken columns he stopped and drew himself up to his full height. "Natalie de Minimis defeated me in hand-to-hand combat. You saw it yourself, and I'm here as her defeated foe and trophy!"

An awed murmur passed through the assembled pixies.

Lloyd sang a final couplet:

I sing you her mother's daughter, de Minimis in green
I sing you a warrior leader, champion and queen

The undergravine applauded and the pixies shrieked with joy. Elisabel stared sourly, and slowly, slowly, the applause died down.

"The rats," Charlie whispered to Thomas. "The pixies aren't watching them."

Thomas grinned. "I'm not afraid of any old rat. What shall we do?"

Without drawing attention to themselves, the two boys drifted to the back of the crowd, past the two kobolds, beyond the rats, and onto a low stone knob.

"Be ready," Charlie whispered to his brother.

"Very well," Elisabel cried, her voice piercing. She pointed at Hezekiah. "Herald!"

Hezekiah, flying much lower than the baroness, met her gaze. Slowly, deliberately, he dropped his rod on the cavern floor, then shrugged out of his tabard and cap and dropped those as well.

"No," he said simply.

"Well, I have accomplishments too!" Elisabel shrieked, pounding her fist against the air. "I led Underthames against the rats!"

"Those rats?" Gnat asked, pointing with the Hound's tooth at the huddled knot of chittering fur beneath Charlie.

"And I made peace with the rats, when the time came!" Elisabel bellowed. "And I found us new weapons, for our war against the humans!"

"You've been deceived!" Gnat cried to the rest of the pixies. "The Anti-Human League is a trick, and my cousin, who murdered my mother and stole her throne, is their puppet!"

"Challenge! Challenge! Challenge!" pixies all around the hall shouted.

With a noise that sounded like ten cats being thrown into

the freezing Thames, Elisabel swooped down at her cousin, her spear raised high—

the crowd fell silent and held its breath—

Gnat leaped into the air as if she had wings, seized her cousin's spear, and flung the other pixie down upon the top of the broken column.

Elisabel struck the rock, bounced once, fell to the stone floor in the center of the worn pillars, and lay still.

Gnat turned in the air and pirouetted as Elisabel had, only without wings and therefore faster. She landed with grace, holding the spear in one hand and the Hound's tooth in the other, both above her head.

Across the cavern, every pixie made a joyous noise. Some banged spears on shields—the rifles had all disappeared. Others fluttered their wings, stamped their feet, clapped their hands, and yelled.

The troll gaoler turned and ran.

"The barony passes!" Lloyd Shankin cried.

"The barony passes!" Hezekiah shouted.

A gray rat, taller than the others and with scars streaking down its face, rose from the mass before Charlie and Thomas. Charlie had seen the rat before—it was Scabies!

"Kill them now, my brothers!" Scabies roared.

Charlie didn't wait. He charged the rats from behind. When he grabbed Scabies by the hind legs and yanked him off his feet, the rat's face splashed into one of the cavern's streams, and he began to shriek.

The other rats hesitated, and Thomas charged them. A few

rats poked Charlie and Thomas with their sticks, but it barely hurt, and then Grim was wading into the rodents from behind, and the undergravine's warriors made short work of any rat that didn't flee.

The clamor of acclamation didn't stop.

Gnat leaped atop a pillar again and faced the crowd. "My mother's people!" she cried. "I must leave you, for a time. I shall return! I would leave you in the care of a lady of great worth, Juliet Edelstein, the Undergravine of Hesse. Undergravine, may I ask you to watch my mother's throne?"

The undergravine nodded solemnly. "Well done, Lady de Minimis."

Seamus smiled at Gnat.

Gnat's facial expression in return was surprisingly cold.

She turned to Grim. "We were released for the challenge," she said. "I'll not do you wrong, Grumblesson. Let us return to the cell."

Seamus's mouth fell open.

Grim looked at Heinrich Zahnkrieger, who stared in turn at the troll and at all the pixie hubbub with a look of astonishment on his face, buttoning and unbuttoning his jacket. "Back to gaol it is!" the hulder bellowed.

The kobold looked to Juliet the undergravine. She arched one eyebrow back at him and said nothing.

O'r gwcw, o'r gwcw, ble buost ti cyd?
Cyn dod i'r gymdogaeth ti aethost yn fud.
Cyn dod i'r gymdogaeth ti aethost yn fud.
O gadw'r gyfrinach, caf heddwch fy hun,
Ffolineb or mwya'f yn dweud wrth un dyn.
Ffolineb or mwya'f yn dweud wrth un dyn.

(O cuckoo, o cuckoo, where have you been so long?
Before you came to the neighborhood, you'd become silent.
Before you came to the neighborhood, you'd become silent.
By keeping the secret, I have peace,
It is great foolishness to tell any man.
It is great foolishness to tell any man.)

—"Y Bardd a'r Gwcw," traditional Welsh song

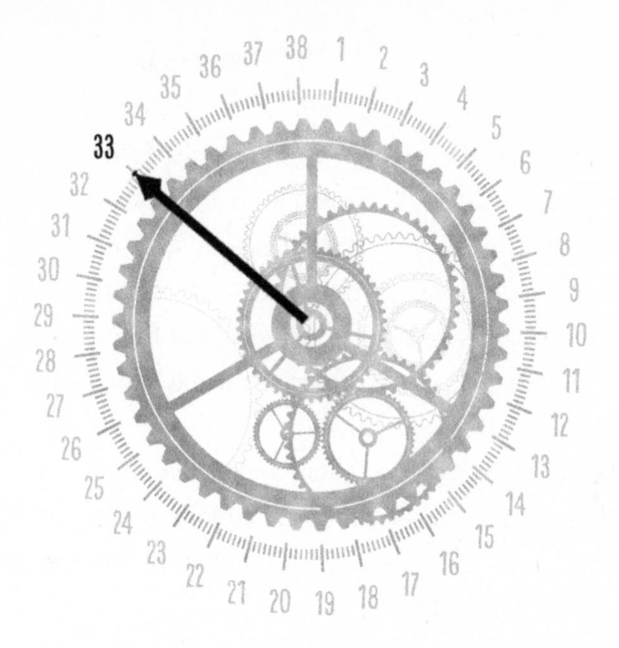

The pixies, other than Gnat, stayed behind, but Lloyd and Hezekiah followed Charlie and his friends to the exit of Underthames.

The rat sentries at the gate were gone, except one that lay dead, impaled on a pixie spear. The pixies stood guard alone now, armed again with spears.

"I'll lead," Grim rumbled, and headed out without waiting for anyone to respond. Charlie and Gnat quickly followed.

"Gnat," Charlie whispered. "What do I call you now?"

Gnat, whose walk had become a high-skipping step, laughed. "Being a young lad made of clockwork, Charlie, and not a pixie at all? You call me Gnat. Though if I'm wearing a nice dress and *don't* have a spear in my hand, perhaps you can call me Natalie."

"But you're the baroness now," Charlie said.

"Aye." She smiled. "Aye, I am."

"Grim, what did you do?" Charlie whispered.

"Only what I had to!" Grim shot back. "Parliament started investigating the Anti-Human League, and I was afraid it might take to locking up innocent hulders and dwarfs, so I volunteered for the committee. And then I found myself locking up hulders and dwarfs, because in fact there *is* an Anti-Human League!"

"I know," Charlie said. "The Undergravine of Hesse—that was her, Juliet, in blue—came here to join it, after Prussia attacked the city where she lived. Only I think Prussia is being manipulated by the Cog."

Grim shook his head. "Ingrid left me."

"I think the Cog invented the Anti-Human League and then invited people to join it," Charlie continued. "As a way to make the elder folk rebel, so they could— What did you say?"

"Ingrid left me," Grim said. "Again. She's a good person, and she can't stand to see me involved in this. I try, you know. I lose prisoners from time to time . . . when I think they're innocent. I delay committee action. I took the job to help, Charlie, and I'm trying my best."

A soft tear trickled down each of the hulder's cheeks.

Charlie took Grim's enormous hand and held it in his own. "It was you who arranged for Gnat and Elisabel to meet, wasn't it?"

Grim sniffed, an enormous sound. "Egil's thugs are idiots. I mentioned to the gaoler that I thought our new pixie prisoner was one of the baroness's warriors from Underthames and a ferocious league soldier, so we'd better not tell anyone we had her prisoner. Naturally, thinking he was doing a favor for the Anti-Human League—or the Iron Cog, or whoever he believes he serves—the moron promptly invited Elisabel to come in and collect her warrior."

Charlie chuckled.

"Egil himself never would have fallen for it, but he makes a point of hiring people stupider than himself. About your powder, Charlie," Grim said. "What if it was dissolved in water and then sprayed on a fire? There's this new pumping station—"

Crack!

"Ouch!" Grim roared. "You hit my head!"

"Go down, you great stinking brute! Down! Down!"

Charlie heard two more loud cracks as a tall, muscular man sprang out of the shadows and hit Grim on the head with a club.

Finally Grim spun in a slow circle, then sank to his knees. Charlie gasped at the sight of his friend's stunned expression and his eyes rolling back into his head, and then Grim collapsed.

"Anti-Human League!" the big man yelled, and raced forward, swinging his club. As he came into the yellow-green light, Charlie saw that he wore a burlap sack over his head, with ragged holes torn in it for eyes. "This is a raid!"

Behind the man came a tall woman wearing a similar bag over her head and also carrying a club. Not a human woman,

Charlie realized, when he saw the long cow's tail bouncing out behind her.

"What?" Heinrich Zahnkrieger tugged at his collar. "Nonsense!"

The tall man clubbed Heinrich several times in the chest. "It ain't nonsense; it's a raid!"

"We're freeing your prisoners!" the hulder woman shouted. She kicked the kobold into the corner.

"Herr Doktor!" Wijmoor cried. The red-haired kobold threw himself to his knees in front of the tall man and pleaded. "Please! Spare us all, but especially spare my poor student Heinrich! He has been badly treated!"

"Ain't no one getting hurt," the big man growled. "We're liberating you! In the name of the Anti-Human League!"

"I am so confused now!" Wijmoor raised a crooked finger up as if trying to pull understanding down from the sky.

And then Charlie recognized the voices of the two attackers. The woman was Ingrid, who had once—or maybe twice—nearly married Grim. The man was Sal, who ran a kind of business called a dairy, where trolls drank milk until it put them into a stupor. He and Grim had butted heads—not literally, because that would have killed Sal—over Sal's business and over Ingrid. Charlie had met them both in Sal's dairy, and later Ingrid had rescued Grim from the Iron Cog by bringing the hulder hue and cry to a gunfight beneath Waterloo Station.

Charlie looked to Grim and found Grim looking back at him.

The troll winked.

"Don't ask too many questions, Meneer Doktor!" Charlie shouted. "We're liberated—that's what counts!"

Ingrid beckoned to Charlie to come with her down a new passageway, and he raced to follow her.

"And stay down!" Sal shouted, smacking Grim once more in the head with his club.

Behind Charlie came Thomas and Gnat in quick succession, and he heard Sal booting and dragging Jan Wijmoor along at the rear.

Grim Grumblesson and Heinrich Zahnkrieger stayed behind, both lying on the ground.

Ingrid quickly led them all to a sewer tunnel, which branched into multiple side passages and slimy brick crossroads. She turned, turned, and turned again, and then threw herself against a wall, breathing hard.

She took off her mask. "We're not supposed to be *members* of the Anti-Human League, Sal. We're supposed to be rescuing these people *from* the Anti-Human League."

Sal yanked off his mask. He still had the ugly snarl Charlie remembered, the short queue of hair tied behind his neck, and the oversized muttonchop side-whiskers. "Yeah, only I figured at the last minute, why not create a little confusion?"

"Maybe leave the last-minute thinking to other people," Ingrid suggested.

"Like your man Grim?" Sal asked.

"You only had to hit him once," she said. "And he's not my man. And before you get any ideas, neither are you."

"He wouldn't go down." Sal shrugged. "If he'd dropped at once like he was supposed to, I wouldn't have had to smack him again. Had to make it look realistic, didn't I?"

Ingrid sighed. "I suppose."

"Thank you," Charlie said.

"Am I to understand," Jan Wijmoor said slowly, "that you two are in league—so to speak—with that troll?"

"Grim Grumblesson," Charlie clarified.

"Now he gets it," Sal said.

"I think I understand why Grim is working for the committee," Charlie said. "But if you're mad at him for doing that . . . why are you helping him now?"

"*Am* I helping Grim?" Ingrid asked. "Or am I helping *you*?"

"You're helping me. Thank you," Charlie said.

"But I'm not angry with Grim," Ingrid went on. "I . . . don't understand his need for crusades, is all. I don't think I can be with someone who always has to have a cause. I want his cause to be *us*, not saving London's elder folk or putting the dairies out of business. Maybe I'm just looking for a farmer after all."

Sal snorted. "I know I could never be with someone whose cause was to put the dairies out of business."

"Shut up, Sal," Ingrid sighed, "or I'll hit *you* in the head. To make it look realistic."

"You freed us," Wijmoor said, "so that the troll could look innocent."

"I freed you because this Anti-Human League stuff is rot!" Sal snarled. "It's all been cooked up so that pixies and trolls and so on will look like they're out to overthrow the government, see? So the government can send those new tin soldiers it has after the pixies and trolls, and get rid of them once and for all."

"I'm a little surprised to see you so concerned about that," Charlie said. "You seemed quite happy to have as many hulders as possible sitting around in a daze in your dairy, slobbering and dreaming."

"Don't you see, Charlie?" Gnat asked. "Sal isn't worried about trolls out of the goodness of his heart. He's worried because if the trolls are killed, or flee London, he won't have any customers. I don't think he's worried about pixies at all."

Sal shrugged. "I got nothing to sell to a pixie."

"I will take any ally I can get, in these straits," Gnat said. "I am Lady de Minimis, Baroness of Underthames."

"Oh yeah? Ingrid here didn't mention you were nobility."

"I didn't know," Ingrid said.

"Where are you supposed to take us?" Gnat said to Ingrid. "We could return to Underthames and my warrior throng."

"Grim wanted us to take you somewhere to meet him." Sal smacked his stick into his palm for emphasis, and for the first time Charlie noticed that it was the same heavy cane he'd seen in the man's hands back at the dairy.

"Pondicherry's shop," Ingrid said.

"Lead the way, sweets." Sal hit his palm again.

"Don't call me that," Ingrid said, "or Odin's missing eye, I'll break your nose." She stepped away from the brick wall and looked both directions. "Only . . . I think I've taken a wrong turn."

Sal laughed. "Oh, this is too good!"

Charlie turned to Gnat. "Are there pixie signs here that would show us the way?"

Gnat shook her head. "But the sewers are large. Surely, all we need to do is find an exit, any exit, and then aboveground we can find our way to where we need to go."

They set out.

"Am I hearing something?" Charlie asked.

"Dripping water?" Thomas said.

"The satisfying rumble of distant machinery?" Wijmoor asked.

"No, I don't think so," Charlie said thoughtfully. "It's something closer, and more animal."

"Yeah," Sal agreed. "I think I hear it too."

"What is it?" Wijmoor asked. "Birds? An owl or a dove, lost and trapped down here in all the filth?"

"It's ghouls," Gnat whispered. "Which direction is it coming from?"

"I can't tell," Charlie said.

"Can we go back the way we came?" Thomas asked.

"Not if we want to protect Grim and escape at the same time," Charlie pointed out. "This way," he suggested, pointing to a low arch beyond which he saw a broad room that seemed to be full of light. The light struck him as hopeful. "I'll go first."

Charlie walked under the arch. The chamber beyond was long and tall, and its ceiling was an iron grate—above, Charlie saw yellow gaslight, and feet treading back and forth across the iron. That was a city street, tantalizingly only a few feet over his head.

Could he jump and reach it?

Perhaps. And Thomas could join him, but then how would the others get out?

He heard the hooting again, nearer, and picked up his pace.

Then he heard another sound, one he'd heard more recently than the hooting of ghouls.

Chittering.

The incessant, mad chittering of London's giant rats.

Charlie took another step forward and then stopped. Through the arch on the far side of the chamber shuffled a single ghoul. In the light from the street overhead, Charlie could clearly see its almost noseless, chimpanzee-like face; its long teeth; its hairless, clammy body.

The ghoul hooted again and again, changing pitch as it did so.

To his surprise, Charlie felt the Babel Card within him slide to work. The ghoul's hoots weren't mere noise; they weren't just the incoherent grunting of an animal. . . . The Babel Card was at least *trying* to interpret the hoots as speech.

"Charlie," Sal said. "Step back." Charlie heard the smack of Sal testing his cane club in the palm of his hand.

"Wait." Charlie raised a cautioning finger.

"Strangers!" the ghoul wailed. "They look dangerous! Hide the nestlings and protect the nest!"

"Wait!" Charlie called. "We're friends! We mean your nestlings no harm!"

"Charlie!" Natalie de Minimis cried. "Are you *hooting,* lad?"

Meneer Doktor Jan Wijmoor snapped his fingers. Charlie turned to see the kobold pointing at the ceiling in glee. "It's the Babel Card, isn't it, Charlie? You're speaking to it!"

"Him," Charlie said. "I'm trying to speak to *him.*"

Two more ghouls popped through the far arch and stood shoulder to shoulder with the first.

The chittering got louder.

"We just want to pass through," Charlie said.

The ghouls glowered at him.

The chittering got louder still.

More ghouls flooded in under the arch.

"Please," Charlie said.

From the arch behind his friends, rats poured into the room.

Mr. William T. Bowen informs this paper that work on the North London Fire Suppression Pumping Station has been completed. The grand opening ceremonies will be held on the twenty-second of July, and the public is invited.

—*Daily Telegraph*, "Pump Station Completed," 21 July 1887

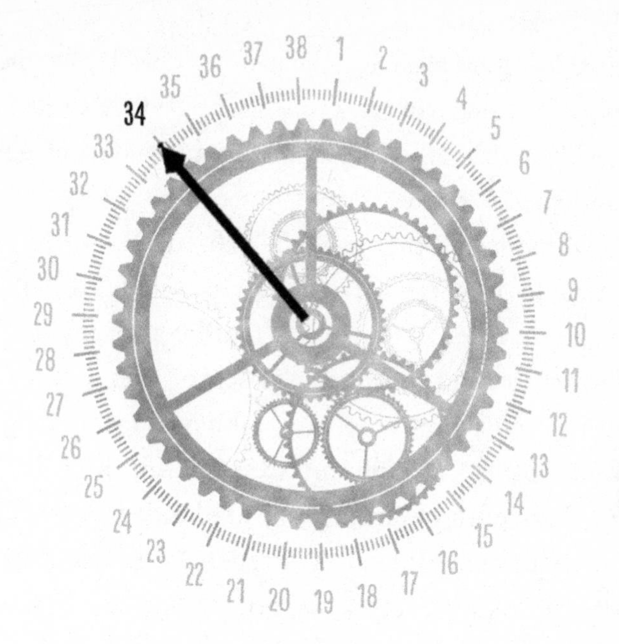

"We're with you!" Charlie hooted to the ghouls.

Thomas joined him. "We're your friends!" Charlie was glad he wasn't the only one with a Babel Card installed.

The wave of ghouls from one end of the hall and the wave of rats from the other rose at the same moment and surged forward.

Charlie turned and charged the rats. "Pondicherry's of Whitechapel!"

Thomas picked up this cry and repeated it.

"De Minimis and Underthames!"

Ingrid and Sal waded into the fight with no battle cry, and Jan Wijmoor pressed himself flat against the wall to avoid the fray completely.

Was this a good idea? Charlie hadn't a clue, but he thought he had just learned, contrary to what he had always believed, that ghouls were a folk. They were a people and had language; they could be talked to.

Surely that meant they could be befriended.

Rats could obviously make friends as well, but Charlie had seen enough treason, trickery, and murder at the hands of the rats to want to avoid getting any closer to them.

The rats' chittering, too, was taking shape as language. Mostly the Babel Card interpreted it as "Kill! Kill! Eat!" But from the back of the swarm of dog-sized rodents rose Scabies, the scarred gray rat. He held a twisted metal fork, as long as he himself was tall, with visibly sharpened tines, and he squealed and chittered and pointed at Charlie.

"Kill that one!" Scabies howled.

The rats rushed at Charlie.

So there it was: his decision was made for him.

Ingrid moved in front of him, swinging her club. She threw back her head and let loose a sound like the moo of a cow, if a cow could sound angry and threatening. She knelt in front of Charlie and turned at the waist, lashing left and right with her weapon, and whenever she hit a rat, she knocked it through the air and it struck a wall, to lie still.

She wasn't nearly Grim's size, but she seemed just as strong.

"We're on your side!" Charlie continued to hoot.

"We do not wish your nestlings harm!" Thomas added.

Sal was dainty by comparison with Ingrid. He chose his targets, usually rats who were distracted or attacking someone else, and he dispatched them with simple bonks to the skull from his cane. He didn't cut the swath Ingrid did, but he knocked down a lot of rats.

Gnat worked with sober efficiency, skewering rats like pigeons for a roasting spit.

But more rats swarmed in, and the wall of rats in front of Ingrid and Sal grew higher, swayed, and leaned forward as if about to collapse, spilling rats all over them.

Then the ghouls attacked.

The first ghoul actually used Charlie as a springboard, leaping up onto his shoulders from behind and hurling itself out over the foremost rats to land in the rear ranks and attack. It was followed by several more, and by ghouls who leaped from Thomas and even Ingrid.

When a ghoul leaped onto Sal's shoulders to springboard from *him,* the big man twisted to shake it off, and they both fell to the ground.

Chittering in rage, half of the first rank of rats turned to attack the ghouls that were suddenly behind their lines. Then the next wave of ghouls attacked. These fighters stayed low to the ground and moved on all fours, which made them appear to gallop more than to run. The ghouls tore into the rats with rage, yanking rat limbs from rat bodies, twisting off rat heads, and tearing out rat throats with ghoul teeth.

"By the Wheel!" Jan Wijmoor whimpered.

Scabies wasn't deterred. He charged through his warriors toward Charlie, sharpened fork tucked under his armpit and clutched in both paws, like a lance. Charlie waited, hands ready.

Scabies stabbed Charlie with his fork. The tines sank into

Charlie's flesh, and it hurt, but it would have hurt a great deal more if Charlie had been flesh and blood. Charlie grabbed Scabies by the neck and muzzle and lifted the rat leader off his feet. With the rat's paws scratching at him, Charlie spun around twice and threw him.

Scabies struck the brick wall above the arch through which he'd entered, then fell to the ground in a heap. Picking himself with chattering teeth and an angry sneer on his muzzle, Scabies turned and ran.

At that sight, the rats fled. Their shrieks of thwarted rage and pain echoed through the sewer's passages, along with the joyous hoots of the ghouls who pursued them.

Charlie pulled the fork out and dropped it to the ground.

Ingrid and Sal stood, shaking themselves. Jan Wijmoor and Thomas stood close to Charlie.

Pursuing ghouls returned, dragging dead rats behind them by the tails.

With a slow tapping sound, a ghoul leaning on a cane approached Charlie. White hair sprouted from her head and back, and a few long strands from her slit nostrils, too. Her eyes were dark yellow with age, and she approached Charlie with a single finger raised in question.

"You are no ghoul, are you?" she asked.

Charlie shook his head, but then he thought that might not be a gesture the ghouls would understand. "No," he added.

She poked him experimentally in the chest until she found one of the holes left by Scabies's fork, and she twisted a rubbery finger inside that hole.

"You're the human who cannot be hurt," she said. "Like the Long Walk Woman."

"I don't know about the Long Walk Woman." That sounded like a story. The ghoul was wrong about Charlie on both counts, but it probably wasn't worth trying to explain that just now. "I can be hurt."

"My people know you," the ghoul crone said. "A moon ago, you were beneath the place the humans call Waterloo Station, and my people met you."

Her people had tried to eat Charlie was what she really meant. And had failed, after gnawing on him at length. And then Charlie had driven them away with rocks.

"Yes," Charlie agreed. "That was me."

"The boy who cannot be eaten."

"Okay," Charlie said. That seemed like a good title to have among ghouls, and then he realized that the pattern of hoots the old ghoul used made it more than just words.

It was Charlie's new name.

"The Boy Who Cannot Be Eaten," Thomas said.

"Charlie," Ingrid asked in a pleasant, relaxed voice. "What's going on?"

"We're talking," he told her.

"The Boy Who Cannot Be Eaten!" the ghouls all hooted.

"That's a lot of noise for just talking," Sal muttered.

"You travel with a pixie," the ghoul observed.

"Not just any pixie," Charlie said. "She's the Baroness de Minimis of Underthames."

"The fairies are our enemies, but for the Boy Who Cannot

Be Eaten, and for her own valor in battle, we will spare her life."

"Thank you," Charlie said.

"And have you come only to aid us in our never-ending war against the rats?"

"I am happy I could help you in your fight today," Charlie said. "But actually, my friends and I are trying to find our way out of the sewers. To someplace safe."

"Safe . . . for your kind," the ghoul crone mused.

"Yes." Was there any such place? Since he'd left Pondicherry's Clockwork Invention & Repair, Charlie hadn't seen a place that was safe for *his* kind. Maybe that was the nature of life. "A place where humans aren't fighting, at least."

The crone bobbed her shoulders up and down, a gesture that looked like a rough nod. "My people will take you to such a place. Eats Too Much! Leaps Higher Backward! One Extra Claw!"

The ghouls shuffled forward, hooting wordlessly. They looked nervous to be in Charlie's presence, and they repeatedly bowed in his direction.

"Take the Boy Who Cannot Be Eaten to the Place of Guarded Meat," the crone directed the three younger ghouls. "Keep him safe, and eat none of his party. On pain of death, mind you."

The ghouls all bobbed their shoulders, hooting. "Yes, Cunning Woman."

The crone fixed her yellow eyes on Gnat, and suddenly she spoke in English. "Baroness de Minimis," she croaked, in a voice that sounded clogged with mud and twigs. "My young men will give you safe passage this one time. You should not expect that this means peace between our peoples."

Gnat showed no reaction to this sudden speech, though Sal took two steps back in surprise.

"Your folk are relentless and hungry," Gnat said.

"And your folk are delicious." The old ghoul laughed suddenly, showing yellowed and broken teeth, but still enough sharp points to tear flesh when she needed to.

Charlie followed the three young ghouls, and his friends followed him.

His feelings were confused and turbulent. The ghouls ate folk—ate *other* folk, since it was clear now the ghouls were themselves thinking people, though perhaps not very nice.

Now these people who ate other folk had given Charlie a name. Had they adopted him as one of their own? It didn't seem so. It seemed more that they recognized him as a strange figure, worth fearing. He had become a sort of bogeyman to the ghouls, and then the bogeyman had showed up to help them win a fight, so they were willing to take him to the Place of Guarded Meat, wherever that was.

A butcher's shop?

Charlie shuddered.

The young ghouls led them through the sewers.

"Charlie," Thomas said in English, "are they leading us in a circle?"

It was true: their path curved through the tunnels.

"Why are we not traveling in a straight line?" Charlie demanded of the ghouls.

The three ghouls looked at each other and hooted nervously.

"Boy Who Cannot Be Eaten," one said, bowing low to scrape his face on the slimy brick, "it is the pixie. We cannot take you in a straight line, because it would allow her to see our warren. Then she and her fairy warriors would kill our nestlings and drive us away with fire."

Charlie thought he might not be sad to see the ghoul warren emptied out by spear and fire, but he bobbed his shoulders like a ghoul in agreement. "I understand."

A few junctions farther on, Charlie saw a bluish light glimmering at the end of a long passage. He had taken a single step toward it when one of the ghouls grabbed his forearm to hold him.

"Don't do that!" the ghoul hooted. "Corpse candle!"

After a few more minutes' walk, the ghouls stopped. Their natural energy became a kind of restless fidget, the three of them hopping back and forth and whimpering.

"We are here," one of the ghouls hooted, then pointed at rusting rungs set into the wall.

"Can we trust them, do you think?" Gnat whispered.

Charlie nodded. "Please go first," he asked the ghouls. "I'll follow."

The ghouls' hopping and hooting intensified, but they climbed the ladder. Charlie followed, and his friends after him.

The ghouls pushed aside a metal disk at the top of the ladder and then climbed out into darkness. Charlie followed, and the cool air of the London night on his skin was a welcome relief. He stood in a narrow alley between two tall brick walls. Steam-carriages passed back and forth past the mouth of the lane.

Where was he?

Jan Wijmoor, last of the group, was still climbing out of the hole when Charlie heard men shouting.

"Ghouls! Ghouls!" A shrill whistle blew. "Wardens!"

Five men charged into the alley. They were dressed in long white coats, bulky because they wore them over heavy leather jackets. On their chests and shoulders was a black-and-white patch bearing a shield split into six sections and the words ST. BARTHOLOMEW'S HOSPITAL. Over their heads and in front of them hung lanterns. The lanterns were suspended from poles anchored to packs strapped between the men's shoulders, and bobbed as they ran.

The men held long poles with a squashed iron circle at the end.

Ghoul wardens! St. Bartholomew's Hospital!

The ghouls called the hospital the Place of Guarded Meat. They must have thought the hospital would be safe for Charlie's kind because the ghoul wardens there protected the hospital's patients from the ghouls themselves.

Charlie felt ill.

"Stop right there!" a warden shouted.

Two wardens each nabbed a ghoul immediately. The third ghoul scampered into a narrow alley and disappeared.

A warden rushed at Charlie with the iron circle at the end of his pole held forward. The squashed-flat side of the iron was a one-way gate, and the moment Charlie saw it, he knew he wouldn't be able to avoid it.

Then suddenly Ingrid was there, knocking Charlie aside. The gate struck her waist—

It gave way, pulling her into the iron ring.

Then the warden yanked at a wire that ran along the pole, and a metal cord inside the iron circle closed tight around Ingrid. He threw the pole to the ground, and it dragged her down.

"Run, Charlie!" she cried.

The warden who had captured Ingrid raised a stubby scattergun hanging from his belt.

"Hey now!" Sal roared. "You leave her alone!" The dairy owner punched one of the wardens in the nose, and two other wardens jumped on him.

"All of you, hold still!" the wardens barked.

Charlie, Gnat, Thomas, and Jan Wijmoor ran after the fleeing ghoul.

Rubrihomo semivisibilis (common name: djinn)—The djinn's most famous feature, its invisibility from all sides other than the front, makes it a fierce predator in savage lands. The notion that djinns subsist on the souls of other living creatures is not scientifically validated, though Mortimer (1827) claims his test subject lived over three hundred days with no visible nourishment, and only the activity of torturing small beasts.

—Smythson, *Almanack*, 1st ed., "Djinn"

Jan Wijmoor had short legs, and might slow them down. Charlie scooped the kobold into his arms and saw Thomas grab Gnat at the same time.

"Stop!" a warden behind them shouted.

The ghoul ahead of them shrieked and dived to the right, into a storm drain with missing iron bars.

"Not that way!" Charlie yelled to Thomas, and turned left.

Boom! The scattergun fired and missed.

This alley was even narrower than the first, but it got them out of sight of the wardens. Charlie looked up, trying to find a fast way to the rooftops.

"Charlie, watch out!" Thomas yelled.

Charlie looked down just in time to avoid running into the

brick wall at the end of the alley. He turned right, down the only available route—and saw another brick wall blocking his way, and a dead end.

But the walls were lower.

"Jump!" he yelled, and leaped for all he was worth.

Jan Wijmoor screamed, but Natalie roared: "De Minimis and Underthames!"

The four of them tumbled into a heap on the flat rooftop. Gnat sprang immediately to her feet.

"Lie flat!" she whispered. Then she crept to the edge of the rooftop.

"Are the wardens there?" Charlie asked.

"Aye." She laughed, softly. "But they didn't see you lads jump. And they look really, really confused." She came back, staying low to the rooftop. "Shall we go to Charlie's shop, then?"

"I don't know the way," Charlie said. "I've been all over the world, in all kinds of odd vehicles and on the backs of strange creatures. Now that I'm in my own city, I have no idea how to find my house."

"That's the dome of St. Paul's, over there, so Whitechapel is that way." Gnat pointed at the church and then eastward.

Whitechapel was where Charlie had lived with his father. He had last seen it from the air in Bob's flyer, taking off to go west to try to save his father's friend, Isambard Kingdom Brunel, from the Iron Cog. He'd failed: Brunel had died.

Gnat must have guessed from Charlie's face what he was thinking. "Let's go see your home, lad."

With Charlie's and Thomas's ability to jump long distances, they traveled by rooftop. This was a perspective Gnat knew well, since she was ordinarily a flyer herself, so she guided them eastward. They hid underneath the tracks of the Sky Trestle—Brunel's great train system, which snaked over London's rooftops—to avoid being seen by passengers when they rolled by.

The sun rose as they traveled, shining a light on London that quickly went from angry red to dull gray.

"Who are those?" Thomas asked, pointing down into a street below.

"Fire bobbies." Charlie knew them because he'd seen them in action, when he had barely escaped from a burning hat manufacturer. "That carriage there is steam-powered, and it's a movable water pump. They spray the water on burning buildings."

"Do they pull water from the Thames?" Thomas asked.

"They used to," Wijmoor said. "That was what your troll friend was talking about. A pumping station at Hampstead Heath, north of the city. That's where the water will come from now."

"What are those long masks?" Thomas asked. "They look like anteaters."

"They look like plague masks," Jan Wijmoor said. "In the Middle Ages, doctors visiting plague patients wore those, and they put sweet flowers in the nose cone of the mask. It was believed to keep the doctor from catching the plague."

Charlie had no idea what the masks were for. "Maybe it

will stop the fire bobbies from breathing in smoke?" And then he remembered why the fire bobbies' masks looked familiar. He'd seen very similar masks on the dwarfs who'd dug the spirit stone out of the floor of the Marburg library.

And again, he'd seen similar masks in his dreams, more than once, dreams in which a city burned.

What had Grim asked? Whether the powdered spirit stone could be dissolved in water and then sprayed on fire?

And something about a brand-new pump? Which was what Jan Wijmoor had just been talking about.

"Speaking of smoke." Jan Wijmoor pointed at a dark smudge on the air behind them, somewhere in the vicinity of the hospital. Then another, beyond St. Paul's.

"Aye, and over there." Gnat pointed at a third.

"Maybe that's smoke from chimneys," Charlie said. "I wish Bob and Ollie were here. They know a lot about chimneys, and they could tell us."

"I doubt it's chimney smoke, Charlie," Gnat said. "I've seen my share of chimney smoke too."

"Well, if it's fires, then it's a good thing you have your fire bobbies," Jan Wijmoor said.

They looked at each other uneasily, and slowly nodded.

"Your alley is just at the end of this block, Charlie," Gnat said. "What did you call it? The Throat?"

"The Gullet," Charlie said.

Charlie recognized the rooftop of Pondicherry's Clockwork Invention & Repair because it still had a hole in its ceiling. This was the opening that Grim and Ingrid had smashed into the roof to allow Charlie and the sweeps to climb out and take off in Bob's flyer. A tarpaulin was nailed across the hole now, but it was a simple matter to pull up two nails and make enough slack for the four of them to slide in.

They came into Charlie's attic. The bare walls of the room hit Charlie like a punch to the stomach—where had the books gone?

Instead, the room was full of tall wooden racks of drying clothing.

He heard shouting from downstairs. "Is someone up there? I warn you, I have a weapon!"

Charlie knew the voice. It belonged to his bap's neighbor, Lucky Wu.

"Mr. Wu?" he called respectfully. "Mr. Wu, it's Charlie Pondicherry. I'm coming down slowly."

Charlie walked down the stairs with his hands up and visible. Lucky Wu stepped into view at the bottom, holding a metal tube with a pump at the base, such as you might use to spray poison to kill insects. It didn't look like a weapon.

"Charlie? You told me I could have the shop." Wu looked suspicious. "Are you here to take it back?"

Rajesh Pondicherry's reception room looked much as it always had, with its table, chairs, and portrait of Queen Victoria.

"You can have it, Mr. Wu." Charlie shrugged. "I'm sorry I surprised you. I didn't expect you'd really take the house. I thought it would be empty."

"I . . . have something for you." Wu reached inside his

waistcoat and produced an envelope. "I wrote my note the day you left. I've kept it with me, hoping I would see you again."

Charlie's friends came down the stairs behind him.

Charlie wasn't used to speaking with Lucky Wu like this. And why would Wu have written him a note? "Thank you." He tucked the envelope inside his coat pocket and found the broken halves of Bap's pipe. "What kind of weapon is that?"

Wu laughed and shook the metal tube. "It's not a weapon. I lied. The fire bobbies passed these out to business owners last week. It's for spraying on flames; it's supposed to douse them. Just in time, since I understand there are several fires in the city today."

At that moment the door was kicked open, and Egil One-Arm crashed into the shop. He held a scattergun in his flesh fingers, and he raised his mechanical hand in a menacing, steam-jetting, three-clawed fist.

After him came burly men and trolls with clubs and guns. Their scarred faces were dirty, and they all wore long brown coats, almost like a uniform, covering their otherwise mismatched clothes.

"Charlie Pondicherry!" Egil bellowed. "You're under arrest!"

Behind Egil and his men came Grim Grumblesson, roaring in protest. "This is outrageous, Egil! I'll have you hauled before the committee, before Parliament, before the Queen's Bench! I'll have you at the Thing by noon, and in prison by sundown! I'll have you tried by pixies, if I have to!"

Grim's hands were locked in manacles before him, and he was pushed by two trolls in brown coats.

Behind Grim came smoke, billowing into the shop.

"Fire," Wu said. "Is my shop on fire?"

"Don't think it's yours," Grim rumbled, but the laundry owner rushed out the door without stopping to listen. The door swung shut behind him.

"You're all under arrest," Egil said to Charlie again. "Conspiracy. Evading officers of the law. Failure to license a dragon. Come along nice and easy, and I'll hurt you less."

"No one's under arrest," Grim growled. "*I'm* in charge here."

Egil and his men chuckled. "Yeah, you look like a real authority, Grumblesson."

"I'm your superior," Grim said. "Duly appointed by Parliament. Unlock me."

"Except you're cheating Parliament," Egil said slowly. "Parliament created the committee to deal with threats like this mechanical boy, and I don't think you're going to do anything about him. He got away from you once already, Grumblesson. Makes a fellow suspicious."

"We can take him in peaceably," Grim said. "And ask Parliament what they want."

Egil laughed. "Pin him."

Four trolls grabbed Grim, two to each arm, and threw him against the wall. Grim bellowed and pushed, but they held him still. Egil approached Grim, opening and closing his mechanical claw and holding it at the level of Grim's eyes. "And if you went missing during an investigation," One-Arm asked, "who would Parliament choose next?"

Knock-knock.

This rapping at the door was polite, but it caused everyone in the room to freeze. Egil looked about the chamber uncertainly, and then he stepped away from Grim and opened the door.

Ollie stood in the alley outside. His face looked tired, but he wore his bowler hat at a jaunty angle. The hat was still thoroughly battered, but Ollie had brushed off all the dust so that it almost looked neat. He stepped in and shut the door behind him.

"Ollie!" Charlie cried. "You're alive!"

"I'm better than alive, mate. I'm here to rescue you."

Charlie thought a look of understanding passed between Ollie and Grim.

"Out of my way!" Egil bellowed, and he seized Ollie.

BAMF! A cloud of yellow gas reeking of rotten eggs filled the room. Men choked, gagged, and coughed, and what Egil grabbed hold of wasn't a red-haired chimney sweep any longer, but a dragon the size of two London buses. Ollie's hindquarters smashed the outer wall of the room, and Pondicherry's Clockwork Invention & Repair groaned and sagged to one side.

Egil's men and trolls scattered. Egil himself tried to hide in the corner of the room.

"I'll be taking my friends now." Ollie the dragon nonchalantly extended a single claw, the size of a scimitar, and snapped Grim's manacles as if he were cutting a chain of paper. "Climb on, my lovelies."

Charlie rushed forward and gave Ollie a hug around his

vast draconic neck before climbing onto his friend. Gnat, Jan Wijmoor, and Thomas sprang onto Ollie's shoulders.

With only a moment's hesitation, Grim followed.

"Oops," Ollie said to Egil. "Now you."

Egil One-Arm had tried to sneak past Ollie, but Ollie had noticed. With one claw, he grabbed the troll by the thigh and held him upside down, dangling above the floor.

Egil responded by roaring and thumping the dragon's paw with his mechanical arm.

"Hey," Ollie the dragon said. "That's annoying." With his other claw he gripped the troll's mechanical arm and plucked it neatly from his body. "There. Now we'll get along much better."

"We're not done here," Egil snarled.

"Yes, we are," Grim shot back. "I'll be making my report to Parliament before the day's up. The committee was always a farce, and now it's over."

Ollie tossed Egil through the room's back door, into the rubble that remained of the rear of the shop. Then he shifted his bulky body, shattering the table and chairs. He pushed his snout out into the Gullet and then snaked his head and neck along after it.

With a grunt, he forced his way through the last of the wall and stood on his hind legs in the alley. Charlie and his friends shrieked and clung to Ollie's long shoulder fur to avoid falling.

"I'm not looking!" Grim shouted.

Ollie hopped, and his hop took him to the rooftop above the Gullet. It sagged under his weight but didn't collapse.

Then, with a final leap, Ollie the dragon sprang into the air, flapped his wings once, and rose into the sky.

"How did you survive?" Charlie shouted into the wind.

"The regimental dragons, you mean?" Ollie asked. "Easy, mate. I turned into the tiniest snake in the world. You know what that is?"

"No!" Charlie shouted.

"It's the *Leptotyphlops carlae.* Read that in the *Almanack*. Thick as a bit of noodle, about the size of a guinea. And I became that tiny thing and just fell."

"What if one of the dragons had noticed you and eaten you?"

"I reckon even if they'd only hit me with the flap of a wing, I'd have been dead. But they didn't, and just before I hit the water I turned into a sea snake. Swam away."

"That doesn't sound all that easy," Charlie said.

"It wasn't, mate. It left me knackered and aching. But I'm proud I did it, and that makes it feel easy after the fact. Know what I mean? Now where am I going?"

"Hampstead Heath!" Grim and Charlie shouted at the same time.

"The new pumping station," Charlie said.

"They're setting fires on purpose," Grim said. "Water from the new pumping station will be pumped by fire bobbies and turn into steam, all over the city."

"If they put that powder in the pumping-station water," Charlie added, "people all over London will breathe it in, in the steam."

"And if they don't breathe it in today, they'll drink it eventually," Grim concluded.

"Not if we can help it!" Charlie cried.

Ollie soared northward, over long rooftops, Sky Trestle tracks, and twisting lanes. Ahead, Charlie saw green. Wind slapped Charlie's hair and face, and to his right the clouds began to scatter, letting in brilliant shafts of yellow sunlight.

"Uh-oh," Ollie rumbled.

"What?" Charlie looked.

Ahead of them, between Ollie and the wooded green hill that was Hampstead Heath, he now saw four dragons. They had large guns mounted on their backs, and they all flew toward Charlie and his friends.

The great fire of 1887 is reported to have arisen from the growing together of numerous lesser conflagrations. Certainly, the blazes that broke out at Blackfriars Bridge and at the Elephant & Castle pub did significant damage and have attracted their share of pyro-enthusiasts. Careful research, though, shows that the fire that broke out at St. Bartholomew's was likely the first fire, and by far the most destructive.

—from Nigel Silversmith, OBE, *History of Unusual Events in Smithfield*, "The Fire of 1887"

Ollie flew faster, and straight toward the dragons.

"This is insane!" Charlie cried.

"I'm not looking!" Grim roared, burying his face in the hair to which he clung.

"Get in close," Gnat cried, brandishing the Hound's tooth, "and I'll board one of them!"

"They can't fire those cannons straight forward," Ollie bellowed. "Or anything north of ten o' clock or two, if you get my meaning. Stops 'em from blowing off their own heads, but what it means is they are best at shooting at targets on their flanks. Like a broadside from the old sailing ships, you know?"

"Don't they also spit fire?" Charlie asked.

"Well, yeah," Ollie admitted. "But I'm a dragon, mate. How's that gonna hurt me?"

"*I* am not a dragon!" Charlie yelled.

"Good point," Ollie agreed. "You should probably stay down."

Charlie and his friends ducked behind Ollie's dragon shoulders just as the lances of flame reached them. Ollie laughed.

Beneath and ahead, Charlie saw where the city abruptly ended and the green of Hampstead Heath began. He saw lines of carriages and people walking on the grass, and an enormous tank like an upside-down teacup. At a platform at one edge of the tank sat a row of dignitaries behind a podium, and a man in bottle green stepping forward to take the lectern. William T. Bowen, the Welsh speculator and member of the Iron Cog who had kidnapped the dwarf child Aldrix? On top of the teacup-shaped tank, he saw a tall man in a long black cape and, beside him, a much shorter person.

The Sinister Man, Gaston St. Jacques. And perhaps a kobold?

He also saw, left and right and beneath him, fires.

"We'll pass them, though," Charlie yelled. "Then what's to stop them from shooting us from behind?"

Ollie laughed, a sound like thunder. "Bob!"

Charlie raised his head to look. At some unimaginably high altitude, he saw a tiny dot. The dot was a dark shadow, an object blotting out the bright sky, but it was rapidly growing in size as it fell. It kept its circular shape, and then Charlie realized what he was seeing.

It was the Pushpaka vimāna. It was ambushing the army's dragons by swooping down on them from directly above.

"Time to dive." Ollie dropped just before reaching the line of oncoming dragons. He passed beneath them, still racing toward the hill and the platform and the tank, and Charlie leaned away from Ollie's body to watch. The attacking dragons angled up, their gunners swiveled their weapons around, the long guns pointed at Ollie—

ZOTTT-T-T-T-t-t-t-t!

Four bolts of lightning slammed into the four dragons. This was no flash, illuminating the sky and then disappearing, but a sustained burning. The dragons twitched and shuddered and then began to lose altitude, arcing away from Ollie and his riders and down toward London.

"Bob!" Charlie cried.

The Pushpaka vimāna spun past Ollie, curved around, and headed north with him toward Hampstead Heath. It moved like nothing Charlie had ever seen, spinning constantly and turning tight corners with ease.

Charlie watched over his shoulder. Two of the dragons crashed into the Thames. The third hit a stone bridge, and the fourth slammed against the side of a large building that looked like a factory.

The vimāna flew just below Ollie. Bob stood at the controls with a broad grin on her face; she wore airman's goggles but no bomber cap, and her long brown hair flew out behind her like a flag, whipping sideways each time Ollie flapped his wings.

Bob shouted something, but the wind snatched away her

words. Then she pointed, and Charlie saw additional regimental dragons rising up into the air on the other side of the hill. Bob shifted her gaze to the dragons, and the Pushpaka vimāna leaped forward. It looked, improbably, like a gigantic golden birthday cake, glittering in the sun as it flew about, hurling lightning bolts out of the spikes protruding from its sides.

"I've got to help Bob," Ollie rumbled. "Where shall I set you down?"

"Grim!" Charlie yelled.

"I'm not opening my eyes!" he roared back.

"I need you to arrest William Bowen," Charlie told him.

"In the name of the same committee that wants you arrested?" Grim asked.

"However you have to do it!" Charlie said. "Ollie—the platform first, and then the tank!"

When Ollie alighted without warning at one end of the stage, William Bowen leaped backward, surprised. The women and men in formal clothing sitting on the stand sprang to their feet and edged away.

The crowd—large, wildly varying, and London to its bones—oohed in wonder. They thought the dragon was part of the show.

Gnat dropped to the stage.

"Are we landed?" Grim asked. In answer, Ollie shrugged one massive shoulder forward and tossed him to the floor too.

Grim stood and stepped to a speaking tube that projected his voice to a loudspeaker. "Please, everyone remain calm.

My name is Grim Grumblesson, I'm deputy chairman of the Committee for the Investigation of Anti-Human Crime, and, for starters, that man there is under arrest."

Gnat leaped to the shoulders of the Welsh incorporator and grabbed him by the ears.

"Go, Charlie!" she cried.

"Ollie!" Charlie cried. "The tank!"

Ollie leaped into the air, carrying himself in a single leap above the water tank. At the height of the dome, Gaston St. Jacques and the shorter person with him worked at something that looked like a hatch with a wheel attached. Charlie saw now that the shorter person was Heinrich Zahnkrieger.

As Ollie glided down to the tank with opened wings, Charlie watched the scene on the stage unfold.

"Listen," Grim continued. "You'll have noticed there are fires breaking out in London."

Gnat dragged Bowen to the floor and stood on his neck, pinning him.

A short man with a blue top hat joined Grim at the podium and leaned forward into the speaking tube. "Good thing we're about to open the new pumping station!"

The crowd cheered.

"No, Your Lordship," Grim said, coughing to hide his feelings of awkwardness. "In fact, I've come with my associates to shut down the pumping station. We'll have to fight the fires the old-fashioned way, I'm afraid. The important thing is that the fires were not started by anything called an Anti-Human League."

"The important thing," the man in the blue hat said, leaning in again and looking at Gnat and Bowen with a frown on his face, "is that we've built this new pumping station, and we'll use it to put out the fires!"

"Sorry, Your Lordship." Grim picked up the man in the blue hat by his jacket, lifted him entirely off his feet, and tossed him off the stage and into the crowd. "Run home!" he called to the crowd. "Fight any fire you find and put it out, but don't use water, and don't call the fire bobbies! Shovels and buckets, my friends, shovels and buckets!"

Ollie landed on the broad, flat top of the dome. The two mechanical boys and Jan Wijmoor slithered down, landing with a series of metallic booms. Above, Bob in the Pushpaka vimāna dodged dragon attacks and fired back with electric bolts. Charlie saw airships closing in on her too, with guns on their decks and rockets bolted onto their sides.

"Careful, Ollie," Thomas said.

"Weather wizards," Charlie said.

"Excuse me?" The dragon looked at Charlie blankly.

"The fires," Charlie said. "The Royal Magical Society is great at changing the weather. If one of you can get away and get a message to the Royal Magical Society . . . maybe they can put out the fires with some hard rain."

Ollie nodded his enormous dragon head and leaped into the sky.

From the very top of the tank, in the center, rose a wheel-shaped metal control. As Charlie and his friends advanced on the Sinister Man and Heinrich Zahnkrieger, St. Jacques finished turning the control wheel and then bent to lift up the hatch.

Zahnkrieger stood beside several large sacks.

Sacks that were together about the size of the white stone in the Marburg Library, the stone that had held the soul of Wilhelm Grimm, the stone out of which a key part of Charlie—his mind, his heart, and his soul—had been fashioned.

"Come on, Thomas!" Charlie cried, and he leaped forward.

Thomas raced with him, and for a moment Charlie felt glee, and a sense that victory and relief were finally within his grasp. Then Heinrich Zahnkrieger said something the Babel Card couldn't make out—

and Charlie and Thomas both fell immobile to the steel under their feet.

"Ah, Charlie." The Sinister Man removed a clasp knife from his pocket and unfolded it. "What a delight you are. From the beginning, you have been so predictable." He slit the tops of the bags, and Charlie saw white sparkling stone inside.

Charlie felt as if he were seeing his own insides.

Lying on his back, Charlie was able to move his head, but nothing else. He watched the Pushpaka vimāna shudder as rockets exploded against its exterior. And what if one of those rockets struck the top of the so-called chariot, where Bob stood unprotected?

"Please!" Jan Wijmoor called. "Don't do this. You don't have to do this."

The Sinister Man placed his foot against one of the bags and kicked it forward. Clouds of white rock dust escaped as it dropped, falling into the tank. "There, it is done." Gaston St. Jacques pulled his long pistol from inside his cloak and pointed it at Wijmoor.

Heinrich Zahnkrieger chuckled and shifted from foot to foot. He couldn't look at Jan Wijmoor, and looked down at the bags of white stone instead. "Perhaps we don't have to kill him."

"I have orders," St. Jacques said. "I carry out my orders. Don't you?"

Zahnkrieger grunted. "But look, just shoot the boys. They're only machines, after all. We can let Wijmoor go."

St. Jacques stepped back, circling around the open hatch. "The thing is, I have orders about you, too, Zahnkrieger."

"No." Zahnkrieger's face showed shock.

"They warned me you might get softhearted," the Sinister Man said. "You should have killed them all while you had the chance, in the Russian pit. Now stand over there with the other gnome."

Jan Wijmoor rushed to Zahnkrieger's side, but he yelled at the Frenchman, "You don't have to do any of this!"

St. Jacques smiled, a grin as wide as a crocodile's. "Some things I don't do because I have to. Some things I do because I want to." He pointed his pistol at the two kobolds and began to fire.

Jan Wijmoor jumped into the path of the bullets, and with a strangled cry he collapsed.

Man is placed between perfection and deficiency, with the power to earn perfection. Man must earn this perfection, however, through his own free will. . . . Man's inclinations are therefore balanced between good (*Yetzer HaTov*) and evil (*Yetzer HaRa*), and he is not compelled toward either of them. He has the power of choice and is able to choose either side knowingly and willingly.

—from Moshe Chaim Luzzatto, *Derech Hashem*

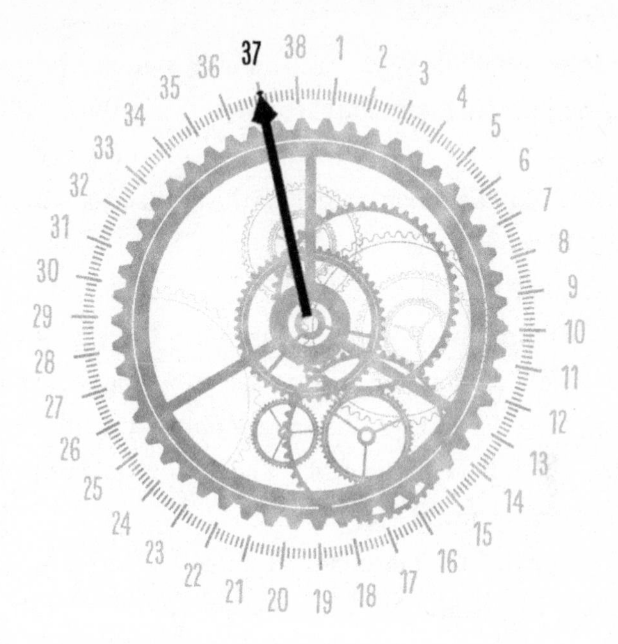

"No!" Heinrich Zahnkrieger cried. The kobold knelt beside his old mentor. "What have you done, St. Jacques? This was completely unnecessary!"

The Sinister Man kicked the rest of the sacks of ground stone down into the water, one at a time. Charlie watched his friends in the sky, who seemed to be slowly losing to the army's airships and dragons, and retreating.

How long until the Royal Aeronautical Navy landed soldiers on top of the tank? Or until the army arrived?

Charlie would be arrested; he might be destroyed. It didn't matter, anyway, since he'd failed to stop the Iron Cog. The stone was in the water now. Whatever Grim told people, the fire bobbies were out trying to extinguish fires. And if their hoses drew water through this pumping station, they would shortly be pumping contaminated water into the air all over the city.

It made Charlie much sadder to think that his failure also doomed Thomas to die.

"I'm sorry," he said.

Only Thomas heard him. "I can move three fingers," his brother said. "It's too late to stop the Iron Cog, but maybe I can drag myself over there and gouge out that man's eyes."

"Not worth it," Charlie said. "They'd probably just replace them with mechanical eyes anyway."

Smoke dirtied the horizon in all directions now. A fire had broken out in a street of row houses just a block from the edge of Hampstead Heath.

"You tried to kill me!" Heinrich stood and faced the Sinister Man.

"Yes." The Frenchman was reloading his pistol. "But I get paid whether you live or die, so yes, I was a little indifferent as to whether I hit you or not. You're not running away right now, so maybe you're indifferent too."

"Paid?" Heinrich Zahnkrieger looked paler than usually.

"Yes, paid!" St. Jacques finished reloading his gun and cackled. "Do you think I long for this better world that the Cog and its minions plan? Do you think I believe they can end poverty and sickness, and put smiles on all the little children's faces? Perhaps I have a sick grandmother, and only the Iron Cog can heal her? No, my tiny little engineer, I have done what I did for you and your friends because I got paid to do it, and nothing more. For money I arranged the kidnapping of Joban Singh. For money I had the Hound and the machine soldiers built. For money I found a shaitan assassin to track and kill the mechanical boys!"

"Your shaitan failed!" Charlie yelled.

"And who fails now?" the Frenchman screamed back.

"You can't treat me like this!" the kobold snapped. "You can't treat my life so casually!"

Jan Wijmoor was dragging himself across the top of the tank. The Sinister Man and his accomplice didn't notice, but Wijmoor was almost to Charlie and Thomas.

He left behind a trail of his own dark blood.

"I'm disappointed that you're even surprised," the Frenchman said. "The Iron Cog treats everyone like this, its own people and others. All folk and all individuals are to live or die, to be fed or starved, according to the complete whim of the Cog and its plans. No individual matters, not Joban Singh, not Queen Victoria, not you. It's a beautiful plan, precisely because it's so consistently ruthless! Shall I kill you or not?"

"I'll see you don't get paid at all," Heinrich snarled.

The Frenchman shook his head slowly. "Those were the stupidest words you have ever spoken." He raised the pistol—

Heinrich muttered—

Click!

The Sinister Man's gun didn't fire. He tried again, and again, grimacing with anger.

Click! Click! Click!

Nothing.

The row-house fire had arrived at the edge of the trees.

Wijmoor reached Charlie. Hands trembling, he popped open Charlie's back and reached inside.

Charlie found he could move.

With an abrupt roar, the Frenchman charged Heinrich Zahnkrieger. He raised his pistol over his head as if it were a club and he intended to beat the kobold to death with it.

Charlie sprang to his feet, and leaped.

He flew through the air headfirst and tackled the Frenchman. They rolled across the steel of the tank, banging elbows and knees on the metal in a clattering racket.

Wijmoor began dragging himself slowly toward Thomas.

Charlie stopped his sideways roll by throwing out a leg, which left him sitting on the Sinister Man's chest. He grabbed the man's arms and thumped him in the nose with his forehead. "It's too late to stop your plan, but I can see to it you go to prison for a long time!"

Gaston St. Jacques laughed. "How, you idiot, since it's too late to stop the plan?"

"It's not too late!" Heinrich Zahnkrieger cried.

The kobold who had once been Raj Pondicherry's business partner began muttering. As he spoke, he took long, deliberate steps toward the control wheel and the open hatch at the top of the tank.

"No, Herr Doktor!" Jan Wijmoor reached out a bloody hand, begging. "No, Heinrich!" Zahnkrieger ignored the other kobold, and his chant grew louder.

"Let him do it!" Thomas shouted.

"Morbleu!" the Frenchman shouted, and threw himself sideways. Distracted, Charlie fell back onto the tank. *Bong!*

What was going on? Heinrich Zahnkrieger had switched sides. He had changed his mind. He was trying to use his red-cap powers to break the pumping station.

And Gaston St. Jacques realized it, and wanted to stop him.

Charlie threw himself forward with his hands and knees—

seized the Sinister Man's cape—

and tugged.

St. Jacques fell backward onto Charlie and cursed as Charlie's head and elbow jabbed him in the back. Charlie pulled the tall man's cape over his face and rolled again, banging the man's head against the tank as they moved.

St. Jacques swung his pistol, and the metal struck Charlie behind the ear.

"Don't do this!" Jan Wijmoor begged. "You can't! The machine is too large; the stress is too great!"

Heinrich Zahnkrieger grunted, taking another step toward the hatch. He continued to chant words Charlie couldn't hear, and when he opened his mouth, a dribble of blood poured out and onto the steel.

Overhead, Charlie thought his friends were losing. The Pushpaka vimāna still danced against Royal Aeronautical Navy craft and the Queen's dragons, delivering and taking blows, but Ollie had disappeared.

Shot down?

Transformed into the world's tiniest snake to hide?

The trees of Hampstead Heath burned. Charlie heard

screaming as the crowd that had come to see the opening of the pumping station now tried to put out a forest fire with no water.

"You stupid little thing!"

This time, St. Jacques smashed his own forehead into Charlie's nose. The move caught Charlie by surprise, and knocked him backward.

St. Jacques jumped on him, kneeing Charlie in the throat. A flesh-and-blood boy, or even a flesh-and-blood man, might have lost consciousness at that. Charlie just got annoyed.

He kicked his foot up and caught the Frenchman in the temple. *"Sacre bleu!"* St. Jacques shouted, and fell. Charlie threw himself on top of the Sinister Man, trying to smother him like a blanket, pressing down his limbs with Charlie's own.

"Heinrich, please!" Jan Wijmoor called his former student. "It's not worth dying for!"

Heinrich Zahnkrieger fell to his knees. Each syllable he spoke came out now as a cough that spattered blood. He paused a moment to look at the other kobold.

"It's the only thing worth dying for," he said.

Then he spoke one last incantation syllable.

CLANG! C-R-R-R-R-AAAAAAK! BOOM!

An unholy racket, like ten factories collapsing simultaneously, came from out of the open hatch.

With a smile on his face, Heinrich Zahnkrieger tumbled forward and lay still.

Charlie saw rain clouds on the horizon.

I have written many strange things here. Many will no doubt be shocked. I have written in the hope that a few might learn.

—Smythson, *Almanack*, 1st ed., "Introduction"

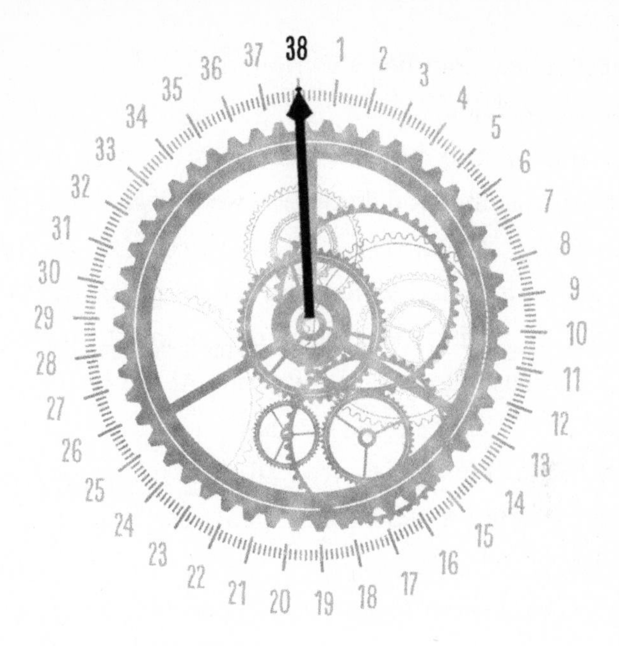

Charlie had been in a landgrave's castle. He'd been in the mansion of a wealthy industrialist. He'd been in the palace of a rajah and even in the floating vimāna of a demon lord, but he'd never been in any place he found as grand as this one.

He stood in the gallery of St. James.

And he was about to see the queen.

Charlie and his friends wore rented clothes that had been described to him as "court costumes." They were old-fashioned; he and Grim and Ollie and Thomas and Jan Wijmoor all wore knee breeches and hose; Gnat and Bob—Roberta, she was calling herself now, but Charlie was having a hard time making the switch—wore silk dresses, each with a long train held over one arm.

Gnat had relinquished the Hound's tooth and the scarf, just for the occasion.

A lord-in-waiting ushered them into the presence chamber. The furnishings and decoration were elegant, but Charlie scarcely noticed them. He felt he was meeting his mother, for the second time in his life. Bob and Gnat dropped their trains, and ladies-in-waiting spread them out behind them with long wands. Thomas followed, and was careful not to step on the trailing fabric. Charlie came very last.

Another lord-in-waiting read all their names off a single card, in the order in which they'd entered. ". . . and Charles Pondicherry."

"Just Charlie, Your Majesty." They bowed and curtsied low.

They'd been warned that, although she had asked for them to be presented, and that this was in itself an unusual thing, Her Majesty the Queen might say very little, or even nothing. But when they came up from their bows, she spoke.

"Natalie de Minimis," she said first. "Baroness of Underthames, you are welcome. Your mother was a fierce warrior. And now your people, along with those of the Undergravine of Hesse, have put down a revolt of our new experimental soldiers. And you did this despite agents of my government having falsely accused you of treason."

"Aye, Your Majesty."

"It is very satisfying to meet such a noble young woman," Victoria said.

Natalie curtsied again.

"Roberta Alice Micklemuch," the queen continued. "I have several admirals as well as an entire working committee of the

Fellows of the Royal Society who wish to speak to you. I have been told you have learned how to make a city fly."

Heaven-Bound Bob grinned, impervious to the solemnity of the occasion. "I reckon I'll be 'appy to 'ear from any of your people, Your Majesty. An' I'd 'ate to disappoint all those learned an' important gents, but if they're 'oping I'll make *London* fly, they're mistaken. I know 'ow to fly all manner of craft, but only the one city, an' it ain't really a city so much as a pyramid."

"A flying pyramid will do.

"Thomas Brunel." It felt strange to hear Thomas's name spoken like that, as if he were his father's flesh-and-blood child. It felt strange, but right. "What a brave young man you are, Thomas. Your father built much of the ironwork on which my kingdom runs. I understand that you very nearly undid his labor, with the nails of the three worlds, in a certain pit in Moscow; I, for one, am glad you chose not to do so. Would you like to follow in your father's footsteps as an engineer?"

"I don't know, Your Majesty." Thomas retreated slightly as he spoke, and a lord-in-waiting stepped behind him to push him back into line. "I've spent all my life focused on a single purpose, and now . . . well, I'll need some time to think about what to do next. And really, I'm still quite a small boy."

The queen nodded. "Mr. Grim Grumblesson. You have come to some notoriety due to your association with a committee created by certain members of my parliament. Whatever its purposes, the committee has done some rather sordid things."

Grim blushed and lowered his head. "Yes, Your Majesty."

"I think you should consider how that notoriety might best be put to use. Perhaps by standing for Parliament yourself. My jotun subjects could always use vigorous representation."

Grim blushed more deeply.

"Also, don't go anywhere. My prosecutors will be happy to have someone of your gravitas to testify against the Frenchman, as well as against certain members of Parliament, who were apparently corrupted by this Iron Cog.

"Meneer Doktor Professor Ingenieur Jan Wijmoor!"

The kobold bowed deeply. "Your Majesty does me too much honor, pronouncing my name, let alone those silly titles."

"Your country is yet at war," the queen said. "I have hopes we may see a short end to the conflict, but in the meantime I pray you will consider an appointment to one of our universities. I understand several have offered."

"I find I favor Oxford, Your Majesty," the kobold said.

"And Oliver. Have you no surname, then?"

"Judging by what they generally yelled after my Christian name in St. Jerome's House for Wayward Youth, Your Majesty, I'd have to guess my full name was Oliver You-Muttonhead."

And then the queen laughed. The lords and ladies in waiting, all tall and elegant and perfectly manicured, laughed with her, warmly.

"You know, Oliver," the queen said, "it was once the custom and sometimes still is to give an orphan child the name of a special saint, or the name of the institution that raised the child. So you have children surnamed Temple, for instance, because they were fostered by the barristers of the Inner or Middle Temple."

Ollie nodded.

"Do you feel it would be too late," the queen continued, "to give you such a surname now?"

"Such as Oliver St. Jerome, Your Majesty? It sounds a bit classy for a lad like me."

"I was thinking perhaps Oliver King."

Ollie turned white as a sheet, and he bowed again. His mouth worked open and shut, but no more words came out.

"And Charlie, not Charles, Pondicherry. I said it once before, Charlie, and I'll say it again now: you are a hero. I believe you have saved my realm, and maybe other realms too, though time will tell. Some people in your place would ask for land and titles, or for great wealth. What gift can the Queen of England give Charlie Pondicherry?"

"Well, Your Majesty," Charlie said. "Nothing, really. I think I'd just like to have some time alone with my brother. With Thomas, that is."

"Of course. I promise I shall not burden you with any official duties, so that your time will remain your own." The Queen of England was generally painted with a solemn expression, which was a pity, because she smiled now at Charlie and Thomas, and her smile was warm and kind and loving. "And anything else?"

"I don't quite know where my bap's buried," Charlie said. "But wherever it is, can it be kept nice? I don't mean a monument, but something? And a stone for Isambard Brunel, with the right dates on it? And Heinrich Zahnkrieger, the kobold who died at the pumping station . . . could he be laid to rest alongside?"

"Done. Fairy godmothers grant three wishes in all the stories I've ever read, Charlie, so I think you'd better ask for one more thing."

Charlie hesitated; his thought seemed silly, but he plunged ahead. "Would it be all right, Your Majesty, if we thought of you as our mum?"

Queen Victoria smiled even more broadly. "I hope that you will."

*

"So you're not going to marry Seamus after all?" Charlie said to Gnat.

Her wings had regrown, and fluttered a brilliant green in the early August sun. Charlie and his friends other than Jan Wijmoor had gathered in a field of yellow flowers at the edge of London to say farewell. Jan Wijmoor was in Oxford—three days after his presentation to the queen, a group of professors had showed up in a cloud of chalk and pipe smoke to escort him to his new appointment, and Charlie hadn't seen or heard from him since. Fortunately, he'd repaired all of Charlie's holes and dings before the professors had arrived.

At Charlie's request, he had *not* repaired Charlie's limp.

Charlie and Thomas had made several trips to the Brompton Cemetery. There, in a lovely shaded corner, three headstones side by side commemorated Joban Singh, Isambard Kingdom Brunel, and Heinrich Zahnkrieger. The boys had left flowers each time.

"Nay, I'll not marry poor Seamus now. 'Tisn't fair to him, to treat him only as my reward for succeeding at my own tasks. He's a person."

"Another way to see that," Grim growled, "is that if he really were your equal, he'd have fought Elisabel tooth and nail, rather than submit as he did." Grim wore a new cravat and a new jacket and hat. He'd come from some sort of political party meeting Charlie didn't understand and didn't try to understand.

"Aye," Gnat agreed. "That's another way to see the matter."

"And will you be traveling back to Hesse with the undergravine?" Charlie asked.

"Aye, someone needs to bring peace to that poor land. And we're kin, if distant."

"Take good care of her, Lloyd," Charlie said.

Natalie de Minimis laughed.

Lloyd laughed too. He wore his tabard and carried his herald's staff, and it occurred to Charlie that he hadn't seen the dewin's eyes shift since the day he'd taken the job. "I'm just a poor singer, boyo, and a reciter of names. And neither the baroness nor the undergravine really need me to take care of them. But I'll do my best, anyway."

"As will I," said Bob. She still dressed in a somewhat boyish fashion, because apparently that was much more convenient for an aeronaut. But her boots were taller and more elegant now, and she wore a small leather vest rather than a peacoat, and her hair hung free. She looked the most changed of all of them. "With the fleet."

"Bob's . . . Roberta's a captain," Ollie said with pride.

"Yeah, well, old Pushpaka won't accept anyone else, will she? But they've got me flying all sorts of other craft as well." Bob grinned. "I insisted."

"Aren't you part of the RMS now, Ollie?" Thomas asked.

"I ain't a Fellow, if that's what you mean." Ollie pretended to frown, but the expression cracked into a big smile. "But let's just say that I'm spending a lot of time with certain Fellows of the Royal Magical Society, and I am . . . expanding my talents."

"You expanded them quite a bit on your own," Charlie said.

"Like I told you," Ollie said, "I decided I was going to write the story and not let it write me. Now that means I have to go with the army into Germany. Try to stop the mechanical Bismarck, and the part of the Cog that's still operating over there. Destroy the transmitter that was supposed to send mind-control orders to everyone in Britain—St. Jacques gave up the location. That'll give me a chance to return Rabbi Rosenbaum's book." He beamed. "They've made me a regimental dragon-wizard. Rank of captain, as it happens."

"What about Ingrid?" Charlie asked Grim.

"Since she agreed to rescue you from me," Grim said, "I haven't seen her. St. Bart's had no record of capturing her, so I expect those ghoul wardens just let her go. I don't think we were ever a very good match, as it happens."

"I don't think she's matched with Sal, either, if that matters," Charlie said.

A single tear came to the corner of Grim's eye. "It does, Charlie. It does."

"An' you lads?" Bob asked. "Up the ol' frog like a couple of dwarfs?"

"Frog and toad, road," Charlie guessed. "Yeah. Though I feel bad. You're all going off to war and politics, and we're going rambling. We could help free Germany instead."

"You're boys," Grim said. "Go do boy things for a while."

"Aye." Gnat smiled at them.

"Where you going, then?" Bob asked.

Charlie shrugged. "We'll pick a direction and just see what we can see."

"Neither one of us has done much traveling," Thomas said.

Ollie laughed. "That's true and it ain't."

They all embraced, and then Charlie and Thomas picked a random direction and walked. On the ridge above the yellow-flowered field, they turned and waved goodbye to their friends.

*

Later in the afternoon, as they sat on a log with their feet in a small brook, Charlie took the envelope and the two halves of his bap's pipe from his pocket.

"What's that?" Thomas asked.

"The pipe was my father's. I keep meaning to get it repaired. Mr. Wu gave me the letter," Charlie said. "He was my neighbor in Whitechapel, and he wrote me a note. Shall we read it together?"

Thomas nodded and scooted closer. To Charlie's surprise, the envelope contained two thin sheets. One had a neat drawing of Charlie's back and his mainspring, with written instructions about how to wind it. The second was a letter from his father. He read:

Dearest Charlie, My Son

I have asked my friend and neighbor Wu Xiang to hold this letter. If you're reading it, I am dead. I think it's likely I was even murdered. This may be a terrible shock to you, and I'm sorry. It's not a surprise to me at all. I made the mistake of associating with wicked people years ago; I have been paying for that mistake ever since.

Here's another surprise for you, Charlie. You are not made of flesh and blood like me, but of springs and gears. I would have told you when you were ready, but I wanted you to feel like a normal boy as long as you could, and I didn't want you to have to keep my secrets.

You'll learn that being a mechanical boy makes you strong, fast, and tough, but it also means you're going to have to depend on other people. Every day or so, someone should wind the spring in your back, to keep you moving. I'm enclosing a diagram of just how one winds the spring. I recommend you show this letter and diagram to Wu; he'll help.

You're a special boy, Charlie. You're powerful, but you're going to need friends, every day of your life. That's not very different from me, really. I needed a friend every day of my life, Son, and that friend was you.

Of all the things I would want you to know after my passing, the one that matters most is this: you are brave, and you can be your own person.

I love you.

Rajesh Pondicherry

Written below the note in a different hand were the words:

I am sorry I did not give this to you earlier. I was angry, because I was afraid. Please forgive me.

Wu Xiang

Charlie folded the note carefully and replaced it in his coat. He'd never forget the words, but he knew he'd want to reread the letter again anyway. He put the pipe back too. Maybe he'd just keep it as it was, broken but still perfect. Still his bap's.

"Well, Thomas," he said. "Where shall we go?"